THE LOST

THE HEROES  OF OLYMPUS

THE LOST HERO

RICK RIORDAN

DISNEP • HYPERION BOOKS
NEW YORK

First Edition

3 5 7 9 10 8 6 4 2

G475-5664-5 10277

Printed in the United States of America

Library of Congress Cataloging-in-Publication Data on file.

ISBN 978-1-4231-1339-3

Reinforced binding

Visit www.hyperionbooksforchildren.com

SUSTAINABLE FORESTRY INITIATIVE

Certified Fiber Sourcing

www.sfiprogram.org

THIS LABEL APPLIES TO TEXT STOCK

For Haley and Patrick, always the first to hear stories.
Without them, Camp Half-Blood would not exist.

THE LOST HERO

JASON

EVEN BEFORE HE GOT ELECTROCUTED, Jason was having a rotten day.

He woke in the backseat of a school bus, not sure where he was, holding hands with a girl he didn't know. That wasn't necessarily the rotten part. The girl was cute, but he couldn't figure out who she was or what he was doing there. He sat up and rubbed his eyes, trying to think.

A few dozen kids sprawled in the seats in front of him, listening to iPods, talking, or sleeping. They all looked around his age...fifteen? Sixteen? Okay, that was scary. He didn't know his own age.

The bus rumbled along a bumpy road. Out the windows, desert rolled by under a bright blue sky. Jason was pretty sure he didn't live in the desert. He tried to think back...the last thing he remembered...

The girl squeezed his hand. "Jason, you okay?"

She wore faded jeans, hiking boots, and a fleece

snowboarding jacket. Her chocolate brown hair was cut choppy and uneven, with thin strands braided down the sides. She wore no makeup like she was trying not to draw attention to herself, but it didn't work. She was seriously pretty. Her eyes seemed to change color like a kaleidoscope—brown, blue, and green.

Jason let go of her hand. "Um, I don't—"

In the front of the bus, a teacher shouted, "All right, cupcakes, listen up!"

The guy was obviously a coach. His baseball cap was pulled low over his hair, so you could just see his beady eyes. He had a wispy goatee and a sour face, like he'd eaten something moldy. His buff arms and chest pushed against a bright orange polo shirt. His nylon workout pants and Nikes were spotless white. A whistle hung from his neck, and a megaphone was clipped to his belt. He would've looked pretty scary if he hadn't been five feet zero. When he stood up in the aisle, one of the students called, "Stand up, Coach Hedge!"

"I heard that!" The coach scanned the bus for the offender. Then his eyes fixed on Jason, and his scowl deepened.

A jolt went down Jason's spine. He was sure the coach knew he didn't belong there. He was going to call Jason out, demand to know what he was doing on the bus—and Jason wouldn't have a clue what to say.

But Coach Hedge looked away and cleared his throat. "We'll arrive in five minutes! Stay with your partner. Don't lose your worksheet. And if any of you precious little cupcakes causes any trouble on this trip, I will personally send you back to campus the hard way."

He picked up a baseball bat and made like he was hitting a homer.

Jason looked at the girl next to him. "Can he talk to us that way?"

She shrugged. "Always does. This is the Wilderness School. 'Where kids are the animals.'"

She said it like it was a joke they'd shared before.

"This is some kind of mistake," Jason said. "I'm not supposed to be here."

The boy in front of him turned and laughed. "Yeah, right, Jason. We've all been framed! I didn't run away six times. Piper didn't steal a BMW."

The girl blushed. "I didn't steal that car, Leo!"

"Oh, I forgot, Piper. What was your story? You 'talked' the dealer into lending it to you?" He raised his eyebrows at Jason like, *Can you believe her?*

Leo looked like a Latino Santa's elf, with curly black hair, pointy ears, a cheerful, babyish face, and a mischievous smile that told you right away this guy should not be trusted around matches or sharp objects. His long, nimble fingers wouldn't stop moving—drumming on the seat, sweeping his hair behind his ears, fiddling with the buttons of his army fatigue jacket. Either the kid was naturally hyper or he was hopped up on enough sugar and caffeine to give a heart attack to a water buffalo.

"Anyway," Leo said, "I hope you've got your worksheet, 'cause I used mine for spit wads days ago. Why are you looking at me like that? Somebody draw on my face again?"

"I don't know you," Jason said.

Leo gave him a crocodile grin. "Sure. I'm not your best friend. I'm his evil clone."

"Leo Valdez!" Coach Hedge yelled from the front. "Problem back there?"

Leo winked at Jason. "Watch this." He turned to the front. "Sorry, Coach! I was having trouble hearing you. Could you use your megaphone, please?"

Coach Hedge grunted like he was pleased to have an excuse. He unclipped the megaphone from his belt and continued giving directions, but his voice came out like Darth Vader's. The kids cracked up. The coach tried again, but this time the megaphone blared: "The cow says moo!"

The kids howled, and the coach slammed down the megaphone. "Valdez!"

Piper stifled a laugh. "My god, Leo. How did you do that?"

Leo slipped a tiny Phillips head screwdriver from his sleeve. "I'm a special boy."

"Guys, seriously," Jason pleaded. "What am I doing here? Where are we going?"

Piper knit her eyebrows. "Jason, are you joking?"

"No! I have no idea—"

"Aw, yeah, he's joking," Leo said. "He's trying to get me back for that shaving cream on the Jell-O thing, aren't you?"

Jason stared at him blankly.

"No, I think he's serious." Piper tried to take his hand again, but he pulled it away.

"I'm sorry," he said. "I don't—I can't—"

"That's it!" Coach Hedge yelled from the front. "The back row has just volunteered to clean up after lunch!"

The rest of the kids cheered.

"There's a shocker," Leo muttered.

But Piper kept her eyes on Jason, like she couldn't decide whether to be hurt or worried. "Did you hit your head or something? You really don't know who we are?"

Jason shrugged helplessly. "It's worse than that. I don't know who *I* am."

The bus dropped them in front of a big red stucco complex like a museum, just sitting in the middle of nowhere. Maybe that's what it was: the National Museum of Nowhere, Jason thought. A cold wind blew across the desert. Jason hadn't paid much attention to what he was wearing, but it wasn't nearly warm enough: jeans and sneakers, a purple T-shirt, and a thin black windbreaker.

"So, a crash course for the amnesiac," Leo said, in a helpful tone that made Jason think this was not going to be helpful. "We go to the 'Wilderness School'"—Leo made air quotes with his fingers. "Which means we're 'bad kids.' Your family, or the court, or whoever, decided you were too much trouble, so they shipped you off to this lovely prison—sorry, 'boarding school'—in Armpit, Nevada, where you learn valuable nature skills like running ten miles a day through the cacti and weaving daisies into hats! And for a special treat we go on 'educational' field trips with Coach Hedge, who keeps order with a baseball bat. Is it all coming back to you now?"

"No." Jason glanced apprehensively at the other kids: maybe twenty guys, half that many girls. None of them looked like hardened criminals, but he wondered what they'd all done to get sentenced to a school for delinquents, and he wondered why he belonged with them.

Leo rolled his eyes. "You're really gonna play this out, huh? Okay, so the three of us started here together this semester. We're totally tight. You do everything I say and give me your dessert and do my chores—"

"Leo!" Piper snapped.

"Fine. Ignore that last part. But we *are* friends. Well, Piper's a little more than your friend, the last few weeks—"

"Leo, stop it!" Piper's face turned red. Jason could feel his face burning too. He thought he'd remember if he'd been going out with a girl like Piper.

"He's got amnesia or something," Piper said. "We've got to tell somebody."

Leo scoffed. "Who, Coach Hedge? He'd try to fix Jason by whacking him upside the head."

The coach was at the front of the group, barking orders and blowing his whistle to keep the kids in line; but every so often he'd glance back at Jason and scowl.

"Leo, Jason needs help," Piper insisted. "He's got a concussion or—"

"Yo, Piper." One of the other guys dropped back to join them as the group was heading into the museum. The new guy wedged himself between Jason and Piper and knocked Leo down. "Don't talk to these bottom-feeders. You're my partner, remember?"

The new guy had dark hair cut Superman style, a deep tan, and teeth so white they should've come with a warning label: DO NOT STARE DIRECTLY AT TEETH. PERMANENT BLINDNESS

MAY OCCUR. He wore a Dallas Cowboys jersey, Western jeans and boots, and he smiled like he was God's gift to juvenile delinquent girls everywhere. Jason hated him instantly.

"Go away, Dylan," Piper grumbled. "I didn't ask to work with you."

"Ah, that's no way to be. This is your lucky day!" Dylan hooked his arm through hers and dragged her through the museum entrance. Piper shot one last look over her shoulder like, *911.*

Leo got up and brushed himself off. "I hate that guy." He offered Jason his arm, like they should go skipping inside together. "I'm Dylan. I'm so cool, I want to date myself, but I can't figure out how! You want to date me instead? You're so lucky!'"

"Leo," Jason said, "you're weird."

"Yeah, you tell me that a lot." Leo grinned. "But if you don't remember me, that means I can reuse all my old jokes. Come on!"

Jason figured that if this was his best friend, his life must be pretty messed up; but he followed Leo into the museum.

They walked through the building, stopping here and there for Coach Hedge to lecture them with his megaphone, which alternately made him sound like a Sith Lord or blared out random comments like "The pig says oink."

Leo kept pulling out nuts, bolts, and pipe cleaners from the pockets of his army jacket and putting them together, like he had to keep his hands busy at all times.

Jason was too distracted to pay much attention to the

exhibits, but they were about the Grand Canyon and the Hualapai tribe, which owned the museum.

Some girls kept looking over at Piper and Dylan and snickering. Jason figured these girls were the popular clique. They wore matching jeans and pink tops and enough makeup for a Halloween party.

One of them said, "Hey, Piper, does your tribe run this place? Do you get in free if you do a rain dance?"

The other girls laughed. Even Piper's so-called partner Dylan suppressed a smile. Piper's snowboarding jacket sleeves hid her hands, but Jason got the feeling she was clenching her fists.

"My dad's Cherokee," she said. "Not Hualapai. 'Course, you'd need a few brain cells to know the difference, Isabel."

Isabel widened her eyes in mock surprise, so that she looked like an owl with a makeup addiction. "Oh, sorry! Was your *mom* in this tribe? Oh, that's right. You never knew your mom."

Piper charged her, but before a fight could start, Coach Hedge barked, "Enough back there! Set a good example or I'll break out my baseball bat!"

The group shuffled on to the next exhibit, but the girls kept calling out little comments to Piper.

"Good to be back on the rez?" one asked in a sweet voice.

"Dad's probably too drunk to work," another said with fake sympathy. "That's why she turned klepto."

Piper ignored them, but Jason was ready to punch them himself. He might not remember Piper, or even who he was, but he knew he hated mean kids.

Leo caught his arm. "Be cool. Piper doesn't like us fighting her battles. Besides, if those girls found out the truth about her dad, they'd be all bowing down to her and screaming, 'We're not worthy!'"

"Why? What about her dad?"

Leo laughed in disbelief. "You're not kidding? You really don't remember that your girlfriend's dad—"

"Look, I wish I did, but I don't even remember *her*, much less her dad."

Leo whistled. "Whatever. We *have* to talk when we get back to the dorm."

They reached the far end of the exhibit hall, where some big glass doors led out to a terrace.

"All right, cupcakes," Coach Hedge announced. "You are about to see the Grand Canyon. Try not to break it. The skywalk can hold the weight of seventy jumbo jets, so you featherweights should be safe out there. If possible, try to avoid pushing each other over the edge, as that would cause me extra paperwork."

The coach opened the doors, and they all stepped outside. The Grand Canyon spread before them, live and in person. Extending over the edge was a horseshoe-shaped walkway made of glass, so you could see right through it.

"Man," Leo said. "That's pretty wicked."

Jason had to agree. Despite his amnesia and his feeling that he didn't belong there, he couldn't help being impressed.

The canyon was bigger and wider than you could appreciate from a picture. They were up so high that birds circled below their feet. Five hundred feet down, a river snaked along the canyon floor. Banks of storm clouds had moved overhead while they'd been inside, casting shadows like angry faces across the cliffs. As far as Jason could see in any direction, red and gray ravines cut through the desert like some crazy god had taken a knife to it.

Jason got a piercing pain behind his eyes. *Crazy gods...* Where had he come up with that idea? He felt like he'd gotten close to something important—something he should know about. He also got the unmistakable feeling he was in danger.

"You all right?" Leo asked. "You're not going to throw up over the side, are you? 'Cause I should've brought my camera."

Jason grabbed the railing. He was shivering and sweaty, but it had nothing to do with heights. He blinked, and the pain behind his eyes subsided.

"I'm fine," he managed. "Just a headache."

Thunder rumbled overhead. A cold wind almost knocked him sideways.

"This can't be safe." Leo squinted at the clouds. "Storm's right over us, but it's clear all the way around. Weird, huh?"

Jason looked up and saw Leo was right. A dark circle of clouds had parked itself over the skywalk, but the rest of the sky in every direction was perfectly clear. Jason had a bad feeling about that.

"All right, cupcakes!" Coach Hedge yelled. He frowned at the storm like it bothered him too. "We may have to cut this short, so get to work! Remember, complete sentences!"

The storm rumbled, and Jason's head began to hurt again. Not knowing why he did it, he reached into his jeans pocket and brought out a coin—a circle of gold the size of a half-dollar, but thicker and more uneven. Stamped on one side was a picture of a battle-ax. On the other was some guy's face wreathed in laurels. The inscription said something like IVLIVS.

"Dang, is that gold?" Leo asked. "You been holding out on me!"

Jason put the coin away, wondering how he'd come to have it, and why he had the feeling he was going to need it soon.

"It's nothing," he said. "Just a coin."

Leo shrugged. Maybe his mind had to keep moving as much as his hands. "Come on," he said. "Dare you to spit over the edge."

They didn't try very hard on the worksheet. For one thing, Jason was too distracted by the storm and his own mixed-up feelings. For another thing, he didn't have any idea how to "name three sedimentary strata you observe" or "describe two examples of erosion."

Leo was no help. He was too busy building a helicopter out of pipe cleaners.

"Check it out." He launched the copter. Jason figured it would plummet, but the pipe-cleaner blades actually spun. The little copter made it halfway across the canyon before it lost momentum and spiraled into the void.

"How'd you do that?" Jason asked.

Leo shrugged. "Would've been cooler if I had some rubber bands."

"Seriously," Jason said, "are we friends?"

"Last I checked."

"You sure? What was the first day we met? What did we talk about?"

"It was..." Leo frowned. "I don't recall exactly. I'm ADHD, man. You can't expect me to remember details."

"But I don't remember you *at all*. I don't remember anyone here. What if—"

"You're right and everyone else is wrong?" Leo asked. "You think you just appeared here this morning, and we've all got fake memories of you?"

A little voice in Jason's head said, *That's exactly what I think.*

But it sounded crazy. Everybody here took him for granted. Everyone acted like he was a normal part of the class—except for Coach Hedge.

"Take the worksheet." Jason handed Leo the paper. "I'll be right back."

Before Leo could protest, Jason headed across the skywalk.

Their school group had the place to themselves. Maybe it was too early in the day for tourists, or maybe the weird weather had scared them off. The Wilderness School kids had spread out in pairs across the skywalk. Most were joking around or talking. Some of the guys were dropping pennies over the side. About fifty feet away, Piper was trying to fill out her worksheet, but her stupid partner Dylan was hitting on her, putting his hand on her shoulder and giving her that blinding white smile. She kept pushing him away, and when she saw Jason she gave him a look like, *Throttle this guy for me.*

Jason motioned for her to hang on. He walked up to Coach Hedge, who was leaning on his baseball bat, studying the storm clouds.

"Did you do this?" the coach asked him.

Jason took a step back. "Do what?" It sounded like the coach had just asked if he'd made the thunderstorm.

Coach Hedge glared at him, his beady little eyes glinting under the brim of his cap. "Don't play games with me, kid. What are you doing here, and why are you messing up my job?"

"You mean . . . you *don't* know me?" Jason said. "I'm not one of your students?"

Hedge snorted. "Never seen you before today."

Jason was so relieved he almost wanted to cry. At least he wasn't going insane. He *was* in the wrong place. "Look, sir, I don't know how I got here. I just woke up on the school bus. All I know is I'm not supposed to be here."

"Got that right." Hedge's gruff voice dropped to a murmur, like he was sharing a secret. "You got a powerful way with the Mist, kid, if you can make all these people think they know you; but you can't fool me. I've been smelling monster for days now. I knew we had an infiltrator, but you don't smell like a monster. You smell like a half-blood. So—who are you, and where'd you come from?"

Most of what the coach said didn't make sense, but Jason decided to answer honestly. "I don't know who I am. I don't have any memories. You've got to help me."

Coach Hedge studied his face like was trying to read Jason's thoughts.

"Great," Hedge muttered. "You're being truthful."

"Of course I am! And what was all that about monsters and half-bloods? Are those code words or something?"

Hedge narrowed his eyes. Part of Jason wondered if the guy was just nuts. But the other part knew better.

"Look, kid," Hedge said, "I don't know who you are. I just know *what* you are, and it means trouble. Now I got to protect three of you rather than two. Are you the special package? Is that it?"

"What are you talking about?"

Hedge looked at the storm. The clouds were getting thicker and darker, hovering right over the skywalk.

"This morning," Hedge said, "I got a message from camp. They said an extraction team is on the way. They're coming to pick up a special package, but they wouldn't give me details. I thought to myself, Fine. The two I'm watching are pretty powerful, older than most. I know they're being stalked. I can smell a monster in the group. I figure that's why the camp is suddenly frantic to pick them up. But then *you* pop up out of nowhere. So, are you the special package?"

The pain behind Jason's eyes got worse than ever. *Half-bloods. Camp. Monsters.* He still didn't know what Hedge was talking about, but the words gave him a massive brain freeze—like his mind was trying to access information that should've been there but wasn't.

He stumbled, and Coach Hedge caught him. For a short guy, the coach had hands like steel. "Whoa, there, cupcake. You say you got no memories, huh? Fine. I'll just have to watch you, too, until the team gets here. We'll let the director figure things out."

"What director?" Jason said. "What camp?"

"Just sit tight. Reinforcements should be here soon. Hopefully nothing happens before—"

Lightning crackled overhead. The wind picked up with a vengeance. Worksheets flew into the Grand Canyon, and the entire bridge shuddered. Kids screamed, stumbling and grabbing the rails.

"I had to say something," Hedge grumbled. He bellowed into his megaphone: "Everyone inside! The cow says moo! Off the skywalk!"

"I thought you said this thing was stable!" Jason shouted over the wind.

"Under normal circumstances," Hedge agreed, "which these aren't. Come on!"

JASON

THE STORM CHURNED INTO A MINIATURE HURRICANE. Funnel clouds snaked toward the skywalk like the tendrils of a monster jellyfish.

Kids screamed and ran for the building. The wind snatched away their notebooks, jackets, hats, and backpacks. Jason skidded across the slick floor.

Leo lost his balance and almost toppled over the railing, but Jason grabbed his jacket and pulled him back.

"Thanks, man!" Leo yelled.

"Go, go, go!" said Coach Hedge.

Piper and Dylan were holding the doors open, herding the other kids inside. Piper's snowboarding jacket was flapping wildly, her dark hair all in her face. Jason thought she must've been freezing, but she looked calm and confident—telling the others it would be okay, encouraging them to keep moving.

Jason, Leo, and Coach Hedge ran toward them, but it was

like running through quicksand. The wind seemed to fight them, pushing them back.

Dylan and Piper pushed one more kid inside, then lost their grip on the doors. They slammed shut, closing off the skywalk.

Piper tugged at the handles. Inside, the kids pounded on the glass, but the doors seemed to be stuck.

"Dylan, help!" Piper shouted.

Dylan just stood there with an idiotic grin, his Cowboys jersey rippling in the wind, like he was suddenly enjoying the storm.

"Sorry, Piper," he said. "I'm done helping."

He flicked his wrist, and Piper flew backward, slamming into the doors and sliding to the skywalk deck.

"Piper!" Jason tried to charge forward, but the wind was against him, and Coach Hedge pushed him back.

"Coach," Jason said, "let me go!"

"Jason, Leo, stay behind me," the coach ordered. "This is my fight. I should've known that was our monster."

"What?" Leo demanded. A rogue worksheet slapped him in the face, but he swatted it away. "What monster?"

The coach's cap blew off, and sticking up above his curly hair were two bumps—like the knots cartoon characters get when they're bonked on the head. Coach Hedge lifted his baseball bat—but it wasn't a regular bat anymore. Somehow it had changed into a crudely shaped tree-branch club, with twigs and leaves still attached.

Dylan gave him that psycho happy smile. "Oh, come on,

Coach. Let the boy attack me! After all, you're getting too old for this. Isn't that why they *retired* you to this stupid school? I've been on your team the entire season, and you didn't even know. You're losing your nose, grandpa."

The coach made an angry sound like an animal bleating. "That's it, cupcake. You're going down."

"You think you can protect three half-bloods at once, old man?" Dylan laughed. "Good luck."

Dylan pointed at Leo, and a funnel cloud materialized around him. Leo flew off the skywalk like he'd been tossed. Somehow he managed to twist in midair, and slammed sideways into the canyon wall. He skidded, clawing furiously for any handhold. Finally he grabbed a thin ledge about fifty feet below the skywalk and hung there by his fingertips.

"Help!" he yelled up at them. "Rope, please? Bungee cord? Something?"

Coach Hedge cursed and tossed Jason his club. "I don't know who you are, kid, but I hope you're good. Keep that *thing* busy"—he stabbed a thumb at Dylan—"while I get Leo."

"Get him how?" Jason demanded. "You going to fly?"

"Not fly. Climb." Hedge kicked off his shoes, and Jason almost had a coronary. The coach didn't have any feet. He had hooves—goat's hooves. Which meant those things on his head, Jason realized, weren't bumps. They were horns.

"You're a faun," Jason said.

"*Satyr!*" Hedge snapped. "Fauns are Roman. But we'll talk about that later."

Hedge leaped over the railing. He sailed toward the canyon wall and hit hooves first. He bounded down the cliff with impossible agility, finding footholds no bigger than postage stamps, dodging whirlwinds that tried to attack him as he picked his way toward Leo.

"Isn't that cute!" Dylan turned toward Jason. "Now it's your turn, boy."

Jason threw the club. It seemed useless with the winds so strong, but the club flew right at Dylan, even curving when he tried to dodge, and smacked him on the head so hard he fell to his knees.

Piper wasn't as dazed as she appeared. Her fingers closed around the club when it rolled next to her, but before she could use it, Dylan rose. Blood—*golden* blood—trickled from his forehead.

"Nice try, boy." He glared at Jason. "But you'll have to do better."

The skywalk shuddered. Hairline fractures appeared in the glass. Inside the museum, kids stopped banging on the doors. They backed away, watching in terror.

Dylan's body dissolved into smoke, as if his molecules were coming unglued. He had the same face, the same brilliant white smile, but his whole form was suddenly composed of swirling black vapor, his eyes like electrical sparks in a living storm cloud. He sprouted black smoky wings and rose above the skywalk. If angels could be evil, Jason decided, they would look exactly like this.

"You're a *ventus*," Jason said, though he had no idea how he knew that word. "A storm spirit."

Dylan's laugh sounded like a tornado tearing off a roof. "I'm glad I waited, demigod. Leo and Piper I've known about for weeks. Could've killed them at any time. But my mistress said a third was coming—someone special. She'll reward me greatly for your death!"

Two more funnel clouds touched down on either side of Dylan and turned into *venti*—ghostly young men with smoky wings and eyes that flickered with lightning.

Piper stayed down, pretending to be dazed, her hand still gripping the club. Her face was pale, but she gave Jason a determined look, and he understood the message: *Keep their attention. I'll brain them from behind.*

Cute, smart, *and* violent. Jason wished he remembered having her as a girlfriend.

He clenched his fists and got ready to charge, but he never got a chance.

Dylan raised his hand, arcs of electricity running between his fingers, and blasted Jason in the chest.

Bang! Jason found himself flat on his back. His mouth tasted like burning aluminum foil. He lifted his head and saw that his clothes were smoking. The lightning bolt had gone straight though his body and blasted off his left shoe. His toes were black with soot.

The storm spirits were laughing. The winds raged. Piper was screaming defiantly, but it all sounded tinny and far away.

Out of the corner of his eye, Jason saw Coach Hedge climbing the cliff with Leo on his back. Piper was on her feet, desperately swinging the club to fend off the two extra storm spirits, but they were just toying with her. The club went right through their bodies like they weren't there. And Dylan, a dark and winged tornado with eyes, loomed over Jason.

"Stop," Jason croaked. He rose unsteadily to his feet, and he wasn't sure who was more surprised: him, or the storm spirits.

"How are you alive?" Dylan's form flickered. "That was enough lightning to kill twenty men!"

"My turn," Jason said.

He reached in his pocket and pulled out the gold coin. He let his instincts take over, flipping the coin in the air like he'd done it a thousand times. He caught it in his palm, and suddenly he was holding a sword—a wickedly sharp double-edged weapon. The ridged grip fit his fingers perfectly, and the whole thing was gold—hilt, handle, and blade.

Dylan snarled and backed up. He looked at his two comrades and yelled, "Well? Kill him!"

The other storm spirits didn't look happy with that order, but they flew at Jason, their fingers crackling with electricity.

Jason swung at the first spirit. His blade passed through it, and the creature's smoky form disintegrated. The second spirit let loose a bolt of lightning, but Jason's blade absorbed the charge. Jason stepped in—one quick thrust, and the second storm spirit dissolved into gold powder.

Dylan wailed in outrage. He looked down as if expecting his comrades to re-form, but their gold dust remains dispersed in the wind. "Impossible! Who *are* you, half-blood?"

Piper was so stunned she dropped her club. "Jason, how...?"

Then Coach Hedge leaped back onto the skywalk and dumped Leo like a sack of flour.

"Spirits, fear me!" Hedge bellowed, flexing his short arms. Then he looked around and realized there was only Dylan.

"Curse it, boy!" he snapped at Jason. "Didn't you leave some for me? I like a challenge!"

Leo got to his feet, breathing hard. He looked completely humiliated, his hands bleeding from clawing at the rocks. "Yo, Coach Supergoat, whatever you are—I just fell down the freaking Grand Canyon! Stop asking for challenges!"

Dylan hissed at them, but Jason could see fear in his eyes. "You have no idea how many enemies you've awakened, half-bloods. My mistress will destroy *all* demigods. This war you *cannot* win."

Above them, the storm exploded into a full-force gale. Cracks expanded in the skywalk. Sheets of rain poured down, and Jason had to crouch to keep his balance.

A hole opened in the clouds—a swirling vortex of black and silver.

"The mistress calls me back!" Dylan shouted with glee. "And you, demigod, will come with me!"

He lunged at Jason, but Piper tackled the monster from behind. Even though he was made of smoke, Piper somehow managed to connect. Both of them went sprawling. Leo, Jason, and the coach surged forward to help, but the spirit screamed with rage. He let loose a torrent that knocked them all backward. Jason and Coach Hedge landed on their butts. Jason's sword skidded across the glass. Leo hit the back of his head and curled on his side, dazed and groaning. Piper got the worst of it. She was thrown off Dylan's back and hit the railing, tumbling over the side until she was hanging by one hand over the abyss.

Jason started toward her, but Dylan screamed, "I'll settle for this one!"

He grabbed Leo's arm and began to rise, towing a half-conscious Leo below him. The storm spun faster, pulling them upward like a vacuum cleaner.

"Help!" Piper yelled. "Somebody!"

Then she slipped, screaming as she fell.

"Jason, go!" Hedge yelled. "Save her!"

The coach launched himself at the spirit with some serious goat fu—lashing out with his hooves, knocking Leo free from the spirit's grasp. Leo dropped safely to the floor, but Dylan grappled the coach's arms instead. Hedge tried to head-butt him, then kicked him and called him a cupcake. They rose into the air, gaining speed.

Coach Hedge shouted down once more, "Save her! I got this!" Then the satyr and the storm spirit spiraled into the clouds and disappeared.

Save her? Jason thought. *She's gone!*

But again his instincts won. He ran to the railing, thinking, *I'm a lunatic,* and jumped over the side.

Jason wasn't scared of heights. He was scared of being smashed against the canyon floor five hundred feet below. He figured he hadn't accomplished anything except for dying along with Piper, but he tucked in his arms and plummeted headfirst. The sides of the canyon raced past like a film on fast-forward. His face felt like it was peeling off.

In a heartbeat, he caught up with Piper, who was flailing wildly. He tackled her waist and closed his eyes, waiting for death. Piper screamed. The wind whistled in Jason's ears. He wondered what dying would feel like. He was thinking, probably not so good. He wished somehow they could never hit bottom.

Suddenly the wind died. Piper's scream turned into a strangled gasp. Jason thought they must be dead, but he hadn't felt any impact.

"J-J-Jason," Piper managed.

He opened his eyes. They weren't falling. They were floating in midair, a hundred feet above the river.

He hugged Piper tight, and she repositioned herself so she was hugging him too. They were nose to nose. Her heart beat so hard, Jason could feel it through her clothes.

Her breath smelled like cinnamon. She said, "How did you—"

"I didn't," he said. "I think I would know if I could fly. . . ."

But then he thought: *I don't even know who I am.*

He imagined going up. Piper yelped as they shot a few feet higher. They weren't exactly floating, Jason decided. He could feel pressure under his feet like they were balancing at the top of a geyser.

"The air is supporting us," he said.

"Well, tell it to support us more! Get us out of here!"

Jason looked down. The easiest thing would be to sink gently to the canyon floor. Then he looked up. The rain had stopped. The storm clouds didn't seem as bad, but they were still rumbling and flashing. There was no guarantee the spirits were gone for good. He had no idea what had happened to Coach Hedge. And he'd left Leo up there, barely conscious.

"We have to help them," Piper said, as if reading his thoughts. "Can you—"

"Let's see." Jason thought *Up*, and instantly they shot skyward.

The fact he was riding the winds might've been cool under different circumstances, but he was too much in shock. As soon as they landed on the skywalk, they ran to Leo.

Piper turned Leo over, and he groaned. His army coat was soaked from the rain. His curly hair glittered gold from rolling around in monster dust. But at least he wasn't dead.

"Stupid...ugly...goat," he muttered.

"Where did he go?" Piper asked.

Leo pointed straight up. "Never came down. Please tell me he didn't actually save my life."

"Twice," Jason said.

Leo groaned even louder. "What happened? The tornado guy, the gold sword...I hit my head. That's it, right? I'm hallucinating?"

Jason had forgotten about the sword. He walked over to where it was lying and picked it up. The blade was well balanced. On a hunch he flipped it. Midspin, the sword shrank back into a coin and landed in his palm.

"Yep," Leo said. "Definitely hallucinating."

Piper shivered in her rain-soaked clothes. "Jason, those things—"

"*Venti,*" he said. "Storm spirits."

"Okay. You acted like...like you'd seen them before. Who *are* you?"

He shook his head. "That's what I've been trying to tell you. I don't know."

The storm dissipated. The other kids from the Wilderness

School were staring out the glass doors in horror. Security guards were working on the locks now, but they didn't seem to be having any luck.

"Coach Hedge said he had to protect three people," Jason remembered. "I think he meant us."

"And that thing Dylan turned into..." Piper shuddered. "God, I can't believe it was *hitting* on me. He called us... what, *demigods*?"

Leo lay on his back, staring at the sky. He didn't seem anxious to get up. "Don't know what *demi* means," he said. "But I'm not feeling too godly. You guys feeling godly?"

There was a brittle sound like dry twigs snapping, and the cracks in the skywalk began to widen.

"We need to get off this thing," Jason said. "Maybe if we—"

"Ohhh-kay," Leo interrupted. "Look up there and tell me if those are flying horses."

At first Jason thought Leo *had* hit his head too hard. Then he saw a dark shape descending from the east—too slow for a plane, too large for a bird. As it got closer he could see a pair of winged animals—gray, four-legged, exactly like horses— except each one had a twenty-foot wingspan. And they were pulling a brightly painted box with two wheels: a chariot.

"Reinforcements," he said. "Hedge told me an extraction squad was coming for us."

"Extraction squad?" Leo struggled to his feet. "That sounds painful."

"And where are they extracting us *to*?" Piper asked.

Jason watched as the chariot landed on the far end of the

skywalk. The flying horses tucked in their wings and cantered nervously across the glass, as if they sensed it was near breaking. Two teenagers stood in the chariot—a tall blond girl maybe a little older than Jason, and a bulky dude with a shaved head and a face like a pile of bricks. They both wore jeans and orange T-shirts, with shields tossed over their backs. The girl leaped off before the chariot had even finished moving. She pulled a knife and ran toward Jason's group while the bulky dude was reining in the horses.

"Where is he?" the girl demanded. Her gray eyes were fierce and a little startling.

"Where's who?" Jason asked.

She frowned like his answer was unacceptable. Then she turned to Leo and Piper. "What about Gleeson? Where is your protector, Gleeson Hedge?"

The coach's first name was Gleeson? Jason might've laughed if the morning hadn't been quite so weird and scary. Gleeson Hedge: football coach, goat man, protector of demigods. Sure. Why not?

Leo cleared his throat. "He got taken by some . . . tornado things."

"*Venti,*" Jason said. "Storm spirits."

The blond girl arched an eyebrow. "You mean *anemoi thuellai*? That's the Greek term. Who are you, and what happened?"

Jason did his best to explain, though it was hard to meet those intense gray eyes. About halfway through the story, the other guy from the chariot came over. He stood there glaring at them, his arms crossed. He had a tattoo of a rainbow on his biceps, which seemed a little unusual.

When Jason had finished his story, the blond girl didn't look satisfied. "No, no, no! She *told* me he would be here. She told me if I came here, I'd find the answer."

"Annabeth," the bald guy grunted. "Check it out." He pointed at Jason's feet.

Jason hadn't thought much about it, but he was still missing his left shoe, which had been blown off by the lightning. His bare foot felt okay, but it looked like a lump of charcoal.

"The guy with one shoe," said the bald dude. "He's the answer."

"No, Butch," the girl insisted. "He can't be. I was tricked." She glared at the sky as though it had done something wrong. "What do you want from me?" she screamed. "What have you done with him?"

The skywalk shuddered, and the horses whinnied urgently.

"Annabeth," said the bald dude, Butch, "we gotta leave. Let's get these three to camp and figure it out there. Those storm spirits might come back."

She fumed for a moment. "Fine." She fixed Jason with a resentful look. "We'll settle this later."

She turned on her heel and marched toward the chariot.

Piper shook her head. "What's *her* problem? What's going on?"

"Seriously," Leo agreed.

"We have to get you out of here," Butch said. "I'll explain on the way."

"I'm not going anywhere with *her*." Jason gestured toward the blonde. "She looks like she wants to kill me."

Butch hesitated. "Annabeth's okay. You gotta cut her some

slack. She had a vision telling her to come here, to find a guy with one shoe. That was supposed to be the answer to her problem."

"What problem?" Piper asked.

"She's been looking for one of our campers, who's been missing three days," Butch said. "She's going out of her mind with worry. She hoped he'd be here."

"Who?" Jason asked.

"Her boyfriend," Butch said. "A guy named Percy Jackson."

III

PIPER

AFTER A MORNING OF STORM SPIRITS, goat men, and flying boyfriends, Piper should've been losing her mind. Instead, all she felt was dread.

It's starting, she thought. *Just like the dream said.*

She stood in back of the chariot with Leo and Jason, while the bald guy, Butch, handled the reins, and the blond girl, Annabeth, adjusted a bronze navigation device. They rose over the Grand Canyon and headed east, icy wind ripping straight through Piper's jacket. Behind them, more storm clouds were gathering.

The chariot lurched and bumped. It had no seat belts and the back was wide open, so Piper wondered if Jason would catch her again if she fell. That had been the most disturbing part of the morning—not that Jason could fly, but that he'd held her in his arms and yet didn't know who she was.

All semester she'd worked on a relationship, trying to get

Jason to notice her as more than a friend. Finally she'd gotten the big dope to kiss her. The last few weeks had been the best of her life. And then, three nights ago, the dream had ruined everything—that horrible voice, giving her horrible news. She hadn't told anyone about it, not even Jason.

Now she didn't even have *him*. It was like someone had wiped his memory, and she was stuck in the worst "do over" of all time. She wanted to scream. Jason stood right next to her: those sky blue eyes, close-cropped blond hair, that cute little scar on his upper lip. His face was kind and gentle, but always a little sad. And he just stared at the horizon, not even noticing her.

Meanwhile, Leo was being annoying, as usual. "This is so cool!" He spit a pegasus feather out of his mouth. "Where are we going?"

"A safe place," Annabeth said. "The *only* safe place for kids like us. Camp Half-Blood."

"Half-Blood?" Piper was immediately on guard. She hated that word. She'd been called a half-blood too many times— half Cherokee, half white—and it was never a compliment. "Is that some kind of bad joke?"

"She means we're demigods," Jason said. "Half god, half mortal."

Annabeth looked back. "You seem to know a lot, Jason. But, yes, demigods. My mom is Athena, goddess of wisdom. Butch here is the son of Iris, the rainbow goddess."

Leo choked. "Your mom is a rainbow goddess?"

"Got a problem with that?" Butch said.

"No, no," Leo said. "Rainbows. Very macho."

"Butch is our best equestrian," Annabeth said. "He gets along great with the pegasi."

"Rainbows, ponies," Leo muttered.

"I'm gonna toss you off this chariot," Butch warned.

"Demigods," Piper said. "You mean you think you're... you think we're—"

Lightning flashed. The chariot shuddered, and Jason yelled, "Left wheel's on fire!"

Piper stepped back. Sure enough, the wheel was burning, white flames lapping up the side of the chariot.

The wind roared. Piper glanced behind them and saw dark shapes forming in the clouds, more storm spirits spiraling toward the chariot—except these looked more like horses than angels.

She started to say, "Why are they—"

"*Anemoi* come in different shapes," Annabeth said. "Sometimes human, sometimes stallions, depending on how chaotic they are. Hold on. This is going to get rough."

Butch flicked the reins. The pegasi put on a burst of speed, and the chariot blurred. Piper's stomach crawled into her throat. Her vision went black, and when it came back to normal, they were in a totally different place.

A cold gray ocean stretched out to the left. Snow-covered fields, roads, and forests spread to the right. Directly below them was a green valley, like an island of springtime, rimmed with snowy hills on three sides and water to the north. Piper saw a cluster of buildings like ancient Greek temples, a big blue mansion, ball courts, a lake, and a climbing wall that seemed to be on fire. But before she could really process all she was seeing, their wheels came off and the chariot dropped out of the sky.

Annabeth and Butch tried to maintain control. The pegasi labored to hold the chariot in a flight pattern, but they seemed exhausted from their burst of speed, and bearing the chariot and the weight of five people was just too much.

"The lake!" Annabeth yelled. "Aim for the lake!"

Piper remembered something her dad had once told her, about hitting water from up high being as bad as hitting cement.

And then—*BOOM.*

The biggest shock was the cold. She was underwater, so disoriented that she didn't know which way was up.

She just had time to think: *This would be a stupid way to die.* Then faces appeared in the green murk—girls with long black hair and glowing yellow eyes. They smiled at her, grabbed her shoulders, and hauled her up.

They tossed her, gasping and shivering, onto the shore. Nearby, Butch stood in the lake, cutting the wrecked harnesses off the pegasi. Fortunately, the horses looked okay, but they were flapping their wings and splashing water everywhere. Jason, Leo, and Annabeth were already on shore, surrounded by kids giving them blankets and asking questions. Somebody took Piper by the arms and helped her stand. Apparently kids fell into the lake a lot, because a detail of campers ran up with big bronze leaf blower–looking things and blasted Piper with hot air; and in about two seconds her clothes were dry.

There were at least twenty campers milling around—the youngest maybe nine, the oldest college age, eighteen or nineteen—and all of them had orange T-shirts like Annabeth's. Piper looked back at the water and saw those strange girls just below the surface, their hair floating in the current. They waved like, *toodle-oo*, and disappeared into the depths. A second later the wreckage of the chariot was tossed from the lake and landed nearby with a wet crunch.

"Annabeth!" A guy with a bow and quiver on his back pushed through the crowd. "I said you could *borrow* the chariot, not destroy it!"

"Will, I'm sorry," Annabeth sighed. "I'll get it fixed, I promise."

Will scowled at his broken chariot. Then he sized up Piper, Leo, and Jason. "These are the ones? Way older than thirteen. Why haven't they been claimed already?"

"Claimed?" Leo asked.

Before Annabeth could explain, Will said, "Any sign of Percy?"

"No," Annabeth admitted.

The campers muttered. Piper had no idea who this guy Percy was, but his disappearance seemed to be a big deal.

Another girl stepped forward—tall, Asian, dark hair in ringlets, plenty of jewelry, and perfect makeup. Somehow she managed to make jeans and an orange T-shirt look glamorous. She glanced at Leo, fixed her eyes on Jason like he might be worthy of her attention, then curled her lip at Piper as if she were a week-old burrito that had just been pulled out of a Dumpster. Piper knew this girl's type. She'd dealt with a lot of girls like this at Wilderness School and every other stupid school her father had sent her to. Piper knew instantly they were going to be enemies.

"Well," the girl said, "I hope they're worth the trouble."

Leo snorted. "Gee, thanks. What are we, your new pets?"

"No kidding," Jason said. "How about some answers before you start judging us—like, what is this place, why are we here, how long do we have to stay?"

Piper had the same questions, but a wave of anxiety washed over her. *Worth the trouble.* If they only knew about her dream. They had no idea. . . .

"Jason," Annabeth said, "I promise we'll answer your questions. And Drew"—she frowned at the glamour girl—"all demigods are worth saving. But I'll admit, the trip didn't accomplish what I hoped."

"Hey," Piper said, "we didn't ask to be brought here."

Drew sniffed. "And nobody *wants* you, hon. Does your hair always look like a dead badger?"

Piper stepped forward, ready to smack her, but Annabeth said, "Piper, stop."

Piper did. She wasn't a bit scared of Drew, but Annabeth didn't seem like somebody she wanted for an enemy.

"We need to make our new arrivals feel welcome," Annabeth said, with another pointed look at Drew. "We'll assign them each a guide, give them a tour of camp. Hopefully by the campfire tonight, they'll be claimed."

"Would somebody tell me what *claimed* means?" Piper asked.

Suddenly there was a collective gasp. The campers backed

away. At first Piper thought she'd done something wrong. Then she realized their faces were bathed in a strange red light, as if someone had lit a torch behind her. She turned and almost forgot how to breathe.

Floating over Leo's head was a blazing holographic image —a fiery hammer.

"That," Annabeth said, "is claiming."

"What'd I do?" Leo backed toward the lake. Then he glanced up and yelped. "Is my hair on fire?" He ducked, but the symbol followed him, bobbing and weaving so it looked like he was trying to write something in flames with his head.

"This can't be good," Butch muttered. "The curse—"

"Butch, shut up," Annabeth said. "Leo, you've just been claimed—"

"By a god," Jason interrupted. "That's the symbol of Vulcan, isn't it?"

All eyes turned to him.

"Jason," Annabeth said carefully, "how did you know that?"

"I'm not sure."

"Vulcan?" Leo demanded. "I don't even LIKE *Star Trek*. What are you talking about?"

"Vulcan is the Roman name for Hephaestus," Annabeth said, "the god of blacksmiths and fire."

The fiery hammer faded, but Leo kept swatting the air like he was afraid it was following him. "The god of *what*? Who?"

Annabeth turned to the guy with the bow. "Will, would you take Leo, give him a tour? Introduce him to his bunkmates in Cabin Nine."

"Sure, Annabeth."

"What's Cabin Nine?" Leo asked. "And I'm not a Vulcan!"

"Come on, Mr. Spock, I'll explain everything." Will put a hand on his shoulder and steered him off toward the cabins.

Annabeth turned her attention back to Jason. Usually Piper didn't like it when other girls checked out her boyfriend, but Annabeth didn't seem to care that he was a good-looking guy. She studied him more like he was a complicated blueprint. Finally she said, "Hold out your arm."

Piper saw what she was looking at, and her eyes widened.

Jason had taken off his windbreaker after his dip in the lake, leaving his arms bare, and on the inside of his right forearm was a tattoo. How had Piper never noticed it before? She'd looked at Jason's arms a million times. The tattoo couldn't have just *appeared*, but it was darkly etched, impossible to miss: a dozen straight lines like a bar code, and over that an eagle with the letters SPQR.

"I've never seen marks like this," Annabeth said. "Where did you get them?"

Jason shook his head. "I'm getting really tired of saying this, but I don't know."

The other campers pushed forward, trying to get a look at Jason's tattoo. The marks seemed to bother them *a lot*—almost like a declaration of war.

"They look burned into your skin," Annabeth noticed.

"They were," Jason said. Then he winced as if his head was aching. "I mean...I think so. I don't remember."

No one said anything. It was clear the campers saw Annabeth as the leader. They were waiting for her verdict.

"He needs to go straight to Chiron," Annabeth decided. "Drew, would you—"

"Absolutely." Drew laced her arm through Jason's. "This way, sweetie. I'll introduce you to our director. He's . . . an *interesting* guy." She flashed Piper a smug look and led Jason toward the big blue house on the hill.

The crowd began to disperse, until only Annabeth and Piper were left.

"Who's Chiron?" Piper asked. "Is Jason in some kind of trouble?"

Annabeth hesitated. "Good question, Piper. Come on, I'll give you a tour. We need to talk."

IV

PIPER

PIPER SOON REALIZED ANNABETH'S HEART wasn't in the tour.

She talked about all this amazing stuff the camp offered—magic archery, pegasus riding, the lava wall, fighting monsters—but she showed no excitement, as if her mind were elsewhere. She pointed out the open-air dining pavilion that overlooked Long Island Sound. (Yes, Long Island, New York; they'd traveled *that* far on the chariot.) Annabeth explained how Camp Half-Blood was mostly a summer camp, but some kids stayed here year-round, and they'd added so many campers it was always crowded now, even in winter.

Piper wondered who ran the camp, and how they'd known Piper and her friends belonged here. She wondered if she'd have to stay full-time, or if she'd be any good at the activities. Could you flunk out of monster fighting? A million questions bubbled in her head, but given Annabeth's mood, she decided to keep quiet.

As they climbed a hill at the edge of camp, Piper turned and got an amazing view of the valley—a big stretch of woods to the northwest, a beautiful beach, the creek, the canoe lake, lush green fields, and the whole layout of the cabins—a bizarre assortment of buildings arranged like a Greek omega, Ω, with a loop of cabins around a central green, and two wings sticking out the bottom on either side. Piper counted twenty cabins in all. One glowed golden, another silver. One had grass on the roof. Another was bright red with barbed wire trenches. One cabin was black with fiery green torches out front.

All of it seemed like a different world from the snowy hills and fields outside.

"The valley is protected from mortal eyes," Annabeth said. "As you can see, the weather is controlled, too. Each cabin represents a Greek god—a place for that god's children to live."

She looked at Piper like she was trying to judge how Piper was handling the news.

"You're saying Mom was a goddess."

Annabeth nodded. "You're taking this awfully calmly."

Piper couldn't tell her why. She couldn't admit that this just confirmed some weird feelings she'd had for years, arguments she'd had with her father about why there were no photos of Mom in the house, and why Dad would never tell her exactly how or why her mom had left them. But mostly, the dream had warned her this was coming. *Soon they will find you, demigod,* that voice had rumbled. *When they do, follow our directions. Cooperate, and your father might live.*

Piper took a shaky breath. "I guess after this morning, it's a little easier to believe. So who's my mom?"

"We should know soon," Annabeth said. "You're what—fifteen? Gods are supposed to claim you when you're thirteen. That was the deal."

"The deal?"

"They made a promise last summer...well, long story ...but they promised not to ignore their demigod children anymore, to claim them by the time they turn thirteen. Sometimes it takes a little longer, but you saw how fast Leo was claimed once he got here. Should happen for you soon. Tonight at the campfire, I bet we'll get a sign."

Piper wondered if she'd have a big flaming hammer over her head, or with her luck, something even more embarrassing. A flaming wombat, maybe. Whoever her mother was, Piper had no reason to think she'd be proud to claim a kleptomaniac daughter with massive problems. "Why thirteen?"

"The older you get," Annabeth said, "the more monsters notice you, try to kill you. 'Round thirteen is usually when it starts. That's why we send protectors into the schools to find you guys, get you to camp before it's too late."

"Like Coach Hedge?"

Annabeth nodded. "He's—he was a satyr: half man, half goat. Satyrs work for the camp, finding demigods, protecting them, bringing them in when the time is right."

Piper had no trouble believing Coach Hedge was half goat. She'd seen the guy eat. She'd never liked the coach much, but she couldn't believe he'd sacrificed himself to save them.

"What happened to him?" she asked. "When we went up into the clouds, did he . . . is he gone for good?"

"Hard to say." Annabeth's expression was pained. "Storm spirits . . . difficult to battle. Even our best weapons, Celestial bronze, will pass right through them unless you can catch them by surprise."

"Jason's sword just turned them to dust," Piper remembered.

"He was lucky, then. If you hit a monster just right, you can dissolve them, send their essence back to Tartarus."

"Tartarus?"

"A huge abyss in the Underworld, where the worst monsters come from. Kind of like a bottomless pit of evil. Anyway, once monsters dissolve, it usually takes months, even years before they can re-form again. But since this storm spirit Dylan got away—well, I don't know why he'd keep Hedge alive. Hedge was a protector, though. He knew the risks. Satyrs don't have mortal souls. He'll be reincarnated as a tree or a flower or something."

Piper tried to imagine Coach Hedge as a clump of very angry pansies. That made her feel even worse.

She gazed at the cabins below, and an uneasy feeling settled over her. Hedge had died to get her here safely. Her mom's cabin was down there somewhere, which meant she had brothers and sisters, more people she'd have to betray. *Do what we tell you*, the voice had said. *Or the consequences will be painful.* She tucked her hands under her arms, trying to stop them from shaking.

"It'll be okay," Annabeth promised. "You have friends

here. We've all been through a lot of weird stuff. We know what you're going through."

I doubt that, Piper thought.

"I've been kicked out of five different schools the past five years," she said. "My dad's running out of places to put me."

"Only five?" Annabeth didn't sound like she was teasing. "Piper, we've all been labeled troublemakers. I ran away from home when I was seven."

"Seriously?"

"Oh, yeah. Most of us are diagnosed with attention deficit disorder or dyslexia, or both—"

"Leo's ADHD," Piper said.

"Right. It's because we're hardwired for battle. Restless, impulsive—we don't fit in with regular kids. You should hear how much trouble Percy—" Her face darkened. "Anyway, demigods get a bad rep. How'd you get in trouble?"

Usually when someone asked that question, Piper started a fight, or changed the subject, or caused some kind of distraction. But for some reason she found herself telling the truth.

"I steal stuff," she said. "Well, not really *steal*..."

"Is your family poor?"

Piper laughed bitterly. "Not even. I did it...I don't know why. For attention, I guess. My dad never had time for me unless I got in trouble."

Annabeth nodded. "I can relate. But you said you didn't really steal? What do you mean?"

"Well...nobody ever believes me. The police, teachers—even the people I took stuff from: they're so embarrassed, they'll deny what happened. But the truth is, I don't steal anything. I just ask people for things. And they give me stuff. Even a BMW convertible. I just asked. And the dealer said, 'Sure. Take it.' Later, he realized what he'd done, I guess. Then the police came after me."

Piper waited. She was used to people calling her a liar, but when she looked up, Annabeth just nodded.

"Interesting. If your *dad* were the god, I'd say you're a child of Hermes, god of thieves. He can be pretty convincing. But your dad is mortal...."

"Very," Piper agreed.

Annabeth shook her head, apparently mystified. "I don't know, then. With luck, your mom will claim you tonight."

Piper almost hoped it wouldn't happen. If her mom were a goddess, would she know about that dream? Would she know what Piper had been asked to do? Piper wondered if Olympian gods ever blasted their kids with lightning for being evil, or grounded them in the Underworld.

Annabeth was studying her. Piper decided she was going to have to be careful what she said from now on. Annabeth was obviously pretty smart. If anyone could figure out Piper's secret...

"Come on," Annabeth said at last. "There's something else I need to check."

They hiked a little farther until they reached a cave near the top of the hill. Bones and old swords littered the ground. Torches flanked the entrance, which was covered in a velvet curtain embroidered with snakes. It looked like the set for some kind of twisted puppet show.

"What's in there?" Piper asked.

Annabeth poked her head inside, then sighed and closed the curtains. "Nothing, right now. A friend's place. I've been expecting her for a few days, but so far, nothing."

"Your friend lives in a cave?"

Annabeth almost managed a smile. "Actually, her family has a luxury condo in Queens, and she goes to a finishing school in Connecticut. But when she's here at camp, yeah, she lives in the cave. She's our oracle, tells the future. I was hoping she could help me—"

"Find Percy," Piper guessed.

All the energy drained out of Annabeth, like she'd been holding it together for as long as she could. She sat down on a rock, and her expression was so full of pain, Piper felt like a voyeur.

She forced herself to look away. Her eyes drifted to the crest of the hill, where a single pine tree dominated the skyline. Something glittered in its lowest branch—like a fuzzy gold bath mat.

No . . . not a bath mat. It was a sheep's fleece.

Okay, Piper thought. Greek camp. They've got a replica of the Golden Fleece.

Then she noticed the base of the tree. At first she thought it was wrapped in a pile of massive purple cables. But the cables had reptilian scales, clawed feet, and a snakelike head with yellow eyes and smoking nostrils.

"That's—a dragon," she stammered. "That's the *actual* Golden Fleece?"

Annabeth nodded, but it was clear she wasn't really

listening. Her shoulders drooped. She rubbed her face and took a shaky breath. "Sorry. A little tired."

"You look ready to drop," Piper said. "How long have been searching for your boyfriend?"

"Three days, six hours, and about twelve minutes."

"And you've got no idea what happened to him?"

Annabeth shook her head miserably. "We were so excited because we both started winter break early. We met up at camp on Tuesday, figured we had three weeks together. It was going to be great. Then after the campfire, he—he kissed me good night, went back to his cabin, and in the morning, he was gone. We searched the whole camp. We contacted his mom. We've tried to reach him every way we know how. Nothing. He just disappeared."

Piper was thinking: *Three days ago.* The same night she'd had her dream. "How long were you guys together?"

"Since August," Annabeth said. "August eighteenth."

"Almost exactly when I met Jason," Piper said. "But we've only been together a few weeks."

Annabeth winced. "Piper . . . about that. Maybe you should sit down."

Piper knew where this was going. Panic started building inside her, like her lungs were filling with water. "Look, I know Jason thought—he thought he just *appeared* at our school today. But that's not true. I've known him for four months."

"Piper," Annabeth said sadly. "It's the Mist."

"Missed . . . what?"

"M-i-s-t. It's a kind of veil separating the mortal world from the magic world. Mortal minds—they can't process strange stuff like gods and monsters, so the Mist bends reality. It makes mortals see things in a way they *can* understand —like their eyes might just skip over this valley completely, or they might look at that dragon and see a pile of cables."

Piper swallowed. "No. You said yourself I'm not a regular mortal. I'm a demigod."

"Even demigods can be affected. I've seen it lots of times. Monsters infiltrate some place like a school, pass themselves off as human, and everyone *thinks* they remember that person. They believe he's always been around. The Mist can change memories, even create memories of things that never happened—"

"But Jason's not a monster!" Piper insisted. "He's a human guy, or demigod, or whatever you want to call him. My memories aren't fake. They're *so* real. The time we set Coach Hedge's pants on fire. The time Jason and I watched a meteor shower on the dorm roof and I finally got the stupid guy to kiss me...."

She found herself rambling, telling Annabeth about her whole semester at Wilderness School. She'd liked Jason from the first week they'd met. He was so nice to her, and so patient, he could even put up with hyperactive Leo and his stupid jokes. He'd accepted her for herself and didn't judge her because of the stupid things she'd done. They'd spent hours talking, looking at the stars, and eventually—*finally*—holding hands. All that *couldn't* be fake.

Annabeth pursed her lips. "Piper, your memories are a lot sharper than most. I'll admit that, and I don't know why that is. But if you know him so well—"

"I do!"

"Then where is he from?"

Piper felt like she'd been hit between the eyes. "He must have told me, but—"

"Did you ever notice his tattoo before today? Did he ever tell you anything about his parents, or his friends, or his last school?"

"I—I don't know, but—"

"Piper, what's his last name?"

Her mind went blank. She didn't know Jason's last name. How could that be?

She started to cry. She felt like a total fool, but she sat down on the rock next to Annabeth and just fell to pieces. It was too much. Did *everything* that was good in her stupid, miserable life have to be taken away?

Yes, the dream had told her. *Yes, unless you do exactly what we say.*

"Hey," Annabeth said. "We'll figure it out. Jason's here now. Who knows? Maybe it'll work out with you guys for real."

Not likely, Piper thought. Not if the dream had told her the truth. But she couldn't say that.

She brushed a tear from her cheek. "You brought me up here so no one would see me blubbering, huh?"

Annabeth shrugged. "I figured it would be hard for you. I know what it's like to lose your boyfriend."

"But I still can't believe . . . I *know* we had something. And now it's just gone, like he doesn't even recognize me. If he really did just show up today, then why? How'd he get there? Why can't he remember anything?"

"Good questions," Annabeth said. "Hopefully Chiron can figure that out. But for now, we need to get you settled. You ready to go back down?"

Piper gazed at the crazy assortment of cabins in the valley. Her new home, a family who supposedly understood her—but soon they'd be just another bunch of people she'd disappointed, just another place she'd been kicked out of. *You'll betray them for us,* the voice had warned. *Or you'll lose everything.*

She didn't have a choice.

"Yeah," she lied. "I'm ready."

On the central green, a group of campers was playing basketball. They were incredible shots. Nothing bounced off the rim. Three-pointers went in automatically.

"Apollo's cabin," Annabeth explained. "Bunch of show-offs with missile weapons—arrows, basketballs."

They walked past a central fire pit, where two guys were hacking at each other with swords.

"Real blades?" Piper noted. "Isn't that dangerous?"

"That's sort of the point," Annabeth said. "Uh, sorry. Bad pun. That's my cabin over there. Number Six." She nodded to a gray building with a carved owl over the door. Through the open doorway, Piper could see bookshelves, weapon displays, and one of those computerized SMART Boards they have in classrooms. Two girls were drawing a map that looked like a battle diagram.

"Speaking of blades," Annabeth said, "come here."

She led Piper around the side of the cabin, to a big metal shed that looked like it was meant for gardening tools. Annabeth unlocked it, and inside were *not* gardening tools, unless you wanted to make war on your tomato plants. The shed was lined with all sorts of weapons—from swords to spears to clubs like Coach Hedge's.

"Every demigod needs a weapon," Annabeth said. "Hephaestus makes the best, but we have a pretty good selection, too. Athena's all about strategy—matching the right weapon to the right person. Let's see . . ."

Piper didn't feel much like shopping for deadly objects, but she knew Annabeth was trying to do something nice for her.

Annabeth handed her a massive sword, which Piper could hardly lift.

"No," they both said at once.

Annabeth rummaged a little farther in the shed and brought out something else.

"A shotgun?" Piper asked.

"Mossberg 500." Annabeth checked the pump action like it was no big deal. "Don't worry. It doesn't hurt humans. It's modified to shoot Celestial bronze, so it only kills monsters."

"Um, I don't think that's my style," Piper said.

"Mmm, yeah," Annabeth agreed. "Too flashy."

She put the shotgun back and started poking through a rack of crossbows when something in the corner of the shed caught Piper's eye.

"What is that?" she said. "A knife?"

Annabeth dug it out and blew the dust off the scabbard. It looked like it hadn't seen the light of day in centuries.

"I don't know, Piper." Annabeth sounded uneasy. "I don't think you want this one. Swords are usually better."

"You use a knife." Piper pointed to the one strapped to Annabeth's belt.

"Yeah, but..." Annabeth shrugged. "Well, take a look if you want."

The sheath was worn black leather, bound in bronze. Nothing fancy, nothing flashy. The polished wood handle fit beautifully in Piper's hand. When she unsheathed it, she found a triangular blade eighteen inches long—bronze gleaming like it had been polished yesterday. The edges were deadly sharp. Her reflection in the blade caught her by surprise. She looked older, more serious, not as scared as she felt.

"It suits you," Annabeth admitted. "That kind of blade is called a parazonium. It was mostly ceremonial, carried by high-ranking officers in the Greek armies. It showed you were a person of power and wealth, but in a fight, it could protect you just fine."

"I like it," Piper said. "Why didn't you think it was right?"

Annabeth exhaled. "That blade has a long story. Most people would be afraid to claim it. Its first owner... well, things didn't turn out too well for her. Her name was Helen."

Piper let that sink in. "Wait, you mean *the* Helen? Helen of Troy?"

Annabeth nodded.

Suddenly Piper felt like she should be handling the dagger with surgical gloves. "And it's just sitting in your toolshed?"

"We're surrounded by Ancient Greek stuff," Annabeth said. "This isn't a museum. Weapons like that—they're meant to be used. They're our heritage as demigods. That was a wedding present from Menelaus, Helen's first husband. She named the dagger Katoptris."

"Meaning?"

"Mirror," Annabeth said. "Looking glass. Probably because that's the only thing Helen used it for. I don't think it's ever seen battle."

Piper looked at the blade again. For a moment, her own image stared up at her, but then the reflection changed. She saw flames, and a grotesque face like something carved from bedrock. She heard the same laughter as in her dream. She saw her dad in chains, tied to a post in front of a roaring bonfire.

She dropped the blade.

"Piper?" Annabeth shouted to the Apollo kids on the court, "Medic! I need some help over here!"

"No, it's—it's okay," Piper managed.

"You sure?"

"Yeah. I just..." She had to control herself. With trembling fingers, she picked up the dagger. "I just got overwhelmed. So much happening today. But...I want to keep the dagger, if that's okay."

Annabeth hesitated. Then she waved off the Apollo kids. "Okay, if you're sure. You turned really pale, there. I thought you were having a seizure or something."

"I'm fine," Piper promised, though her heart was still racing. "Is there...um, a phone at camp? Can I call my dad?"

Annabeth's gray eyes were almost as unnerving as the dagger blade. She seemed to be calculating a million possibilities, trying to read Piper's thoughts.

"We aren't allowed phones," she said. "Most demigods, if they use a cell phone, it's like sending up a signal, letting monsters know where you are. But...I've got one." She slipped it out of her pocket. "Kind of against the rules, but if it can be our secret..."

Piper took it gratefully, trying not to let her hands shake. She stepped away from Annabeth and turned to face the commons area.

She called her dad's private line, even though she knew what would happen. Voice mail. She'd been trying for three days, ever since the dream. Wilderness School only allowed phone privileges once a day, but she'd called every evening, and gotten nowhere.

Reluctantly she dialed the other number. Her dad's personal assistant answered immediately. "Mr. McLean's office."

"Jane," Piper said, gritting her teeth. "Where's my dad?"

Jane was silent for a moment, probably wondering if she could get away with hanging up. "Piper, I thought you weren't supposed to call from school."

"Maybe I'm not at school," Piper said. "Maybe I ran away to live among the woodland creatures."

"Mmm." Jane didn't sound concerned. "Well, I'll tell him you called."

"Where is he?"

"Out."

"You don't know, do you?" Piper lowered her voice, hoping Annabeth was too nice to eavesdrop. "When are you going to call the police, Jane? He could be in trouble."

"Piper, we are not going to turn this into a media circus. I'm sure he's fine. He does take off occasionally. He always comes back."

"So it's true. You *don't* know—"

"I have to go, Piper," Jane snapped. "Enjoy school."

The line went dead. Piper cursed. She walked back to Annabeth and handed her the phone.

"No luck?" Annabeth asked.

Piper didn't answer. She didn't trust herself not to start crying again.

Annabeth glanced at the phone display and hesitated. "Your last name is McLean? Sorry, it's not my business. But that sounds really familiar."

"Common name."

"Yeah, I guess. What does your dad do?"

"He's got a degree in the arts," Piper said automatically. "He's a Cherokee artist."

Her standard response. Not a lie, just not the whole truth. Most people, when they heard that, figured her dad sold Indian souvenirs at a roadside stand on a reservation. Sitting Bull bobble-heads, wampum necklaces, Big Chief tablets—that kind of thing.

"Oh." Annabeth didn't look convinced, but she put the phone away. "You feeling okay? Want to keep going?"

Piper fastened her new dagger to her belt and promised

herself that later, when she was alone, she'd figure out how it worked. "Sure," she said. "I want to see everything."

All the cabins were cool, but none of them struck Piper as *hers*. No burning signs—wombats or otherwise—appeared over her head.

Cabin Eight was entirely silver and glowed like moonlight. "Artemis?" Piper guessed.

"You know Greek mythology," Annabeth said.

"I did some reading when my dad was working on a project last year."

"I thought he did Cherokee art."

Piper bit back a curse. "Oh, right. But—you know, he does other stuff too."

Piper thought she'd blown it: McLean, Greek mythology. Thankfully, Annabeth didn't seem to make the connection.

"Anyway," Annabeth continued, "Artemis is goddess of the moon, goddess of hunting. But no campers. Artemis was an eternal maiden, so she doesn't have any kids."

"Oh." That kind of bummed Piper out. She'd always liked the stories of Artemis, and figured she would make a cool mom.

"Well, there *are* the Hunters of Artemis," Annabeth amended. "They visit sometimes. They're not the children of Artemis, but they're her handmaidens—this band of immortal teenage girls who adventure together and hunt monsters and stuff."

Piper perked up. "That sounds cool. They get to be immortal?"

"Unless they die in combat, or break their vows. Did I mention they have to swear off boys? No dating—ever. For eternity."

"Oh," Piper said. "Never mind."

Annabeth laughed. For a moment she looked almost happy, and Piper thought she'd be a cool friend to hang out with in better times.

Forget it, Piper reminded herself. You're not going to make any friends here. Not once they find out.

They passed the next cabin, Number Ten, which was decorated like a Barbie house with lace curtains, a pink door, and potted carnations in the windows. They walked by the doorway, and the smell of perfume almost made Piper gag.

"Gah, is that where supermodels go to die?"

Annabeth smirked. "Aphrodite's cabin. Goddess of love. Drew is the head counselor."

"Figures," Piper grumbled.

"They're not all bad," Annabeth said. "The last head counselor we had was great."

"What happened to her?"

Annabeth's expression darkened. "We should keep moving."

They looked at the other cabins, but Piper just got more depressed. She wondered if she could be the daughter of Demeter, the farming goddess. Then again, Piper killed every plant she ever touched. Athena was cool. Or maybe Hecate, the magic goddess. But it didn't really matter. Even here, where everyone was supposed to find a lost parent, she knew she would still end up the unwanted kid. She was not looking forward to the campfire tonight.

"We started with the twelve Olympian gods," Annabeth explained. "Male gods on the left, female on the right. Then last year, we added a whole bunch of new cabins for the other gods who didn't have thrones on Olympus—Hecate, Hades, Iris—"

"What are the two big ones on the end?" Piper asked.

Annabeth frowned. "Zeus and Hera. King and queen of the gods."

Piper headed that way, and Annabeth followed, though she didn't act very excited. The Zeus cabin reminded Piper of a bank. It was white marble with big columns out front and polished bronze doors emblazoned with lightning bolts.

Hera's cabin was smaller but done in the same style, except the doors were carved with peacock feather designs, shimmering in different colors.

Unlike the other cabins, which were all noisy and open and full of activity, the Zeus and Hera cabins looked closed and silent.

"Are they empty?" Piper asked.

Annabeth nodded. "Zeus went a long time without having any children. Well, mostly. Zeus, Poseidon, and Hades, the eldest brothers among the gods—they're called the Big Three. Their kids are really powerful, really dangerous. For the last seventy years or so, they tried to avoid having demigod children."

"*Tried* to avoid it?"

"Sometimes they…um, cheated. I've got a friend, Thalia

Grace, who's the daughter of Zeus. But she gave up camp life and became a Hunter of Artemis. My boyfriend, Percy, he's a son of Poseidon. And there's a kid who shows up sometimes, Nico—son of Hades. Except for them, there are no demigod children of the Big Three gods. At least, not that we know of."

"And Hera?" Piper looked at the peacock-decorated doors. The cabin bothered her, though she wasn't sure why.

"Goddess of marriage." Annabeth's tone was carefully controlled, like she was trying to avoid cursing. "She doesn't have kids with anyone but Zeus. So, yeah, no demigods. The cabin's just honorary."

"You don't like her," Piper noticed.

"We have a long history," Annabeth admitted. "I thought we'd made peace, but when Percy disappeared... I got this weird dream vision from her."

"Telling you to come get us," Piper said. "But you thought Percy would be there."

"It's probably better I don't talk about it," Annabeth said. "I've got nothing good to say about Hera right now."

Piper looked down the base of the doors. "So who goes in here?"

"No one. The cabin is just honorary, like I said. No one goes in."

"Someone does." Piper pointed at a footprint on the dusty threshold. On instinct, she pushed the doors and they swung open easily.

Annabeth stepped back. "Um, Piper, I don't think we should—"

"We're supposed to do dangerous stuff, right?" And Piper walked inside.

Hera's cabin was not someplace Piper would want to live. It was as cold as a freezer, with a circle of white columns around a central statue of the goddess, ten feet tall, seated on a throne in flowing golden robes. Piper had always thought of Greek statues as white with blank eyes, but this one was brightly painted so it looked almost human—except huge. Hera's piercing eyes seemed to follow Piper.

At the goddess's feet, a fire burned in a bronze brazier. Piper wondered who tended it if the cabin was always empty. A stone hawk sat on Hera's shoulder, and in her hand was a staff topped with a lotus flower. The goddess's hair was done in black plaits. Her face smiled, but the eyes were cold and calculating, as if she were saying: *Mother knows best. Now don't cross me or I will have to step on you.*

There was nothing else in the cabin—no beds, no furniture, no bathroom, no windows, nothing that anyone could actually use to live. For a goddess of home and marriage, Hera's place reminded Piper of a tomb.

No, this wasn't her mom. At least Piper was sure of *that*. She hadn't come in here because she felt a *good* connection, but because her sense of dread was stronger here. Her dream—that horrible ultimatum she'd been handed—had something to do with this cabin.

She froze. They weren't alone. Behind the statue, at a little altar in the back, stood a figure covered in a black shawl. Only her hands were visible, palms up. She seemed to be chanting something like a spell or a prayer.

Annabeth gasped. "Rachel?"

The other girl turned. She dropped her shawl, revealing a mane of curly red hair and a freckled face that didn't go with the seriousness of the cabin or the black shawl at all. She looked about seventeen, a totally normal teen in a green blouse and tattered jeans covered with marker doodles. Despite the cold floor, she was barefoot.

"Hey!" She ran to give Annabeth a hug. "I'm so sorry! I came as fast as I could."

They talked for a few minutes about Annabeth's boy-friend and how there was no news, et cetera, until finally Annabeth remembered Piper, who was standing there feeling uncomfortable.

"I'm being rude," Annabeth apologized. "Rachel, this is Piper, one of the half-bloods we rescued today. Piper, this is Rachel Elizabeth Dare, our oracle."

"The friend who lives in the cave," Piper guessed.

Rachel grinned. "That's me."

"So you're an oracle?" Piper asked. "You can tell the future?"

"More like the future mugs me from time to time," Rachel said. "I speak prophecies. The oracle's spirit kind of hijacks me every once in a while and speaks important stuff that doesn't make any sense to anybody. But yeah, the prophecies tell the future."

"Oh." Piper shifted from foot to foot. "That's cool."

Rachel laughed. "Don't worry. Everybody finds it a little creepy. Even me. But usually I'm harmless."

"You're a demigod?"

"Nope," Rachel said. "Just mortal."

"Then what are you . . ." Piper waved her hand around the room.

Rachel's smile faded. She glanced at Annabeth, then back at Piper. "Just a hunch. Something about this cabin and Percy's disappearance. They're connected somehow. I've learned to follow my hunches, especially the last month, since the gods went silent."

"Went silent?" Piper asked.

Rachel frowned at Annabeth. "You haven't told her yet?"

"I was getting to that," Annabeth said. "Piper, for the last month . . . well, it's normal for the gods not to talk to their children very much, but usually we can count on some messages now and then. Some of us can even visit Olympus. I spent practically all semester at the Empire State Building."

"Excuse me?"

"The entrance to Mount Olympus these days."

"Oh," Piper said. "Sure, why not?"

"Annabeth was redesigning Olympus after it was damaged in the Titan War," Rachel explained. "She's an amazing architect. You should see the salad bar—"

"Anyway," Annabeth said, "starting about a month ago, Olympus fell silent. The entrance closed, and no one could get in. Nobody knows why. It's like the gods have sealed themselves off. Even my mom won't answer my prayers, and our camp director, Dionysus, was recalled."

"Your camp director was the god of . . . wine?"

"Yeah, it's a—"

"Long story," Piper guessed. "Right. Go on."

"That's it, really," Annabeth said. "Demigods still get claimed, but nothing else. No messages. No visits. No sign the gods are even listening. It's like something has happened —something *really* bad. Then Percy disappeared."

"And Jason showed up on our field trip," Piper supplied. "With no memory."

"Who's Jason?" Rachel asked.

"My—" Piper stopped herself before she could say "boyfriend," but the effort made her chest hurt. "My friend. But Annabeth, you said Hera sent you a dream vision."

"Right," Annabeth said. "The first communication from a god in a month, and it's Hera, the least helpful goddess, and she contacts me, her least favorite demigod. She tells me I'll find out what happened to Percy if I go to the Grand Canyon skywalk and look for a guy with one shoe. Instead, I find you guys, and the guy with one shoe is Jason. It doesn't make sense."

"Something bad is happening," Rachel agreed. She looked at Piper, and Piper felt an overwhelming desire to tell them about her dream, to confess that *she* knew what was happening—at least part of the story. And the bad stuff was only beginning.

"Guys," she said. "I—I need to—"

Before she could continue, Rachel's body stiffened. Her eyes began to glow with a greenish light, and she grabbed Piper by the shoulders.

Piper tried to back away, but Rachel's hands were like steel clamps.

Free me, she said. But it wasn't Rachel's voice. It sounded like an older woman, speaking from somewhere far away, down a long, echoing pipe. *Free me, Piper McLean, or the earth shall swallow us. It must be by the solstice.*

The room started spinning. Annabeth tried to separate Piper from Rachel, but it was no use. Green smoke enveloped them, and Piper was no longer sure if she was awake or dreaming. The giant statue of the goddess seemed to rise from its throne. It leaned over Piper, its eyes boring into her. The statue's mouth opened, its breath like horribly thick perfume. It spoke in the same echoing voice: *Our enemies stir. The fiery one is only the first. Bow to his will, and their king shall rise, dooming us all. FREE ME!*

Piper's knees buckled, and everything went black.

V

LEO

Leo's tour was going great until he learned about the dragon.

The archer dude, Will Solace, seemed pretty cool. Everything he showed Leo was so amazing, it should've been illegal. Real Greek warships moored at the beach that sometimes had practice fights with flaming arrows and explosives? Sweet! Arts & crafts sessions where you could make sculptures with chain saws and blowtorches? Leo was like, *Sign me up!* The woods were stocked with dangerous monsters, and no one should ever go in there alone? Nice! And the camp was overflowing with fine-looking girls. Leo didn't quite understand the whole related-to-the-gods business, but he hoped that didn't mean he was cousins with all these ladies. That would suck. At the very least, he wanted to check out those underwater girls in the lake again. They were definitely worth drowning for.

Will showed him the cabins, the dining pavilion, and the sword arena.

"Do I get a sword?" Leo asked.

Will glanced at him like he found the idea disturbing. "You'll probably make your own, seeing as how you're in Cabin Nine."

"Yeah, what's up with that? Vulcan?"

"Usually we don't call the gods by their Roman names," Will said. "The original names are Greek. Your dad is Hephaestus."

"Festus?" Leo had heard somebody say that before, but he was still dismayed. "Sounds like the god of cowboys."

"*He*-phaestus," Will corrected. "God of blacksmiths and fire."

Leo had heard that too, but he was trying not to think about it. The god of fire . . . seriously? Considering what had happened to his mom, that seemed like a sick joke.

"So the flaming hammer over my head," Leo said. "Good thing, or bad thing?"

Will took a while to answer. "You were claimed almost immediately. That's usually good."

"But that Rainbow Pony dude, Butch—he mentioned a curse."

"Ah . . . look, it's nothing. Since Cabin Nine's last head counselor died—"

"Died? Like, painfully?"

"I ought to let your bunkmates tell you about it."

"Yeah, where *are* my home dawgs? Shouldn't their counselor be giving me the VIP tour?"

"He, um, can't. You'll see why." Will forged ahead before Leo could ask anything else.

"Curses and death," Leo said to himself. "This just gets better and better."

He was halfway across the green when he spotted his old babysitter. And she was *not* the kind of person he expected to see at a demigod camp.

Leo froze in his tracks.

"What's wrong?" Will asked.

Tía Callida—*Auntie* Callida. That's what she'd called herself, but Leo hadn't seen her since he was five years old. She was just standing there, in the shadow of a big white cabin at the end of the green, watching him. She wore her black linen widow's dress, with a black shawl pulled over her hair. Her face hadn't changed—leathery skin, piercing dark eyes. Her withered hands were like claws. She looked ancient, but no different than Leo remembered.

"That old lady..." Leo said. "What's she doing here?"

Will tried to follow his gaze. "What old lady?"

"Dude, *the* old lady. The one in black. How many old ladies do you see over there?"

Will frowned. "I think you've had a long day, Leo. The Mist could still be playing tricks on your mind. How about we head straight to your cabin now?"

Leo wanted to protest, but when he looked back toward the big white cabin, Tía Callida was gone. He was *sure* she'd been there, almost as if thinking about his mom had summoned Callida back from the past.

And that wasn't good, because Tía Callida had tried to kill him.

"Just messing with you, man." Leo pulled some gears and levers from his pockets and started fiddling with them to calm his nerves. He couldn't have everybody at camp thinking he was crazy. At least, not crazier than he really was.

"Let's go see Cabin Nine," he said. "I'm in the mood for a good curse."

From the outside, the Hephaestus cabin looked like an oversize RV with shiny metal walls and metal-slatted windows. The entrance was like a bank vault door, circular and several feet thick. It opened with lots of brass gears turning and hydraulic pistons blowing smoke.

Leo whistled. "They got a steampunk theme going on, huh?"

Inside, the cabin seemed deserted. Steel bunks were folded against the walls like high-tech Murphy beds. Each had a digital control panel, blinking LED lights, glowing gems, and interlocking gears. Leo figured each camper had his own combination lock to release his bed, and there was probably an alcove behind it with storage, maybe some traps to keep out unwanted visitors. At least, that's the way Leo would've designed it. A fire pole came down from the second floor, even though the cabin didn't appear to *have* a second floor from the outside. A circular staircase led down into some kind of basement. The walls were lined with every kind of power tool Leo could imagine, plus a huge assortment of knives, swords, and other implements of destruction. A large workbench overflowed with scrap metal—screws, bolts, washers, nails, rivets, and a million other machine parts. Leo had a strong urge to shovel them all into his coat pockets. He loved that kind of stuff. But he'd need a hundred more coats to fit it all.

Looking around, he could almost imagine he was back in his mom's machine shop. Not the weapons, maybe—but the tools, the piles of scrap, the smell of grease and metal and hot engines. She would've loved this place.

He pushed that thought away. He didn't like painful memories. *Keep moving*—that was his motto. Don't dwell on things. Don't stay in one place too long. It was the only way to stay ahead of the sadness.

He picked a long implement from the wall. "A weed whacker? What's the god of fire want with a weed whacker?"

A voice in the shadows said, "You'd be surprised."

At the back of the room, one of the bunk beds was occupied. A curtain of dark camouflage material retracted, and Leo could see the guy who'd been invisible a second before. It was hard to tell much about him because he was covered in a body cast. His head was wrapped in gauze except for his face, which was puffy and bruised. He looked like the Pillsbury Doughboy after a beat-down.

"I'm Jake Mason," the guy said. "I'd shake your hand, but..."

"Yeah," Leo said. "Don't get up."

The guy cracked a smile, then winced like it hurt to move his face. Leo wondered what had happened to him, but he was afraid to ask.

"Welcome to Cabin Nine," Jake said. "Been almost a year since we had any new kids. I'm head counselor for now."

"For now?" Leo asked.

Will Solace cleared his throat. "So where is everybody, Jake?"

"Down at the forges," Jake said wistfully. "They're working on . . . you know, that problem."

"Oh." Will changed the subject. "So, you got a spare bed for Leo?"

Jake studied Leo, sizing him up. "You believe in curses, Leo? Or ghosts?"

I just saw my evil babysitter Tía Callida, Leo thought. She's *got* to be dead after all these years. And I can't go a day without remembering my mom in that machine shop fire. Don't talk to me about ghosts, doughboy.

But aloud, he said, "Ghosts? Pfft. Nah. I'm cool. A storm spirit chucked me down the Grand Canyon this morning, but you know, all in a day's work, right?"

Jake nodded. "That's good. Because I'll give you the best bed in the cabin—Beckendorf's."

"Whoa, Jake," Will said. "You sure?"

Jake called out: "Bunk 1-A, please."

The whole cabin rumbled. A circular section of the floor spiraled open like a camera lens, and a full-size bed popped up. The bronze frame had a built-in game station at the footboard, a stereo system in the headboard, a glass-door refrigerator mounted into the base, and a whole bunch of control panels running down the side.

Leo jumped right in and lay back with arms behind his head. "I can handle this."

"It retracts into a private room below," Jake said.

"Oh, heck, yes," Leo said. "See y'all. I'll be down in the Leo Cave. Which button do I press?"

"Hold on," Will Solace protested. "You guys have private underground rooms?"

Jake probably would've smiled if it didn't hurt so much. "We got lots of secrets, Will. You Apollo guys can't have all the fun. Our campers have been excavating the tunnel system under Cabin Nine for almost a century. We still haven't found the end. Anyway, Leo, if you don't mind sleeping in a dead man's bed, it's yours."

Suddenly Leo didn't feel like kicking back. He sat up, careful not to touch any of the buttons. "The counselor who died—this was his bed?"

"Yeah," Jake said. "Charles Beckendorf."

Leo imagined saw blades coming through the mattress, or maybe a grenade sewn inside the pillows. "He didn't, like, die *in* this bed, did he?"

"No," Jake said. "In the Titan War, last summer."

"The Titan War," Leo repeated, "which has *nothing* to do with this very fine bed?"

"The Titans," Will said, like Leo was an idiot. "The big powerful guys that ruled the world before the gods. They tried to make a comeback last summer. Their leader, Kronos, built a new palace on top of Mount Tam in California. Their armies came to New York and almost destroyed Mount Olympus. A lot of demigods died trying to stop them."

"I'm guessing this wasn't on the news?" Leo said.

It seemed like a fair question, but Will shook his head in

disbelief. "You didn't hear about Mount St. Helens erupting, or the freak storms across the country, or that building collapsing in St. Louis?"

Leo shrugged. Last summer, he'd been on the run from another foster home. Then a truancy officer caught him in New Mexico, and the court sentenced him to the nearest correctional facility—the Wilderness School. "Guess I was busy."

"Doesn't matter," Jake said. "You were lucky to miss it. The thing is, Beckendorf was one of the first casualties, and ever since then—"

"Your cabin's been cursed," Leo guessed.

Jake didn't answer. Then again, the dude was in a body cast. That *was* an answer. Leo started noticing little things that he hadn't seen before—an explosion mark on the wall, a stain on the floor that might've been oil... or blood. Broken swords and smashed machines kicked into the corners of the room, maybe out of frustration. The place *did* feel unlucky.

Jake sighed halfheartedly. "Well, I should get some sleep. I hope you like it here, Leo. It used to be...really nice."

He closed his eyes, and the camouflage curtain drew itself across the bed.

"Come on, Leo," Will said. "I'll take you to the forges."

As they were leaving, Leo looked back at his new bed, and he could almost imagine a dead counselor sitting there —another ghost who wasn't going to leave Leo alone.

VI

LEO

"How did he die?" Leo asked. "I mean Beckendorf."

Will Solace trudged ahead. "Explosion. Beckendorf and Percy Jackson blew up a cruise ship full of monsters. Beckendorf didn't make it out."

There was that name again—Percy Jackson, Annabeth's missing boyfriend. That guy must've been into everything around here, Leo thought.

"So Beckendorf was pretty popular?" Leo asked. "I mean —before he blew up?"

"He was awesome," Will agreed. "It was hard on the whole camp when he died. Jake—he became head counselor in the middle of the war. Same as I did, actually. Jake did his best, but he never wanted to be leader. He just likes building stuff. Then after the war, things started to go wrong. Cabin Nine's chariots blew up. Their automatons went haywire. Their inventions started to malfunction. It was like a curse, and eventually people started calling it that—the Curse of Cabin Nine. Then Jake had his accident—"

"Which had something to do with the problem he mentioned," Leo guessed.

"They're working on it," Will said without enthusiasm. "And here we are."

The forge looked like a steam-powered locomotive had smashed into the Greek Parthenon and they had fused together. White marble columns lined the soot-stained walls. Chimneys pumped smoke over an elaborate gable carved with a bunch of gods and monsters. The building sat at the edge of a stream, with several waterwheels turning a series of bronze gears. Leo heard machinery grinding inside, fires roaring, and hammers ringing on anvils.

They stepped through the doorway, and a dozen guys and girls who'd been working on various projects all froze. The noise died down to the roar of the forge and the *click-click-click* of gears and levers.

"'Sup, guys," Will said. "This is your new brother, Leo —um, what's your last name?"

"Valdez." Leo looked around at the other campers. Was he really related to all of them? His cousins came from some big families, but he'd always just had his mom—until she died.

Kids came up and started shaking hands and introducing themselves. Their names blurred together: Shane, Christopher, Nyssa, Harley (yeah, like the motorcycle). Leo knew he'd never keep everybody straight. Too many of them. Too overwhelming.

None of them looked like the others—all different face types, skin tone, hair color, height. You'd never think, *Hey, look, it's the Hephaestus Bunch!* But they all had powerful hands, rough with calluses and stained with engine grease. Even little Harley, who couldn't have been more than eight, looked like he could go six rounds with Chuck Norris without breaking a sweat.

And all the kids shared a sad kind of seriousness. Their shoulders slumped like life had beaten them down pretty hard. Several looked like they'd been physically beaten up, too. Leo counted two arm slings, one pair of crutches, an eye patch, six Ace bandages, and about seven thousand Band-Aids.

"Well, all right!" Leo said. "I hear this is the party cabin!"

Nobody laughed. They all just stared at him.

Will Solace patted Leo's shoulder. "I'll leave you guys to get acquainted. Somebody show Leo to dinner when it's time?"

"I got it," one of the girls said. Nyssa, Leo remembered. She wore camo pants, a tank top that showed off her buff arms, and a red bandanna over a mop of dark hair. Except for the smiley-face Band-Aid on her chin, she looked like one of those female action heroes, like any second she was going to grab a machine gun and start mowing down evil aliens.

"Cool," Leo said. "I always wanted a sister who could beat me up."

Nyssa didn't smile. "Come on, joker boy. I'll show you around."

• • •

Leo was no stranger to workshops. He'd grown up around grease monkeys and power tools. His mom used to joke that his first pacifier was a lug wrench. But he'd never seen any place like the camp forge.

One guy was working on a battle-ax. He kept testing the blade on a slab of concrete. Each time he swung, the ax cut into the slab like it was warm cheese, but the guy looked unsatisfied and went back to honing the edge.

"What's he planning to kill with that thing?" Leo asked Nyssa. "A battleship?"

"You never know. Even with Celestial bronze—"

"That's the metal?"

She nodded. "Mined from Mount Olympus itself. Extremely rare. Anyway, it usually disintegrates monsters on contact, but big powerful ones have notoriously tough hides. Drakons, for instances—"

"You mean dragons?"

"Similar species. You'll learn the difference in monster-fighting class."

"Monster-fighting class. Yeah, I already got my black belt in that."

She didn't crack a smile. Leo hoped she wasn't this serious all the time. His dad's side of the family had to have *some* sense of humor, right?

They passed a couple of guys making a bronze windup toy. At least that's what it looked like. It was a six-inch-tall centaur—half man, half horse—armed with a miniature bow. One of the campers cranked the centaur's tail, and it whirred to life. It galloped across the table, yelling, "Die, mosquito! Die, mosquito!" and shooting everything in sight.

Apparently this had happened before, because everybody knew to hit the floor except Leo. Six needle-sized arrows embedded themselves in his shirt before a camper grabbed a hammer and smashed the centaur to pieces.

"Stupid curse!" The camper waved his hammer at the sky. "I just want a magic bug killer! Is that too much to ask?"

"Ouch," Leo said.

Nyssa pulled the needles out of his shirt. "Ah, you're fine. Let's move on before they rebuild it."

Leo rubbed his chest as they walked. "That sort of thing happen a lot?"

"Lately," Nyssa said, "everything we build turns to junk."

"The curse?"

Nyssa frowned. "I don't believe in curses. But *something's* wrong. And if we don't figure out the dragon problem, it's gonna get even worse."

"The dragon problem?" Leo hoped she was talking about a miniature dragon, maybe one that killed cockroaches, but he got the feeling he wasn't going to be so lucky.

Nyssa took him over to a big wall map that a couple of girls were studying. The map showed the camp—a semicircle of land with Long Island Sound on the north shore, the woods to the west, the cabins to the east, and a ring of hills to the south.

"It's got to be in the hills," the first girl said.

"We *looked* in the hills," the second argued. "The woods are a better hiding place."

"But we already set traps—"

"Hold up," Leo said. "You guys lost a dragon? A *real* full-size dragon?"

"It's a bronze dragon," Nyssa said. "But yes, it's a life-size automaton. Hephaestus cabin built it years ago. Then it was lost in the woods until a few summers back, when Beckendorf found it in pieces and rebuilt it. It's been helping protect the camp, but, um, it's a little unpredictable."

"Unpredictable," Leo said.

"It goes haywire and smashes down cabins, sets people on fire, tries to eat the satyrs."

"That's pretty unpredictable."

Nyssa nodded. "Beckendorf was the only one who could control it. Then he died, and the dragon just got worse and worse. Finally it went berserk and ran off. Occasionally it shows up, demolishes something, and runs away again. Everyone expects us to find it and destroy it—"

"*Destroy* it?" Leo was appalled. "You've got a life-size bronze dragon, and you want to *destroy* it?"

"It breathes fire," Nyssa explained. "It's deadly and out of control."

"But it's a dragon! Dude, that's so awesome. Can't you try talking to it, controlling it?"

"We tried. Jake Mason tried. You saw how well that worked."

Leo thought about Jake, wrapped in a body cast, lying alone on his bunk. "Still—"

"There's no other option." Nyssa turned to the other girls. "Let's try more traps in the woods—here, here, and here. Bait them with thirty-weight motor oil."

"The dragon drinks that?" Leo asked.

"Yeah." Nyssa sighed regretfully. "He used to like it with a little Tabasco sauce, right before bed. If he springs a trap, we can come in with acid sprayers—should melt through his hide. Then we get metal cutters and ... and finish the job."

They all looked sad. Leo realized they didn't want to kill the dragon any more than he did.

"Guys," he said. "There has to be another way."

Nyssa looked doubtful, but a few other campers stopped what they were working on and drifted over to hear the conversation.

"Like what?" one asked. "The thing breathes fire. We can't even get close."

Fire, Leo thought. Oh, man, the things he could tell them about fire. . . . But he had to be careful, even if these were his brothers and sisters. *Especially* if he had to live with them.

"Well ..." He hesitated. "Hephaestus is the god of fire, right? So don't any of you have like fire resistance or something?"

Nobody acted as if it was a crazy question, which was a relief, but Nyssa shook her head gravely.

"That's a Cyclops ability, Leo. Demigod children of Hephaestus ... we're just good with our hands. We're build-ers, craftsmen, weaponsmiths—stuff like that."

Leo's shoulders slumped. "Oh."

A guy in back said, "Well, a long *time* ago—"

"Yeah, okay," Nyssa conceded. "A long time ago some children of Hephaestus were born with power over fire. But that ability was very, very rare. And always dangerous. No

demigod like that has been born in centuries. The last one..."
She looked at one of the other kids for help.

"Sixteen sixty-six," the girl offered. "Guy named Thomas Faynor. He started the Great Fire of London, destroyed most of the city."

"Right," Nyssa said. "When a child of Hephaestus like that appears, it usually means something catastrophic is about to happen. And we don't need any more catastrophes."

Leo tried to keep his face clear of emotion, which wasn't his strong suit. "I guess I see your point. Too bad, though. If you could resist flames, you could get close to the dragon."

"Then it would kill you with its claws and fangs," Nyssa said. "Or simply step on you. No, we've got to destroy it. Trust me, if anyone *could* figure out another answer..."

She didn't finish, but Leo got the message. This was the cabin's big test. If they could do something only Beckendorf could do, if they could subdue the dragon without killing it, then maybe their curse would be lifted. But they were stumped for ideas. Any camper who figured out how would be a hero.

A conch horn blew in the distance. Campers started putting up their tools and projects. Leo hadn't realized it was getting so late, but he looked through the windows and saw the sun going down. His ADHD did that to him sometimes. If he was bored, a fifty-minute class seemed like six hours. If he was interested in something, like touring a demigod camp, hours slipped away and *bam*—the day was over.

"Dinner," Nyssa said. "Come on, Leo."

"Up at the pavilion, right?" he asked.

She nodded.

"You guys go ahead," Leo said. "Can you . . . give me a second?"

Nyssa hesitated. Then her expression softened. "Sure. It's a lot to process. I remember my first day. Come up when you're ready. Just don't touch anything. Almost every project in here can kill you if you're not careful."

"No touching," Leo promised.

His cabinmates filed out of the forge. Soon Leo was alone with the sounds of the bellows, the waterwheels, and small machines clicking and whirring.

He stared at the map of camp—the locations where his newfound siblings were going to put traps to catch a dragon. It was wrong. Plain wrong.

Very rare, he thought. And always dangerous.

He held out his hand and studied his fingers. They were long and thin, not callused like the other Hephaestus campers'. Leo had never been the biggest or the strongest kid. He'd survived in tough neighborhoods, tough schools, tough foster homes by using his wits. He was the class clown, the court jester, because he'd learned early that if you cracked jokes and pretended you weren't scared, you usually didn't get beat up. Even the baddest gangster kids would tolerate you, keep you around for laughs. Plus, humor was a good way to hide the pain. And if that didn't work, there was always Plan B. Run away. Over and over.

There *was* a Plan C, but he'd promised himself never to use it again.

He felt an urge to try it now—something he hadn't done since the accident, since his mom's death.

He extended his fingers and felt them tingle, like they were waking up—pins and needles. Then flames flickered to life, curls of red-hot fire dancing across his palm.

VII

JASON

As soon as Jason saw the house, he knew he was a dead man.

"Here we are!" Drew said cheerfully. "The Big House, camp headquarters."

It didn't look threatening, just a four-story manor painted baby blue with white trim. The wraparound porch had lounge chairs, a card table, and an empty wheelchair. Wind chimes shaped like nymphs turned into trees as they spun. Jason could imagine old people coming here for summer vacation, sitting on the porch and sipping prune juice while they watched the sunset. Still, the windows seemed to glare down at him like angry eyes. The wide-open doorway looked ready to swallow him. On the highest gable, a bronze eagle weathervane spun in the wind and pointed straight in his direction, as if telling him to turn around.

Every molecule in Jason's body told him he was on enemy ground.

"I am *not* supposed to be here," he said.

Drew circled her arm through his. "Oh, please. You're *perfect* here, sweetie. Believe me, I've seen a lot of heroes."

Drew smelled like Christmas—a strange combination of pine and nutmeg. Jason wondered if she always smelled like that, or if it was some kind of special perfume for the holidays. Her pink eyeliner was really distracting. Every time she blinked, he felt compelled to look at her. Maybe that was the point, to show off her warm brown eyes. She was pretty. No doubt about that. But she made Jason feel uncomfortable.

He slipped his arm away as gently as he could. "Look, I appreciate—"

"Is it that girl?" Drew pouted. "Oh, please, tell me you are *not* dating the Dumpster Queen."

"You mean Piper? Um..."

Jason wasn't sure how to answer. He didn't think he'd ever seen Piper before today, but he felt strangely guilty about it. He knew he shouldn't be in this place. He shouldn't befriend these people, and certainly he shouldn't date one of them. Still...Piper had been holding his hand when he woke up on that bus. She believed she was his girlfriend. She'd been brave on the skywalk, fighting those *venti*, and when Jason had caught her in midair and they'd held each other face-to-face, he couldn't pretend he wasn't a little tempted to kiss her. But that wasn't right. He didn't even know his own story. He couldn't play with her emotions like that.

Drew rolled her eyes. "Let me help you decide, sweetie. You can do better. A guy with your looks and obvious talent?"

She wasn't looking at him, though. She was staring at a spot right above his head.

"You're waiting for a sign," he guessed. "Like what popped over Leo's head."

"What? No! Well...yes. I mean, from what I heard, you're pretty powerful, right? You're going to be important at camp, so I figure your parent will claim you right away. And I'd love to see that. I wanna be with you every step of the way! So is your dad or mom the god? Please tell me it's not your mom. I would hate it if you were an *Aphrodite* kid."

"Why?"

"Then you'd be my half brother, silly. You can't date somebody from your own cabin. Yuck!"

"But aren't all the gods related?" Jason asked. "So isn't everyone here your cousin or something?"

"Aren't you cute! Sweetie, the godly side of your family doesn't count except for your parent. So anybody from another cabin—they're fair game. So who's your godly parent—mom or dad?"

As usual, Jason didn't have an answer. He looked up, but no glowing sign popped above his head. At the top of the Big House, the weathervane was still pointing his direction, that bronze eagle glaring as if to say, *Turn around, kid, while you still can.*

Then he heard footsteps on the front porch. No—not footsteps—*hooves.*

"Chiron!" Drew called. "This is Jason. He's totally awesome!"

Jason backed up so fast he almost tripped. Rounding the corner of the porch was a man on horseback. Except he wasn't on horseback—he was part of the horse. From the waist up he was human, with curly brown hair and a well-trimmed beard. He wore a T-shirt that said *World's Best Centaur*, and had a quiver and bow strapped to his back. His head was so high up he had to duck to avoid the porch lights, because from the waist down, he was a white stallion.

Chiron started to smile at Jason. Then the color drained from his face.

"You..." The centaur's eyes flared like a cornered animal's. "You should be dead."

Chiron ordered Jason—well, *invited*, but it sounded like an order—to come inside the house. He told Drew to go back to her cabin, which Drew didn't look happy about.

The centaur trotted over to the empty wheelchair on the porch. He slipped off his quiver and bow and backed up to the chair, which opened like a magician's box. Chiron gingerly stepped into it with his back legs and began scrunching himself into a space that should've been much too small. Jason imagined a truck's reversing noises—*beep, beep, beep*—as the centaur's lower half disappeared and the chair folded up, popping out a set of fake human legs covered in a blanket, so Chiron appeared to be a regular mortal guy in a wheelchair.

"Follow me," he ordered. "We have lemonade."

The living room looked like it had been swallowed by a rain forest. Grapevines curved up the walls and across the ceiling, which Jason found a little strange. He didn't think plants grew like that inside, especially in the winter, but these were leafy green and bursting with bunches of red grapes.

Leather couches faced a stone fireplace with a crackling fire. Wedged in one corner, an old-style Pac-Man arcade game beeped and blinked. Mounted on the walls was an assortment of masks—smiley/frowny Greek theater types, feathered Mardi Gras masks, Venetian *Carnevale* masks with big beaklike noses, carved wooden masks from Africa. Grapevines grew through their mouths so they seemed to have leafy tongues. Some had red grapes bulging through their eyeholes.

But the weirdest thing was the stuffed leopard's head above the fireplace. It looked so real, its eyes seemed to follow Jason. Then it snarled, and Jason nearly leaped out of his skin.

"Now, Seymour," Chiron chided. "Jason is a friend. Behave yourself."

"That thing is alive!" Jason said.

Chiron rummaged through the side pocket of his wheelchair and brought out a package of Snausages. He threw one to the leopard, who snapped it up and licked his lips.

"You must excuse the décor," Chiron said. "All this was a parting gift from our old director before he was recalled to Mount Olympus. He thought it would help us to remember him. Mr. D has a strange sense of humor."

"Mr. D," Jason said. "Dionysus?"

"Mmm hmm." Chiron poured lemonade, though his hands were trembling a little. "As for Seymour, well, Mr. D liberated him from a Long Island garage sale. The leopard is

Mr. D's sacred animal, you see, and Mr. D was appalled that someone would stuff such a noble creature. He decided to grant it life, on the assumption that life as a mounted head was better than no life at all. I must say it's a kinder fate than Seymour's previous owner got."

Seymour bared his fangs and sniffed the air, as if hunting for more Snausages.

"If he's only a head," Jason said, "where does the food go when he eats?"

"Better not to ask," Chiron said. "Please, sit."

Jason took some lemonade, though his stomach was fluttering. Chiron sat back in his wheelchair and tried for a smile, but Jason could tell it was forced. The old man's eyes were as deep and dark as wells.

"So, Jason," he said, "would you mind telling me—ah—where you're from?"

"I wish I knew." Jason told him the whole story, from waking up on the bus to crash-landing at Camp Half-Blood. He didn't see any point in hiding the details, and Chiron was a good listener. He didn't react to the story, other than to nod encouragingly for more.

When Jason was done, the old man sipped his lemonade.

"I see," Chiron said. "And you must have questions for me."

"Only one," Jason admitted. "What did you mean when you said that I should be dead?"

Chiron studied him with concern, as if he expected Jason to burst into flames. "My boy, do you know what those marks on your arm mean? The color of your shirt? Do you remember anything?"

Jason looked at the tattoo on his forearm: SPQR, the eagle, twelve straight lines.

"No," he said. "Nothing."

"Do you know where you are?" Chiron asked. "Do you understand what this place is, and who I am?"

"You're Chiron the centaur," Jason said. "I'm guessing you're the same one from the old stories, who used to train the Greek heroes like Heracles. This is a camp for demigods, children of the Olympian gods."

"So you believe those gods still exist?"

"Yes," Jason said immediately. "I mean, I don't think we should *worship* them or sacrifice chickens to them or anything, but they're still around because they're a powerful part of civilization. They move from country to country as the center of power shifts—like they moved from Ancient Greece to Rome."

"I couldn't have said it better." Something about Chiron's voice had changed. *"So you already know the gods are real. You have already been claimed, haven't you?"*

"Maybe," Jason answered. *"I'm not really sure."*

Seymour the leopard snarled.

Chiron waited, and Jason realized what had just happened. The centaur had switched to another language and Jason had understood, automatically answering in the same tongue.

"Quis erat—" Jason faltered, then made a conscious effort to speak English. "What was that?"

"You know Latin," Chiron observed. "Most demigods recognize a few phrases, of course. It's in their blood, but not as much as Ancient Greek. None can speak Latin fluently without practice."

Jason tried to wrap his mind around what that meant, but too many pieces were missing from his memory. He still had the feeling that he shouldn't be here. It was wrong—and dangerous. But at least Chiron wasn't threatening. In fact the centaur seemed concerned for him, afraid for his safety.

The fire reflected in Chiron's eyes, making them dance fretfully. "I taught your namesake, you know, the original Jason. He had a hard path. I've seen many heroes come and go. Occasionally, they have happy endings. Mostly, they don't. It breaks my heart, like losing a child each time one of my pupils dies. But you—you are not like any pupil I've ever taught. Your presence here could be a disaster."

"Thanks," Jason said. "You must be an inspiring teacher."

"I am sorry, my boy. But it's true. I had hoped that after Percy's success—"

"Percy Jackson, you mean. Annabeth's boyfriend, the one who's missing."

Chiron nodded. "I hoped that after he succeeded in the Titan War and saved Mount Olympus, we might have some peace. I might be able to enjoy one final triumph, a happy ending, and perhaps retire quietly. I should have known better. The last chapter approaches, just as it did before. The worst is yet to come."

In the corner, the arcade game made a sad *pew-pew-pew-pew* sound, like a Pac-Man had just died.

"Ohh-kay," Jason said. "So—last chapter, happened before,

worst yet to come. Sounds fun, but can we go back to the part where I'm supposed to be dead? I don't like that part."

"I'm afraid I can't explain, my boy. I swore on the River Styx and on all things sacred that I would never..." Chiron frowned. "But you're here, in violation of the same oath. That too, should not be possible. I don't understand. Who would've done such a thing? Who—"

Seymour the leopard howled. His mouth froze, half open. The arcade game stopped beeping. The fire stopped crackling, its flames hardening like red glass. The masks stared down silently at Jason with their grotesque grape eyes and leafy tongues.

"Chiron?" Jason asked. "What's going—"

The old centaur had frozen, too. Jason jumped off the couch, but Chiron kept staring at the same spot, his mouth open mid-sentence. His eyes didn't blink. His chest didn't move.

Jason, a voice said.

For a horrible moment, he thought the leopard had spoken. Then dark mist boiled out of Seymour's mouth, and an even worse thought occurred to Jason: *storm spirits*.

He grabbed the golden coin from his pocket. With a quick flip, it changed into a sword.

The mist took the form of a woman in black robes. Her face was hooded, but her eyes glowed in the darkness. Over her shoulders she wore a goatskin cloak. Jason wasn't sure how he knew it was goatskin, but he recognized it and knew it was important.

Would you attack your patron? the woman chided. Her voice echoed in Jason's head. *Lower your sword.*

"Who are you?" he demanded. "How did you—"

Our time is limited, Jason. My prison grows stronger by the hour. It took me a full month to gather enough energy to work even the smallest magic through its bonds. I've managed to bring you here, but now I have little time left, and even less power. This may be the last time I can speak to you.

"You're in prison?" Jason decided maybe he wouldn't lower his sword. "Look, I don't know you, and you're not my patron."

You know me, she insisted. *I have known you since your birth.*

"I don't remember. I don't remember anything."

No, you don't, she agreed. *That also was necessary. Long ago, your father gave me your life as a gift to placate my anger. He named you Jason, after my favorite mortal. You belong to me.*

"Whoa," Jason said. "I don't belong to anyone."

Now is the time to pay your debt, she said. *Find my prison. Free me, or their king will rise from the earth, and I will be destroyed. You will never retrieve your memory.*

"Is that a threat? You *took* my memories?"

You have until sunset on the solstice, Jason. Four short days. Do not fail me.

The dark woman dissolved, and the mist curled into the leopard's mouth.

Time unfroze. Seymour's howl turned into a cough like he'd sucked in a hair ball. The fire crackled to life, the arcade machine beeped, and Chiron said, "—would dare to bring you here?"

"Probably the lady in the mist," Jason offered.

Chiron looked up in surprise. "Weren't you just sitting . . . why do you have a sword drawn?"

"I hate to tell you this," Jason said, "but I think your leopard just ate a goddess."

He told Chiron about the frozen-in-time visit, the dark misty figure that disappeared into Seymour's mouth.

"Oh, dear," Chiron murmured. "That does explain a lot."

"Then why don't you explain a lot to me?" Jason said. "Please."

Before Chiron could say anything, footsteps reverberated on the porch outside. The front door blew open, and Annabeth and another girl, a redhead, burst in, dragging Piper between them. Piper's head lolled like she was unconscious.

"What happened?" Jason rushed over. "What's wrong with her?"

"Hera's cabin," Annabeth gasped, like they'd run all the way. "Vision. Bad."

The redheaded girl looked up, and Jason saw that she'd been crying.

"I think . . ." The redheaded girl gulped. "I think I may have killed her."

VIII

JASON

JASON AND THE REDHEAD, WHO INTRODUCED herself as Rachel, put Piper on the couch while Annabeth rushed down the hall to get a med kit. Piper was still breathing, but she wouldn't wake up. She seemed to be in some kind of coma.

"We've got to heal her," Jason insisted. "There's a way, right?"

Seeing her so pale, barely breathing, Jason felt a surge of protectiveness. Maybe he didn't really know her. Maybe she wasn't his girlfriend. But they'd survived the Grand Canyon together. They'd come all this way. He'd left her side for a little while, and *this* had happened.

Chiron put his hand on her forehead and grimaced. "Her mind is in a fragile state. Rachel, what happened?"

"I wish I knew," she said. "As soon as I got to camp, I had a premonition about Hera's cabin. I went inside. Annabeth and Piper came in while I was there. We talked, and then—I just blanked out. Annabeth said I spoke in a different voice."

"A prophecy?" Chiron asked.

"No. The spirit of Delphi comes from within. I know how that feels. This was like long distance, a power trying to speak through me."

Annabeth ran in with a leather pouch. She knelt next to Piper. "Chiron, what happened back there—I've never seen anything like it. I've heard Rachel's prophecy voice. This was different. She sounded like an older woman. She grabbed Piper's shoulders and told her—"

"To free her from a prison?" Jason guessed.

Annabeth stared at him. "How did you know that?"

Chiron made a three-fingered gesture over his heart, like a ward against evil.

"Jason, tell them. Annabeth, the medicine bag, please."

Chiron trickled drops from a medicine vial into Piper's mouth while Jason explained what had happened when the room froze—the dark misty woman who had claimed to be Jason's patron.

When he was done, no one spoke, which made him more anxious.

"So does this happen often?" he asked. "Supernatural phone calls from convicts demanding you bust them out of jail?"

"Your patron," Annabeth said. "Not your godly parent?"

"No, she said *patron*. She also said my dad had given her my life."

Annabeth frowned. "I've never of heard anything like that before. You said the storm spirit on the skywalk—he claimed to be working for some mistress who was giving him orders, right? Could it be this woman you saw, messing with your mind?"

"I don't think so," Jason said. "If she were my enemy, why would she be asking for my help? She's imprisoned. She's worried about some enemy getting more powerful. Something about a king rising from the earth on the solstice—"

Annabeth turned to Chiron. "Not Kronos. Please tell me it's not that."

The centaur looked miserable. He held Piper's wrist, checking her pulse.

At last he said, "It is not Kronos. That threat is ended. But..."

"But what?" Annabeth asked.

Chiron closed the medicine bag. "Piper needs rest. We should discuss this later."

"Or now," Jason said. "Sir, Mr. Chiron, you told me the greatest threat was coming. The last chapter. You can't possibly mean something worse than an army of Titans, right?"

"Oh," Rachel said in a small voice. "Oh, dear. The woman was Hera. Of course. Her cabin, her voice. She showed herself to Jason at the same moment."

"Hera?" Annabeth's snarl was even fiercer than Seymour's. "*She* took you over? She did this to Piper?"

"I think Rachel's right," Jason said. "The woman did seem like a goddess. And she wore this—this goatskin cloak. That's a symbol of Juno, isn't it?"

"It is?" Annabeth scowled. "I've never heard that."

Chiron nodded reluctantly. "Of Juno, Hera's Roman

aspect, in her most warlike state. The goatskin cloak was a symbol of the Roman soldier."

"So Hera is imprisoned?" Rachel asked. "Who could do that to the queen of the gods?"

Annabeth crossed her arms. "Well, whoever they are, maybe we should thank them. If they can shut up Hera—"

"Annabeth," Chiron warned, "she is still one of the Olympians. In many ways, she is the glue that holds the gods' family together. If she truly has been imprisoned and is in danger of destruction, this could shake the foundations of the world. It could unravel the stability of Olympus, which is never great even in the best of times. And if Hera has asked Jason for help—"

"Fine," Annabeth grumbled. "Well, we know Titans can capture a god, right? Atlas captured Artemis a few years ago. And in the old stories, the gods captured each other in traps all the time. But something worse than a Titan...?"

Jason looked at the leopard's head. Seymour was smacking his lips like the goddess had tasted much better than a Snausage. "Hera said she'd been trying to break through her prison bonds for a month."

"Which is how long Olympus has been closed," Annabeth said. "So the gods must know something bad is going on."

"But why use her energy to send me here?" Jason asked. "She wiped my memory, plopped me into the Wilderness School field trip, and sent you a dream vision to come pick me up. Why am I so important? Why not just send up an emergency flare to the other gods—let them know where she is so they bust her out?"

"The gods need heroes to do their will down here on earth," Rachel said. "That's right, isn't it? Their fates are always intertwined with demigods."

"That's true," Annabeth said, "but Jason's got a point. Why him? Why take his memory?"

"And Piper's involved somehow," Rachel said. "Hera sent her the same message—*Free me*. And, Annabeth, this must have something to do with Percy's disappearing."

Annabeth fixed her eyes on Chiron. "Why are you so quiet, Chiron? What is it we're facing?"

The old centaur's face looked like it had aged ten years in a matter of minutes. The lines around his eyes were deeply etched. "My dear, in this, I cannot help you. I am so sorry."

Annabeth blinked. "You've never...you've *never* kept information from me. Even the last great prophecy—"

"I will be in my office." His voice was heavy. "I need some time to think before dinner. Rachel, will you watch the girl? Call Argus to bring her to the infirmary, if you'd like. And Annabeth, you should speak with Jason. Tell him about—about the Greek and Roman gods."

"But..."

The centaur turned his wheelchair and rolled off down the hallway. Annabeth's eyes turned stormy. She muttered something in Greek, and Jason got the feeling it wasn't complimentary toward centaurs.

"I'm sorry," Jason said. "I think my being here—I don't know. I've messed things up coming to the camp, somehow. Chiron said he'd sworn an oath and couldn't talk about it."

"What oath?" Annabeth demanded. "I've never seen him

act this way. And why would he tell me to talk to you about the gods..."

Her voice trailed off. Apparently she'd just noticed Jason's sword sitting on the coffee table. She touched the blade gingerly, like it might be hot.

"Is this gold?" she said. "Do you remember where you got it?"

"No," Jason said. "Like I said, I don't remember anything."

Annabeth nodded, like she'd just come up with a rather desperate plan. "If Chiron won't help, we'll need to figure things out ourselves. Which means...Cabin Fifteen. Rachel, you'll keep an eye on Piper?"

"Sure," Rachel promised. "Good luck, you two."

"Hold on," Jason said. "What's in Cabin Fifteen?"

Annabeth stood. "Maybe a way to get your memory back."

They headed toward a newer wing of cabins in the southwest corner of the green. Some were fancy, with glowing walls or blazing torches, but Cabin Fifteen was not so dramatic. It looked like an old-fashioned prairie house with mud walls and a rush roof. On the door hung a wreath of crimson flowers —red poppies, Jason thought, though he wasn't sure how he knew.

"You think this is my parent's cabin?" he asked.

"No," Annabeth said. "This is the cabin for Hypnos, the god of sleep."

"Then why—"

"You've forgotten everything," she said. "If there's any god who can help us figure out memory loss, it's Hypnos."

Inside, even though it was almost dinnertime, three kids

were sound asleep under piles of covers. A warm fire crackled in the hearth. Above the mantel hung a tree branch, each twig dripping white liquid into a collection of tin bowls. Jason was tempted to catch a drop on his finger just to see what it was, but he held himself back.

Soft violin music played from somewhere. The air smelled like fresh laundry. The cabin was so cozy and peaceful that Jason's eyelids started to feel heavy. A nap sounded like a great idea. He was exhausted. There were plenty of empty beds, all with feather pillows and fresh sheets and fluffy quilts and—

Annabeth nudged him. "Snap out of it."

Jason blinked. He realized his knees had been starting to buckle.

"Cabin Fifteen does that to everyone," Annabeth warned. "If you ask me, this place is even more dangerous than the Ares cabin. At least with Ares, you can learn where the land mines are."

"Land mines?"

She walked up to the nearest snoring kid and shook his shoulder. "Clovis! Wake up!"

The kid looked like a baby cow. He had a blond tuft of hair on a wedge-shaped head, with thick features and a thick neck. His body was stocky, but he had spindly little arms like he'd never lifted anything heavier than a pillow.

"Clovis!" Annabeth shook harder, then finally knocked on his forehead about six times.

"Wh-wh-what?" Clovis complained, sitting up and squinting. He yawned hugely, and both Annabeth and Jason yawned too.

"Stop that!" Annabeth said. "We need your help."

"I was sleeping."

"You're *always* sleeping."

"Good night."

Before he could pass out, Annabeth yanked his pillow off the bed.

"That's not fair," Clovis complained meekly. "Give it back."

"First help," Annabeth said. "Then sleep."

Clovis sighed. His breath smelled like warm milk. "Fine. What?"

Annabeth explained about Jason's problem. Every once in a while she'd snap her fingers under Clovis's nose to keep him awake.

Clovis must have been really excited, because when Annabeth was done, he didn't pass out. He actually stood and stretched, then blinked at Jason. "So you don't remember anything, huh?"

"Just impressions," Jason said. "Feelings, like . . ."

"Yes?" Clovis said.

"Like I know I shouldn't be here. At this camp. I'm in danger."

"Hmm. Close your eyes."

Jason glanced at Annabeth, but she nodded reassuringly.

Jason was afraid he'd end up snoring in one of the bunks forever, but he closed his eyes. His thoughts became murky, as if he were sinking into a dark lake.

The next thing he knew, his eyes snapped open. He was sitting in a chair by the fire. Clovis and Annabeth knelt next to him.

"—serious, all right," Clovis was saying.

"What happened?" Jason said. "How long—"

"Just a few minutes," Annabeth said. "But it was tense. You almost dissolved."

Jason hoped she didn't mean *literally*, but her expression was solemn.

"Usually," Clovis said, "memories are lost for a good reason. They sink under the surface like dreams, and with a good sleep, I can bring them back. But this..."

"Lethe?" Annabeth asked.

"No," Clovis said. "Not even Lethe."

"Lethe?" Jason asked.

Clovis pointed to the tree branch dripping milky drops above the fireplace. "The River Lethe in the Underworld. It dissolves your memories, wipes your mind clean permanently. That's the branch of a poplar tree from the Underworld, dipped into the Lethe. It's the symbol of my father, Hypnos. Lethe is not a place you want to go swimming."

Annabeth nodded. "Percy went there once. He told me it was powerful enough to wipe the mind of a Titan."

Jason was suddenly glad he hadn't touched the branch. "But... that's not my problem?"

"No," Clovis agreed. "Your mind wasn't wiped, and your memories weren't buried. They've been stolen."

The fire crackled. Drops of Lethe water plinked into the tin cups on the mantel. One of the other Hypnos campers muttered in his sleep—something about a duck.

"Stolen," Jason said. "How?"

"A god," Clovis said. "Only a god would have that kind of power."

"We know that," said Jason. "It was Juno. But how did she do it, and why?"

Clovis scratched his neck. "Juno?"

"He means Hera," Annabeth said. "For some reason, Jason likes the Roman names."

"Hmm," Clovis said.

"What?" Jason asked. "Does that mean something?"

"Hmm," Clovis said again, and this time Jason realized he was snoring.

"Clovis!" he yelled.

"What? What?" His eyes fluttered open. "We were talking about pillows, right? No, gods. I remember. Greek and Roman. Sure, could be important."

"But they're the same gods," Annabeth said. "Just different names."

"Not exactly," Clovis said.

Jason sat forward, now very much awake. "What do you mean, not exactly?"

"Well..." Clovis yawned. "Some gods are only Roman. Like Janus, or Pompona. But even the major Greek gods—it's not just their names that changed when they moved to Rome. Their appearances changed. Their attributes changed. They even had slightly different personalities."

"But..." Annabeth faltered. "Okay, so maybe people saw them differently through the centuries. That doesn't change who they are."

"Sure it does." Clovis began to nod off, and Jason snapped his fingers under his nose.

"Coming, Mother!" he yelped. "I mean... Yeah, I'm

awake. So, um, personalities. The gods change to reflect their host cultures. You know that, Annabeth. I mean, these days, Zeus likes tailored suits, reality television, and that Chinese food place on East Twenty-eighth Street, right? It was the same in Roman times, and the gods were Roman almost as long as they were Greek. It was a big empire, lasted for centuries. So of course their Roman aspects are still a big part of their character."

"Makes sense," Jason said.

Annabeth shook her head, mystified. "But how do you know all this, Clovis?"

"Oh, I spend a lot of time dreaming. I see the gods there all the time—always shifting forms. Dreams are fluid, you know. You can be in different places at once, always changing identities. It's a lot like being a god, actually. Like recently, I dreamed I was watching a Michael Jackson concert, and then I was onstage *with* Michael Jackson, and we were singing this duet, and I could *not* remember the words for 'The Girl Is Mine.' Oh, man, it was so embarrassing, I—"

"Clovis," Annabeth interrupted. "Back to Rome?"

"Right, Rome," Clovis said. "So we call the gods by their Greek names because that's their original form. But saying their Roman aspects are exactly the same—that's not true. In Rome, they became more warlike. They didn't mingle with mortals as much. They were harsher, more powerful—the gods of an empire."

"Like the dark side of the gods?" Annabeth asked.

"Not exactly," Clovis said. "They stood for discipline, honor, strength—"

"Good things, then," Jason said. For some reason, he felt the need to speak up for the Roman gods, though wasn't sure why it mattered to him. "I mean, discipline is important, right? That's what made Rome last so long."

Clovis gave him a curious look. "That's true. But the Roman gods weren't very friendly. For instance, my dad, Hypnos...he didn't do much except sleep in Greek times. In Roman times, they called him Somnus. He liked killing people who didn't stay alert at their jobs. If they nodded off at the wrong time, *boom*—they never woke up. He killed the helmsman of Aeneas when they were sailing from Troy."

"Nice guy," Annabeth said. "But I still don't understand what it has to do with Jason."

"Neither do I," Clovis said. "But if Hera took your memory, only she can give it back. And if I had to meet the queen of the gods, I'd hope she was more in a Hera mood than a Juno mood. Can I go back to sleep now?"

Annabeth stared at the branch above the fire, dripping Lethe water into the cups. She looked so worried, Jason wondered if she was considering a drink to forget her troubles. Then she stood and tossed Clovis his pillow. "Thanks, Clovis. We'll see you at dinner."

"Can I get room service?" Clovis yawned and stumbled to his bunk. "I feel like...zzzz..." He collapsed with his butt in the air and his face buried in pillow.

"Won't he suffocate?" Jason asked.

"He'll be fine," Annabeth said. "But I'm beginning to think that you are in serious trouble."

PIPER

Piper DREAMED ABOUT HER LAST DAY with her dad.

They were on the beach near Big Sur, taking a break from surfing. The morning had been so perfect, Piper knew something had to go wrong soon—a rabid horde of paparazzi, or maybe a great white shark attack. No way her luck could hold.

But so far, they'd had excellent waves, an overcast sky, and a mile of oceanfront completely to themselves. Dad had found this out-of-the-way spot, rented a beachfront villa *and* the properties on either side, and somehow managed to keep it secret. If he stayed there too long, Piper knew the photographers would find him. They always did.

"Nice job out there, Pipes." He gave her the smile he was famous for: perfect teeth, dimpled chin, a twinkle in his dark eyes that always made grown women scream and ask him to sign their bodies in permanent marker. (*Seriously*, Piper thought, *get a life*.) His close-cropped black hair gleamed with salt water. "You're getting better at hanging ten."

Piper flushed with pride, though she suspected Dad was just being nice. She still spent most of her time wiping out. It took special talent to run over yourself with a surfboard. Her *dad* was the natural surfer—which made no sense since he'd been raised a poor kid in Oklahoma, hundreds of miles from the ocean—but he was amazing on the curls. Piper would've given up surfing a long time ago except it let her spend time with him. There weren't many ways she could do that.

"Sandwich?" Dad dug into the picnic basket his chef, Arno, had made. "Let's see: turkey pesto, crabcake wasabi —ah, a Piper special. Peanut butter and jelly."

She took the sandwich, though her stomach was too upset to eat. She always asked for PB&J. Piper was vegetarian, for one thing. She had been ever since they'd driven past that slaughterhouse in Chino and the smell had made her insides want to come outside. But it was more than that. PB&J was simple food, like a regular kid would have for lunch. Sometimes she pretended her dad had actually made it for her, not a personal chef from France who liked to wrap the sandwich in gold leaf paper with a light-up sparkler instead of a toothpick.

Couldn't anything be simple? That's why she turned down the fancy clothes Dad always offered, the designer shoes, the trips to the salon. She cut her own hair with a pair of plastic Garfield safety scissors, deliberately making it uneven. She preferred to wear beat-up running shoes, jeans, a T-shirt, and her old Polartec jacket from the time they went snowboarding.

And she hated the snobby private schools Dad thought were good for her. She kept getting herself kicked out. He kept finding more schools.

Yesterday, she'd pulled her biggest heist yet—driving that "borrowed" BMW out of the dealership. She *had* to pull a bigger stunt each time, because it took more and more to get Dad's attention.

Now she regretted it. Dad didn't know yet.

She'd meant to tell him that morning. Then he'd surprised her with this trip, and she couldn't ruin it. It was the first time they'd had a day together in what—three months?

"What's wrong?" He passed her a soda.

"Dad, there's something—"

"Hold on, Pipes. That's a serious face. Ready for Any Three Questions?"

They'd been playing that game for years—her dad's way of staying connected in the shortest possible amount of time. They could ask each other any three questions. Nothing off-limits, and you had to answer honestly. The rest of the time, Dad promised to stay out of her business—which was easy, since he was never around.

Piper knew most kids would find a Q&A like this with their parents totally mortifying. But she looked forward to it. It was like surfing—not easy, but a way to feel like she actually had a father.

"First question," she said. "Mom."

No surprise. That was always one of her topics.

Her dad shrugged with resignation. "What do you want to know, Piper? I've already told you—she disappeared. I don't know why, or where she went. After you were born, she simply left. I never heard from her again."

"Do you think she's still alive?"

It wasn't a real question. Dad was allowed to say he didn't know. But she wanted to hear how he'd answer.

He stared at the waves.

"Your Grandpa Tom," he said at last, "he used to tell me that if you walked far enough toward the sunset, you'd come to Ghost Country, where you could talk to the dead. He said a long time ago, you could bring the dead back; but then mankind messed up. Well, it's a long story."

"Like the Land of the Dead for the Greeks," Piper remembered. "It was in the west, too. And Orpheus—he tried to bring his wife back."

Dad nodded. A year before, he'd had his biggest role as an Ancient Greek king. Piper had helped him research the myths—all those old stories about people getting turned to stone and boiled in lakes of lava. They'd had a fun time reading together, and it made Piper's life seem not so bad. For a while she'd felt closer to her dad, but like everything, it didn't last.

"Lot of similarities between Greek and Cherokee," Dad agreed. "Wonder what your grandpa would think if he saw us now, sitting at the end of the western land. He'd probably think we're ghosts."

"So you're saying you believe those stories? You think Mom is dead?"

His eyes watered, and Piper saw the sadness behind them. She figured that's why women were so attracted to him. On the surface, he seemed confident and rugged, but his eyes held so much sadness. Women wanted to find out why. They wanted to comfort him, and they never could. Dad told

Piper it was a Cherokee thing—they all had that darkness inside them from generations of pain and suffering. But Piper thought it was more than that.

"I don't believe the stories," he said. "They're fun to tell, but if I really believed in Ghost Country, or animal spirits, or Greek gods...I don't think I could sleep at night. I'd always be looking for somebody to blame."

Somebody to blame for Grandpa Tom dying of lung cancer, Piper thought, before Dad got famous and had the money to help. For Mom—the only woman he'd ever loved —abandoning him without even a good-bye note, leaving him with a newborn girl he wasn't ready to care for. For his being so successful, and yet still not happy.

"I don't know if she's alive," he said. "But I do think she might as well be in Ghost Country, Piper. There's no getting her back. If I believed otherwise...I don't think I could stand that, either."

Behind them, a car door opened. Piper turned, and her heart sank. Jane was marching toward them in her business suit, wobbling over the sand in her high heels, her PDA in hand. The look on her face was partly annoyed, partly triumphant, and Piper knew she'd been in touch with the police.

Please fall down, Piper prayed. *If there's any animal spirit or Greek god that can help, make Jane take a header. I'm not asking for permanent damage, just knock her out for the rest of the day, please?*

But Jane kept advancing.

"Dad," Piper said quickly. "Something happened yesterday...."

But he'd seen Jane, too. He was already reconstructing his business face. Jane wouldn't be here if it wasn't serious. A studio head called—a project fell through—or Piper had messed up again.

"We'll get back to that, Pipes," he promised. "I'd better see what Jane wants. You know how she is."

Yes—Piper knew. Dad trudged across the sand to meet her. Piper couldn't hear them talking, but she didn't need to. She was good at reading faces. Jane gave him the facts about the stolen car, occasionally pointing at Piper like she was a disgusting pet that had whizzed on the carpet.

Dad's energy and enthusiasm drained away. He gestured for Jane to wait. Then he walked back to Piper. She couldn't stand that look in his eyes—like she'd betrayed his trust.

"You told me you would try, Piper," he said.

"Dad, I hate that school. I can't do it. I wanted to tell you about the BMW, but—"

"They've expelled you," he said. "A car, Piper? You're sixteen next year. I would buy you any car you want. How could you—"

"You mean *Jane* would buy me a car?" Piper demanded. She couldn't help it. The anger just welled up and spilled out of her. "Dad, just listen for once. Don't make me wait for you to ask your stupid three questions. I want to go to regular school. I want *you* to take me to parents' night, not Jane. Or homeschool me! I learned so much when we read about Greece together. We could do that all the time! We could—"

"Don't make this about me," her dad said. "I do the best I can, Piper. We've had this conversation."

No, she thought. *You've cut off this conversation. For years.*

Her dad sighed. "Jane's talked to the police, brokered a deal. The dealership won't press charges, but you have to agree to go to a boarding school in Nevada. They specialize in problems... in kids with tough issues."

"That's what I am." Her voice trembled. "A problem."

"Piper... you said you'd try. You let me down. I don't know what else to do."

"Do anything," she said. "But do it yourself! Don't let Jane handle it for you. You can't just send me away."

Dad looked down at the picnic basket. His sandwich sat uneaten on a piece of gold leaf paper. They'd planned for a whole afternoon in the surf. Now that was ruined.

Piper couldn't believe he'd really give in to Jane's wishes. Not this time. Not on something as huge as boarding school.

"Go see her," Dad said. "She's got the details."

"Dad..."

He looked away, gazing at the ocean like he could see all the way to Ghost Country. Piper promised herself she wouldn't cry. She headed up the beach toward Jane, who smiled coldly and held up a plane ticket. As usual, she'd already arranged everything. Piper was just another problem of the day that Jane could now check off her list.

Piper's dream changed.

She stood on a mountaintop at night, city lights glimmering below. In front of her, a bonfire blazed. Purplish flames seemed to cast more shadows than light, but the heat was so intense, her clothes steamed.

"This is your second warning," a voice rumbled, so powerful it shook the earth. Piper had heard that voice before in her dreams. She'd tried to convince herself it wasn't as scary as she remembered, but it was worse.

Behind the bonfire, a huge face loomed out of the darkness. It seemed to float above the flames, but Piper knew it must be connected to an enormous body. The crude features might've been chiseled out of rock. The face hardly seemed alive except for its piercing white eyes, like raw diamonds, and its horrible frame of dreadlocks, braided with human bones. It smiled, and Piper shivered.

"You'll do what you're told," the giant said. "You'll go on the quest. Do our bidding, and you may walk away alive. Otherwise—"

He gestured to one side of the fire. Piper's father was hanging unconscious, tied to a stake.

She tried to cry out. She wanted to call to her dad, and demand the giant let him go, but her voice wouldn't work.

"I'll be watching," the giant said. "Serve me, and you both live. You have the word of Enceladus. Fail me . . . well, I've slept for millennia, young demigod. I am *very* hungry. Fail, and I'll eat well."

The giant roared with laughter. The earth trembled. A crevice opened at Piper's feet, and she tumbled into darkness.

She woke feeling like she'd been trampled by an Irish step-dancing troupe. Her chest hurt, and she could barely breathe. She reached down and closed her hand around the hilt of the dagger Annabeth had given her—Katoptris, Helen of Troy's weapon.

So Camp Half-Blood hadn't been a dream.

"How are you feeling?" someone asked.

Piper tried to focus. She was lying in a bed with a white curtain on one side, like in a nurse's office. That redheaded girl, Rachel Dare, sat next to her. On the wall was a poster of a cartoon satyr who looked disturbingly like Coach Hedge with a thermometer sticking out of his mouth. The caption read: *Don't let sickness get your goat!*

"Where—" Piper's voice died when she saw the guy at the door.

He looked like a typical California surfer dude—buff and tan, blond hair, dressed in shorts and a T-shirt. But he had hundreds of blue eyes all over his body—along his arms, down his legs, and all over his face. Even his feet had eyes, peering up at her from between the straps of his sandals.

"That's Argus," Rachel said, "our head of security. He's just keeping an eye on things . . . so to speak."

Argus nodded. The eye on his chin winked.

"Where—?" Piper tried again, but she felt like she was talking through a mouthful of cotton.

"You're in the Big House," Rachel said. "Camp offices. We brought you here when you collapsed."

"You grabbed me," Piper remembered. "Hera's voice—"

"I'm so sorry about that," Rachel said. "Believe me, it was *not* my idea to get possessed. Chiron healed you with some nectar—"

"Nectar?"

"The drink of the gods. In small amounts, it heals demigods, if it doesn't—ah—burn you to ashes."

"Oh. Fun."

Rachel sat forward. "Do you remember your vision?"

Piper had a moment of dread, thinking she meant the dream about the giant. Then she realized Rachel was talking about what happened in Hera's cabin.

"Something's wrong with the goddess," Piper said. "She told me to free her, like she's trapped. She mentioned the earth swallowing us, and a fiery one, and something about the solstice."

In the corner, Argus made a rumbling sound in his chest. His eyes all fluttered at once.

"Hera created Argus," Rachel explained. "He's actually very sensitive when it comes to her safety. We're trying to keep him from crying, because last time that happened... well, it caused quite a flood."

Argus sniffled. He grabbed a fistful of Kleenex from the bedside table and started dabbing eyes all over his body.

"So..." Piper tried not to stare as Argus wiped the tears from his elbows. "What's happened to Hera?"

"We're not sure," Rachel said. "Annabeth and Jason were here for you, by the way. Jason didn't want to leave you, but Annabeth had an idea—something that might restore his memories."

"That's... that's great."

Jason had been here for her? She wished she'd been conscious for that. But if he got his memories back, would that be a good thing? She was still holding out hope that they really did know each other. She didn't want their relationship to be just a trick of the Mist.

Get over yourself, she thought. If she was going to save her dad, it didn't matter whether Jason liked her or not. He would hate her eventually. Everyone here would.

She looked down at the ceremonial dagger strapped to her side. Annabeth had said it was a sign of power and status, but not normally used in battle. All show and no substance. A fake, just like Piper. And its name was Katoptris, looking glass. She didn't dare unsheathe it again, because she couldn't bear to see her own reflection.

"Don't worry." Rachel squeezed her arm. "Jason seems like a good guy. He had a vision too, a lot like yours. Whatever's happening with Hera—I think you two are meant to work together."

Rachel smiled like this was good news, but Piper's spirits plunged even further. She'd thought that this quest—whatever it was—would involve nameless people. Now Rachel was basically telling her: *Good news! Not only is your dad being held ransom by a cannibal giant, you also get to betray the guy you like! How awesome is that?*

"Hey," Rachel said. "No need to cry. You'll figure it out."

Piper wiped her eyes, trying to get control of herself. This wasn't like her. She was supposed to be tough—a hardened car thief, the scourge of L.A. private schools. Here she was, crying like a baby. "How can you know what I'm facing?"

Rachel shrugged. "I know it's a hard choice, and your options aren't great. Like I said, I get hunches sometimes.

But you're going to be claimed at the campfire. I'm almost sure. When you know who your godly parent is, things might be clearer."

Clearer, Piper thought. Not necessarily better.

She sat up in bed. Her forehead ached like someone had driven a spike between her eyes. *There's no getting your mother back*, her dad had told her. But apparently, tonight, her mom might claim her. For the first time, Piper wasn't sure she wanted that.

"I hope it's Athena." She looked up, afraid Rachel might make fun of her, but the oracle just smiled.

"Piper, I don't blame you. Truthfully? I think Annabeth is hoping that too. You guys are a lot alike."

The comparison made Piper feel even guiltier. "Another hunch? You don't know anything about me."

"You'd be surprised."

"You're just saying that because you're an oracle, aren't you? You're supposed to sound all mysterious."

Rachel laughed. "Don't be giving away my secrets, Piper. And don't worry. Things will work out—just maybe not the way you plan."

"That's not making me feel better."

Somewhere in the distance, a conch horn blew. Argus grumbled and opened the door.

"Dinner?" Piper guessed.

"You slept through it," Rachel said. "Time for the campfire. Let's go find out who you are."

X

PIPER

THE WHOLE CAMPFIRE IDEA FREAKED PIPER OUT. It made her think of that huge purple bonfire in the dreams, and her father tied to a stake.

What she got instead was almost as terrifying: a sing-along. The amphitheater steps were carved into the side of a hill, facing a stone-lined fire pit. Fifty or sixty kids filled the rows, clustered into groups under various banners.

Piper spotted Jason in the front next to Annabeth. Leo was nearby, sitting with a bunch of burly-looking campers under a steel gray banner emblazoned with a hammer. Standing in front of the fire, half a dozen campers with guitars and strange, old-fashioned harps—lyres?—were jumping around, leading a song about pieces of armor, something about how their grandma got dressed for war. Everybody was singing with them and making gestures for the pieces of armor and joking around. It was quite possibly the weirdest thing Piper had ever seen—one of those campfire songs that would've been completely embarrassing in daylight; but in the dark, with everybody participating, it was kind of corny and fun. As the energy level got higher, the flames did too, turning from red to orange to gold.

Finally the song ended with a lot of rowdy applause. A guy on a horse trotted up. At least in the flickering light, Piper *thought* it was a guy on a horse. Then she realized it was a centaur—his bottom half a white stallion, his top half a middle-aged guy with curly hair and a trimmed beard. He brandished a spear impaled with toasted marshmallows. "Very nice! And a special welcome to our new arrivals. I am Chiron, camp activities director, and I'm happy you have all arrived here alive and with most of your limbs attached. In a moment, I promise we'll get to the s'mores, but first—"

"What about capture the flag?" somebody yelled. Grumbling broke out among some kids in armor, sitting under a red banner with the emblem of a boar's head.

"Yes," the centaur said. "I know the Ares cabin is anxious to return to the woods for our regular games."

"And kill people!" one of them shouted.

"However," Chiron said, "until the dragon is brought under control, that won't be possible. Cabin Nine, anything to report on that?"

He turned to Leo's group. Leo winked at Piper and shot her with a finger gun. The girl next to him stood uncomfortably. She wore an army jacket a lot like Leo's, with her hair covered in a red bandanna. "We're working on it."

More grumbling.

"How, Nyssa?" an Ares kid demanded.

"Really hard," the girl said.

Nyssa sat down to a lot of yelling and complaining, which caused the fire to sputter chaotically. Chiron stamped his hoof against the fire pit stones—*bang, bang, bang*—and the campers fell silent.

"We will have to be patient," Chiron said. "In the meantime, we have more pressing matters to discuss."

"Percy?" someone asked. The fire dimmed even further, but Piper didn't need the mood flames to sense the crowd's anxiety.

Chiron gestured to Annabeth. She took a deep breath and stood.

"I didn't find Percy," she announced. Her voice caught a little when she said his name. "He wasn't at the Grand Canyon like I thought. But we're not giving up. We've got teams everywhere. Grover, Tyson, Nico, the Hunters of Artemis —everyone's out looking. We *will* find him. Chiron's talking about something different. A new quest."

"It's the Great Prophecy, isn't it?" a girl called out.

Everyone turned. The voice had come from a group in back, sitting under a rose-colored banner with a dove emblem. They'd been chatting among themselves and not paying much attention until their leader stood up: Drew.

Everyone else looked surprised. Apparently Drew didn't address the crowd very often.

"Drew?" Annabeth said. "What do you mean?"

"Well, *come on.*" Drew spread her hands like the truth was obvious. "Olympus is closed. Percy's disappeared. Hera sends you a vision and you come back with three new demigods in one day. I mean, something weird is going on. The Great Prophecy has started, right?"

Piper whispered to Rachel, "What's she talking about—the Great Prophecy?"

Then she realized everyone else was looking at Rachel, too.

"Well?" Drew called down. "You're the oracle. Has it started or not?"

Rachel's eyes looked scary in the firelight. Piper was afraid she might clench up and start channeling a freaky peacock goddess again, but she stepped forward calmly and addressed the camp.

"Yes," she said. "The Great Prophecy has begun."

Pandemonium broke out.

Piper caught Jason's eye. He mouthed, *You all right?* She nodded and managed a smile, but then looked away. It was too painful seeing him and not being with him.

When the talking finally subsided, Rachel took another step toward the audience, and fifty-plus demigods leaned away from her, as if one skinny redheaded mortal was more intimidating than all of them put together.

"For those of you who have not heard it," Rachel said, "the Great Prophecy was my first prediction. It arrived in August. It goes like this:

> *"Seven half-bloods shall answer the call.*
> *To storm or fire the world must fall—"*

Jason shot to his feet. His eyes looked wild, like he'd just been tasered.

Even Rachel seemed caught off guard. "J-Jason?" she said. "What's—"

"*Ut cum spiritu postrema sacramentum dejuremus,*" he chanted. "*Et hostes ornamenta addent ad ianuam necem.*"

An uneasy silence settled on the group. Piper could see from their faces that several of them were trying to translate the lines. She could tell it was Latin, but she wasn't sure why her hopefully future boyfriend was suddenly chanting like a Catholic priest.

"You just... finished the prophecy," Rachel stammered. "*—An oath to keep with a final breath/And foes bear arms to the Doors of Death.* How did you—"

"I know those lines." Jason winced and put his hands to his temples. "I don't know how, but I *know* that prophecy."

"In Latin, no less," Drew called out. "Handsome *and* smart."

There was some giggling from the Aphrodite cabin. God, what a bunch of losers, Piper thought. But it didn't do much to break the tension. The campfire was burning a chaotic, nervous shade of green.

Jason sat down, looking embarrassed, but Annabeth put a hand on his shoulder and muttered something reassuring. Piper felt a pang of jealousy. It should have been *her* next to him, comforting him.

Rachel Dare still looked a little shaken. She glanced back at Chiron for guidance, but the centaur stood grim and silent, as if he were watching a play he couldn't interrupt—a tragedy that ended with a lot of people dead onstage.

"Well," Rachel said, trying to regain her composure. "So,

yeah, that's the Great Prophecy. We hoped it might not happen for years, but I fear it's starting now. I can't give you proof. It's just a feeling. And like Drew said, some weird stuff is happening. The seven demigods, whoever they are, have not been gathered yet. I get the feeling some are here tonight. Some are not here."

The campers began to stir and mutter, looking at each other nervously, until a drowsy voice in the crowd called out, "I'm here! Oh...were you calling roll?"

"Go back to sleep, Clovis," someone yelled, and a lot of people laughed.

"Anyway," Rachel continued, "we don't know what the Great Prophecy means. We don't know what challenge the demigods will face, but since the *first* Great Prophecy predicted the Titan War, we can guess the *second* Great Prophecy will predict something at least that bad."

"Or worse," Chiron murmured.

Maybe he didn't mean everyone to overhear, but they did. The campfire immediately turned dark purple, the same color as Piper's dream.

"What we *do* know," Rachel said, "is that the first phase has begun. A major problem has arisen, and we need a quest to solve it. Hera, the queen of the gods, has been taken."

Shocked silence. Then fifty demigods started talking at once.

Chiron pounded his hoof again, but Rachel still had to wait before she could get back their attention.

She told them about the incident on the Grand Canyon skywalk—how Gleeson Hedge had sacrificed himself when the storm spirits attacked, and the spirits had warned it was only the beginning. They apparently served some great mistress who would destroy all demigods.

Then Rachel told them about Piper passing out in Hera's cabin. Piper tried to keep a calm expression, even when she noticed Drew in the back row, pantomiming a faint, and her friends giggling. Finally Rachel told them about Jason's vision in the living room of the Big House. The message Hera had delivered there was so similar that Piper got a chill. The only difference: Hera had warned Piper not to betray her: *Bow to his will, and their king shall rise, dooming us all.* Hera *knew* about the giant's threat. But if that was true, why hadn't she warned Jason, and exposed Piper as an enemy agent?

"Jason," Rachel said. "Um . . . do you remember your last name?"

He looked self-conscious, but he shook his head.

"We'll just call you Jason, then," Rachel said. "It's clear Hera herself has issued you a quest."

Rachel paused, as if giving Jason a chance to protest his destiny. Everyone's eyes were on him; there was so much pressure, Piper thought she would've buckled in his position. Yet he looked brave and determined. He set his jaw and nodded. "I agree."

"You must save Hera to prevent a great evil," Rachel continued. "Some sort of king from rising. For reasons we don't yet understand, it must happen by the winter solstice, only four days from now."

"That's the council day of the gods," Annabeth said. "If the gods don't *already* know Hera's gone, they will definitely notice her absence by then. They'll probably break out fighting, accusing each other of taking her. That's what they usually do."

"The winter solstice," Chiron spoke up, "is also the time of greatest darkness. The gods gather that day, as mortals always have, because there is strength in numbers. The solstice is a day when evil magic is strong. *Ancient* magic, older than the gods. It is a day when things...stir."

The way he said it, stirring sounded absolutely sinister— like it should be a first-degree felony, not something you did to cookie dough.

"Okay," Annabeth said, glaring at the centaur. "Thank you, Captain Sunshine. Whatever's going on, I agree with Rachel. Jason has been chosen to lead this quest, so—"

"Why hasn't he been claimed?" somebody yelled from the Ares cabin. "If he's so important—"

"He has been claimed," Chiron announced. "Long ago. Jason, give them a demonstration."

At first, Jason didn't seem to understand. He stepped forward nervously, but Piper couldn't help thinking how amazing he looked with his blond hair glowing in the firelight, his regal features like a Roman statue's. He glanced at Piper, and she nodded encouragingly. She mimicked flipping a coin.

Jason reached into his pocket. His coin flashed in the air, and when he caught it in his hand, he was holding a lance—a rod of gold about seven feet long, with a spear tip at one end.

The other demigods gasped. Rachel and Annabeth stepped back to avoid the point, which looked sharp as an ice pick.

"Wasn't that . . ." Annabeth hesitated. "I thought you had a sword."

"Um, it came up tails, I think," Jason said. "Same coin, long-range weapon form."

"Dude, I want one!" yelled somebody from Ares cabin.

"Better than Clarisse's electric spear, Lamer!" one of his brothers agreed.

"Electric," Jason murmured, like that was a good idea. "Back away."

Annabeth and Rachel got the message. Jason raised his javelin, and thunder broke open the sky. Every hair on Piper's arms stood straight up. Lightning arced down through the golden spear point and hit the campfire with the force of an artillery shell.

When the smoke cleared, and the ringing in Piper's ears subsided, the entire camp sat frozen in shock, half blind, covered in ashes, staring at the place where the fire had been. Cinders rained down everywhere. A burning log had impaled itself a few inches from the sleeping kid Clovis, who hadn't even stirred.

Jason lowered his lance. "Um . . . sorry."

Chiron brushed some burning coals out of his beard. He grimaced as if his worst fears had been confirmed. "A little overkill, perhaps, but you've made your point. And I believe we know who your father is."

"Jupiter," Jason said. "I mean Zeus. Lord of the Sky."

Piper couldn't help smiling. It made perfect sense. The most powerful god, the father of all the greatest heroes in the ancient myths—no one else could possibly be Jason's dad.

Apparently, the rest of the camp wasn't so sure. Everything broke into chaos, with dozens of people asking questions until Annabeth raised her arms.

"Hold it!" she said. "How can he be the son of Zeus? The Big Three...their pact not to have mortal kids...how could we not have known about him sooner?"

Chiron didn't answer, but Piper got the feeling he knew. And the truth was not good.

"The important thing," Rachel said, "is that Jason's here now. He has a quest to fulfill, which means he will need his own prophecy."

She closed her eyes and swooned. Two campers rushed forward and caught her. A third ran to the side of the amphitheater and grabbed a bronze three-legged stool, like they'd been trained for this duty. They eased Rachel onto the stool in front of the ruined hearth. Without the fire, the night was dark, but green mist started swirling around Rachel's feet. When she opened her eyes, they were glowing. Emerald smoke issued from her mouth. The voice that came out was raspy and ancient—the sound a snake would make if it could talk:

> *"Child of lightning, beware the earth,*
> *The giants' revenge the seven shall birth,*
> *The forge and dove shall break the cage,*
> *And death unleash through Hera's rage."*

On the last word, Rachel collapsed, but her helpers were waiting to catch her. They carried her away from the hearth and laid her in the corner to rest.

"Is that normal?" Piper asked. Then she realized she'd spoken into the silence, and everyone was looking at her. "I mean . . . does she spew green smoke a lot?"

"Gods, you're dense!" Drew sneered. "She just issued a prophecy—Jason's prophecy to save Hera! Why don't you just—"

"Drew," Annabeth snapped. "Piper asked a fair question. Something about that prophecy *definitely* isn't normal. If breaking Hera's cage unleashes her rage and causes a bunch of death . . . why would we free her? It might be a trap, or—or maybe Hera will turn on her rescuers. She's never been kind to heroes."

Jason rose. "I don't have much choice. Hera took my memory. I need it back. Besides, we can't just *not* help the queen of the heavens if she's in trouble."

A girl from Hephaestus cabin stood up—Nyssa, the one with the red bandanna. "Maybe. But you should listen to Annabeth. Hera can be vengeful. She threw her own son— our dad—down a mountain just because he was ugly."

"*Real* ugly," snickered someone from Aphrodite.

"Shut up!" Nyssa growled. "Anyway, we've also got to think —why beware the earth? And what's the giants' revenge? What are we dealing with here that's powerful enough to kidnap the queen of the heavens?"

No one answered, but Piper noticed Annabeth and Chiron having a silent exchange. Piper thought it went something like:

Annabeth: *The giants' revenge . . . no, it can't be.*
Chiron: *Don't speak of it here. Don't scare them.*

Annabeth: *You're kidding me! We can't be that unlucky.*

Chiron: *Later, child. If you told them everything, they would be too terrified to proceed.*

Piper knew it was crazy to think she could read their expressions so well—two people she barely knew. But she was absolutely positive she understood them, and it scared the jujubes out of her.

Annabeth took a deep breath. "It's Jason's quest," she announced, "so it's Jason's choice. Obviously, he's the child of lightning. According to tradition, he may choose any two companions."

Someone from the Hermes cabin yelled, "Well, you, obviously, Annabeth. You've got the most experience."

"No, Travis," Annabeth said. "First off, I'm *not* helping Hera. Every time I've tried, she's deceived me, or it's come back to bite me later. Forget it. No way. Secondly, I'm leaving first thing in the morning to find Percy."

"It's connected," Piper blurted out, not sure how she got the courage. "You know that's true, don't you? This whole business, your boyfriend's disappearance—it's all connected."

"How?" demanded Drew. "If you're so smart, how?"

Piper tried to form an answer, but she couldn't.

Annabeth saved her. "You may be right, Piper. If this is connected, I'll find out from the other end—by searching for Percy. As I said, I'm not about to rush off to rescue Hera, even if her disappearance sets the rest of the Olympians fighting again. But there's another reason I can't go. The prophecy says otherwise."

"It says who *I* pick," Jason agreed. "*The forge and dove shall break the cage.* The forge is the symbol of Vul—Hephaestus."

Under the Cabin Nine banner, Nyssa's shoulders slumped, like she'd just been given a heavy anvil to carry. "If you have to beware the earth," she said, "you should avoid traveling overland. You'll need air transport."

Piper was about to call out that Jason could fly. But then she thought better of it. That was for Jason to tell them, and he wasn't volunteering the information. Maybe he figured he'd freaked them out enough for one night.

"The flying chariot's broken," Nyssa continued, "and the pegasi, we're using them to search for Percy. But maybe Hephaestus cabin can help figure out something else to help. With Jake incapacitated, I'm senior camper. I can volunteer for the quest."

She didn't sound enthusiastic.

Then Leo stood up. He'd been so quiet, Piper had almost forgotten he was there, which was totally *not* like Leo.

"It's me," he said.

His cabinmates stirred. Several tried to pull him back to his seat, but Leo resisted.

"No, it's me. I know it is. I've got an idea for the transportation problem. Let me try. I can fix this!"

Jason studied him for a moment. Piper was sure he was going to tell Leo no. Then he smiled. "We started this together, Leo. Seems only right you come along. You find us a ride, you're in."

"Yes!" Leo pumped his fist.

"It'll be dangerous," Nyssa warned him. "Hardship, monsters, terrible suffering. Possibly none of you will come back alive."

"Oh." Suddenly Leo didn't look so excited. Then he remembered everyone was watching. "I mean...Oh, cool! Suffering? I love suffering! Let's do this."

Annabeth nodded. "Then, Jason, you only need to choose the third quest member. The dove—"

"Oh, absolutely!" Drew was on her feet and flashing Jason a smile. "The dove is Aphrodite. Everybody knows that. I am *totally* yours."

Piper's hands clenched. She stepped forward. "No."

Drew rolled her eyes. "Oh, please, Dumpster girl. Back off."

"*I* had the vision of Hera; not you. I have to do this."

"Anyone can have a vision," Drew said. "You were just at the right place at the right time." She turned to Jason. "Look, fighting is all fine, I suppose. And people who build things..." She looked at Leo in disdain. "Well, I suppose someone has to get their hands dirty. But you need *charm* on your side. I can be very persuasive. I could help a lot."

The campers started murmuring about how Drew *was* pretty persuasive. Piper could see Drew winning them over. Even Chiron was scratching his beard, like Drew's participation suddenly made sense to him.

"Well..." Annabeth said. "Given the wording of the prophecy—"

"No!" Piper's own voice sounded strange in her ears—more insistent, richer in tone. "I'm supposed to go."

Then the weirdest thing happened. Everyone started nodding, muttering that hmm, Piper's point of view made sense too. Drew looked around, incredulous. Even some of her own campers were nodding.

"Get over it!" Drew snapped at the crowd. "What can Piper do?"

Piper tried to respond, but her confidence started to wane. What *could* she offer? She wasn't a fighter, or a planner, or a fixer. She had no skills except getting into trouble and occasionally convincing people to do stupid things.

Plus, she was a liar. She needed to go on this quest for reasons that went way beyond Jason—and if she did go, she'd end up betraying everyone there. She heard that voice from the dream: *Do our bidding, and you may walk away alive.* How could she make a choice like that—between helping her father and helping Jason?

"Well," Drew said smugly, "I guess that settles it."

Suddenly there was collective gasp. Everyone stared at Piper like she'd just exploded. She wondered what she'd done wrong. Then she realized there was a reddish glow around her.

"What?" she demanded.

She looked above her, but there was no burning symbol like the one that appeared over Leo. Then she looked down and yelped.

Her clothes...what in the world was she *wearing*? She despised dresses. She didn't *own* a dress. But now she was adorned in a beautiful white sleeveless gown that went down to her ankles, with a V-neck so low it was totally embarrassing. Delicate gold armbands circled her biceps. An intricate necklace of amber, coral, and gold flowers glittered on her chest, and her hair...

"Oh, god," she said. "What's happened?"

A stunned Annabeth pointed at Piper's dagger, which was now oiled and gleaming, hanging at her side on a golden cord. Piper didn't want to draw it. She was afraid of what she would see. But her curiosity won out. She unsheathed Katoptris and stared at her reflection in the polished metal blade. Her hair was perfect: lush and long and chocolate brown, braided with gold ribbons down one side so it fell across her shoulder. She even wore makeup, better than Piper would ever know how to do herself—subtle touches that made her lips cherry red and brought out all the different colors in her eyes.

She was...she was...

"Beautiful," Jason exclaimed. "Piper, you...you're a knockout."

Under different circumstances, that would've been the happiest moment of her life. But now everyone was staring at her like she was a freak. Drew's face was full of horror and revulsion. "No!" she cried. "Not possible!"

"This isn't me," Piper protested. "I—don't understand."

Chiron the centaur folded his front legs and bowed to her, and all the campers followed his example.

"Hail, Piper McLean," Chiron announced gravely, as if he were speaking at her funeral. "Daughter of Aphrodite, lady of the doves, goddess of love."

LEO

LEO DIDN'T STICK AROUND AFTER PIPER turned beautiful.
Sure, it was amazing and all—*She's got makeup! It's a miracle!*
—but Leo had problems to deal with. He ducked out of the
amphitheater and ran into the darkness, wondering what he'd
gotten himself into.

He'd stood up in front of a bunch of stronger, braver demigods and volunteered—*volunteered*—for a mission that would
probably get him killed.

He hadn't mentioned seeing Tía Callida, his old babysitter,
but as soon as he'd heard about Jason's vision—the lady in the
black dress and shawl—Leo knew it was the same woman.
Tía Callida was Hera. His evil babysitter was the queen of the
gods. Stuff like that could really deep-fry your brain.

He trudged toward the woods and tried not to think about
his childhood—all the messed-up things that had led to his
mother's death. But he couldn't help it.

• • •

The first time Tía Callida tried to kill him, he must've been about two. Tía Callida was looking after him while his mother was at the machine shop. She wasn't really his aunt, of course —just one of the old women in the community, a generic *tía* who helped watch the kids. She smelled like a honey-baked ham, and always wore a widow's dress with a black shawl.

"Let's set you down for a nap," she said. "Let's see if you are my brave little hero, eh?"

Leo was sleepy. She nestled him into his blankets in a warm mound of red and yellow—pillows? The bed was like a cubbyhole in the wall, made of blackened bricks, with a metal slot over his head and a square hole far above, where he could see the stars. He remembered resting comfortably, grabbing at sparks like fireflies. He dozed, and dreamed of a boat made of fire, sailing through the cinders. He imagined himself on board, navigating the sky. Somewhere nearby, Tía Callida sat in her rocking chair—*creak, creak, creak*—and sang a lullaby. Even at two, Leo knew the difference between English and Spanish, and he remembered being puzzled because Tía Callida was singing in a language that was neither.

Everything was fine until his mother came home. She screamed and raced over to snatch him up, yelling at Tía Callida, "How could you?" But the old lady had disappeared.

Leo remembered looking over his mother's shoulder at the flames curling around his blankets. Only years later had he realized he'd been sleeping in a blazing fireplace.

The weirdest thing? Tía Callida hadn't been arrested or even banished from their house. She appeared again several times over the next few years. Once when Leo was three, she let him play with knives. "You must learn your blades early," she insisted, "if you are to be my hero someday." Leo managed not to kill himself, but he got the feeling Tía Callida wouldn't have cared one way or the other.

When Leo was four, Tía found a rattlesnake for him in a nearby cow pasture. She gave him a stick and encouraged him to poke the animal. "Where is your bravery, little hero? Show me the Fates were right to choose you." Leo stared down at those amber eyes, hearing the dry *shh-shh-ssh* of the snake's rattle. He couldn't bring himself to poke the snake. It didn't seem fair. Apparently the snake felt the same way about biting a little kid. Leo could've sworn it looked at Tía Callida like, *Are you nuts, lady?* Then it disappeared into the tall grass.

The last time she babysat him, Leo was five. She brought him a pack of crayons and a pad of paper. They sat together at the picnic table in back of the apartment complex, under an old pecan tree. While Tía Callida sang her strange songs, Leo drew a picture of the boat he'd seen in the flames, with colorful sails and rows of oars, a curved stern, and an awesome masthead. When he was almost done, about to sign his name the way he'd learned in kindergarten, a wind snatched the picture away. It flew into the sky and disappeared.

Leo wanted to cry. He'd spent so much time on that picture—but Tía Callida just clucked with disappointment.

"It isn't time yet, little hero. Someday, you'll have your quest. You'll find your destiny, and your hard journey will finally make sense. But first you must face many sorrows. I regret that, but heroes cannot be shaped any other way. Now, make me a fire, eh? Warm these old bones."

A few minutes later, Leo's mom came out and shrieked with horror. Tía Callida was gone, but Leo sat in the middle of a smoking fire. The pad of paper was reduced to ashes. Crayons had melted into a bubbling puddle of multicolored goo, and Leo's hands were ablaze, slowly burning through the picnic table. For years afterward, people in the apartment complex would wonder how someone had seared the impressions of a five-year-old's hands an inch deep into solid wood.

Now Leo was sure that Tía Callida, his psychotic babysitter, had been Hera all along. That made her, what—his godly grandmother? His family was even more messed up than he realized.

He wondered if his mother had known the truth. Leo remembered after that last visit, his mom took him inside and had a long talk with him, but he only understood some of it.

"She can't come back again." His mom had a beautiful face with kind eyes, and curly dark hair, but she looked older than she was because of hard work. The lines around her eyes were deeply etched. Her hands were callused. She was the first person from their family to graduate from college. She had a degree in mechanical engineering and could design anything, fix anything, build anything.

No one would hire her. No company would take her seriously, so she ended up in the machine shop, trying to make enough money to support the two of them. She always smelled of machine oil, and when she talked with Leo, she switched from Spanish to English constantly—using them like complementary tools. It took Leo years to realize that not everyone spoke that way. She'd even taught him Morse code as a kind of game, so they could tap messages to each other when they were in different rooms: *I love you. You okay?* Simple things like that.

"I don't care what Callida says," his mom told him. "I don't care about destiny and the Fates. You're too young for that. You're still my baby."

She took his hands, looking for burn marks, but of course there weren't any. "Leo, listen to me. Fire is a tool, like anything else, but it's more dangerous than most. You don't know your limits. Please, promise me—no more fire until you meet your father. Someday, *mijo*, you *will* meet him. He'll explain everything."

Leo had heard that since he could remember. Someday he would meet his dad. His mom wouldn't answer any questions about him. Leo had never met him, never even seen pictures, but she talked like he'd just gone to the store for some milk and he'd be back any minute. Leo tried to believe her. Someday, everything would make sense.

For the next couple of years, they were happy. Leo almost forgot about Tía Callida. He still dreamed of the flying boat, but the other strange events seemed like a dream too.

It all came apart when he was eight. By then, he was spending every free hour at the shop with his mom. He knew how to use the machines. He could measure and do math better than most adults. He'd learned to think three-dimensionally, solving mechanical problems in his head the way his mom did.

One night, they stayed late because his mom was finishing

a drill bit design she hoped to patent. If she could sell the prototype, it might change their lives. She'd finally get a break.

As she worked, Leo passed her supplies and told her corny jokes, trying to keep her spirits up. He loved it when he could make her laugh. She'd smile and say, "Your father would be proud of you, *mijo*. You'll meet him soon, I'm sure."

Mom's workspace was at the very back of the shop. It was kind of creepy at night, because they were the only ones there. Every sound echoed through the dark warehouse, but Leo didn't mind as long as he was with his mom. If he did wander the shop, they could always keep in touch with Morse code taps. Whenever they were ready to leave, they had to walk through the entire shop, through the break room, and out to the parking lot, locking the doors behind them.

That night after finishing up, they'd just gotten to the break room when his mom realized she didn't have her keys.

"That's funny." She frowned. "I know I had them. Wait here, *mijo*. I'll only be a minute."

She gave him one more smile—the last one he'd ever get —and she went back into the warehouse.

She'd only been gone a few heartbeats when the interior door slammed shut. Then the exterior door locked itself.

"Mom?" Leo's heart pounded. Something heavy crashed inside the warehouse. He ran to the door, but no matter how hard he pulled or kicked, it wouldn't open. "Mom!" Frantically, he tapped a message on the wall: *You okay?*

"She can't hear you," a voice said.

Leo turned and found himself facing a strange woman. At

first he thought it was Tía Callida. She was wrapped in black robes, with a veil covering her face.

"Tía?" he said.

The woman chuckled, a slow gentle sound, as if she were half asleep. "I am not your guardian. Merely a family resemblance."

"What—what do you want? Where's my mom?"

"Ah...loyal to your mother. How nice. But you see, I have children too...and I understand you will fight them someday. When they try to wake me, you will prevent them. I cannot allow that."

"I don't know you. I don't want to fight anybody."

She muttered like a sleepwalker in a trance, "A wise choice."

With a chill, Leo realized the woman was, in fact, asleep. Behind the veil, her eyes were closed. But even stranger: her clothes were not made of cloth. They were made of *earth*—dry black dirt, churning and shifting around her. Her pale, sleeping face was barely visible behind a curtain of dust, and he had the horrible sense that she'd had just risen from the grave. If the woman was asleep, Leo wanted her to stay that way. He knew that fully awake, she would be even more terrible.

"I cannot destroy you yet," the woman murmured. "The Fates will not allow it. But they not do protect your mother, and they cannot stop me from breaking your spirit. Remember this night, little hero, when they ask you to oppose me."

"Leave my mother alone!" Fear rose in his throat as the woman shuffled forward. She moved more like an avalanche than a person, a dark wall of earth shifting toward him.

"How will you stop me?" she whispered.

She walked straight through a table, the particles of her body reassembling on the other side.

She loomed over Leo, and he knew she would pass right through him, too. He was the only thing between her and his mother.

His hands caught fire.

A sleepy smile spread across the woman's face, as if she'd already won. Leo screamed with desperation. His vision turned red. Flames washed over the earthen woman, the walls, the locked doors. And Leo lost consciousness.

When he woke, he was in an ambulance.

The paramedic tried to be kind. She told him the warehouse had burned down. His mother hadn't made it out. The paramedic said she was sorry, but Leo felt hollow. He'd lost control, just like his mother had warned. Her death was his fault.

Soon the police came to get him, and they weren't as nice. The fire had started in the break room, they said, right where Leo was standing. He'd survived by some miracle, but what kind of child locked the doors of his mother's workplace, knowing she was inside, and started a fire?

Later, his neighbors at the apartment complex told the police what a strange boy he was. They talked about the burned handprints on the picnic table. They'd always known something was wrong with Esperanza Valdez's son.

His relatives wouldn't take him in. His Aunt Rosa called him a *diablo* and shouted at the social workers to take him away. So Leo went to his first foster home. A few days later, he ran away. Some foster homes lasted longer than others. He would joke around, make a few friends, pretend that nothing bothered him, but he always ended up running sooner or later. It was the only thing that made the pain better—feeling like he was moving, getting farther and farther away from the ashes of that machine shop.

He'd promised himself he would never play with fire again. He hadn't thought about Tía Callida, or the sleeping woman wrapped in earthen robes, for a long time.

He was almost to the woods when he imagined Tía Callida's voice: *It wasn't your fault, little hero. Our enemy wakes. It's time to stop running.*

"Hera," Leo muttered, "you're not even here, are you? You're in a cage somewhere."

There was no answer.

But now, at least, Leo understood something. Hera had been watching him his entire life. Somehow, she'd known that one day she would need him. Maybe those Fates she mentioned could tell the future. Leo wasn't sure. But he knew he was *meant* to go on this quest. Jason's prophecy warned them to beware the earth, and Leo knew it had something to do with that sleeping woman in the shop, wrapped in robes of shifting dirt.

You'll find your destiny, Tía Callida had promised, *and your hard journey will finally make sense.*

Leo might find out what that flying boat in his dreams meant. He might meet his father, or even get to avenge his mother's death.

But first things first. He'd promised Jason a flying ride.

Not the boat from his dreams—not yet. There wasn't time to build something that complicated. He needed a quicker solution. He needed a dragon.

He hesitated at the edge of the woods, peering into absolute blackness. Owls hooted, and something far away hissed like a chorus of snakes.

Leo remembered what Will Solace had told him: No one should go in the woods alone, definitely not unarmed. Leo had nothing—no sword, no flashlight, no help.

He glanced back at the lights of the cabins. He could turn around now and tell everyone he'd been joking. *Psych!* Nyssa could go on the quest instead. He could stay at camp and learn to be part of the Hephaestus cabin, but he wondered how long it would be before he looked like his bunkmates—sad, dejected, convinced of his own bad luck.

They cannot stop me from breaking your spirit, the sleeping woman had said. *Remember this night, little hero, when they ask you to oppose me.*

"Believe me, lady," Leo muttered, "I remember. And whoever you are, I'm gonna face-plant you hard, Leo-style."

He took a deep breath and plunged into the forest.

XII

LEO

THE WOODS WEREN'T LIKE ANYPLACE he'd been before. Leo had been raised in a north Houston apartment complex. The wildest things he'd ever seen were that rattlesnake in the cow pasture and his Aunt Rosa in her nightgown, until he was sent to Wilderness School.

Even there, the school had been in the desert. No trees with gnarled roots to trip over. No streams to fall into. No branches casting dark, creepy shadows and owls looking down at him with their big reflective eyes. This was the Twilight Zone.

He stumbled along until he was sure no one back at the cabins could possibly see him. Then he summoned fire. Flames danced along his fingertips, casting enough light to see. He hadn't tried to keep a sustained burn going since he was five, at that picnic table. Since his mom's death, he'd been too afraid to try anything. Even this tiny fire made him feel guilty.

He kept walking, looking for dragon-type clues—giant

footprints, trampled trees, swaths of burning forest. Some-thing that big couldn't exactly sneak around, right? But he saw *nada*. Once he glimpsed a large, furry shape like a wolf or a bear, but it stayed away from his fire, which was fine by Leo.

Then, at the bottom of a clearing, he saw the first trap—a hundred-foot-wide crater ringed with boulders.

Leo had to admit it was pretty ingenious. In the center of the depression, a metal vat the size of a hot tub had been filled with bubbly dark liquid—Tabasco sauce and motor oil. On a pedestal suspended over the vat, an electric fan rotated in a circle, spreading the fumes across the forest. Could metal dragons smell?

The vat seemed to be unguarded. But Leo looked closely, and in the dim light of the stars and his handheld fire, he could see the glint of metal beneath the dirt and leaves—a bronze net lining the entire crater. Or maybe *see* wasn't the right word—he could sense it there, as if the mechanism was emitting heat, revealing itself to him. Six large strips of bronze stretched out from the vat like the spokes of a wheel. They would be pressure sensitive, Leo guessed. As soon as the dragon stepped on one, the net would spring closed, and *voilà*—one gift-wrapped monster.

Leo edged closer. He put his foot on the nearest trig-ger strip. As he expected, nothing happened. They had to have set the net for something really heavy. Otherwise they could catch an animal, human, smaller monster, whatever. He doubted there was anything else as heavy as a metal dragon in these woods. At least, he hoped there wasn't.

He picked his way down the crater and approached the

vat. The fumes were almost overpowering, and his eyes started watering. He remembered a time when Tía Callida (Hera, whatever) had made him chop jalapeños in the kitchen and he'd gotten the juice in his eyes. Serious pain. But of course she'd been like, "Endure it, little hero. The Aztecs of your mother's homeland used to punish bad children by holding them over a fire filled with chili peppers. They raised many heroes that way."

A total psycho, that lady. Leo was so glad he was on a quest to rescue her.

Tía Callida would've loved this vat, because it was *way* worse than jalapeño juice. Leo looked for a trigger—something that would disable the net. He didn't see anything.

He had a moment of panic. Nyssa had said there were several traps like this in the woods, and they were planning more. What if the dragon had already stepped into another one? How could Leo possibly find them all?

He continued to search, but he didn't see any release mechanism. No large button labeled OFF. It occurred to him that there might not *be* one. He started to despair—and then he heard the sound.

It was more of a tremor—the deep sort of rumbling you hear in your gut rather than your ears. It gave him the jitters, but he didn't look around for the source. He just kept examining the trap, thinking, *Must be a long way off. It's pounding its way through the woods. I gotta hurry.*

Then he heard a grinding snort, like steam forced out of a metal barrel.

His neck tingled. He turned slowly. At the edge of the pit,

fifty feet away, two glowing red eyes were staring at him. The creature gleamed in the moonlight, and Leo couldn't believe something that huge had sneaked up on him so fast. Too late, he realized its gaze was fixed on the fire in his hand, and he extinguished the flames.

He could still see the dragon just fine. It was about sixty feet long, snout to tail, its body made of interlocking bronze plates. Its claws were the size of butcher knives, and its mouth was lined with hundreds of dagger-sharp metal teeth. Steam came out of its nostrils. It snarled like a chain saw cutting through a tree. It could've bitten Leo in half, easy, or stomped him flat. It was the most beautiful thing he'd ever seen, except for one problem that completely ruined Leo's plan.

"You don't have wings," Leo said.

The dragon's snarl died. It tilted its head as if to say, *Why aren't you running away in terror?*

"Hey, no offense," Leo said. "You're amazing! Good god, who *made* you? Are you hydraulic or nuclear-powered or what? But if it was me, I would've put wings on you. What kind of dragon doesn't have wings? I guess maybe you're too heavy to fly? I should've thought of that."

The dragon snorted, more confused now. It was supposed to trample Leo. This conversation thing wasn't part of the plan. It took a step forward, and Leo shouted, "No!"

The dragon snarled again.

"It's a trap, bronze brain," Leo said. "They're trying to catch you."

The dragon opened its mouth and blew fire. A column of white-hot flames billowed over Leo, more than he'd ever tried to endure before. He felt as if he were being hosed down with a powerful, very hot fire hose. It stung a little, but he stood his ground. When the flames died, he was perfectly fine. Even his clothes were okay, which Leo didn't understand, but for which he was grateful. He liked his army jacket, and having his pants seared off would've been pretty embarrassing.

The dragon stared at Leo. Its face didn't actually change, being made of metal and all, but Leo thought he could read its expression: *Why no crispy critter?* A spark flew out of its neck like it was about to short-circuit.

"You can't burn me," Leo said, trying to sound stern and calm. He'd never had a dog before, but he talked to the dragon the way he thought you'd talk to a dog. "Stay, boy. Don't come any closer. I don't want you to get caught. See, they think you're broken and have to be scrapped. But I don't believe that. I can fix you if you'll let me—"

The dragon creaked, roared, and charged. The trap sprang. The floor of the crater erupted with a sound like a thousand trash can lids banging together. Dirt and leaves flew, metal net flashing. Leo was knocked off his feet, turned upside down, and doused in Tabasco sauce and oil. He found himself sandwiched between the vat and the dragon as it thrashed, trying to free itself from the net that had wrapped around them both.

The dragon blew flames in every direction, lighting up the sky and setting trees on fire. Oil and sauce burned all over them. It didn't hurt Leo, but it left a nasty taste in his mouth.

"Will you stop that!" he yelled.

The dragon kept squirming. Leo realized he would get

crushed if he didn't move. It wasn't easy, but he managed to wriggle out from between the dragon and the vat. He squirmed his way through the net. Fortunately the holes were plenty big enough for a skinny kid.

He ran to the dragon's head. It tried to snap at him, but its teeth were tangled in the mesh. It blew fire again, but seemed to be running out of energy. This time the flames were only orange. They sputtered before they even reached Leo's face.

"Listen, man," Leo said, "you're just going to show them where you are. Then they'll come and break out the acid and the metal cutters. Is that what you want?"

The dragon's jaw made a creaking sound, like it was trying to talk.

"Okay, then," Leo said. "You'll have to trust me."

And Leo set to work.

It took him almost an hour to find the control panel. It was right behind the dragon's head, which made sense. He'd elected to keep the dragon in the net, because it was easier to work with the dragon constrained, but the dragon didn't like it.

"Hold still!" Leo scolded.

The dragon made another creaking sound that might've been a whimper.

Leo examined the wires inside the dragon's head. He was distracted by a sound in the woods, but when he looked up it was just a tree spirit—a dryad, Leo thought they were called—putting out the flames in her branches. Fortunately, the dragon hadn't started an all-out forest fire, but still the dryad wasn't too pleased. The girl's dress was smoking. She smothered the flames with a silky blanket, and when she saw Leo looking at her, she made a gesture that was probably very rude in Dryad. Then she disappeared in a green poof of mist.

Leo returned his attention to the wiring. It was ingenious, definitely, and it made sense to him. This was the motor control relay. This processed sensory input from the eyes. This disk...

"Ha," he said. "Well, no wonder."

Creak? the dragon asked with its jaw.

"You've got a corroded control disk. Probably regulates your higher reasoning circuits, right? Rusty brain, man. No wonder you're a little...confused." He almost said *crazy*, but he caught himself. "I wish I had a replacement disk, but... this is a complicated piece of circuitry. I'm gonna have to take it out and clean it. Only be a minute." He pulled out the disk, and the dragon went absolutely still. The glow died in its eyes. Leo slid off its back and began polishing the disk. He mopped up some oil and Tabasco sauce with his sleeve, which helped cut through the grime, but the more he cleaned, the more concerned he got. Some of the circuits were beyond repair. He could make it better, but not perfect. For that, he'd need a completely new disk, and he had no idea how to build one.

He tried to work quickly. He wasn't sure how long the dragon's control disk could be off without damaging it— maybe forever—but he didn't want to take chances. Once he'd done the best he could, he climbed back up to the dragon's head and started cleaning the wiring and gearboxes, getting himself filthy in the process.

"Clean hands, dirty equipment," he muttered, something

his mother used to say. By the time he was through, his hands were black with grease and his clothes looked like he'd just lost a mud-wrestling contest, but the mechanisms looked a lot better. He slipped in the disk, connected the last wire, and sparks flew. The dragon shuddered. Its eyes began to glow.

"Better?" Leo asked.

The dragon made a sound like a high-speed drill. It opened its mouth and all its teeth rotated.

"I guess that's a *yes*. Hold on, I'll free you."

Another thirty minutes to find the release clamps for the net and untangle the dragon, but finally it stood and shook the last bit of netting off its back. It roared triumphantly and shot fire at the sky.

"Seriously," Leo said. "Could you not show off?"

Creak? the dragon asked.

"You need a name," Leo decided. "I'm calling you Festus."

The dragon whirred its teeth and grinned. At least Leo hoped it was a grin.

"Cool," Leo said. "But we still have a problem, because you don't have wings."

Festus tilted his head and snorted steam. Then he lowered his back in an unmistakable gesture. He wanted Leo to climb on.

"Where we going?" Leo asked.

But he was too excited to wait for an answer. He climbed onto the dragon's back, and Festus bounded off into the woods.

• • •

Leo lost track of time and all sense of direction. It seemed impossible the woods could be so deep and wild, but the dragon traveled until the trees were like skyscrapers and the canopy of leaves completely blotted out the stars. Even the fire in Leo's hand couldn't have lit the way, but the dragon's glowing red eyes acted like headlights.

Finally they crossed a stream and came to a dead end, a limestone cliff a hundred feet tall—a solid, sheer mass the dragon couldn't possibly climb.

Festus stopped at the base and lifted one leg like a dog pointing.

"What is it?" Leo slid to the ground. He walked up to the cliff—nothing but solid rock. The dragon kept pointing.

"It's not going to move out of your way," Leo told him.

The loose wire in the dragon's neck sparked, but otherwise he stayed still. Leo put his hand on the cliff. Suddenly his fingers smoldered. Lines of fire spread from his fingertips like ignited gunpowder, sizzling across the limestone. The burning lines raced across the cliff face until they had outlined a glowing red door five times as tall as Leo. He backed up and the door swung open, disturbingly silently for such a big slab of rock.

"Perfectly balanced," he muttered. "That's some first-rate engineering."

The dragon unfroze and marched inside, as if he were coming home.

Leo stepped through, and the door began to close. He had a moment of panic, remembering that night in the machine shop long ago, when he'd been locked in. What if he got stuck in here? But then lights flickered on—a combination of electric fluorescents and wall-mounted torches. When Leo saw the cavern, he forgot about leaving.

"Festus," he muttered. "What *is* this place?"

The dragon stomped to the center of the room, leaving tracks in the thick dust, and curled up on a large circular platform.

The cave was the size of an airplane hangar, with endless worktables and storage cages, rows of garage-sized doors along either wall, and staircases that led up to a network of catwalks high above. Equipment was everywhere—hydraulic lifts, welding torches, hazard suits, air-spades, forklifts, plus something that looked suspiciously like a nuclear reaction chamber. Bulletin boards were covered with tattered, faded blueprints. And weapons, armor, shields—war supplies all over the place, a lot of them only partially finished.

Hanging from chains far above the dragon's platform was an old tattered banner almost too faded to read. The letters were Greek, but Leo somehow knew what they said: BUNKER 9.

Did that mean nine as in the Hephaestus cabin, or nine as in there were eight others? Leo looked at Festus, still curled up on the platform, and it occurred to him that the dragon looked so content because it *was* home. It had probably been built on that pad.

"Do the other kids know . . . ?" Leo's question died as he asked it. Clearly, this place had been abandoned for decades. Cobwebs and dust covered everything. The floor revealed no footprints except for his, and the huge paw prints of the dragon. He was the first one in this bunker since . . . since a long time ago. Bunker 9 had been abandoned with a lot of projects half finished on the tables. Locked up and forgotten, but why?

Leo looked at a map on the wall—a battle map of camp, but the paper was as cracked and yellow as onionskin. A date at the bottom read, 1864.

"No way," he muttered.

Then he spotted a blueprint on a nearby bulletin board, and his heart almost leaped out of his throat. He ran to the worktable and stared up at a white-line drawing almost faded beyond recognition: a Greek ship from several different angles. Faintly scrawled words underneath it read: PROPHECY? UNCLEAR. FLIGHT?

It was the ship he'd seen in his dreams—the flying ship. Someone had tried to build it here, or at least sketched out the idea. Then it was left, forgotten . . . a prophecy yet to come. And weirdest of all, the ship's masthead was exactly like the one Leo had drawn when he was five—the head of a dragon.

"Looks like you, Festus," he murmured. "That's creepy."

The masthead gave him an uneasy feeling, but Leo's mind spun with too many other questions to think about it for long. He touched the blueprint, hoping he could take it down to study, but the paper crackled at his touch, so he left it alone. He looked around for other clues. No boats. No pieces that looked like parts of this project, but there were so many doors and storerooms to explore.

Festus snorted like he was trying to get Leo's attention, reminding him they didn't have all night. It was true. Leo figured it would be morning in a few hours, and he'd gotten completely sidetracked. He'd saved the dragon, but it wasn't going to help him on the quest. He needed something that would fly.

Festus nudged something toward him—a leather tool belt that had been left next to his construction pad. Then the dragon switched on his glowing red eye beams and turned them toward the ceiling. Leo looked up to where the spotlights were pointing, and yelped when he recognized the shapes hanging above them in the darkness.

"Festus," he said in a small voice. "We've got work to do."

XIII

JASON

JASON DREAMED OF WOLVES.

He stood in a clearing in the middle of a redwood forest. In front of him rose the ruins of a stone mansion. Low gray clouds blended with the ground fog, and cold rain hung in the air. A pack of large gray beasts milled around him, brushing against his legs, snarling and baring their teeth. They gently nudged him toward the ruins.

Jason had no desire to become the world's largest dog biscuit, so he decided to do what they wanted.

The ground squelched under his boots as he walked. Stone spires of chimneys, no longer attached to anything, rose up like totem poles. The house must've been enormous once, multi-storied with massive log walls and a soaring gabled roof, but now nothing remained but its stone skeleton. Jason passed under a crumbling doorway and found himself in a kind of courtyard.

Before him was a drained reflecting pool, long and

rectangular. Jason couldn't tell how deep it was, because the bottom was filled with mist. A dirt path led all the way around, and the house's uneven walls rose on either side. Wolves paced under the archways of rough red volcanic stone.

At the far end of the pool sat a giant she-wolf, several feet taller than Jason. Her eyes glowed silver in the fog, and her coat was the same color as the rocks—warm chocolaty red.

"I know this place," Jason said.

The wolf regarded him. She didn't exactly speak, but Jason could understand her. The movements of her ears and whiskers, the flash of her eyes, the way she curled her lips—all of these were part of her language.

Of course, the she-wolf said. *You began your journey here as a pup. Now you must find your way back. A new quest, a new start.*

"That isn't fair," Jason said. But as soon as he spoke, he knew there was no point complaining to the she-wolf.

Wolves didn't feel sympathy. They never expected fairness. The wolf said: *Conquer or die. This is always our way.*

Jason wanted to protest that he couldn't conquer if he didn't know who he was, or where he was supposed to go. But he knew this wolf. Her name was simply Lupa, the Mother Wolf, the greatest of her kind. Long ago she'd found him in this place, protected him, nurtured him, *chosen* him, but if Jason showed weakness, she would tear him to shreds. Rather than being her pup, he would become her dinner. In the wolf pack, weakness was not an option.

"Can you guide me?" Jason asked.

Lupa made a rumbling noise deep in her throat, and the mist in the pool dissolved.

At first Jason wasn't sure what he was seeing. At opposite ends of the pool, two dark spires had erupted from the cement floor like the drill bits of some massive tunneling machines boring through the surface. Jason couldn't tell if the spires were made of rock or petrified vines, but they were formed of thick tendrils that came together in a point at the top. Each spire was about five feet tall, but they weren't identical. The one closest to Jason was darker and seemed like a solid mass, its tendrils fused together. As he watched, it pushed a little farther out of the earth and expanded a little wider.

On Lupa's end of the pool, the second spire's tendrils were more open, like the bars of a cage. Inside, Jason could vaguely see a misty figure struggling, shifting within its confines.

"Hera," Jason said.

The she-wolf growled in agreement. The other wolves circled the pool, their fur standing up on their backs as they snarled at the spires.

The enemy has chosen this place to awaken her most powerful son, the giant king, Lupa said. *Our sacred place, where demigods are claimed—the place of death or life. The burned house. The house of the wolf. It is an abomination. You must stop her.*

"Her?" Jason was confused. "You mean, Hera?"

The she-wolf gnashed her teeth impatiently. *Use your senses, pup. I care nothing for Juno, but if she falls, our enemy wakes. And that will be the end for all of us. You know this place. You can find it again. Cleanse our house. Stop this before it is too late.*

The dark spire grew slowly larger, like the bulb of some horrible flower. Jason sensed that if it ever opened, it would release something he did *not* want to meet.

"Who am I?" Jason asked the she-wolf. "At least tell me that."

Wolves don't have much of a sense of humor, but Jason could tell the question amused Lupa, as if Jason were a cub just trying out his claws, practicing to be the alpha male.

You are our saving grace, as always. The she-wolf curled her lip, as if she had just made a clever joke. *Do not fail, son of Jupiter.*

XIV

JASON

JASON WOKE TO THE SOUND OF THUNDER. Then he remembered where he was. It was always thundering in Cabin One.

Above his cot, the domed ceiling was decorated with a blue-and-white mosaic like a cloudy sky. The cloud tiles shifted across the ceiling, changing from white to black. Thunder rumbled through the room, and gold tiles flashed like veins of lightning.

Except for the cot that the other campers had brought him, the cabin had no regular furniture—no chairs, tables, or dressers. As far as Jason could tell, it didn't even have a bathroom. The walls were carved with alcoves, each holding a bronze brazier or a golden eagle statue on a marble pedestal. In the center of the room, a twenty-foot-tall, full-color statue of Zeus in classic Greek robes stood with a shield at his side and a lightning bolt raised, ready to smite somebody.

Jason studied the statue, looking for anything he had in common with the Lord of the Sky. Black hair? Nope. Grumbly expression? Well, maybe. Beard? No thanks. In his robes and sandals, Zeus looked like a really buff, really angry hippie.

Yeah, Cabin One. A big honor, the other campers had told him. Sure, if you liked sleeping in a cold temple by yourself with Hippie Zeus frowning down at you all night.

Jason got up and rubbed his neck. His whole body was stiff from bad sleep and summoning lightning. That little trick last night hadn't been as easy as he had let on. It had almost made him pass out.

Next to the cot, new clothes were laid out for him: jeans, sneakers, and an orange Camp Half-Blood shirt. He definitely needed a change of clothes, but looking down at his tattered purple shirt, he was reluctant to change. It felt wrong somehow, putting on the camp shirt. He still couldn't believe he belonged here, despite everything they'd told him.

He thought about his dream, hoping more memories would come back to him about Lupa, or that ruined house in the redwoods. He knew he'd been there before. The wolf was real. But his head ached when he tried to remember. The marks on his forearm seemed to burn.

If he could find those ruins, he could find his past. Whatever was growing inside that rock spire, Jason had to stop it.

He looked at Hippie Zeus. "You're welcome to help."

The statue said nothing.

"Thanks, Pops," Jason muttered.

He changed clothes and checked his reflection in Zeus's shield. His face looked watery and strange in the metal, like he was dissolving in a pool of gold. Definitely he didn't look as good as Piper had last night after she'd suddenly been transformed.

Jason still wasn't sure how he felt about that. He'd acted like an idiot, announcing in front of everyone that she was a knockout. Not like there'd been anything wrong with her *before*. Sure, she looked great after Aphrodite zapped her, but she also didn't look like herself, not comfortable with the attention.

Jason had felt bad for her. Maybe that was crazy, considering she'd just been claimed by a goddess and turned into the most gorgeous girl at camp. Everybody had started fawning over her, telling her how amazing she was and how obviously *she* should be the one who went on the quest—but that attention had nothing to do with who she was. New dress, new makeup, glowing pink aura, and *boom*: suddenly people liked her. Jason felt like he understood that.

Last night when he'd called down lightning, the other campers' reactions had seemed familiar to him. He was pretty sure he'd been dealing with that for a long time—people looking at him in awe just because he was the son of Zeus, treating him special, but it didn't have anything to do with *him*. Nobody cared about *him*, just his big scary daddy standing behind him with the doomsday bolt, as if to say, *Respect this kid or eat voltage!*

After the campfire, when people started heading back to their cabins, Jason had gone up to Piper and formally asked her to come with him on the quest.

She'd still been in a state of shock, but she nodded, rubbing her arms, which must've been cold in that sleeveless dress.

"Aphrodite took my snowboarding jacket," she muttered. "Mugged by my own mom."

In the first row of the amphitheater, Jason found a blanket and wrapped it around her shoulders. "We'll get you a new jacket," he promised.

She managed a smile. He wanted to wrap his arms around her, but he restrained himself. He didn't want her to think he was as shallow as everyone else—trying to make a move on her because she'd turned all beautiful.

He was glad Piper was going with him on the quest. Jason had tried to act brave at the campfire, but it was just that— an act. The idea of going up against an evil force powerful enough to kidnap Hera scared him witless, especially since he didn't even know his own past. He'd need help, and it felt right: Piper should be with him. But things were already complicated without figuring out how much he liked her, and why. He'd already messed with her head enough.

He slipped on his new shoes, ready to get out of that cold, empty cabin. Then he spotted something he hadn't noticed the night before. A brazier had been moved out of one of the alcoves to create a sleeping niche, with a bedroll, a backpack, even some pictures taped to the wall.

Jason walked over. Whoever had slept there, it had been a long time ago. The bedroll smelled musty. The backpack was covered with a thin film of dust. Some of the photos once taped to the wall had lost their stickiness and fallen to the floor.

One picture showed Annabeth—much younger, maybe eight, but Jason could tell it was she: same blond hair and gray eyes, same distracted look like she was thinking a million things at once. She stood next to a sandy-haired guy about fourteen or fifteen, with a mischievous smile and ragged leather armor over a T-shirt. He was pointing to an alley behind them, like he was telling the photographer, *Let's go meet things in a dark alley and kill them!* A second photo showed Annabeth and the same guy sitting at a campfire, laughing hysterically.

Finally Jason picked up one of the photos that had fallen. It was a strip of pictures like you'd take in a do-it-yourself photo booth: Annabeth and the sandy-haired guy, but with another girl between them. She was maybe fifteen, with black hair—choppy like Piper's—a black leather jacket, and silver jewelry, so she looked kind of goth; but she was caught mid-laugh, and it was clear she was with her two best friends.

"That's Thalia," someone said.

Jason turned.

Annabeth was peering over his shoulder. Her expression was sad, like the picture bought back hard memories. "She's the other child of Zeus who lived here—but not for long. Sorry, I should've knocked."

"It's fine," Jason said. "Not like I think of this place as home."

Annabeth was dressed for travel, with a winter coat over her camp clothes, her knife at her belt, and a backpack across her shoulder.

Jason said, "Don't suppose you've changed your mind about coming with us?"

She shook her head. "You got a good team already. I'm off to look for Percy."

Jason was a little disappointed. He would've appreciated having somebody on the trip who knew what they were doing, so he wouldn't feel like he was leading Piper and Leo off a cliff.

"Hey, you'll do fine," Annabeth promised. "Something tells me this isn't your first quest."

Jason had a vague suspicion she was right, but that didn't make him feel any better. Everyone seemed to think he was so brave and confident, but they didn't see how lost he really felt. How could they trust him when he didn't even know who he was?

He looked at the pictures of Annabeth smiling. He wondered how long it had been since she'd smiled. She must really like this Percy guy to search for him so hard, and that made Jason a little envious. Was anyone searching for *him* right now? What if somebody cared for *him* that much and was going out of her mind with worry, and he couldn't even remember his old life?

"You know who I am," he guessed. "Don't you?"

Annabeth gripped the hilt of her dagger. She looked for a chair to sit on, but of course there weren't any. "Honestly, Jason . . . I'm not sure. My best guess, you're a loner. It happens sometimes. For one reason or another, the camp never found you, but you survived anyway by constantly moving around. Trained yourself to fight. Handled the monsters on your own. You beat the odds."

"The first thing Chiron said to me," Jason remembered, "was *you should be dead.*"

"That could be why," Annabeth said. "Most demigods

would never make it on their own. And a child of Zeus—
I mean, it doesn't get any more dangerous than that. The
chances of your reaching age fifteen without finding Camp
Half-Blood or dying—microscopic. But like I said, it does
happen. Thalia ran away when she was young. She survived
on her own for years. Even took care of me for a while. So
maybe you were a loner too."

Jason held out his arm. "And these marks?"

Annabeth glanced at the tattoos. Clearly, they bothered
her. "Well, the eagle is the symbol of Zeus, so that makes
sense. The twelve lines—maybe they stand for years, if you'd
been making them since you were three years old. SPQR—
that's the motto of the old Roman Empire: *Senatus Populusque
Romanus*, the Senate and the People of Rome. Though why
you would burn that on your own arm, I don't know. Unless
you had a *really* harsh Latin teacher..."

Jason was pretty sure that wasn't the reason. It also didn't
seem possible he'd been on his own his whole life. But what
else made sense? Annabeth had been pretty clear—Camp
Half-Blood was the only safe place in the world for demigods.

"I, um...had a weird dream last night," he said. It seemed
like a stupid thing to confide, but Annabeth didn't look
surprised.

"Happens all the time to demigods," she said. "What did
you see?"

He told her about the wolves and the ruined house and
the two rock spires. As he talked, Annabeth started pacing,
looking more and more agitated.

"You don't remember where this house is?" she asked.

Jason shook his head. "But I'm sure I've been there before."

"Redwoods," she mused. "Could be northern California. And the she-wolf...I've studied goddesses, spirits, and monsters my whole life. I've never heard of Lupa."

"She said the enemy was a 'her.' I thought maybe it was Hera, but—"

"I wouldn't trust Hera, but I don't think she's the enemy. And that thing rising out of the earth—" Annabeth's expression darkened. "You've got to stop it."

"You know what it is, don't you?" he asked. "Or at least, you've got a guess. I saw your face last night at the campfire. You looked at Chiron like it was suddenly dawning on you, but you didn't want to scare us."

Annabeth hesitated. "Jason, the thing about prophecies... the more you know, the more you try to change them, and that can be disastrous. Chiron believes it's better that you find your own path, find out things in your own time. If he'd told me everything he knew before my first quest with Percy ...I've got to admit, I'm not sure I would've been able to go through with it. For your quest, it's even more important."

"That bad, huh?"

"Not if you succeed. At least...I hope not."

"But I don't even know where to start. Where am I supposed to go?"

"Follow the monsters," Annabeth suggested.

Jason thought about that. The storm spirit who'd attacked him at the Grand Canyon had said he was being recalled to his boss. If Jason could track the storm spirits, he might be able to find the person controlling them. And maybe that would lead him to Hera's prison.

"Okay," he said. "How do I find storm winds?"

"Personally, I'd ask a wind god," Annabeth said. "Aeolus is the master of all the winds, but he's a little ... unpredictable. No one finds him unless he wants to be found. I'd try one of the four seasonal wind gods that work for Aeolus. The nearest one, the one who has the most dealings with heroes, is Boreas, the North Wind."

"So if I looked him up on Google maps—"

"Oh, he's not hard to find," Annabeth promised. "He settled in North America like all the other gods. So of course he picked the oldest northern settlement, about as far north as you can go."

"Maine?" Jason guessed.

"Farther."

Jason tried to envision a map. What was farther north than Maine? The oldest northern settlement ...

"Canada," he decided. "Quebec."

Annabeth smiled. "I hope you speak French."

Jason actually felt a spark of excitement. Quebec—at least now he had a goal. Find the North Wind, track down the storm spirits, find out who they worked for and where that ruined house was. Free Hera. All in four days. Cake.

"Thanks, Annabeth." He looked at the photo booth pictures still in his hand. "So, um ... you said it was dangerous being a child of Zeus. What ever happened to Thalia?"

"Oh, she's fine," Annabeth said. "She became a Hunter of

Artemis—one of the handmaidens of the goddess. They roam around the country killing monsters. We don't see them at camp very often."

Jason glanced over at the huge statue of Zeus. He understood why Thalia had slept in this alcove. It was the only place in the cabin not in Hippie Zeus's line of sight. And even that hadn't been enough. She'd chosen to follow Artemis and be part of a group rather than stay in this cold drafty temple alone with her twenty-foot-tall dad—*Jason's dad*—glowering down at her. *Eat voltage!* Jason didn't have any trouble understanding Thalia's feelings. He wondered if there was a Hunters group for guys.

"Who's the other kid in the photo?" he asked. "The sandy-haired guy."

Annabeth's expression tightened. Touchy subject.

"That's Luke," she said. "He's dead now."

Jason decided it was best not to ask more, but the way Annabeth said Luke's name, he wondered if maybe Percy Jackson wasn't the only boy Annabeth had ever liked.

He focused again on Thalia's face. He kept thinking this photo of her was important. He was missing something.

Jason felt a strange sense of connection to this other child of Zeus—someone who might understand his confusion, maybe even answer some questions. But another voice inside him, an insistent whisper, said: *Dangerous. Stay away.*

"How old is she now?" he asked.

"Hard to say. She was a tree for a while. Now she's immortal."

"What?"

His expression must've been pretty good, because Annabeth laughed. "Don't worry. It's not something all children of Zeus go through. It's a long story, but . . . well, she was out of commission for a long time. If she'd aged regularly, she'd be in her twenties now, but she still looks the same as in that picture, like she's about . . . well, about your age. Fifteen or sixteen?"

Something the she-wolf had said in his dream nagged at Jason. He found himself asking, "What's her last name?"

Annabeth looked uneasy. "She didn't use a last name, really. If she had to, she'd use her mom's, but they didn't get along. Thalia ran away when she was pretty young."

Jason waited.

"Grace," Annabeth said. "Thalia Grace."

Jason's fingers went numb. The picture fluttered to the floor.

"You okay?" Annabeth asked.

A shred of memory had ignited—maybe a tiny piece that Hera had forgotten to steal. Or maybe she'd left it there on purpose—just enough for him to remember that name, and know that digging up his past was terribly, terribly dangerous.

You should be dead, Chiron had said. It wasn't a comment about Jason beating the odds as a loner. Chiron knew something specific—something about Jason's family.

The she-wolf's words in his dream finally made sense to him, her clever joke at his expense. He could imagine Lupa growling a wolfish laugh.

"What is it?" Annabeth pressed.

Jason couldn't keep this to himself. It would kill him, and

he had to get Annabeth's help. If she knew Thalia, maybe she could advise him.

"You have to swear not to tell anyone else," he said.

"Jason—"

"Swear it," he urged. "Until I figure out what's going on, what this all means—" He rubbed the burned tattoos on his forearm. "You have to keep a secret."

Annabeth hesitated, but her curiosity won out. "All right. Until you tell me it's okay, I won't share what you say with anyone else. I swear on the River Styx."

Thunder rumbled, even louder than usual for the cabin.

You are our saving Grace, the wolf had snarled.

Jason picked up the photo from the floor.

"My last name is Grace," he said. "This is my sister."

Annabeth turned pale. Jason could see her wrestling with dismay, disbelief, anger. She thought he was lying. His claim was impossible. And part of him felt the same way, but as soon as he spoke the words, he knew they were true.

Then the doors of the cabin burst open. Half a dozen campers spilled in, led by the bald guy from Iris, Butch.

"Hurry!" he said, and Jason couldn't tell if his expression was excitement or fear. "The dragon is back."

X V

PIPER

PIPER WOKE UP AND IMMEDIATELY GRABBED a mirror. There were plenty of those in the Aphrodite cabin. She sat on her bunk, looked at her reflection and groaned.

She was *still* gorgeous.

Last night after the campfire, she'd tried everything. She messed up her hair, washed the makeup off her face, cried to make her eyes red. Nothing worked. Her hair popped back to perfection. The magic makeup reapplied itself. Her eyes refused to get puffy or bloodshot.

She would've changed clothes, but she had nothing to change into. The other Aphrodite campers offered her some (laughing behind her back, she was sure), but each outfit was even more fashionable and ridiculous than what she had on.

Now, after a horrible night's sleep, still no change. Piper normally looked like a zombie in the morning, but her hair was styled like a supermodel's and her skin was perfect. Even that horrible zit at the base of her nose, which she'd had for so many days she'd started to call it Bob, had disappeared.

She growled in frustration and raked her fingers through her hair. No use. The do just popped back into place. She looked like Cherokee Barbie.

From across the cabin, Drew called, "Oh, honey, it won't go away." Her voice dripped with false sympathy. "Mom's blessing will last *at least* another day. Maybe a week if you're lucky."

Piper gritted her teeth. "A *week?*"

The other Aphrodite kids—about dozen girls and five guys—smirked and snickered at her discomfort. Piper knew she should play cool, not let them get under her skin. She'd dealt with shallow, popular kids plenty of times. But this was different. These were her brothers and sisters, even if she had *nothing* in common with them, and how Aphrodite had managed to have so many kids so close in age . . . Never mind. She didn't want to know.

"Don't worry, hon." Drew blotted her fluorescent lipstick. "You're thinking you don't belong here? We couldn't agree more. Isn't that right, *Mitchell?*"

One of the guys flinched. "Um, yeah. Sure."

"Mmm-hmm." Drew took out her mascara and checked her lashes. Everyone else watched, not daring to speak. "So anyways, people, fifteen minutes until breakfast. The cabin's not going to clean itself! And Mitchell, I think you've learned your lesson. Right, sweetie? So you're on garbage patrol just for today, mm-kay? Show Piper how it's done, 'cause I have a feeling she'll have that job soon—*if* she survives her *quest*. Now, get to work, everybody! It's my bathroom time!"

Everybody started rushing around, making beds and folding clothes, while Drew scooped up her makeup kit, hair dryer, and brush and marched into the bathroom.

Someone inside yelped, and a girl about eleven was kicked out, hastily wrapped in towels with shampoo still in her hair.

The door slammed shut, and the girl started to cry. A couple of older campers comforted her and wiped the bubbles out of her hair.

"Seriously?" Piper said to no one in particular. "You let Drew treat you like this?"

A few kids shot Piper nervous looks, like they might actually agree, but they said nothing.

The campers kept working, though Piper couldn't see why the cabin needed much cleaning. It was a life-size dollhouse, with pink walls and white window trim. The lace curtains were pastel blue and green, which of course matched the sheets and feather comforters on all the beds.

The guys had one row of bunks separated by a curtain, but their section of the cabin was just as neat and orderly as the girls'. Something was *definitely* unnatural about that. Every camper had a wooden camp chest at the foot of their bunk with their name painted on it, and Piper guessed that the clothes in each chest were neatly folded and color coordinated. The only bit of individualism was how the campers decorated their private bunk spaces. Each had slightly different pictures tacked up of whatever celebrities they thought were hot. A few had personal photos, too, but most were actors or singers or whatever.

Piper hoped she might not see *The Poster*. It had been almost a year since the movie, and she thought by now surely everyone had torn down those old tattered advertisements and tacked up something newer. But no such luck. She spotted one on the wall by the storage closet, in the middle of a collage of famous heartthrobs.

The title was lurid red: KING OF SPARTA. Under that, the poster showed the leading man—a three-quarters shot of bare-chested bronze flesh, with ripped pectorals and six-pack abs. He was clad in only a Greek war kilt and a purple cape, sword in hand. He looked like he'd just been rubbed in oil, his short black hair gleaming and rivulets of sweat pouring off his rugged face, those dark sad eyes facing the camera as if to say, *I will kill your men and steal your women! Ha-ha!*

It was the most ridiculous poster of all time. Piper and her dad had had a good laugh over it the first time they saw it. Then the movie made a bajillion dollars. The poster graphic popped up everywhere. Piper couldn't get away from it at school, walking down the street, even online. It became *The Poster*, the most embarrassing thing in her life. And yeah, it was a picture of her dad.

She turned away so no one would think she was staring at it. Maybe when everyone went to breakfast she could tear it down and they wouldn't notice.

She tried to look busy, but she didn't have any extra clothes to fold. She straightened her bed, then realized the top blanket was the one Jason had wrapped around her shoulders last night. She picked it up and pressed it to her face. It smelled of wood smoke, but unfortunately not of Jason. He was the *only* person who'd been genuinely nice to her after the claiming, like he cared about how she felt, not just about her stupid new clothes. God, she'd wanted to kiss him, but he'd seemed so uncomfortable, almost scared of her. She couldn't really blame him. She'd been glowing pink.

"'Scuse me," said a voice by her feet. The garbage patrol guy, Mitchell, was crawling around on all fours, picking up chocolate wrappers and crumpled notes from under the bunk beds. Apparently the Aphrodite kids weren't one hundred percent neat freaks after all.

She moved out of his way. "What'd you do to make Drew mad?"

He glanced over at the bathroom door to make sure it was still closed. "Last night, after you were claimed, I said you might not be so bad."

It wasn't much of a compliment, but Piper was stunned. An Aphrodite kid had actually stood up for her?

"Thanks," she said.

Mitchell shrugged. "Yeah, well. See where it got me. But for what it's worth, welcome to Cabin Ten."

A girl with blond pigtails and braces raced up with a pile of clothes in her arms. She looked around furtively like she was delivering nuclear materials.

"I brought you these," she whispered.

"Piper, meet Lacy," Mitchell said, still crawling around on the floor.

"Hi," Lacy said breathlessly. "You *can* change clothes. The blessing won't stop you. This is just, you know, a backpack, some rations, ambrosia and nectar for emergencies, some jeans, a few extra shirts, and a warm jacket. The boots might be a little snug. But—well—we took up a collection. Good luck on your quest!"

Lacy dumped the things on the bed and started to hurry away, but Piper caught her arm. "Hold on. At least let me thank you! Why are you rushing off?"

Lacy looked like she might shake apart from nervousness. "Oh, well—"

"Drew might find out," Mitchell explained.

"I might have to wear the shoes of shame!" Lacy gulped.

"The what?" Piper asked.

Lacy and Mitchell both pointed to a black shelf mounted in the corner of the room, like an altar. Displayed on it were a hideous pair of orthopedic nurse's shoes, bright white with thick soles.

"I had to wear them for a week once," Lacy whimpered. "They don't go with *anything*!"

"And there're worse punishments," Mitchell warned. "Drew can charmspeak, see? Not many Aphrodite kids have that power; but if she tries hard enough, she can get you to do some pretty embarrassing things. Piper, you're the first person I've seen in a long time who is able to resist her."

"Charmspeak..." Piper remembered last night, the way the crowd at the campfire had swayed back and forth between Drew's opinion and hers. "You mean, like, you could talk someone into doing things. Or...giving you things. Like a car?"

"Oh, don't give Drew any ideas!" Lacy gasped.

"But yeah," Mitchell said. "She could do that."

"So that's why she's head counselor," Piper said. "She convinced you all?"

Mitchell picked a nasty wad of gum from under Piper's bed. "Nah, she inherited the post when Silena Beauregard died in the war. Drew was second oldest. Oldest camper automatically gets the post, unless somebody with more years or more completed quests wants to challenge, in which case there's a duel, but that hardly ever happens. Anyway, we've been stuck with Drew in charge since August. She decided to make some, ah, *changes* in the way the cabin is run."

"Yes, I did!" Suddenly Drew was there, leaning against the bunk. Lacy squeaked like a guinea pig and tried to run, but Drew put an arm out to stop her. She looked down at Mitchell. "I think you missed some trash, sweetie. You'd better make another pass."

Piper glanced toward the bathroom and saw that Drew had dumped everything from the bathroom waste bin—some pretty *nasty* things—all over the floor.

Mitchell sat up on his haunches. He glared at Drew like he was about to attack (which Piper would've paid money to see), but finally he snapped, "Fine."

Drew smiled. "See, Piper, hon, we're a good cabin here. A good family! Silena Beauregard, though . . . you could take a warning from her. She was secretly passing information to Kronos in the Titan War, helping the *enemy*."

Drew smiled all sweet and innocent, with her glittery pink makeup and her blow-dried hair lush and smelling like nutmeg. She looked like any popular teenage girl from any high school. But her eyes were as cold as steel. Piper got the feeling Drew was looking straight into her soul, pulling out her secrets.

Helping the enemy.

"Oh, none of the other cabins talk about it," Drew confided. "They act like Silena Beauregard was a hero."

"She sacrificed her life to make things right," Mitchell grumbled. "She *was* a hero."

"Mmm-hmm," Drew said. "Another day on garbage patrol, Mitchell. But *anyways*, Silena lost track of what this cabin is about. We match up cute couples at camp! Then we break them apart and start over! It's the best fun ever. We don't have any business getting involved in other stuff like wars and quests. *I* certainly haven't been on any quests. They're a waste of time!"

Lacy raised her hand nervously. "But last night you said you wanted to go on a—"

Drew glared at her, and Lacy's voice died.

"Most of all," Drew continued, "we certainly don't need our image tarnished by spies, do we, *Piper*?"

Piper tried to answer, but she couldn't. There was no way Drew could know about her dreams or her dad's kidnapping, was there?

"It's too bad you won't be around," Drew sighed. "But if you survive your little quest, don't worry, I'll find *somebody* to match up with you. Maybe one of those gross Hephaestus guys. Or Clovis? He's pretty repulsive." Drew looked her over with a mix of pity and disgust. "Honestly, I didn't think it was *possible* for Aphrodite to have an ugly child, but...who *was* your father? Was he some sort of mutant, or—"

"Tristan McLean," Piper snapped.

As soon as she said it, she hated herself. She never, *ever* played the "famous dad" card. But Drew had driven her over the edge. "My dad's Tristan McLean."

The stunned silence was gratifying for a few seconds, but Piper felt ashamed of herself. Everybody turned and looked at *The Poster*, her dad flexing his muscles for the whole world to see.

"Oh my god!" half the girls screamed at once.

"Sweet!" a guy said. "The dude with the sword who killed that other dude in that movie?"

"He is *so* hot for an old guy," a girl said, and then she blushed. "I mean I'm sorry. I know he's your *dad*. That's *so* weird!"

"It's weird, all right," Piper agreed.

"Do you think you could get me his autograph?" another girl asked.

Piper forced a smile. She couldn't say, *If my dad survives....*

"Yeah, no problem," she managed.

The girl squealed in excitement, and more kids surged forward, asking a dozen questions at once.

"Have you ever been on the set?"

"Do you live in a mansion?"

"Do you have lunch with movie stars?"

"Have you had your rite of passage?"

That one caught Piper off guard. "Rite of what?" she asked.

The girls and guys giggled and shoved each other around like this was an embarrassing topic.

"The rite of passage for an Aphrodite child," one explained. "You get someone to fall in love with you. Then you break their heart. Dump them. Once you do that, you've proven yourself worthy of Aphrodite."

Piper stared at the crowd to see if they were joking. "Break someone's heart on purpose? That's terrible!"

The others looked confused.

"Why?" a guy asked.

"Oh my god!" a girl said. "I bet Aphrodite broke your *dad's* heart! I bet he never loved anyone again, did he? That's so romantic! When you have your rite of passage, you can be just like Mom!"

"Forget it!" Piper yelled, a little louder than she'd intended. The other kids backed away. "I'm *not* breaking somebody's heart just for a stupid rite of passage!"

Which of course gave Drew a chance to take back control. "Well, there you go!" she cut in. "Silena said the same thing. She broke the tradition, fell in love with that Beckendorf boy, and *stayed* in love. If you ask me, that's why things ended tragically for her."

"That's not true!" Lacy squeaked, but Drew glared at her, and she immediately melted back into the crowd.

"Hardly matters," Drew continued, "because, Piper, hon, you couldn't break anyone's heart anyway. And this nonsense about your dad being Tristan McLean—that's *so* begging for attention."

Several of the kids blinked uncertainly.

"You mean he's *not* her dad?" one asked.

Drew rolled her eyes. "Please. Now, it's time for breakfast, people, and Piper here has to start that little quest. So let's get her packed and get her out of here!"

Drew broke up the crowd and got everyone moving. She called them "hon" and "dear," but her tone made it clear she expected to be obeyed. Mitchell and Lacy helped Piper pack. They even guarded the bathroom while Piper went in and changed into a better traveling outfit. The hand-me-downs weren't fancy—thank god—just well-worn jeans, a T-shirt, a comfortable winter coat, and hiking boots that fit perfectly. She strapped her dagger, Katoptris, to her belt.

When Piper came out, she felt almost normal again. The other campers were standing at their bunks while Drew came around and inspected. Piper turned to Mitchell and Lacy and mouthed, *Thank you.* Mitchell nodded grimly. Lacy flashed a full-braces smile. Piper doubted Drew had ever thanked them for anything. She also noticed that the *King of Sparta* poster had been wadded up and thrown in the trash. Drew's orders, no doubt. Even though Piper had wanted to take the poster down herself, now she was totally steamed.

When Drew spotted her, she clapped in mock applause. "Very nice! Our little quest girl all dressed in Dumpster clothes again. Now, off you go! No need to eat breakfast with us. Good luck with . . . whatever. Bye!"

Piper shouldered her bag. She could feel everyone else's eyes on her as she walked to the door. She could just leave and forget about it. That would've been the easy thing. What did she care about this cabin, these shallow kids?

Except that some of them had tried to help her. Some of them had even stood up to Drew for her.

She turned at the door. "You know, you all don't have to follow Drew's orders."

The other kids shifted. Several glanced at Drew, but she looked too stunned to respond.

"Umm," one managed, "she's our head counselor."

"She's a tyrant," Piper corrected. "You can think for yourselves. There's got to be more to Aphrodite than *this*."

"More than this," one kid echoed.

"Think for ourselves," a second muttered.

"People!" Drew screeched. "Don't be stupid! She's charmspeaking you."

"No," Piper said. "I'm just telling the truth."

At least, Piper thought that was the case. She didn't understand exactly how this charmspeaking business worked, but she didn't feel like she was putting any special power into her words. She didn't want to win an argument by tricking people. That would make her no better than Drew. Piper simply meant what she said. Besides, even if she tried charmspeaking, she had a feeling it wouldn't work very well on another charmspeaker like Drew.

Drew sneered at her. "You may have a little power, Miss Movie Star. But you don't know the first thing about Aphrodite. You have such great ideas? What do you think this cabin is about, then? Tell them. Then maybe I'll tell them a few things about *you*, huh?"

Piper wanted to make a withering retort, but her anger turned to panic. She was a spy for the enemy, just like Silena

Beauregard. An Aphrodite traitor. Did Drew know about that, or was she bluffing? Under Drew's glare, her confidence began to crumble.

"Not this," Piper managed. "Aphrodite is not about this."

Then she turned and stormed out before the others could see her blushing.

Behind her, Drew started laughing. "*Not this?* Hear that, people? She doesn't have a clue!"

Piper promised herself she would never *ever* go back to that cabin. She blinked away her tears and stormed across the green, not sure where she was going—until she saw the dragon swooping down from the sky.

XVI

PIPER

"LEO?" SHE YELLED.

Sure enough, there he was, sitting atop a giant bronze death machine and grinning like a lunatic. Even before he landed, the camp alarm went up. A conch horn blew. All the satyrs started screaming, "Don't kill me!" Half the camp ran outside in a mixture of pajamas and armor. The dragon set down right in the middle of the green, and Leo yelled, "It's cool! Don't shoot!"

Hesitantly, the archers lowered their bows. The warriors backed away, keeping their spears and swords ready. They made a loose wide ring around the metal monster. Other demigods hid behind their cabin doors or peeped out the windows. Nobody seemed anxious to get close.

Piper couldn't blame them. The dragon was huge. It glistened in the morning sun like a living penny sculpture —different shades of copper and bronze—a sixty-foot-long serpent with steel talons and drill-bit teeth and glowing ruby eyes. It had bat-shaped wings twice its length that unfurled like metallic sails, making a sound like coins cascading out of a slot machine every time they flapped.

"It's beautiful," Piper muttered. The other demigods stared at her like she was insane.

The dragon reared its head and shot a column of fire into the sky. Campers scrambled away and hefted their weapons, but Leo slid calmly off the dragon's back. He held up his hands like he was surrendering, except he still had that crazy grin on his face.

"People of Earth, I come in peace!" he shouted. He looked like he'd been rolling around in the campfire. His army coat and his face were smeared with soot. His hands were grease-stained, and he wore a new tool belt around his waist. His eyes were bloodshot. His curly hair was so oily it stuck up in porcupine quills, and he smelled strangely of Tabasco sauce. But he looked absolutely delighted. "Festus is just saying hello!"

"That thing is dangerous!" an Ares girl shouted, brandishing her spear. "Kill it now!"

"Stand down!" someone ordered.

To Piper's surprise, it was Jason. He pushed through the crowd, flanked by Annabeth and that girl from the Hephaestus cabin, Nyssa.

Jason gazed up at the dragon and shook his head in amazement. "Leo, what have you done?"

"Found a ride!" Leo beamed. "You said I could go on the quest if I got you a ride. Well, I got you a class-A metallic flying bad boy! Festus can take us anywhere!"

"It—has wings," Nyssa stammered. Her jaw looked like it might drop off her face.

"Yeah!" Leo said. "I found them and reattached them."

"But it never had wings. Where did you find them?"

Leo hesitated, and Piper could tell he was hiding something.

"In...the woods," he said. "Repaired his circuits, too, mostly, so no more problems with him going haywire."

"Mostly?" Nyssa asked.

The dragon's head twitched. It tilted to one side and a stream of black liquid—maybe oil, *hopefully* just oil—poured out of its ear, all over Leo.

"Just a few kinks to work out," Leo said.

"But how did you survive...?" Nyssa was still staring at the creature in awe. "I mean, the fire breath..."

"I'm quick," Leo said. "And lucky. Now, am I on this quest, or what?"

Jason scratched his head. "You named him Festus? You know that in Latin, 'festus' means 'happy'? You want us to ride off to save the world on Happy the Dragon?"

The dragon twitched and shuddered and flapped his wings.

"That's a yes, bro!" Leo said. "Now, um, I'd really suggest we get going, guys. I already picked up some supplies in the —um, in the woods. And all these people with weapons are making Festus nervous."

Jason frowned. "But we haven't planned anything yet. We can't just—"

"Go," Annabeth said. She was the only one who didn't look nervous at all. Her expression was sad and wistful, like this reminded her of better times. "Jason, you've only got three days until the solstice now, and you should never keep a nervous dragon waiting. This is certainly a good omen. Go!"

Jason nodded. Then he smiled at Piper. "You ready, partner?"

Piper looked at the bronze dragon wings shining against the sky, and those talons that could've shredded her to pieces.

"You bet," she said.

Flying on the dragon was the most amazing experience ever, Piper thought.

Up high, the air was freezing cold; but the dragon's metal hide generated so much heat, it was like they were flying in a protective bubble. Talk about seat warmers! And the grooves in the dragon's back were designed like high-tech saddles, so they weren't uncomfortable at all. Leo showed them how to hook their feet in the chinks of the armor, like in stirrups, and use the leather safety harnesses cleverly concealed under the exterior plating. They sat single file: Leo in front, then Piper, then Jason, and Piper was very aware of Jason right behind her. She wished he would hold on to her, maybe wrap his arms around her waist; but sadly, he didn't.

Leo used the reins to steer the dragon into the sky like he'd been doing it all his life. The metal wings worked perfectly, and soon the coast of Long Island was just a hazy line behind them. They shot over Connecticut and climbed into the gray winter clouds.

Leo grinned back at them. "Cool, right?"

"What if we get spotted?" Piper asked.

"The Mist," Jason said. "It keeps mortals from seeing magic things. If they spot us, they'll probably mistake us for a small plane or something."

Piper glanced over her shoulder. "You sure about that?"

"No," he admitted. Then Piper saw he was clutching a photo in his hand—a picture of a girl with dark hair.

She gave Jason a quizzical look, but he blushed and put the photo in his pocket. "We're making good time. Probably get there by tonight."

Piper wondered who the girl in the picture was, but she didn't want to ask; and if Jason didn't volunteer the information, that wasn't a good sign. Had he remembered something about his life before? Was that a photo of his real girlfriend?

Stop it, she thought. You'll just torture yourself.

She asked a safer question. "Where are we heading?"

"To find the god of the North Wind," Jason said. "And chase some storm spirits."

XVII

LEO

LEO WAS TOTALLY BUZZING.

The expression on everyone's faces when he flew the dragon into camp? Priceless! He thought his cabinmates were going to bust a lug nut.

Festus had been awesome too. He hadn't blowtorched a single cabin or eaten any satyrs, even if he did dribble a little oil from his ear. Okay, a *lot* of oil. Leo could work on that later.

So maybe Leo didn't seize the chance to tell everybody about Bunker 9 or the flying boat design. He needed some time to think about all that. He could tell them when he came back.

If I come back, part of him thought.

Nah, he'd come back. He'd scored a sweet magic tool belt from the bunker, plus a lot of cool supplies now safely stowed in his backpack. Besides, he had a fire-breathing, only slightly leaky dragon on his side. What could go wrong?

Well, the control disk could bust, the bad part of him suggested. *Festus could eat you.*

Okay, so the dragon wasn't *quite* as fixed as Leo might've let on. He'd worked all night attaching those wings, but he hadn't found an extra dragon brain anywhere in the bunker. Hey, they were under a time limit! Three days until the solstice. They had to get going. Besides, Leo had cleaned the disk pretty well. Most of the circuits were still good. It would just have to hold together.

His bad side started to think, *Yeah, but what if—*

"Shut up, me," Leo said aloud.

"What?" Piper asked.

"Nothing," he said. "Long night. I think I'm hallucinating. It's cool."

Sitting in front, Leo couldn't see their faces, but he assumed from their silence that his friends were not pleased to have a sleepless, hallucinating dragon driver.

"Just joking." Leo decided it might be good to change the subject. "So what's the plan, bro? You said something about catching wind, or breaking wind, or something?"

As they flew over New England, Jason laid out the game plan: First, find some guy named Boreas and grill him for information—

"His name is *Boreas?*" Leo had to ask. "What is he, the God of Boring?"

Second, Jason continued, they had to find those *venti* that had attacked them at the Grand Canyon—

"Can we just call them storm spirits?" Leo asked. "*Venti* makes them sound like evil espresso drinks."

And third, Jason finished, they had to find out who the storm spirits worked for, so they could find Hera and free her.

"So you want to look for Dylan, the nasty storm dude, *on purpose*," Leo said. "The guy who threw me off the skywalk and sucked Coach Hedge into the clouds."

"That's about it," Jason said. "Well . . . there may be a wolf involved, too. But I think she's friendly. She probably won't eat us, unless we show weakness."

Jason told them about his dream—the big nasty mother wolf and a burned-out house with stone spires growing out of the swimming pool.

"Uh-huh," Leo said. "But you don't know where this place is."

"Nope," Jason admitted.

"There's also giants," Piper added. "The prophecy said *the giants' revenge*."

"Hold on," Leo said. "Giants—like more than one? Why can't it be just one giant who wants revenge?"

"I don't think so," Piper said. "I remember in some of the old Greek stories, there was something about an army of giants."

"Great," Leo muttered. "Of course, with our luck, it's an army. So you know anything else about these giants? Didn't you do a bunch of myth research for that movie with your dad?"

"Your dad's an actor?" Jason asked.

Leo laughed. "I keep forgetting about your amnesia. Heh. Forgetting about amnesia. That's funny. But yeah, her dad's Tristan McLean."

"Uh— Sorry, what was he in?"

"It doesn't matter," Piper said quickly. "The giants—well, there were lots of giants in Greek mythology. But if I'm thinking of the right ones, they were bad news. Huge, almost impossible to kill. They could throw mountains and stuff. I think they were related to the Titans. They rose from the earth after Kronos lost the war—I mean the *first* Titan war, thousands of years ago—and they tried to destroy Olympus. If we're talking about the same giants—"

"Chiron said it was happening again," Jason remembered. "The last chapter. That's what he meant. No wonder he didn't want us to know all the details."

Leo whistled. "So...giants who can throw mountains. Friendly wolves that will eat us if we show weakness. Evil espresso drinks. Gotcha. Maybe this isn't the time to bring up my psycho babysitter."

"Is that another joke?" Piper asked.

Leo told them about Tía Callida, who was really Hera, and how she'd appeared to him at camp. He didn't tell them about his fire abilities. That was still a touchy subject, especially after Nyssa had told him fire demigods tended to destroy cities and stuff. Besides, then Leo would have to get into how he'd caused his mom's death, and...No. He wasn't ready to go there. He did manage to tell about the night she died, not mentioning the fire, just saying the machine shop collapsed. It was easier without having to look at his friends, just keeping his eyes straight ahead as they flew.

And he told them about the strange woman in earthen

robes who seemed to be asleep, and seemed to know the future.

Leo estimated the whole state of Massachusetts passed below them before his friends spoke.

"That's ... disturbing," Piper said.

"'Bout sums it up," Leo agreed. "Thing is, everybody says don't trust Hera. She hates demigods. And the prophecy said we'd cause death if we unleash her rage. So I'm wondering ... why are we doing this?"

"She chose us," Jason said. "All three of us. We're the first of the seven who have to gather for the Great Prophecy. This quest is the beginning of something much bigger."

That didn't make Leo feel any better, but he couldn't argue with Jason's point. It *did* feel like this was the start of something huge. He just wished that if there were four more demigods destined to help them, they'd show up quick. Leo didn't want to hog all the terrifying life-threatening adventures.

"Besides," Jason continued, "helping Hera is the only way I can get back my memory. And that dark spire in my dream seemed to be feeding on Hera's energy. If that thing unleashes a king of the giants by destroying Hera—"

"Not a good trade-off," Piper agreed. "At least Hera is on our side—mostly. Losing her would throw the gods into chaos. She's the main one who keeps peace in the family. And a war with the giants could be even more destructive than the Titan War."

Jason nodded. "Chiron also talked about worse forces stirring on the solstice, with it being a good time for dark magic, and all—something that could awaken if Hera were sacrificed on that day. And this mistress who's controlling the storm spirits, the one who wants to kill all the demigods—"

"Might be that weird sleeping lady," Leo finished. "Dirt Woman fully awake? Not something I want to see."

"But who is she?" Jason asked. "And what does she have to do with giants?"

Good questions, but none of them had answers. They flew in silence while Leo wondered if he'd done the right thing, sharing so much. He'd never told anyone about that night at the warehouse. Even if he hadn't give them the whole story, it still felt strange, like he'd opened up his chest and taken out all the gears that made him tick. His body was shaking, and not from the cold. He hoped Piper, sitting behind him, couldn't tell.

The forge and dove shall break the cage. Wasn't that the prophecy line? That meant Piper and he would have to figure out how to break into that magic rock prison, assuming they could find it. Then they'd unleash Hera's rage, causing a lot of death. Well, that sounded fun! Leo had seen Tía Callida in action; she liked knives, snakes, and putting babies in roaring fires. Yeah, definitely let's unleash her rage. Great idea.

Festus kept flying. The wind got colder, and below them snowy forests seemed to go on forever. Leo didn't know exactly where Quebec was. He'd told Festus to take them to the palace of Boreas, and Festus kept going north. Hopefully, the dragon knew the way, and they wouldn't end up at the North Pole.

"Why don't you get some sleep?" Piper said in his ear. "You were up all night."

Leo wanted to protest, but the word *sleep* sounded really good. "You won't let me fall off?"

Piper patted his shoulder. "Trust me, Valdez. Beautiful people never lie."

"Right," he muttered. He leaned forward against the warm bronze of the dragon's neck, and closed his eyes.

XVIII

LEO

It seemed he slept only for seconds, but when Piper shook him awake, the daylight was fading.

"We're here," she said.

Leo rubbed the sleep out of his eyes. Below them, a city sat on a cliff overlooking a river. The plains around it were dusted with snow, but the city itself glowed warmly in the winter sunset. Buildings crowded together inside high walls like a medieval town, way older than any place Leo had seen before. In the center was an actual castle—at least Leo assumed it was a castle—with massive red brick walls and a square tower with a peaked, green gabled roof.

"Tell me that's Quebec and not Santa's workshop," Leo said.

"Yeah, Quebec City," Piper confirmed. "One of the oldest cities in North America. Founded around sixteen hundred or so?"

Leo raised an eyebrow. "Your dad do a movie about that too?"

She made a face at him, which Leo was used to, but it didn't quite work with her new glamorous makeup. "I *read* sometimes, okay? Just because Aphrodite claimed me, doesn't mean I have to be an airhead."

"Feisty!" Leo said. "So you know so much, what's that castle?"

"A hotel, I think."

Leo laughed. "No way."

But as they got closer, Leo saw she was right. The grand entrance was bustling with doormen, valets, and porters taking bags. Sleek black luxury cars idled in the drive. People in elegant suits and winter cloaks hurried to get out of the cold.

"The North Wind is staying in a hotel?" Leo said. "That can't be—"

"Heads up, guys," Jason interrupted. "We got company!"

Leo looked below and saw what Jason meant. Rising from the top of the tower were two winged figures—angry angels, with nasty-looking swords.

Festus didn't like the angel guys. He swooped to a halt in midair, wings beating and talons bared, and made a rumbling sound in his throat that Leo recognized. He was getting ready to blow fire.

"Steady, boy," Leo muttered. Something told him the angels would not take kindly to getting torched.

"I don't like this," Jason said. "They look like storm spirits."

At first Leo thought he was right, but as the angels got closer, he could see they were much more solid than *venti*. They looked like regular teenagers except for their icy white hair and feathery purple wings. Their bronze swords were jagged, like icicles. Their faces looked similar enough that they might've been brothers, but they definitely weren't twins.

One was the size of an ox, with a bright red hockey jersey, baggy sweatpants, and black leather cleats. The guy clearly had been in too many fights, because both his eyes were black, and when he bared his teeth, several of them were missing.

The other guy looked like he'd just stepped off one of Leo's mom's 1980s rock album covers—Journey, maybe, or Hall & Oates, or something even lamer. His ice-white hair was long and feathered into a mullet. He wore pointy-toed leather shoes, designer pants that were way too tight, and a god-awful silk shirt with the top three buttons open. Maybe he thought he looked like a groovy love god, but the guy couldn't have weighed more than ninety pounds, and he had a bad case of acne.

The angels pulled up in front of the dragon and hovered there, swords at the ready.

The hockey ox grunted. "No clearance."

"'Scuse me?" Leo said.

"You have no flight plan on file," explained the groovy love god. On top of his other problems, he had a French accent so bad Leo was sure it was fake. "This is restricted airspace."

"Destroy them?" The ox showed off his gap-toothed grin.

The dragon began to hiss steam, ready to defend them. Jason summoned his golden sword, but Leo cried, "Hold on!

Let's have some manners here, boys. Can I at least find out who has the honor of destroying me?"

"I am Cal!" the ox grunted. He looked very proud of himself, like he'd taken a long time to memorize that sentence.

"That's short for Calais," the love god said. "Sadly, my brother cannot say words with more than two syllables—"

"Pizza! Hockey! Destroy!" Cal offered.

"—which includes his own name," the love god finished.

"I am Cal," Cal repeated. "And this is Zethes! My brother!"

"Wow," Leo said. "That was almost three sentences, man! Way to go."

Cal grunted, obviously pleased with himself.

"Stupid buffoon," his brother grumbled. "They make fun of you. But no matter. I am Zethes, which is short for Zethes. And the lady there—" He winked at Piper, but the wink was more like a facial seizure. "She can call me anything she likes. Perhaps she would like to have dinner with a famous demigod before we must destroy you?"

Piper made a sound like gagging on a cough drop. "That's ... a truly horrifying offer."

"It is no problem." Zethes wiggled his eyebrows. "We are a very romantic people, we Boreads."

"Boreads?" Jason cut in. "Do you mean, like, the sons of Boreas?"

"Ah, so you've heard of us!" Zethes looked pleased. "We are our father's gatekeepers. So you understand, we cannot have unauthorized people flying in his airspace on creaky dragons, scaring the silly mortal peoples."

He pointed below, and Leo saw that the mortals were

starting to take notice. Several were pointing up—not with alarm, yet—more with confusion and annoyance, like the dragon was a traffic helicopter flying too low.

"Which is sadly why, unless this is an emergency landing," Zethes said, brushing his hair out of his acne-covered face, "we will have to destroy you painfully."

"Destroy!" Cal agreed, with a little more enthusiasm than Leo thought necessary.

"Wait!" Piper said. "This *is* an emergency landing."

"Awww!" Cal looked so disappointed, Leo almost felt sorry for him.

Zethes studied Piper, which of course he'd already been doing. "How does the pretty girl decide this is an emergency, then?"

"We have to see Boreas. It's totally urgent! Please?" She forced a smile, which Leo figured must've been killing her; but she still had that blessing of Aphrodite thing going on, and she looked great. Something about her voice, too—Leo found himself believing every word. Jason was nodding, looking absolutely convinced.

Zethes picked at his silk shirt, probably making sure it was still open wide enough. "Well . . . I hate to disappoint a lovely lady, but you see, my sister, she would have an avalanche if we allowed you—"

"And our dragon is malfunctioning!" Piper added. "It could crash any minute!"

Festus shuddered helpfully, then turned his head and spilled gunk out of his ear, splattering a black Mercedes in the parking lot below.

"No destroy?" Cal whimpered.

Zethes pondered the problem. Then he gave Piper another spasmodic wink. "Well, you are pretty. I mean, you're *right*. A malfunctioning dragon—this could be an emergency."

"Destroy them later?" Cal offered, which was probably as close to friendly as he ever got.

"It will take some explaining," Zethes decided. "Father has not been kind to visitors lately. But, yes. Come, faulty dragon people. Follow us."

The Boreads sheathed their swords and pulled smaller weapons from their belts—or at least Leo thought they were weapons. Then the Boreads switched them on, and Leo realized they were flashlights with orange cones, like the ones traffic controller guys use on a runway. Cal and Zethes turned and swooped toward the hotel's tower.

Leo turned to his friends. "I love these guys. Follow them?"

Jason and Piper didn't look eager.

"I guess," Jason decided. "We're here now. But I wonder why Boreas hasn't been kind to visitors."

"Pfft, he just hasn't met us." Leo whistled. "Festus, after those flashlights!"

As they got closer, Leo worried they'd crash into the tower. The Boreads made right for the green gabled peak and didn't slow down. Then a section of the slanted roof slid open, revealing an entrance easily wide enough for Festus. The top and bottom were lined with icicles like jagged teeth.

"This cannot be good," Jason muttered, but Leo spurred the dragon downward, and they swooped in after the Boreads.

They landed in what must have been the penthouse suite; but the place had been hit by a flash freeze. The entry hall had vaulted ceilings forty feet high, huge draped windows, and lush oriental carpets. A staircase at the back of the room led up to another equally massive hall, and more corridors branched off to the left and right. But the ice made the room's beauty a little frightening. When Leo slid off the dragon, the carpet crunched under his feet. A fine layer of frost covered the furniture. The curtains didn't budge because they were frozen solid, and the ice-coated windows let in weird watery light from the sunset. Even the ceiling was furry with icicles. As for the stairs, Leo was sure he'd slip and break his neck if he tried to climb them.

"Guys," Leo said, "fix the thermostat in here, and I would totally move in."

"Not me." Jason looked uneasily at the staircase. "Something feels wrong. Something up there..."

Festus shuddered and snorted flames. Frost started to form on his scales.

"No, no, no." Zethes marched over, though how he could walk in those pointy leather shoes, Leo had no idea. "The dragon must be deactivated. We can't have fire in here. The heat ruins my hair."

Festus growled and spun his drill-bit teeth.

"'S'okay, boy." Leo turned to Zethes. "The dragon's a little touchy about the whole *deactivation* concept. But I've got a better solution."

"Destroy?" Cal suggested.

"No, man. You gotta stop with the *destroy* talk. Just wait."

"Leo," Piper said nervously, "what are you—"

"Watch and learn, beauty queen. When I was repairing Festus last night, I found all kinds of buttons. Some, you do *not* want to know what they do. But others ... Ah, here we go."

Leo hooked his fingers behind the dragon's left foreleg. He pulled a switch, and the dragon shuddered from head to toe. Everyone backed away as Festus folded like origami. His bronze plating stacked together. His neck and tail contracted into his body. His wings collapsed and his trunk compacted until he was a rectangular metal wedge the size of a suitcase.

Leo tried to lift it, but the thing weighed about six billion pounds. "Um ... yeah. Hold on. I think—aha."

He pushed another button. A handle flipped up on the top, and wheels clicked out on the bottom.

"Ta-da!" he announced. "The world's heaviest carry-on bag!"

"That's impossible," Jason said. "Something that big couldn't—"

"Stop!" Zethes ordered. He and Cal both drew their swords and glared at Leo.

Leo raised his hands. "Okay ... what'd I do? Stay calm, guys. If it bothers you that much, I don't *have* to take the dragon as carry-on—"

"Who are you?" Zethes shoved the point of his sword against Leo's chest. "A child of the South Wind, spying on us?"

"What? No!" Leo said. "Son of Hephaestus. Friendly blacksmith, no harm to anyone!"

Cal growled. He put his face up to Leo's, and he definitely

wasn't any prettier at point-blank, with his bruised eyes and bashed-in mouth. "Smell fire," he said. "Fire is bad."

"Oh." Leo's heart raced. "Yeah, well...my clothes are kind of singed, and I've been working with oil, and—"

"No!" Zethes pushed Leo back at sword point. "We can *smell* fire, demigod. We assumed it was from the creaky dragon, but now the dragon is a suitcase. And I still smell fire...on *you.*"

If it hadn't been like three degrees in the penthouse, Leo would've started sweating. "Hey...look...I don't know—" He glanced at his friends desperately. "Guys, a little help?"

Jason already had his gold coin in his hand. He stepped forward, his eyes on Zethes. "Look, there's been a mistake. Leo isn't a fire guy. Tell them, Leo. Tell them you're not a fire guy."

"Um..."

"Zethes?" Piper tried her dazzling smile again, though she looked a little too nervous and cold to pull it off. "We're all friends here. Put down your swords and let's talk."

"The girl is pretty," Zethes admitted, "and of course she cannot help being attracted to my amazingness; but sadly, I cannot romance her at this time." He poked his sword point farther into Leo's chest, and Leo could feel the frost spreading across his shirt, turning his skin numb.

He wished he could reactivate Festus. He needed some backup. But it would've taken several minutes, even if he could reach the button, with two purple-winged crazy guys in his path.

"Destroy him now?" Cal asked his brother.

Zethes nodded. "Sadly, I think—"

"No," Jason insisted. He sounded calm enough, but Leo figured he was about two seconds away from flipping that coin and going into full gladiator mode. "Leo's just a son of Hephaestus. He's no threat. Piper here is a daughter of Aphrodite. I'm the son of Zeus. We're on a peaceful..."

Jason's voice faltered, because both Boreads had suddenly turned on him.

"What did you say?" Zethes demanded. "You are the son of Zeus?"

"Um...yeah," Jason said. "That's a good thing, right? My name is Jason."

Cal looked so surprised, he almost dropped his sword. "Can't be Jason," he said. "Doesn't look the same."

Zethes stepped forward and squinted at Jason's face. "No, he is not *our* Jason. Our Jason was more stylish. Not as much as me—but stylish. Besides, our Jason died millennia ago."

"Wait," Jason said. "*Your* Jason...you mean the original Jason? The Golden Fleece guy?"

"Of course," Zethes said. "We were his crewmates aboard his ship, the *Argo*, in the old times, when we were mortal demigods. Then we accepted immortality to serve our father, so I could look this good for all time, and my silly brother could enjoy pizza and hockey."

"Hockey!" Cal agreed.

"But Jason—*our* Jason—he died a mortal death," Zethes said. "You can't be him."

"I'm not," Jason agreed.

"So, destroy?" Cal asked. Clearly the conversation was giving his two brain cells a serious workout.

"No," Zethes said regretfully. "If he is a son of Zeus, he could be the one we've been watching for."

"Watching for?" Leo asked. "You mean like in a good way: you'll shower him with fabulous prizes? Or watching for like in a *bad* way: he's in trouble?"

A girl's voice said, "That depends on my father's will."

Leo looked up the staircase. His heart nearly stopped. At the top stood a girl in a white silk dress. Her skin was unnaturally pale, the color of snow, but her hair was a lush mane of black, and her eyes were coffee brown. She focused on Leo with no expression, no smile, no friendliness. But it didn't matter. Leo was in love. She was the most dazzling girl he'd ever seen.

Then she looked at Jason and Piper, and seemed to understand the situation immediately.

"Father will want to see the one called Jason," the girl said.

"Then it *is* him?" Zethes asked excitedly.

"We'll see," the girl said. "Zethes, bring our guests."

Leo grabbed the handle of his bronze dragon suitcase. He wasn't sure how he'd lug it up the stairs, but he *had* to get next to that girl and ask her some important questions—like her e-mail address and phone number.

Before he could take a step, she froze him with a look. Not *literally* froze, but she might as well have.

"Not you, Leo Valdez," she said.

In the back of his mind, Leo wondered how she knew his

name; but mostly he was just concentrating on how crushed he felt.

"Why not?" He probably sounded like a whiny kindergartner, but he couldn't help it.

"You cannot be in the presence of my father," the girl said. "Fire and ice—it would not be wise."

"We're going together," Jason insisted, putting his hand on Leo's shoulder, "or not at all."

The girl tilted her head, like she wasn't used to people refusing her orders. "He will not be harmed, Jason Grace, unless you make trouble. Calais, keep Leo Valdez here. Guard him, but do not kill him."

Cal pouted. "Just a little?"

"No," the girl insisted. "And take care of his interesting suitcase, until Father passes judgment."

Jason and Piper looked at Leo, their expressions asking him a silent question: *How do you want to play this?*

Leo felt a surge of gratitude. They were ready to fight for him. They wouldn't leave him alone with the hockey ox. Part of him wanted to go for it, bust out his new tool belt and see what he could do, maybe even summon a fireball or two and warm this place up. But the Boread guys scared him. And that gorgeous girl scared him more, even if he still wanted her number.

"It's fine, guys," he said. "No sense causing trouble if we don't have to. You go ahead."

"Listen to your friend," the pale girl said. "Leo Valdez will be perfectly safe. I wish I could say the same for you, son of Zeus. Now come, King Boreas is waiting."

XIX

JASON

JASON DIDN'T WANT TO LEAVE LEO, but he was starting to think that hanging out with Cal the hockey jock might be the *least* dangerous option in this place.

As they climbed the icy staircase, Zethes stayed behind them, his blade drawn. The guy might've looked like a disco-era reject, but there was nothing funny about his sword. Jason figured one hit from that thing would probably turn him into a Popsicle.

Then there was the ice princess. Every once in a while she'd turn and give Jason a smile, but there was no warmth in her expression. She regarded Jason like he was an especially inter-esting science specimen—one she couldn't wait to dissect.

If these were Boreas's kids, Jason wasn't sure he wanted to meet Daddy. Annabeth had told him Boreas was the friend-liest of the wind gods. Apparently that meant he didn't kill heroes quite as fast as the others did.

Jason worried that he'd led his friends into a trap. If things went bad, he wasn't sure he could get them out alive. Without thinking about it, he took Piper's hand for reassurance.

She raised her eyebrows, but she didn't let go.

"It'll be fine," she promised. "Just a talk, right?"

At the top of the stairs, the ice princess looked back and noticed them holding hands. Her smile faded. Suddenly Jason's hand in Piper's turned ice cold—*burning* cold. He let go, and his fingers were smoking with frost. So were Piper's.

"Warmth is not a good idea here," the princess advised, "especially when *I* am your best chance of staying alive. Please, this way."

Piper gave him a nervous frown like, *What was that about?*

Jason didn't have an answer. Zethes poked him in the back with his icicle sword, and they followed the princess down a massive hallway decked in frosty tapestries.

Freezing winds blew back and forth, and Jason's thoughts moved almost as fast. He'd had a lot of time to think while they rode the dragon north, but he felt as confused as ever.

Thalia's picture was still in his pocket, though he didn't need to look at it anymore. Her image had burned itself into his mind. It was bad enough not remembering his past, but to know he had a sister out there somewhere who might have answers and to have no way of finding her—that just drove him up the wall.

In the picture, Thalia looked nothing like him. They both had blue eyes, but that was it. Her hair was black. Her complexion was more Mediterranean. Her facial features were sharper—like a hawk's.

Still, Thalia looked *so* familiar. Hera had left him just

enough memory that he could be certain Thalia was his sister. But Annabeth had acted completely surprised when he'd told her, like she'd never heard of Thalia's having a brother. Did Thalia even know about him? How had they been separated?

Hera had taken those memories. She'd stolen everything from Jason's past, plopped him into a new life, and now she expected him to save her from some prison just so he could get back what she'd taken. It made Jason so angry, he wanted to walk away, let Hera rot in that cage: but he couldn't. He was hooked. He had to know more, and that made him even more resentful.

"Hey." Piper touched his arm. "You still with me?"

"Yeah . . . yeah, sorry."

He was grateful for Piper. He needed a friend, and he was glad she'd started losing the Aphrodite blessing. The makeup was fading. Her hair was slowly going back to its old choppy style with the little braids down the sides. It made her look more real, and as far as Jason was concerned, more beautiful.

He was sure now that they'd never known each other before the Grand Canyon. Their relationship was just a trick of the Mist in Piper's mind. But the longer he spent with her, the more he wished it had been real.

Stop that, he told himself. It wasn't fair to Piper, thinking that way. Jason had no idea what was waiting for him back in his old life—or *who* might be waiting. But he was pretty sure his past wouldn't mix with Camp Half-Blood. After this quest, who knew what would happen? Assuming they even survived.

At the end of the hallway they found themselves in front

of a set of oaken doors carved with a map of the world. In each corner was a man's bearded face, blowing wind. Jason was pretty sure he'd seen maps like this before. But in this version, all the wind guys were Winter, blowing ice and snow from every corner of the world.

The princess turned. Her brown eyes glittered, and Jason felt like he was a Christmas present she was hoping to open.

"This is the throne room," she said. "Be on your best behavior, Jason Grace. My father can be... chilly. I will translate for you, and try to encourage him to hear you out. I do hope he spares you. We could have such fun."

Jason guessed this girl's definition of fun was not the same as his.

"Um, okay," he managed. "But really, we're just here for a little talk. We'll be leaving right afterward."

The girl smiled. "I love heroes. So blissfully ignorant."

Piper rested her hand on her dagger. "Well, how about you enlighten us? You say you're going to translate for us, and we don't even know who you are. What's your name?"

The girl sniffed with distaste. "I suppose I shouldn't be surprised you don't recognize me. Even in the ancient times the Greeks did not know me well. Their island homes were too warm, too far from my domain. I am Khione, daughter of Boreas, goddess of snow."

She stirred the air with her finger, and a miniature blizzard swirled around her—big, fluffy flakes as soft as cotton.

"Now, come," Khione said. The oaken doors blew open, and cold blue light spilled out of the room. "Hopefully you will survive your little talk."

XX

JASON

IF THE ENTRY HALL HAD BEEN COLD, the throne room was like a meat locker.

Mist hung in the air. Jason shivered, and his breath steamed. Along the walls, purple tapestries showed scenes of snowy forests, barren mountains, and glaciers. High above, ribbons of colored light—the aurora borealis—pulsed along the ceiling. A layer of snow covered the floor, so Jason had to step carefully. All around the room stood life-size ice sculpture warriors—some in Greek armor, some medieval, some in modern camouflage—all frozen in various attack positions, swords raised, guns locked and loaded.

At least Jason *thought* they were sculptures. Then he tried to step between two Greek spearmen, and they moved with surprising speed, their joints cracking and spraying ice crystals as they crossed their javelins to block Jason's path.

From the far end of the hall, a man's voice rang out in a language that sounded like French. The room was so long and misty, Jason couldn't see the other end; but whatever the man said, the ice guards uncrossed their javelins.

"It's fine," Khione said. "My father has ordered them not to kill you just yet."

"Super," Jason said.

Zethes prodded him in the back with his sword. "Keep moving, Jason Junior."

"Please don't call me that."

"My father is not a patient man," Zethes warned, "and the beautiful Piper, sadly, is losing her magic hairdo very fast. Later, perhaps, I can lend her something from my wide assortment of hair products."

"Thanks," Piper grumbled.

They kept walking, and the mist parted to reveal a man on an ice throne. He was sturdily built, dressed in a stylish white suit that seemed woven from snow, with dark purple wings that spread out to either side. His long hair and shaggy beard were encrusted with icicles, so Jason couldn't tell if his hair was gray or just white with frost. His arched eyebrows made him look angry, but his eyes twinkled more warmly than his daughter's—as if he might have a sense of humor buried somewhere under that permafrost. Jason hoped so.

"Bienvenu," the king said. *"Je suis Boreas le Roi. Et vous?"*

Khione the snow goddess was about to speak, but Piper stepped forward and curtsied.

"Votre Majesté," she said, *"je suis Piper McLean. Et c'est Jason, fils de Zeus."*

The king smiled with pleasant surprise. *"Vous parlez français? Très bien!"*

"Piper, you speak French?" Jason asked.

Piper frowned. "No. Why?"

"You just spoke French."

Piper blinked. "I did?"

The king said something else, and Piper nodded. *"Oui, Votre Majesté."*

The king laughed and clapped his hands, obviously delighted. He said a few more sentences then swept his hand toward his daughter as if shooing her away.

Khione looked miffed. "The king says—"

"He says I'm a daughter of Aphrodite," Piper interrupted, "so naturally I can speak French, which is the language of love. I had no idea. His Majesty says Khione won't have to translate now."

Behind them, Zethes snorted, and Khione shot him a murderous look. She bowed stiffly to her father and took a step back.

The king sized up Jason, and Jason decided it would be a good idea to bow. "Your Majesty, I'm Jason Grace. Thank you for, um, not killing us. May I ask...why does a Greek god speak French?"

Piper had another exchange with the king.

"He speaks the language of his host country," Piper translated. "He says all gods do this. Most Greek gods speak English, as they now reside in the United States, but Boreas was never welcomed in their realm. His domain was always far to the north. These days he likes Quebec, so he speaks French."

The king said something else, and Piper turned pale.

"The king says..." She faltered. "He says—"

"Oh, allow me," Khione said. "My father says he has orders to kill you. Did I not mention that earlier?"

Jason tensed. The king was still smiling amiably, like he'd just delivered great news.

"Kill us?" Jason said. "Why?"

"Because," the king said, in heavily accented English, "my lord Aeolus has commanded it."

Boreas rose. He stepped down from his throne and furled his wings against his back. As he approached, Khione and Zethes bowed. Jason and Piper followed their example.

"I shall deign to speak your language," Boreas said, "as Piper McLean has honored me in mine. *Toujours*, I have had a fondness for the children of Aphrodite. As for you, Jason Grace, my master Aeolus would not expect me to kill a son of Lord Zeus . . . without first hearing you out."

Jason's gold coin seemed to grow heavy in his pocket. If he were forced to fight, he didn't like his chances. Two seconds at least to summon his blade. Then he'd be facing a god, two of his children, and an army of freeze-dried warriors.

"Aeolus is the master of the winds, right?" Jason asked. "Why would he want us dead?"

"You are demigods," Boreas said, as if this explained everything. "Aeolus's job is to contain the winds, and demigods have always caused him many headaches. They ask him for favors. They unleash winds and cause chaos. But the final insult was the battle with Typhon last summer. . . ."

Boreas waved his hand, and a sheet of ice like a flat-screen TV appeared in the air. Images of a battle flickered across the surface—a giant wrapped in storm clouds, wading across a river toward the Manhattan skyline. Tiny, glowing figures —the gods, Jason guessed—swarmed around him like angry wasps, pounding the monster with lightning and fire. Finally the river erupted in a massive whirlpool, and the smoky form sank beneath the waves and disappeared.

"The storm giant, Typhon," Boreas explained. "The first time the gods defeated him, eons ago, he did not die quietly. His death released a host of storm spirits—wild winds that answered to no one. It was Aeolus's job to track them all down and imprison them in his fortress. The other gods—they did not help. They did not even apologize for the inconvenience. It took Aeolus centuries to track down all the storm spirits, and naturally this irritated him. Then, last summer, Typhon was defeated again—"

"And his death released another wave of *venti*," Jason guessed. "Which made Aeolus even angrier."

"*C'est vrai*," Boreas agreed.

"But, Your Majesty," Piper said, "the gods had no choice but to battle Typhon. He was going to destroy Olympus! Besides, why punish demigods for that?"

The king shrugged. "Aeolus cannot take out his anger on the gods. They are his bosses, and very powerful. So he gets even with the demigods who helped them in the war. He issued orders to us: demigods who come to us for aid are no longer to be tolerated. We are to crush your little mortal faces."

There was an uncomfortable silence.

"That sounds . . . extreme," Jason ventured. "But you're not going to crush our faces yet, right? You're going to listen to us first, 'cause once you hear about our quest—"

"Yes, yes," the king agreed. "You see, Aeolus also said that a son of Zeus might seek my aid, and if this happened, I should listen to you before destroying you, as you might— how did he put it?—make all our lives very interesting. I am only obligated to *listen*, however. After that, I am free to pass judgment as I see fit. But I *will* listen first. Khione wishes this also. It may be that we will not kill you."

Jason felt like he could almost breathe again. "Great. Thanks."

"Do not thank me." Boreas smiled. "There are many ways you could make our lives interesting. Sometimes we keep demigods for our amusement, as you can see."

He gestured around the room to the various ice statues.

Piper made a strangled noise. "You mean—they're all demigods? Frozen demigods? They're alive?"

"An interesting question," Boreas conceded, as if it had never occurred to him before. "They do not move unless they are obeying my orders. The rest of the time, they are merely frozen. Unless they were to melt, I suppose, which would be very messy."

Khione stepped behind Jason and put her cold fingers on his neck. "My father gives me such lovely presents," she murmured in his ear. "Join our court. Perhaps I'll let your friends go."

"What?" Zethes broke in. "If Khione gets this one, then I deserve the girl. Khione always gets more presents!"

"Now, children," Boreas said sternly. "Our guests will think you are spoiled! Besides, you moved too fast. We have not even heard the demigod's story yet. Then we will decide what to do with them. Please, Jason Grace, entertain us."

Jason felt his brain shutting down. He didn't look at Piper for fear he'd completely lose it. He'd gotten them into this, and now they were going die—or worse, they'd be amusements for Boreas's children and end up frozen forever in this throne room, slowly corroding from freezer burn.

Khione purred and stroked his neck. Jason didn't plan it, but electricity sparked along his skin. There was loud *pop*, and Khione flew backward, skidding across the floor.

Zethes laughed. "That is good! I'm glad you did that, even though I have to kill you now."

For a moment, Khione was too stunned to react. Then the air around her began to swirl with a micro-blizzard. "You dare—"

"Stop," Jason ordered, with as much force as he could muster. "You're not going to kill us. And you're not going to keep us. We're on a quest for the queen of the gods herself, so unless you want Hera busting down your doors, you're going to let us go."

He sounded a lot more confident than he felt, but it got their attention. Khione's blizzard swirled to a stop. Zethes lowered his sword. They both looked uncertainly at their father.

"Hmm," Boreas said. His eyes twinkled, but Jason couldn't tell if it was with anger or amusement. "A son of Zeus, favored by Hera? This is definitely a first. Tell us your story."

Jason would've botched it right there. He hadn't been expecting to get the chance to talk, and now that he could, his voice abandoned him.

Piper saved him. "Your Majesty." She curtsied again with incredible poise, considering her life was on the line. She told Boreas the whole story, from the Grand Canyon to the prophecy, much better and faster than Jason could have.

"All we ask for is guidance," Piper concluded. "These storm spirits attacked us, and they're working for some evil mistress. If we find them, maybe we can find Hera."

The king stroked the icicles in his beard. Out the windows, night had fallen, and the only light came from the aurora borealis overhead, washing everything in red and blue.

"I know of these storm spirits," Boreas said. "I know where they are kept, and of the prisoner they took."

"You mean Coach Hedge?" Jason asked. "He's alive?"

Boreas waved aside the question. "For now. But the one who controls these storm winds...It would be madness to oppose her. You would be better staying here as frozen statues."

"Hera's in trouble," Jason said. "In three days she's going to be—I don't know—consumed, destroyed, something. And a giant is going to rise."

"Yes," Boreas agreed. Was it Jason's imagination, or did he shoot Khione an angry look? "Many horrible things are waking. Even my children do not tell me all the news they should. The Great Stirring of monsters that began with Kronos—your father Zeus foolishly believed it would end when the Titans were defeated. But just as it was before, so it is now. The final

battle is yet to come, and the one who will wake is more terrible than any Titan. Storm spirits—these are only beginning.
The earth has many more horrors to yield up. When monsters
no longer stay in Tartarus, and souls are no longer confined
to Hades . . . Olympus has good reason to fear."

Jason wasn't sure what all this meant, but he didn't like the
way Khione was smiling—like *this* was her definition of fun.

"So you'll help us?" Jason asked the king.

Boreas scowled. "I did not say that."

"Please, Your Majesty," Piper said.

Everyone's eyes turned toward her. She had to be scared
out of her mind, but she looked beautiful and confident—and
it had nothing to do with the blessing of Aphrodite. She
looked herself again, in day-old traveling clothes with choppy
hair and no makeup. But she almost glowed with warmth in
that cold throne room. "If you tell us where the storm spirits
are, we can capture them and bring them to Aeolus. You'd
look good in front of your boss. Aeolus might pardon us and
the other demigods. We could even rescue Gleeson Hedge.
Everyone wins."

"She's pretty," Zethes mumbled. "I mean, she's right."

"Father, don't listen to her," Khione said. "She's a child of
Aphrodite. She dares to charmspeak a god? Freeze her now!"

Boreas considered this. Jason slipped his hand in his pocket
and got ready to bring out the gold coin. If things went wrong,
he'd have to move fast.

The movement caught Boreas's eye. "What is that on your
forearm, demigod?"

Jason hadn't realized his coat sleeve had gotten pushed

up, revealing the edge of his tattoo. Reluctantly, he showed Boreas his marks.

The god's eyes widened. Khione actually hissed and stepped away.

Then Boreas did something unexpected. He laughed so loudly, an icicle cracked from the ceiling and crashed next to his throne. The god's form began to flicker. His beard disappeared. He grew taller and thinner, and his clothes changed into a Roman toga, lined with purple. His head was crowned with a frosty laurel wreath, and a gladius—a Roman sword like Jason's—hung at his side.

"Aquilon," Jason said, though where he got the god's Roman name from, he had no idea.

The god inclined his head. "You recognize me better in this form, yes? And yet you said you came from Camp Half-Blood?"

Jason shifted his feet. "Uh...yes, Your Majesty."

"And Hera sent you there...." The winter god's eyes were full of mirth. "I understand now. Oh, she plays a dangerous game. Bold, but dangerous! No wonder Olympus is closed. They must be trembling at the gamble she has taken."

"Jason," Piper said nervously, "why did Boreas change shape? The toga, the wreath. What's going on?"

"It's his Roman form," Jason said. "But what's going on—I don't know."

The god laughed. "No, I'm sure you don't. This should be very interesting to watch."

"Does that mean you'll let us go?" Piper asked.

"My dear," Boreas said, "there is no reason for me to kill

you. If Hera's plan fails, which I think it will, you will tear each other apart. Aeolus will never have to worry about demi-gods again."

Jason felt as if Khione's cold fingers were on his neck again, but it wasn't her—it was just the feeling that Boreas was right. That sense of wrongness which had bothered Jason since he got to Camp Half-Blood, and Chiron's comment about his arrival being disastrous—Boreas knew what they meant.

"I don't suppose you could explain?" Jason asked.

"Oh, perish the thought! It is not for me to interfere in Hera's plan. No wonder she took your memory." Boreas chuckled, apparently still having a great time imagining demigods tearing each other apart. "You know, I have a reputation as a helpful wind god. Unlike my brethren, I've been known to fall in love with mortals. Why, my sons Zethes and Calais started as demigods—"

"Which explains why they are idiots," Khione growled.

"Stop it!" Zethes snapped back. "Just because you were born a full goddess—"

"Both of you, freeze," Boreas ordered. Apparently, that word carried a lot of weight in the household, because the two siblings went absolutely still. "Now, as I was saying, I have a good reputation, but it is rare that Boreas plays an important role in the affairs of gods. I sit here in my palace, at the edge of civilization, and so rarely have amusements. Why, even that fool Notus, the South Wind, gets spring break in Cancún. What do I get? A winter festival with naked Québécois rolling around in the snow!"

"I like the winter festival," Zethes muttered.

"My point," Boreas snapped, "is that I now have a chance to be the center. Oh, yes, I will let you go on this quest. You will find your storm spirits in the windy city, of course. Chicago—"

"Father!" Khione protested.

Boreas ignored his daughter. "If you can capture the winds, you may be able to gain safe entrance to the court of Aeolus. If by some miracle you succeed, be sure to tell him you captured the winds on my orders."

"Okay, sure," Jason said. "So Chicago is where we'll find this lady who's controlling the winds? She's the one who's trapped Hera?"

"Ah." Boreas grinned. "Those are two different questions, son of Jupiter."

Jupiter, Jason noticed. *Before, he called me son of Zeus.*

"The one who controls the winds," Boreas continued, "yes, you will find her in Chicago. But *she* is only a servant—a servant who is very likely to destroy you. If you succeed against her and take the winds, then you may go to Aeolus. Only he has knowledge of all the winds on the earth. All secrets come to his fortress eventually. If anyone can tell you where Hera is imprisoned, it is Aeolus. As for who you will meet when you finally find Hera's cage—truly, if I told you that, you would beg me to freeze you."

"Father," Khione protested, "you can't simply let them—"

"I can do what I like," he said, his voice hardening. "I am still master here, am I not?"

The way Boreas glared at his daughter, it was obvious they had some ongoing argument. Khione's eyes flashed with anger, but she clenched her teeth. "As you wish, Father."

"Now go, demigods," Boreas said, "before I change my mind. Zethes, escort them out safely."

They all bowed, and the god of the North Wind dissolved into mist.

Back in the entry hall, Cal and Leo were waiting for them. Leo looked cold but unharmed. He'd even gotten cleaned up, and his clothes looked newly washed, like he'd used the hotel's valet service. Festus the dragon was back in normal form, snorting fire over his scales to keep himself defrosted.

As Khione led them down the stairs, Jason noticed that Leo's eyes followed her. Leo started combing his hair back with his hands. Uh-oh, Jason thought. He made a mental note to warn Leo about the snow goddess later. She was not someone to get a crush on.

At the bottom step, Khione turned to Piper. "You have fooled my father, girl. But you have not fooled me. We are not done. And you, Jason Grace, I will see you as a statue in the throne room soon enough."

"Boreas is right," Jason said. "You're a spoiled kid. See you around, ice princess."

Khione's eyes flared pure white. For once, she seemed at a loss for words. She stormed back up the stairs—literally. Halfway up, she turned into a blizzard and disappeared.

"Be careful," Zethes warned. "She never forgets an insult."

Cal grunted in agreement. "Bad sister."

"She's the goddess of snow," Jason said. "What's she going to do, throw snowballs at us?" But as he said it, Jason had a feeling Khione could do a whole lot worse.

Leo looked devastated. "What happened up there? You made her mad? Is she mad at me too? Guys, that was my prom date!"

"We'll explain later," Piper promised, but when she glanced at Jason, he realized she expected *him* to explain.

What *had* happened up there? Jason wasn't sure. Boreas had turned into Aquilon, his Roman form, as if Jason's presence caused him to go schizophrenic.

The idea that Jason had been sent to Camp Half-Blood seemed to amuse the god, but Boreas/Aquilon hadn't let them go out of kindness. Cruel excitement had danced in his eyes, as if he'd just placed a bet on a dogfight.

You will tear each other apart, he'd said with delight. *Aeolus will never have to worry about demigods again.*

Jason looked away from Piper, trying not to show how unnerved he was. "Yeah," he agreed, "we'll explain later."

"Be careful, pretty girl," Zethes said. "The winds between here and Chicago are bad-tempered. Many other evil things are stirring. I am sorry you will not be staying. You would make a lovely ice statue, in which I could check my reflection."

"Thanks," Piper said. "But I'd sooner play hockey with Cal."

"Hockey?" Cal's eyes lit up.

"Joking," Piper said. "And the storm winds aren't our worst problem, are they?"

"Oh, no," Zethes agreed. "Something else. Something worse."

"Worse," Cal echoed.

"Can you tell me?" Piper gave them a smile.

This time, the charm didn't work. The purple-winged Boreads shook their heads in unison. The hangar doors opened onto a freezing starry night, and Festus the dragon stomped his feet, anxious to fly.

"Ask Aeolus what is worse," Zethes said darkly. "He knows. Good luck."

He almost sounded like he cared what happened to them, even though a few minutes ago he'd wanted to make Piper into an ice sculpture.

Cal patted Leo on the shoulder. "Don't get destroyed," he said, which was probably the longest sentence he'd ever attempted. "Next time—hockey. Pizza."

"Come on, guys." Jason stared out at the dark. He was anxious to get out of that cold penthouse, but he had a feeling it was the most hospitable place they'd see for a while. "Let's go to Chicago and try not to get destroyed."

XXI

PIPER

PIPER DIDN'T RELAX UNTIL THE GLOW OF Quebec City faded behind them.

"You were amazing," Jason told her.

The compliment should've made her day. But all she could think about was the trouble ahead. *Evil things are stirring,* Zethes had warned them. She knew that firsthand. The closer they got to the solstice, the less time Piper had to make her decision.

She told Jason in French: "If you knew the truth about me, you wouldn't think I was so amazing."

"What'd you say?" he asked.

"I said I only talked to Boreas. It wasn't so amazing."

She didn't turn to look, but she imagined him smiling.

"Hey," he said, "you saved me from joining Khione's sub-zero hero collection. I owe you one."

That was definitely the easy part, she thought. There was no way Piper would've let that ice witch keep Jason. What bothered Piper more was the way Boreas had changed form, and why he'd let them go. It had something to do with Jason's past, those tattoos on his arm. Boreas assumed Jason was some sort of Roman, and Romans didn't mix with Greeks. She kept waiting for Jason to offer an explanation, but he clearly didn't want to talk about it.

Until now, Piper had been able to dismiss Jason's feeling that he didn't belong at Camp Half-Blood. Obviously he was a demigod. Of course he belonged. But now . . . what if he was something else? What if he really was an enemy? She couldn't stand that idea any more than she could stand Khione.

Leo passed them some sandwiches from his pack. He'd been quiet ever since they'd told him what happened in the throne room. "I still can't believe Khione," he said. "She looked so nice."

"Trust me, man," Jason said. "Snow may be pretty, but up close it's cold and nasty. We'll find you a better prom date."

Piper smiled, but Leo didn't look pleased. He hadn't said much about his time in the palace, or why the Boreads had singled him out for smelling like fire. Piper got the feeling he was hiding something. Whatever it was, his mood seemed to be affecting Festus, who grumbled and steamed as he tried to keep himself warm in the cold Canadian air. Happy the Dragon was not so happy.

They ate their sandwiches as they flew. Piper had no idea how Leo had stocked up on supplies, but he'd even remembered to bring veggie rations for her. The cheese and avocado sandwich was awesome.

Nobody talked. Whatever they might find in Chicago,

they all knew Boreas had only let them go because he figured they were already on a suicide mission.

The moon rose and stars turned overhead. Piper's eyes started to feel heavy. The encounter with Boreas and his children had scared her more than she wanted to admit. Now that she had a full stomach, her adrenaline was fading.

Suck it up, cupcake! Coach Hedge would've yelled at her. *Don't be a wimp!*

Piper had been thinking about the coach ever since Boreas mentioned he was still alive. She'd never liked Hedge, but he'd leaped off a cliff to save Leo, and he'd sacrificed himself to protect them on the skywalk. She now realized that all the times at school the coach had pushed her, yelled at her to run faster or do more push-ups, or even when he'd turned his back and let her fight her own battles with the mean girls, the old goat man had been trying to help her in his own irritating way—trying to prepare her for life as a demigod.

On the skywalk, Dylan the storm spirit had said something about the coach, too: how he'd been retired to Wilderness School because he was getting too old, like it was some sort of punishment. Piper wondered what that was about, and if it explained why the coach was always so grumpy. Whatever the truth, now that Piper knew Hedge was alive, she had a strong compulsion to save him.

Don't get ahead of yourself, she chided. You've got bigger problems. This trip won't have a happy ending.

She was a traitor, just like Silena Beauregard. It was only a matter of time before her friends found out.

She looked up at the stars and thought about a night

long ago when she and her dad had camped out in front of Grandpa Tom's house. Grandpa Tom had died years before, but Dad had kept his house in Oklahoma because it was where he grew up.

They'd gone back for a few days, with the idea of getting the place fixed up to sell, although Piper wasn't sure who'd want to buy a run-down cabin with shutters instead of windows and two tiny rooms that smelled like cigars. The first night had been so stifling hot—no air conditioning in the middle of August—that Dad suggested they sleep outside.

They'd spread their sleeping bags and listened to the cicadas buzzing in the trees. Piper pointed out the constellations she'd been reading about—Hercules, Apollo's lyre, Sagittarius the centaur.

Her dad crossed his arms behind his head. In his old T-shirt and jeans he looked like just another guy from Tahlequah, Oklahoma, a Cherokee who might've never left tribal lands. "Your grandpa would say those Greek patterns are a bunch of bull. He told me the stars were creatures with glowing fur, like magic hedgehogs. Once, long ago, some hunters even captured a few in the forest. They didn't know what they'd done until nighttime, when the star creatures began to glow. Golden sparks flew from their fur, so the Cherokee released them back into the sky."

"You believe in magic hedgehogs?" Piper asked.

Her dad laughed. "I think Grandpa Tom was full of bull, too, just like the Greeks. But it's a big sky. I suppose there's room for Hercules and hedgehogs."

They sat for a while, until Piper got the nerve to ask a

question that had been bugging her. "Dad, why don't you ever play Native American parts?"

The week before, he'd turned down several million dollars to play Tonto in a remake of *The Lone Ranger*. Piper was still trying to figure out why. He'd played all kinds of roles—a Latino teacher in a tough L.A. school, a dashing Israeli spy in an action-adventure blockbuster, even a Syrian terrorist in a James Bond movie. And, of course, he would always be known as the King of Sparta. But if the part was Native American—it didn't matter what *kind* of role it was—Dad turned it down.

He winked at her. "Too close to home, Pipes. Easier to pretend I'm something I'm not."

"Doesn't that get old? Aren't you ever tempted, like, if you found the perfect part that could change people's opinions?"

"If there's a part like that, Pipes," he said sadly, "I haven't found it."

She looked at the stars, trying to imagine them as glowing hedgehogs. All she saw were the stick figures she knew—Hercules running across the sky, on his way to kill monsters. Dad was probably right. The Greeks and the Cherokee were equally crazy. The stars were just balls of fire.

"Dad," she said, "if you don't like being close to home, why are we sleeping in Grandpa Tom's yard?"

His laughter echoed in the quiet Oklahoma night. "I think you know me too well, Pipes."

"You're not really going to sell this place, are you?"

"Nope," he sighed. "I'm probably not."

Piper blinked, shaking herself out of the memory. She

realized she'd been falling asleep on the dragon's back. How could her dad pretend to be so many things he wasn't? She was trying to do that now, and it was tearing her apart.

Maybe she could pretend for a little while longer. She could dream of finding a way to save her father without betraying her friends—even if right now a happy ending seemed about as likely as magic hedgehogs.

She leaned back against Jason's warm chest. He didn't complain. As soon she closed her eyes, she drifted off to sleep.

In her dream, she was back on the mountaintop. The ghostly purple bonfire cast shadows across the trees. Piper's eyes stung from smoke, and the ground was so warm, the soles of her boots felt sticky.

A voice from the dark rumbled, "You forget your duty."

Piper couldn't see him, but it was definitely her least favorite giant—the one who called himself Enceladus. She looked around for any sign of her father, but the pole where he'd been chained was no longer there.

"Where is he?" she demanded. "What've you done with him?"

The giant's laugh was like lava hissing down a volcano. "His body is safe enough, though I fear the poor man's mind can't take much more of my company. For some reason he finds me—disturbing. You must hurry, girl, or I fear there will be little left of him to save."

"Let him go!" she screamed. "Take me instead. He's just a mortal!"

"But, my dear," the giant rumbled, "we must prove our love

for our parents. That's what *I'm* doing. Show me you value your father's life by doing what I ask. Who's more important —your father, or a deceitful goddess who used you, toyed with your emotions, manipulated your memories, eh? What is Hera to you?"

Piper began to tremble. So much anger and fear boiled inside her, she could hardly talk. "You're asking me to betray my friends."

"Sadly, my dear, your friends are destined to die. Their quest is impossible. Even if you succeeded, you heard the prophecy: unleashing Hera's rage would mean your destruction. The only question now—will you die with your friends, or live with your father?"

The bonfire roared. Piper tried to step back, but her feet were heavy. She realized the ground was pulling her down, clinging to her boots like wet sand. When she looked up, a shower of purple sparks had spread across the sky, and the sun was rising in the east. A patchwork of cities glowed in the valley below, and far to the west, over a line of rolling hills, she saw a familiar landmark rising from a sea of fog.

"Why are you showing me this?" Piper asked. "You're revealing where you are."

"Yes, you know this place," the giant said. "Lead your friends here instead of their true destination, and I will deal with them. Or even better, arrange their deaths before you arrive. I don't care which. Just be at the summit by noon on the solstice, and you may collect your father and go in peace."

"I can't," Piper said. "You can't ask me—"

"To betray that foolish boy Valdez, who always irritated

you and is now hiding secrets from you? To give up a boyfriend you never really had? Is that more important than your
own father?"

"I'll find a way to defeat you," Piper said. "I'll save my
father *and* my friends."

The giant growled in the shadows. "I was once proud too.
I thought the gods could never defeat me. Then they hurled
a mountain on top of me, crushed me into the ground, where
I struggled for eons, half-conscious in pain. That taught me
patience, girl. It taught me not to act rashly. Now I've clawed
my way back with the help of the waking earth. I am only
the first. My brethren will follow. We will not be denied our
vengeance—not this time. And you, Piper McLean, need a
lesson in humility. I'll show you how easily your rebellious
spirit can be brought to earth."

The dream dissolved. And Piper woke up screaming, free-
falling through the air.

XXII

PIPER

PIPER TUMBLED THROUGH THE SKY. Far below she saw city lights glimmering in the early dawn, and several hundred yards away the body of the bronze dragon spinning out of control, its wings limp, fire flickering in its mouth like a badly wired lightbulb.

A body shot past her—Leo, screaming and frantically grabbing at the clouds. "Not coooooool!"

She tried to call to him, but he was already too far below.

Somewhere above her, Jason yelled, "Piper, level out! Extend your arms and legs!"

It was hard to control her fear, but she did what he said and regained some balance. She fell spread-eagle like a skydiver, the wind underneath her like a solid block of ice. Then Jason was there, wrapping his arms around her waist.

Thank god, Piper thought. But part of her also thought: Great. Second time this week he's hugged me, and both times it's because I'm plummeting to my death.

"We have to get Leo!" she shouted.

Their fall slowed as Jason controlled the winds, but they still lurched up and down like the winds didn't want to cooperate.

"Gonna get rough," Jason warned. "Hold on!"

Piper locked her arms around him, and Jason shot toward the ground. Piper probably screamed, but the sound was ripped from her mouth. Her vision blurred.

And then, *thump!* They slammed into another warm body —Leo, still wriggling and cursing.

"Stop fighting!" Jason said. "It's me!"

"My dragon!" Leo yelled. "You gotta save Festus!"

Jason was already struggling to keep the three of them aloft, and Piper knew there was no way he could help a fifty-ton metal dragon. But before she could try to reason with Leo, she heard an explosion below them. A fireball rolled into the sky from behind a warehouse complex, and Leo sobbed, "Festus!"

Jason's face reddened with strain as he tried to maintain an air cushion beneath them, but intermittent slow-downs were the best he could manage. Rather than free-falling, it felt like they were bouncing down a giant staircase, a hundred feet at a time, which wasn't doing Piper's stomach any favors.

As they wobbled and zigzagged, Piper could make out details of the factory complex below—warehouses, smoke-stacks, barbed-wire fences, and parking lots lined with snow-covered vehicles. They were still high enough so that hitting the ground would flatten them into roadkill—or skykill— when Jason groaned, "I can't—"

And they dropped like stones.

They hit the roof of the largest warehouse and crashed through into darkness.

Unfortunately, Piper tried to land on her feet. Her feet didn't like that. Pain flared in her left ankle as she crumpled against a cold metal surface.

For a few seconds she wasn't conscious of anything but pain—pain so bad that her ears rang and her vision went red.

Then she heard Jason's voice somewhere below, echoing through the building. "Piper! Where's Piper?"

"Ow, bro!" Leo groaned. "That's my back! I'm not a sofa! Piper, where'd you go?"

"Here," she managed, her voice a whimper.

She heard shuffling and grunting, then feet pounding on metal steps.

Her vision began to clear. She was on a metal catwalk that ringed the warehouse interior. Leo and Jason had landed on ground level, and were now coming up the stairs toward her. She looked at her foot, and wave of nausea swept over her. Her toes weren't supposed to point that way, were they?

Oh, god. She forced herself to look away before she threw up. Focus on something else. Anything else.

The hole they'd made in the roof was a ragged starburst twenty feet above. How they'd even survived that drop, she had no idea. Hanging from the ceiling, a few electric bulbs flickered dimly, but they didn't do much to light the enormous space. Next to Piper, the corrugated metal wall was emblazoned with a company logo, but it was almost completely spray-painted over with graffiti. Down in the shadowy warehouse, she could make out huge machines, robotic arms, half-finished trucks on an assembly line. The place looked like it had been abandoned for years.

Jason and Leo reached her side.

Leo started to ask, "You okay...?" Then he saw her foot. "Oh no, you're not."

"Thanks for the reassurance," Piper groaned.

"You'll be fine," Jason said, though Piper could hear the worry in his voice. "Leo, you got any first aid supplies?"

"Yeah—yeah, sure." He dug around in his tool belt and pulled out a wad of gauze and a roll of duct tape—both of which seemed too big for the belt's pockets. Piper had noticed the tool belt yesterday morning, but she hadn't thought to ask Leo about it. It didn't look like anything special—just one of those wraparound leather aprons with a bunch of pockets, like a blacksmith or a carpenter might wear. And it seemed to be empty.

"How did you—" Piper tried to sit up, and winced. "How did pull that stuff from an empty belt?"

"Magic," Leo said. "Haven't figure it out completely, but I can summon just about any regular tool out of the pockets, plus some other helpful stuff." He reached into another pocket and pulled out a little tin box. "Breath mint?"

Jason snatched away the mints. "That's great, Leo. Now, can you fix her foot?"

"I'm a mechanic, man. Maybe if she was a car..." He snapped his fingers. "Wait, what was that godly healing stuff they fed you at camp—Rambo food?"

"Ambrosia, dummy," Piper said through gritted teeth. "There should be some in my bag, if it's not crushed."

Jason carefully pulled her backpack off her shoulders. He rummaged through the supplies the Aphrodite kids had packed for her, and found a Ziploc full of smashed pastry squares like lemon bars. He broke off a piece and fed it to her.

The taste was nothing like she expected. It reminded her of Dad's black bean soup from when she was a little girl. He used to feed it to her whenever she got sick. The memory relaxed her, though it made her sad. The pain in her ankle subsided.

"More," she said.

Jason frowned. "Piper, we shouldn't risk it. They said too much could burn you up. I think I should try to set your foot."

Piper's stomach fluttered. "Have you ever done that before?"

"Yeah...I think so."

Leo found an old piece of wood and broke it in half for a splint. Then he got the gauze and duct tape ready.

"Hold her leg still," Jason told him. "Piper, this is going to hurt."

When Jason set the foot, Piper flinched so hard she punched Leo in the arm, and he yelled almost as much as she did. When her vision cleared and she could breathe normally again, she found that her foot was pointing the right way, her ankle splinted with plywood, gauze, and duct tape.

"Ow," she said.

"Jeez, beauty queen!" Leo rubbed his arm. "Glad my face wasn't there."

"Sorry," she said. "And don't call me 'beauty queen,' or I'll punch you again."

"You both did great." Jason found a canteen in Piper's pack and gave her some water. After a few minutes, her stomach began to calm down.

Once she wasn't screaming in pain, she could hear the wind howling outside. Snowflakes fluttered through the hole in the roof, and after their meeting with Khione, snow was the last thing Piper wanted to see.

"What happened to the dragon?" she asked. "Where are we?"

Leo's expression turned sullen. "I don't know with Festus. He just jerked sideways like he hit an invisible wall and started to fall."

Piper remembered Enceladus's warning: *I'll show you how easily your rebellious spirit can be brought to earth.* Had he managed to strike them down from so far away? It seemed impossible. If he were that powerful, why would he need her to betray her friends when he could just kill them himself? And how could the giant be keeping an eye on her in a snowstorm thousands of miles away?

Leo pointed to the logo on the wall. "As far as where we are..." It was hard to see through the graffiti, but Piper could make out a large red eye with the stenciled words: MONOCLE MOTORS, ASSEMBLY PLANT 1.

"Closed car plant," Leo said. "I'm guessing we crash-landed in Detroit."

Piper had heard about closed car plants in Detroit, so that

made sense. But it seemed like a pretty depressing place to land. "How far is that from Chicago?"

Jason handed her the canteen. "Maybe three-fourths of the way from Quebec? The thing is, without the dragon, we're stuck traveling overland."

"No way," Leo said. "It isn't safe."

Piper thought about the way the ground had pulled at her feet in the dream, and what King Boreas had said about the earth yielding up more horrors. "He's right. Besides, I don't know if I can walk. And three people—Jason, you can't fly that many across country by yourself."

"No way," Jason said. "Leo, are you sure the dragon didn't malfunction? I mean, Festus is old, and—"

"And I might not have repaired him right?"

"I didn't say that," Jason protested. "It's just—maybe you could fix it."

"I don't know." Leo sounded crestfallen. He pulled a few screws out of his pockets and started fiddling with them. "I'd have to find where he landed, if he's even in one piece."

"It was my fault." Piper said without thinking. She just couldn't stand it anymore. The secret about her father was heating up inside her like too much ambrosia. If she kept lying to her friends, she felt like she'd burn to ashes.

"Piper," Jason said gently, "you were asleep when Festus conked out. It couldn't be your fault."

"Yeah, you're just shaken up," Leo agreed. He didn't even try to make a joke at her expense. "You're in pain. Just rest."

She wanted to tell them everything, but the words stuck

in her throat. They were both being so kind to her. Yet if Enceladus was watching her somehow, saying the wrong thing could get her father killed.

Leo stood. "Look, um, Jason, why don't you stay with her, bro? I'll scout around for Festus. I think he fell outside the warehouse somewhere. If I can find him, maybe I can figure out what happened and fix him."

"It's too dangerous," Jason said. "You shouldn't go by yourself."

"Ah, I got duct tape and breath mints. I'll be fine," Leo said, a little too quickly, and Piper realized he was a lot more shaken up than he was letting on. "You guys just don't run off without me."

Leo reached into his magic tool belt, pulled out a flashlight, and headed down the stairs, leaving Piper and Jason alone.

Jason gave her a smile, though he looked kind of nervous. It was the exact expression he'd had on his face after he'd kissed her the first time, up on the Wilderness School dorm roof—that cute little scar on his lip curving into a crescent. The memory gave her a warm feeling. Then she remembered that the kiss had never really happened.

"You look better," Jason offered.

Piper wasn't sure if he meant her foot, or the fact that she wasn't magically beautified anymore. Her jeans were tattered from the fall through the roof. Her boots were splattered with melted dirty snow. She didn't know what her face looked like, but probably horrible.

Why did it matter? She'd never cared about things like that before. She wondered if it was her stupid mother, the goddess of love, messing with her thoughts. If Piper started getting urges to read fashion magazines, she was going to have to find Aphrodite and smack her.

She decided to focus on her ankle instead. As long as she didn't move it, the pain wasn't bad. "You did a good job," she told Jason. "Where'd you learn first aid?"

He shrugged. "Same answer as always. I don't know."

"But you're starting to have some memories, aren't you? Like that prophecy in Latin back at camp, or that dream about the wolf."

"It's fuzzy," he said. "Like déjà vu. Ever forgotten a word or a name, and you know it should be on the tip of your tongue, but it isn't? It's like that—only with my whole life."

Piper sort of knew what he meant. The last three months —a life she thought she'd had, a relationship with Jason—had turned out to be Mist.

A boyfriend you never really had, Enceladus had said. *Is that more important than your own father?*

She should've kept her mouth shut, but she voiced the question that had been on her mind since yesterday.

"That photo in your pocket," she said. "Is that someone from your past?"

Jason pulled back.

"I'm sorry," she said. "None of my business. Forget it."

"No—it's okay." His features relaxed. "Just, I'm trying to figure things out. Her name's Thalia. She's my sister. I don't remember any details. I'm not even sure how I know, but— um, why are you smiling?"

"Nothing." Piper tried to kill the smile. *Not* an old

girlfriend. She felt ridiculously happy. "Um, it's just—that's great you remembered. Annabeth told me she became a Hunter of Artemis, right?"

Jason nodded. "I get the feeling I'm supposed to find her. Hera left me that memory for a reason. It's got something to do with this quest. But...I also have the feeling it could be dangerous. I'm not sure I *want* to find out the truth. Is that crazy?"

"No," Piper said. "Not at all."

She stared at the logo on the wall: MONOCLE MOTORS, the single red eye. Something about that logo bothered her.

Maybe it was the idea Enceladus was watching her, holding her father for leverage. She had to save him, but how could she betray her friends?

"Jason," she said. "Speaking of the truth, I need to tell you something—something about my dad—"

She didn't get the chance. Somewhere below, metal clanged against metal, like a door slamming shut. The sound echoed through the warehouse.

Jason stood. He took out his coin and flipped it, snatching his golden sword out of the air. He peered over the railing. "Leo?" he called.

No answer.

He crouched next to Piper. "I don't like this."

"He could be in trouble," Piper said. "Go check."

"I can't leave you alone."

"I'll be fine." She felt terrified, but she wasn't about to admit it. She drew her dagger Katoptris and tried to look confident. "Anyone gets close, I'll skewer them."

Jason hesitated. "I'll leave you the pack. If I'm not back in five minutes—"

"Panic?" she suggested.

He managed a smile. "Glad you're back to normal. The makeup and the dress were a lot more intimidating than the dagger."

"Get going, Sparky, before I skewer *you*."

"Sparky?"

Even offended, Jason looked hot. It wasn't fair. Then he made his way to the stairs and disappeared into the dark.

Piper counted her breaths, trying to gauge how much time had passed. She lost track at around forty-three. Then something in the warehouse went *bang!*

The echo died. Piper's heart pounded, but she didn't call out. Her instincts told her it might not be a good idea.

She stared at her splinted ankle. *It's not like I can run.* Then she looked up again at the Monocle Motors sign. A little voice in her head pestered her, warning of danger. Something from Greek mythology . . .

Her hand went to her backpack. She took out the ambrosia squares. Too much would burn her up, but would a little more fix her ankle?

Boom. The sound was closer this time, directly below her. She dug out a whole square of ambrosia and stuffed it in her mouth. Her heart raced faster. Her skin felt feverish.

Hesitantly, she flexed her ankle against the splint. No pain, no stiffness at all. She cut through the duct tape with her dagger and heard heavy steps on the stairs—like metal boots.

Had it been five minutes? Longer? The steps didn't sound

like Jason, but maybe he was carrying Leo. Finally she couldn't stand it. Gripping her dagger, she called out, "Jason?"

"Yeah," he said from the darkness. "On my way up."

Definitely Jason's voice. So why did all her instincts say *Run?*

With effort, she got to her feet.

The steps came closer.

"It's okay," Jason's voice promised.

At the top of the stairs, a face appeared out of the darkness —a hideous black grin, a smashed nose, and a single blood-shot eye in the middle of his forehead.

"It's fine," the Cyclops said, in a perfect imitation of Jason's voice. "You're just in time for dinner."

XXIII

LEO

LEO WISHED THE DRAGON HADN'T LANDED on the toilets.

Of all the places to crash, a line of Porta-Potties would not have been his first choice. A dozen of the blue plastic boxes had been set up in the factory yard, and Festus had flattened them all. Fortunately, they hadn't been used in a long time, and the fireball from the crash incinerated most of the contents; but still, there were some pretty gross chemicals leaking out of the wreckage. Leo had to pick his way through and try not to breathe through his nose. Heavy snow was coming down, but the dragon's hide was still steaming hot. Of course, that didn't bother Leo.

After a few minutes climbing over Festus's inanimate body, Leo started to get irritated. The dragon looked perfectly fine. Yes, it had fallen out of the sky and landed with a big *ka-boom*, but its body wasn't even dented. The fireball had apparently come from built up gasses inside the toilet units, not from the dragon itself. Festus's wings were intact. Nothing seemed broken. There was no reason it should have stopped.

"Not my fault," he muttered. "Festus, you're making me look bad."

Then he opened the control panel on the dragon's head, and Leo's heart sank. "Oh, Festus, what the heck?"

The wiring had frozen over. Leo knew it had been okay yesterday. He'd worked so hard to repair the corroded lines, but something had caused a flash freeze inside the dragon's skull, where it should've been too hot for ice to form. The ice had caused the wiring to overload and char the control disk. Leo couldn't see any reason that would've happened. Sure, the dragon was old, but still, it didn't make sense.

He could replace the wires. That wasn't the problem. But the charred control disk was not good. The Greek letters and pictures carved around the edges, which probably held all kinds of magic, were blurred and blackened.

The one piece of hardware Leo couldn't replace—and it was damaged. *Again.*

He imagined his mom's voice: *Most problems look worse than they are,* mijo. *Nothing is unfixable.*

His mom could repair just about anything, but Leo was pretty sure she'd never worked on a fifty-year-old magic metal dragon.

He clenched his teeth and decided he had to try. He wasn't walking from Detroit to Chicago in a snowstorm, and he wasn't going to be responsible for stranding his friends.

"Right," he muttered, brushing the snow off his shoulders.

"Gimme a nylon bristle detail brush, some nitrile gloves, and maybe a can of that aerosol cleaning solvent."

The tool belt obliged. Leo couldn't help smiling as he pulled out the supplies. The belt's pockets did have limits. They wouldn't give him anything magic, like Jason's sword, or anything huge, like a chain saw. He'd tried asking for both. And if he asked for too many things at once, the belt needed a cooldown time before it could work again. The more complicated the request, the longer the cooldown. But anything small and simple like you might find around a workshop—all Leo had to do was ask.

He began cleaning off the control disk. While he worked, snow collected on the cooling dragon. Leo had to stop from time to time to summon fire and melt it away, but mostly he went into autopilot mode, his hands working by themselves as his thoughts wandered.

Leo couldn't believe how stupid he'd acted back at Boreas's palace. He should've figured a family of winter gods would hate him on sight. Son of the fire god flying a fire-breathing dragon into an ice penthouse—yeah, maybe not the best move. Still, he hated feeling like a reject. Jason and Piper got to visit the throne room. Leo got to wait in the lobby with Cal, the demigod of hockey and major head injuries.

Fire is bad, Cal had told him.

That pretty much summed it up. Leo knew he couldn't keep the truth from his friends much longer. Ever since Camp Half-Blood, one line of that Great Prophecy kept coming back to him: *To storm or fire the world must fall.*

And Leo was the fire guy, the first one since 1666 when London had burned down. If he told his friends what he could really do—*Hey, guess what, guys? I might destroy the world!*—why would anyone welcome him back at camp? Leo would have to go on the run again. Even though he knew that drill, the idea depressed him.

Then there was Khione. Dang, that girl was fine. Leo knew he'd acted like a total fool, but he couldn't help himself. He'd had his clothes cleaned with the one-hour valet service —which had been totally sweet, by the way. He'd combed his hair—never an easy job—and even discovered the tool bag could make breath mints, all in hopes that he could get close to her. Naturally, no such luck.

Getting frozen out—story of his life—by his relatives, foster homes, you name it. Even at Wilderness School, Leo had spent the last few weeks feeling like a third wheel as Jason and Piper, his only friends, became a couple. He was happy for them and all, but still it made him feel like they didn't need him anymore.

When he'd found out that Jason's whole time at school had been an illusion—a kind of a memory burp—Leo had been secretly excited. It was a chance for a reset. Now Jason and Piper were heading toward being a couple again—that was obvious from the way they'd acted in the warehouse just now, like they wanted to talk in private without Leo around. What had he expected? He'd wind up the odd man out again. Khione had just given him the cold shoulder a little quicker than most.

"Enough, Valdez," he scolded himself. "Nobody's going

to play any violins for you just because you're not important. Fix the stupid dragon."

He got so involved with his work, he wasn't sure how much time had passed before he heard the voice.

You're wrong, Leo, it said.

He fumbled his brush and dropped it into the dragon's head. He stood, but he couldn't see who'd spoken. Then he looked at the ground. Snow and chemical sludge from the toilets, even the asphalt itself was shifting like it was turning to liquid. A ten-foot-wide area formed eyes, a nose, and a mouth—the giant face of a sleeping woman.

She didn't exactly speak. Her lips didn't move. But Leo could hear her voice in his head, as if the vibrations were coming through the ground, straight into his feet and resonating up his skeleton.

They need you desperately, she said. *In some ways, you are the most important of the seven—like the control disk in the dragon's brain. Without you, the power of the others means nothing. They will never reach me, never stop me. And I will fully wake.*

"You." Leo was shaking so badly he wasn't sure he'd spoken aloud. He hadn't heard that voice since he was eight, but it was her: the earthen woman from the machine shop. "You killed my mom."

The face shifted. The mouth formed a sleepy smile like it was having a pleasant dream. *Ah, but Leo. I am your mother too—the First Mother. Do not oppose me. Walk away now. Let my son Porphyrion rise and become king, and I will ease your burdens. You will tread lightly on the earth.*

Leo grabbed the nearest thing he could find—a Porta-Potty seat—and threw it at the face. "Leave me alone!"

The toilet seat sank into the liquid earth. Snow and sludge rippled, and the face dissolved.

Leo stared at the ground, waiting for the face to reappear. But it didn't. Leo wanted to think he'd imagined it.

Then from the direction of the factory, he heard a crash —like two dump trucks slamming together. Metal crumpled and groaned, and the noise echoed across the yard. Instantly Leo knew that Jason and Piper were in trouble.

Walk away now, the voice had urged.

"Not likely," Leo growled. "Gimme the biggest hammer you got."

He reached into his tool belt and pulled out a three-pound club hammer with a double-faced head the size of a baked potato. Then he jumped off the dragon's back and ran toward the warehouse.

XXIV

LEO

LEO STOPPED AT THE DOORS AND TRIED to control his breathing. The voice of the earth woman still rang in his ears, reminding him of his mother's death. The last thing he wanted to do was plunge into another dark warehouse. Suddenly he felt eight years old again, alone and helpless as someone he cared about was trapped and in trouble.

Stop it, he told himself. That's how she wants you to feel.

But that didn't make him any less scared. He took a deep breath and peered inside. Nothing looked different. Gray morning light filtered through the hole in the roof. A few lightbulbs flickered, but most of the factory floor was still lost in shadows. He could make out the catwalk above, the dim shapes of heavy machinery along the assembly line, but no movement. No sign of his friends.

He almost called out, but something stopped him—a sense he couldn't identify. Then he realized it was *smell*. Something smelled wrong—like burning motor oil and sour breath.

Something not human was inside the factory. Leo was certain. His body shifted into high gear, all his nerves tingling.

Somewhere on the factory floor, Piper's voice cried out: "Leo, help!"

But Leo held his tongue. How could Piper have gotten off the catwalk with her broken ankle?

He slipped inside and ducked behind a cargo container. Slowly, gripping his hammer, he worked his way toward the center of the room, hiding behind boxes and hollow truck chassis. Finally he reached the assembly line. He crouched behind the nearest piece of machinery—a crane with a robotic arm.

Piper's voice called out again: "Leo?" Less certain this time, but very close.

Leo peeked around the machinery. Hanging directly above the assembly line, suspended by a chain from a crane on the opposite side, was a massive truck engine—just dangling thirty feet up, as if it had been left there when the factory was abandoned. Below it on the conveyor belt sat a truck chassis, and clustered around it were three dark shapes the size of forklifts. Nearby, dangling from chains on two other robotic arms, were two smaller shapes—maybe more engines, but one of them was twisting around as if it were alive.

Then one of the forklift shapes rose, and Leo realized it was a humanoid of massive size. "Told you it was nothing," the thing rumbled. Its voice was too deep and feral to be human.

One of the other forklift-sized lumps shifted, and called out in Piper's voice: "Leo, help me! Help—" Then the voice changed, becoming a masculine snarl. "Bah, there's nobody out there. No demigod could be that quiet, eh?"

The first monster chuckled. "Probably ran away, if he knows what's good for him. Or the girl was lying about a third demigod. Let's get cooking."

Snap. A bright orange light sizzled to life—an emergency flare—and Leo was temporarily blinded. He ducked behind the crane until the spots cleared from his eyes. Then he took another peep and saw a nightmare scene even Tía Callida couldn't have dreamed up.

The two smaller things dangling from crane arms weren't engines. They were Jason and Piper. Both hung upside down, tied by their ankles and cocooned with chains up to their necks. Piper was flailing around, trying to free herself. Her mouth was gagged, but at least she was alive. Jason didn't look so good. He hung limply, his eyes rolled up in his head. A red welt the size of an apple had swollen over his left eyebrow.

On the conveyor belt, the bed of the unfinished pickup truck was being used as a fire pit. The emergency flare had ignited a mixture of tires and wood, which, from the smell of it, had been doused in kerosene. A big metal pole was suspended over the flames—a spit, Leo realized, which meant this was a cooking fire.

But most terrifying of all were the cooks.

Monocle Motors: that single red eye logo. Why hadn't Leo realized?

Three massive humanoids gathered around the fire. Two

were standing, stoking the flames. The largest one crouched with his back to Leo. The two facing him were each ten feet tall, with hairy muscular bodies and skin that glowed red in the firelight. One of the monsters wore a chain mail loincloth that looked really uncomfortable. The other wore a ragged fuzzy toga made of fiberglass insulation, which also would not have made Leo's top ten wardrobe ideas. Other than that, the two monsters could've been twins. Each had a brutish face with a single eye in the center of his forehead. The cooks were Cyclopes.

Leo's legs started quaking. He'd seen some weird things so far—storm spirits and winged gods and a metal dragon that liked Tabasco sauce. But this was different. These were actual, flesh-and-blood, ten-foot-tall living monsters who wanted to eat his friends for dinner.

He was so terrified he could hardly think. If only he had Festus. He could use a fire-breathing sixty-foot-long tank about now. But all he had was a tool belt and a backpack. His three-pound club hammer looked awfully small compared to those Cyclopes.

This is what the sleeping earth lady had been talking about. She wanted Leo to walk away and leave his friends to die.

That decided it. No way was Leo going to let that earth lady make him feel powerless—never again. Leo slipped off his backpack and quietly started to unzip it.

The Cyclops in the chain mail loincloth walked over to Piper, who squirmed and tried to head-butt him in the eye. "Can I take her gag off now? I like it when they scream."

The question was directed at the third Cyclops, apparently

the leader. The crouching figure grunted, and Loincloth ripped the gag off Piper's mouth.

She didn't scream. She took a shaky breath like she was trying to keep herself calm.

Meanwhile, Leo found what he wanted in the pack: a stack of tiny remote control units he'd picked up in Bunker 9. At least he *hoped* that's what they were. The robotic crane's maintenance panel was easy to find. He slipped a screwdriver from his tool belt and went to work, but he had to go slowly. The leader Cyclops was only twenty feet in front of him. The monsters obviously had excellent senses. Pulling off his plan without making noise seemed impossible, but he didn't have much choice.

The Cyclops in the toga poked at the fire, which was now blazing away and billowing noxious black smoke toward the ceiling. His buddy Loincloth glowered at Piper, waiting for her to do something entertaining. "Scream, girl! I like funny screaming!"

When Piper finally spoke, her tone was calm and reasonable, like she was correcting a naughty puppy. "Oh, Mr. Cyclops, you don't want to kill us. It would be much better if you let us go."

Loincloth scratched his ugly head. He turned to his friend in the fiberglass toga. "She's kind of pretty, Torque. Maybe I should let her go."

Torque, the dude in the toga, growled. "I saw her first, Sump. *I'll* let her go!"

Sump and Torque started to argue, but the third Cyclops rose and shouted, "Fools!"

Leo almost dropped his screwdriver. The third Cyclops was a *female*. She was several feet taller than Torque or Sump, and even beefier. She wore a tent of chain mail cut like one of those sack dresses Leo's mean Aunt Rosa used to wear. What'd they call that—a muumuu? Yeah, the Cyclops lady had a chain mail muumuu. Her greasy black hair was matted in pigtails, woven with copper wires and metal washers. Her nose and mouth were thick and smashed together, like she spent her free time ramming her face into walls; but her single red eye glittered with evil intelligence.

The woman Cyclops stalked over to Sump and pushed him aside, knocking him over the conveyor belt. Torque backed up quickly.

"The girl is Venus spawn," the lady Cyclops snarled. "She's using charmspeak on you."

Piper started to say, "Please, ma'am—"

"Rarr!" The lady Cyclops grabbed Piper around the waist. "Don't try your pretty talk on me, girl! I'm Ma Gasket! I've eaten heroes tougher than you for lunch!"

Leo feared Piper would get crushed, but Ma Gasket just dropped her and let her dangle from her chain. Then she started yelling at Sump about how stupid he was.

Leo's hands worked furiously. He twisted wires and turned switches, hardly thinking about what he was doing. He finished attaching the remote. Then he crept over to the next robotic arm while the Cyclopes were talking.

"—eat her last, Ma?" Sump was saying.

"Idiot!" Ma Gasket yelled, and Leo realized Sump and Torque must be her sons. If so, ugly definitely ran in the family. "I should've thrown you out on the streets when you were babies, like *proper* Cyclops children. You might have learned some useful skills. Curse my soft heart that I kept you!"

"Soft heart?" Torque muttered.

"What was that, you ingrate?"

"Nothing, Ma. I said you got a soft heart. We get to work for you, feed you, file your toenails—"

"And you should be grateful!" Ma Gasket bellowed. "Now, stoke the fire, Torque! And Sump, you idiot, my case of salsa is in the other warehouse. Don't tell me you expect me to eat these demigods without salsa!"

"Yes, Ma," Sump said. "I mean no, Ma. I mean—"

"Go get it!" Ma Gasket picked up a nearby truck chassis and slammed it over Sump's head. Sump crumpled to his knees. Leo was sure a hit like that would kill him, but Sump apparently got hit by trucks a lot. He managed to push the chassis off his head. Then he staggered to his feet and ran off to fetch the salsa.

Now's the time, Leo thought. While they're separated.

He finished wiring the second machine and moved toward a third. As he dashed between robotic arms, the Cyclopes didn't see him, but Piper did. Her expression turned from terror to disbelief, and she gasped.

Ma Gasket turned to her. "What's the matter, girl? So fragile I broke you?"

Thankfully, Piper was a quick thinker. She looked away from Leo and said, "I think it's my ribs, ma'am. If I'm busted up inside, I'll taste terrible."

Ma Gasket bellowed with laughter. "Good one. The last hero we ate—remember him, Torque? Son of Mercury, wasn't he?"

"Yes, Ma," Torque said. "Tasty. Little bit stringy."

"He tried a trick like that. Said he was on medication. But he tasted fine!"

"Tasted like mutton," Torque recalled. "Purple shirt. Talked in Latin. Yes, a bit stringy, but good."

Leo's fingers froze on the maintenance panel. Apparently, Piper was having the same thought he was, because she asked, "Purple shirt? Latin?"

"Good eating," Ma Gasket said fondly. "Point is, girl, we're not as dumb as people think! We're not falling for those stupid tricks and riddles, not us northern Cyclopes."

Leo forced himself back to work, but his mind was racing. A kid who spoke Latin had been caught here—in a purple shirt like Jason's? He didn't know what that meant, but he had to leave the interrogation to Piper. If he was going to have any chance of defeating these monsters, he had to move fast before Sump came back with the salsa.

He looked up at the engine block suspended right above the Cyclopes' campsite. He wished he could use that—it would make a great weapon. But the crane holding it was on the opposite side of the conveyor belt. There was no way Leo could get over there without being seen, and besides, he was running short on time.

The last part of his plan was the trickiest. From his tool belt he summoned some wires, a radio adapter, and a smaller screwdriver and started to build a universal remote. For the first time, he said a silent thank-you to his dad—Hephaestus —for the magic tool belt. *Get me out of here,* he prayed, *and maybe you're not such a jerk.*

Piper kept talking, laying on the praise. "Oh, I've heard about the northern Cyclopes!" Which Leo figured was bull, but she sounded convincing. "I never knew you were so big and clever!"

"Flattery won't work either," Ma Gasket said, though she sounded pleased. "It's true, you'll be breakfast for the best Cyclopes around."

"But aren't Cyclopes good?" Piper asked. "I thought you made weapons for the gods."

"Bah! I'm very good. Good at eating people. Good at smashing. And good at building things, yes, but not for the gods. Our cousins, the elder Cyclopes, they do this, yes. Thinking they're so high and mighty 'cause they're a few thousand years older. Then there's our southern cousins, living on islands and tending sheep. Morons! But we Hyperborean Cyclopes, the northern clan, we're the best! Founded Monocle Motors in this old factory—the best weapons, armor, chariots, fuel-efficient SUVs! And yet—bah! Forced to shut down. Laid off most of our tribe. The war was too quick. Titans lost. No good! No more need for Cyclops weapons."

"Oh, no," Piper sympathized. "I'm sure you made some amazing weapons."

Torque grinned. "Squeaky war hammer!" He picked up a large pole with an accordion-looking metal box on the end.

He slammed it against the floor and the cement cracked, but there was also a sound like the world's largest rubber ducky getting stomped.

"Terrifying," Piper said.

Torque looked pleased. "Not as good as the exploding ax, but this one can be used more than once."

"Can I see it?" Piper asked. "If you could just free my hands—"

Torque stepped forward eagerly, but Ma Gasket said, "Stupid! She's tricking you again. Enough talk! Slay the boy first before he dies on his own. I like my meat fresh."

No! Leo's fingers flew, connecting the wires for the remote. *Just a few more minutes!*

"Hey, wait," Piper said, trying to get the Cyclopes' attention. "Hey, can I just ask—"

The wires sparked in Leo's hand. The Cyclopes froze and turned in his direction. Then Torque picked up a truck and threw it at him.

Leo rolled as the truck steamrolled over the machinery. If he'd been a half-second slower, he would've been smashed.

He got to his feet, and Ma Gasket spotted him. She yelled, "Torque, you pathetic excuse for a Cyclops, get him!"

Torque barreled toward him. Leo frantically gunned the toggle on his makeshift remote.

Torque was fifty feet away. Twenty feet.

Then the first robotic arm whirred to life. A three-ton yellow metal claw slammed the Cyclops in the back so hard, he landed flat on his face. Before Torque could recover, the robotic hand grabbed him by one leg and hurled him straight up.

"AHHHHH!" Torque rocketed into the gloom. The ceiling was too dark and too high up to see exactly what happened, but judging from the harsh metal *clang*, Leo guessed the Cyclops had hit one of the support girders.

Torque never came down. Instead, yellow dust rained to the floor. Torque had disintegrated.

Ma Gasket stared at Leo in shock. "My son... You... You..."

As if on cue, Sump lumbered into the firelight with a case of salsa. "Ma, I got the extra-spicy—"

He never finished his sentence. Leo spun the remote's toggle, and the second robotic arm whacked Sump in the chest. The salsa case exploded like a piñata and Sump flew backward, right into the base of Leo's third machine. Sump may have been immune to getting hit with truck chasses, but he wasn't immune to robotic arms that could deliver ten thousand pounds of force. The third crane arm slammed him against the floor so hard, he exploded into dust like a broken flour sack.

Two Cyclopes down. Leo was beginning to feel like Commander Tool Belt when Ma Gasket locked her eye on him. She grabbed the nearest crane arm and ripped it off its pedestal with a savage roar. "You busted my boys! Only *I* get to bust my boys!"

Leo punched a button, and the two remaining arms swung into action. Ma Gasket caught the first one and tore it in half. The second arm smacked her in the head, but that only seemed to make her mad. She grabbed it by the clamps, ripped it free, and swung it like a baseball bat. It missed Piper and Jason by an inch. Then Ma Gasket let it go—spinning it toward Leo. He yelped and rolled to one side as it demolished the machine next to him.

Leo started to realize that an angry Cyclops mother was not something you wanted to fight with a universal remote and a screwdriver. The future for Commander Tool Belt was not looking so hot.

She stood about twenty feet from him now, next to the cooking fire. Her fists were clenched, her teeth bared. She looked ridiculous in her chain mail muumuu and her greasy pigtails—but given the murderous glare in her huge red eye and the fact that she was twelve feet tall, Leo wasn't laughing.

"Any more tricks, demigod?" Ma Gasket demanded.

Leo glanced up. The engine block suspended on the chain —if only he'd had time to rig it. If only he could get Ma Gasket to take one step forward. The chain itself... that one link... Leo shouldn't have been able to see it, especially from so far down, but his senses told him there was metal fatigue.

"Heck, yeah, I got tricks!" Leo raised his remote control. "Take one more step, and I'll destroy you with fire!"

Ma Gasket laughed. "Would you? Cyclopes are immune to fire, you idiot. But if you wish to play with flames, let me help!"

She scooped red-hot coals into her bare hands and flung them at Leo. They landed all around his feet.

"You missed," he said incredulously. Then Ma Gasket

grinned and picked up a barrel next to the truck. Leo just had time to read the stenciled word on the side—KEROSENE —before Ma Gasket threw it. The barrel split on the floor in front of him, spilling lighter fluid everywhere.

Coals sparked. Leo closed his eyes, and Piper screamed, "No!"

A firestorm erupted around him. When Leo opened his eyes he was bathed in flames swirling twenty feet into the air.

Ma Gasket shrieked with delight, but Leo didn't offer the fire any good fuel. The kerosene burned off, dying down to small fiery patches on the floor.

Piper gasped. "Leo?"

Ma Gasket looked astonished. "You live?" Then she took that extra step forward, which put her right where Leo wanted. "What are you?"

"The son of Hephaestus," Leo said. "And I warned you I'd destroy you with fire."

He pointed one finger in the air and summoned all his will. He'd never tried to do anything so focused and intense —but he shot a bolt of white-hot flames at the chain suspending the engine block above the Cyclops's head—aiming for the link that looked weaker than rest.

The flames died. Nothing happened. Ma Gasket laughed. "An impressive try, son of Hephaestus. It's been many centuries since I saw a fire user. You'll make a spicy appetizer!"

The chain snapped—that single link heated beyond its tolerance point—and the engine block fell, deadly and silent.

"I don't think so," Leo said.

Ma Gasket didn't even have time to look up.

Smash! No more Cyclops—just a pile of dust under a five-ton engine block.

"Not immune to engines, huh?" Leo said. "Boo-yah!"

Then he fell to his knees, his head buzzing. After a few minutes he realized Piper was calling his name.

"Leo! Are you all right? Can you move?"

He stumbled to his feet. He'd never tried to summon such an intense fire before, and it had left him completely drained.

It took him a long time to get Piper down from her chains. Then together they lowered Jason, who was still unconscious. Piper managed to trickle a little nectar into his mouth, and he groaned. The welt on his head started to shrink. His color came back a little.

"Yeah, he's got a nice thick skull," Leo said. "I think he's gonna be fine."

"Thank god," Piper sighed. Then she looked at Leo with something like fear. "How did you—the fire—have you always...?"

Leo looked down. "Always," he said. "I'm a freaking menace. Sorry, I should've told you guys sooner but—"

"Sorry?" Piper punched his arm. When he looked up, she was grinning. "That was amazing, Valdez! You saved our lives. What are you sorry about?"

Leo blinked. He started to smile, but his sense of relief was ruined when he noticed something next to Piper's foot.

Yellow dust—the powdered remains of one of the Cyclopes, maybe Torque—was shifting across the floor like an invisible wind was pushing it back together.

"They're forming again," Leo said. "Look."

Piper stepped away from the dust. "That's not possible. Annabeth told me monsters dissipate when they're killed. They go back to Tartarus and can't return for a long time."

"Well, nobody told the dust that." Leo watched as it collected into a pile, then very slowly spread out, forming a shape with arms and legs.

"Oh, god." Piper turned pale. "Boreas said something about this—the earth yielding up horrors. 'When monsters no longer stay in Tartarus, and souls are no longer confined to Hades.' How long do you think we have?"

Leo thought about the face that had formed in the ground outside—the sleeping woman who was *definitely* a horror from the earth.

"I don't know," he said. "But we need to get out of here."

JASON

JASON DREAMED HE WAS WRAPPED in chains, hanging upside down like a hunk of meat. Everything hurt—his arms, his legs, his chest, his head. Especially his head. It felt like an overinflated water balloon.

"If I'm dead," he murmured, "why does it hurt so much?"

"You're not dead, my hero," said a woman's voice. "It is not your time. Come, speak with me."

Jason's thoughts floated away from his body. He heard monsters yelling, his friends screaming, fiery explosions, but it all seemed to be happening on another plane of existence —getting farther and farther away.

He found himself standing in an earthen cage. Tendrils of tree roots and stone whirled together, confining him. Outside the bars, he could see the floor of a dry reflecting pool, another earthen spire growing at the far end, and above them, the ruined red stones of a burned-out house.

Next to him in the cage, a woman sat cross-legged in black

robes, her head covered by a shroud. She pushed aside her veil, revealing a face that was proud and beautiful—but also hardened with suffering.

"Hera," Jason said.

"Welcome to my prison," said the goddess. "You will not die today, Jason. Your friends will see you through—for now."

"For now?" he asked.

Hera gestured at the tendrils of her cage. "There are worse trials to come. The very earth stirs against us."

"You're a goddess," Jason said. "Why can't you just escape?"

Hera smiled sadly. Her form began to glow, until her brilliance filled the cage with painful light. The air hummed with power, molecules splitting apart like a nuclear explosion. Jason suspected if he were actually there in the flesh, he would've been vaporized.

The cage should've been blasted to rubble. The ground should've split and the ruined house should've been leveled. But when the glow died, the cage hadn't budged. Nothing outside the bars had changed. Only Hera looked different—a little more stooped and tired.

"Some powers are even greater than the gods," she said. "I am not easily contained. I can be in many places at once. But when the greater part of my essence is caught, it is like a foot in a bear trap, you might say. I can't escape, and I am concealed from the eyes of the other gods. Only you can find me, and I grow weaker by the day."

"Then why did you come here?" Jason asked. "How were you caught?"

The goddess sighed. "I could not stay idle. Your father

Jupiter believes he can withdraw from the world, and thus lull our enemies back to sleep. He believes we Olympians have become too involved in the affairs of mortals, in the fates of our demigod children, especially since we agreed to claim them all after the war. He believes this is what has caused our enemies to stir. That is why he closed Olympus."

"But you don't agree."

"No," she said. "Often I do not understand my husband's moods or his decisions, but even for Zeus, this seemed paranoid. I cannot fathom why he was so insistent and so convinced. It was...unlike him. As Hera, I might have been content to follow my lord's wishes. But I am also Juno." Her image flickered, and Jason saw armor under her simple black robes, a goatskin cloak—the symbol of a Roman warrior—across her bronze mantle. "Juno Moneta they once called me —Juno, the One Who Warns. I was guardian of the state, patron of Eternal Rome. I could not sit by while the descendants of my people were attacked. I sensed danger at this sacred spot. A voice—" She hesitated. "A voice told me I should come here. Gods do not have what you might call a conscience, nor do we have dreams; but the voice was like that—soft and persistent, warning me to come here. And so the same day Zeus closed Olympus, I slipped away without telling him my plans, so he could not stop me. And I came here to investigate."

"It was a trap," Jason guessed.

The goddess nodded. "Only too late did I realize how quickly the earth was stirring. I was even more foolish than Jupiter—a slave to my own impulses. This is exactly how it happened the first time. I was taken captive by the giants, and my imprisonment started a war. Now our enemies rise again. The gods can only defeat them with the help of the greatest living heroes. And the one whom the giants serve . . . *she* cannot be defeated at all—only kept asleep."

"I don't understand."

"You will soon," Hera said.

The cage began to constrict, the tendrils spiraling tighter. Hera's form shivered like a candle flame in the breeze. Outside the cage, Jason could see shapes gathering at the edge of the pool—lumbering humanoids with hunched backs and bald heads. Unless Jason's eyes were tricking him—they had more than one set of arms. He heard wolves too, but not the wolves he'd seen with Lupa. He could tell from their howls this was a different pack—hungrier, more aggressive, out for blood.

"Hurry, Jason," Hera said. "My keepers approach, and you begin to wake. I will not be strong enough to appear to you again, even in dreams."

"Wait," he said. "Boreas told us you'd made a dangerous gamble. What did he mean?"

Hera's eyes looked wild, and Jason wondered if she really *had* done something crazy.

"An exchange," she said. "The only way to bring peace. The enemy counts on our divisions, and if we are divided, we *will* be destroyed. You are my peace offering, Jason—a bridge to overcome millennia of hatred."

"What? I don't—"

"I cannot tell you more," Hera said. "You have only lived

this long because I have taken your memory. Find this place. Return to your starting point. Your sister will help."

"Thalia?"

The scene began to dissolve. "Good-bye, Jason. Beware Chicago. Your most dangerous mortal enemy waits there. If you are to die, it will be by her hand."

"Who?" he demanded.

But Hera's image faded, and Jason awoke.

His eyes snapped open. "Cyclops!"

"Whoa, sleepyhead." Piper sat behind him on the bronze dragon, holding his waist to keep him balanced. Leo sat in front, driving. They flew peacefully through the winter sky as if nothing had happened.

"D-Detroit," Jason stammered. "Didn't we crash-land? I thought—"

"It's okay," Leo said. "We got away, but you got a nasty concussion. How you feeling?"

Jason's head throbbed. He remembered the factory, then walking down the catwalk, then a creature looming over him —a face with one eye, a massive fist—and everything went black.

"How did you—the Cyclops—"

"Leo ripped them apart," Piper said. "He was amazing. He can summon fire—"

"It was nothing," Leo said quickly.

Piper laughed. "Shut up, Valdez. I'm going to tell him. Get over it."

And she did—how Leo single-handedly defeated the Cyclopes family; how they freed Jason, then noticed the Cyclopes starting to re-form; how Leo had replaced the dragon's wiring and gotten them back in the air just as they'd started to hear the Cyclopes roaring for vengeance inside the factory.

Jason was impressed. Taking out three Cyclopes with nothing but a tool kit? Not bad. It didn't exactly scare him to hear how close he'd come to death, but it did make him feel horrible. He'd stepped right into an ambush and spent the whole fight knocked out while his friends fended for themselves. What kind of quest leader was he?

When Piper told him about the other kid the Cyclopes claimed to have eaten, the one in the purple shirt who spoke Latin, Jason felt like his head was going to explode. A son of Mercury...Jason felt like he should know that kid, but the name was missing from his mind.

"I'm not alone, then," he said. "There are others like me."

"Jason," Piper said, "you were never alone. You've got us."

"I—I know...but something Hera said. I was having a dream...."

He told them what he'd seen, and what the goddess had said inside her cage.

"An exchange?" Piper asked. "What does that mean?"

Jason shook his head. "But Hera's gamble is *me.* Just by sending me to Camp Half-Blood, I have a feeling she broke some kind of rule, something that could blow up in a big way—"

"Or save us," Piper said hopefully. "That bit about the sleeping enemy—that sounds like the lady Leo told us about."

Leo cleared his throat. "About that . . . she kind of appeared to me back in Detroit, in a pool of Porta-Potty sludge."

Jason wasn't sure he'd heard that right. "Did you say . . . Porta-Potty?"

Leo told them about the big face in the factory yard. "I don't know if she's completely unkillable," he said, "but she cannot be defeated by toilet seats. I can vouch for that. She wanted me to betray you guys, and I was like, 'Pfft, right, I'm gonna listen to a face in the potty sludge.'"

"She's trying to divide us." Piper slipped her arms from around Jason's waist. He could sense her tension without even looking at her.

"What's wrong?" he asked.

"I just . . . Why are they toying with us? Who is this lady, and how is she connected to Enceladus?"

"Enceladus?" Jason didn't think he'd heard that name before.

"I mean . . ." Piper's voice quavered. "That's one of the giants. Just one of the names I could remember."

Jason got the feeling there was a lot more bothering her, but he decided he not to press her. She'd had a rough morning.

Leo scratched his head. "Well, I dunno about Enchiladas—"

"Enceladus," Piper corrected.

"Whatever. But Old Potty Face mentioned another name. Porpoise Fear, or something?"

"Porphyrion?" Piper asked. "He was the giant king, I think."

Jason envisioned that dark spire in the old reflecting pool —growing larger as Hera got weaker. "I'm going to take wild guess," he said. "In the old stories, Porphyrion kidnapped Hera. That was the first shot in the war between the giants and the gods."

"I think so," Piper agreed. "But those myths are really garbled and conflicted. It's almost like nobody wanted that story to survive. I just remember there was a war, and the giants were almost impossible to kill."

"Heroes and gods had to work together," Jason said. "That's what Hera told me."

"Kind of hard to do," Leo grumbled, "if the gods won't even talk to us."

They flew west, and Jason became lost in his thoughts—all of them bad. He wasn't sure how much time passed before the dragon dove through a break in the clouds, and below them, glittering in the winter sun, was a city at the edge of a massive lake. A crescent of skyscrapers lined the shore. Behind them, stretching out to the western horizon, was a vast grid of snow-covered neighborhoods and roads.

"Chicago," Jason said.

He thought about what Hera had said in his dream. His worst mortal enemy would be waiting here. If he was going to die, it would be by her hand.

"One problem down," Leo said. "We got here alive. Now, how do we find the storm spirits?"

Jason saw a flash of movement below them. At first he thought it was a small plane, but it was too small, too dark and fast. The thing spiraled toward the skyscrapers, weaving and changing shape—and, just for a moment it became the smoky figure of a horse.

"How about we follow that one," Jason suggested, "and see where it goes?"

XXVI

JASON

JASON WAS AFRAID THEY'D LOSE THEIR TARGET. The *ventus* moved like . . . well, like the wind.

"Speed up!" he urged.

"Bro," Leo said, "if I get any closer, he'll spot us. Bronze dragon ain't exactly a stealth plane."

"Slow down!" Piper yelped.

The storm spirit dove into the grid of downtown streets. Festus tried to follow, but his wingspan was way too wide. His left wing clipped the edge of a building, slicing off a stone gargoyle before Leo pulled up.

"Get above the buildings," Jason suggested. "We'll track him from there."

"You want to drive this thing?" Leo grumbled, but he did what Jason asked.

After a few minutes, Jason spotted the storm spirit again, zipping through the streets with no apparent purpose—blowing over pedestrians, ruffling flags, making cars swerve.

"Oh great," Piper said. "There're two."

She was right. A second *ventus* blasted around the corner of the Renaissance Hotel and linked up with the first. They wove together in a chaotic dance, shooting to the top of a skyscraper, bending a radio tower, and diving back down toward the street.

"Those guys do *not* need any more caffeine," Leo said.

"I guess Chicago's a good place to hang out," Piper said. "Nobody's going to question a couple more evil winds."

"More than a couple," Jason said. "Look."

The dragon circled over a wide avenue next to a lakeside park. Storm spirits were converging—at least a dozen of them, whirling around a big public art installation.

"Which one do you think is Dylan?" Leo asked. "I wanna throw something at him."

But Jason focused on the art installation. The closer they got to it, the faster his heart beat. It was just a public fountain, but it was unpleasantly familiar. Two five-story monoliths rose from either end of a long granite reflecting pool. The monoliths seemed to be built of video screens, flashing the combined image of a giant face that spewed water into the pool.

Maybe it was just a coincidence, but it looked like a high-tech, super-size version of that ruined reflecting pool he'd seen in his dreams, with those two dark masses jutting from either end. As Jason watched, the image on the screens changed to a woman's face with her eyes closed.

"Leo..." he said nervously.

"I see her," Leo said. "I don't like her, but I see her."

Then the screens went dark. The *venti* swirled together into a single funnel cloud and skittered across the fountain, kicking up a waterspout almost as high as the monoliths. They got to its center, popped off a drain cover, and disappeared underground.

"Did they just go down a drain?" Piper asked. "How are we supposed to follow them?"

"Maybe we shouldn't," Leo said. "That fountain thing is giving me seriously bad vibes. And aren't we supposed to, like, beware the earth?"

Jason felt the same way, but they had to follow. It was their only way forward. They had to find Hera, and they now had only two days until the solstice.

"Put us down in that park," he suggested. "We'll check it out on foot."

Festus landed in an open area between the lake and the skyline. The signs said Grant Park, and Jason imagined it would've been a nice place in the summer; but now it was a field of ice, snow, and salted walkways. The dragon's hot metal feet hissed as they touched down. Festus flapped his wings unhappily and shot fire into the sky, but there was no one around to notice. The wind coming off the lake was bitter cold. Anyone with sense would be inside. Jason's eyes stung so badly, he could barely see.

They dismounted, and Festus the dragon stomped his feet. One of his ruby eyes flickered, so it looked like he was blinking.

"Is that normal?" Jason asked.

Leo pulled a rubber mallet from his tool bag. He whacked the dragon's bad eye, and the light went back to normal. "Yes," Leo said. "Festus can't hang around here, though, in the middle of the park. They'll arrest him for loitering. Maybe if I had a dog whistle..."

He rummaged in his tool belt, but came up with nothing.

"Too specialized?" he guessed. "Okay, give me a safety whistle. They got that in lots of machine shops."

This time, Leo pulled out a big plastic orange whistle. "Coach Hedge would be jealous! Okay, Festus, listen." Leo blew the whistle. The shrill sound probably rolled all the way across Lake Michigan. "You hear that, come find me, okay? Until then, you fly wherever you want. Just try not to barbecue any pedestrians."

The dragon snorted—hopefully in agreement. Then he spread his wings and launched into the air.

Piper took one step and winced. "Ah!"

"Your ankle?" Jason felt bad he'd forgotten about her injury back in the Cyclops factory. "That nectar we gave you might be wearing off."

"It's fine." She shivered, and Jason remembered his promise to get her a new snowboarding coat. He hoped he lived long enough to find her one. She took a few more steps with only a slight limp, but Jason could tell she was trying not to grimace.

"Let's get out of the wind," he suggested.

"Down a drain?" Piper shuddered. "Sounds cozy."

They wrapped themselves up as best they could and headed toward the fountain.

• • •

According to the plaque, it was called Crown Fountain. All the water had emptied out except for a few patches that were starting to freeze. It didn't seem right to Jason that the fountain would have water in it in the winter anyway. Then again, those big monitors had flashed the face of their mysterious enemy Dirt Woman. Nothing about this place was right.

They stepped to the center of the pool. No spirits tried to stop them. The giant monitor walls stayed dark. The drain hole was easily big enough for a person, and a maintenance ladder led down into the gloom.

Jason went first. As he climbed, he braced himself for horrible sewer smells, but it wasn't that bad. The ladder dropped into a brickwork tunnel running north to south. The air was warm and dry, with only a trickle of water on the floor.

Piper and Leo climbed down after him.

"Are all sewers this nice?" Piper wondered.

"No," Leo said. "Trust me."

Jason frowned. "How do you know—"

"Hey, man, I ran away six times. I've slept in some weird places, okay? Now, which way do we go?"

Jason tilted his head, listening, then pointed south. "That way."

"How can you be sure?" Piper asked.

"There's a draft blowing south," Jason said. "Maybe the *venti* went with the flow."

It wasn't much of a lead, but nobody offered anything better.

Unfortunately, as soon as they started walking, Piper stumbled. Jason had to catch her.

"Stupid ankle," she cursed.

"Let's rest," Jason decided. "We could all use it. We've been going nonstop for over a day. Leo, can you pull any food from that tool belt besides breath mints?"

"Thought you'd never ask. Chef Leo is on it!"

Piper and Jason sat on a brick ledge while Leo shuffled through his pack.

Jason was glad to rest. He was still tired and dizzy, and hungry, too. But mostly, he wasn't eager to face whatever lay ahead. He turned his gold coin in his fingers.

If you are to die, Hera had warned, *it will be by her hand.*

Whoever "her" was. After Khione, the Cyclops mother, and the weird sleeping lady, the last thing Jason needed was another psycho villainess in his life.

"It wasn't your fault," Piper said.

He looked at her blankly. "What?"

"Getting jumped by the Cyclopes," she said. "It wasn't your fault."

He looked down at the coin in his palm. "I was stupid. I left you alone and walked into a trap. I should've known...."

He didn't finish. There were too many things he should have known—who he was, how to fight monsters, how Cyclopes lured their victims by mimicking voices and hiding in shadows and a hundred other tricks. All that information was supposed to be in his head. He could feel the places it should be—like empty pockets. If Hera wanted him to succeed, why had she stolen the memories that could help him? She claimed his amnesia had kept him alive, but that made no sense. He was starting to understand why Annabeth had wanted to leave the goddess in her cage.

"Hey." Piper nudged his arm. "Cut yourself some slack. Just because you're the son of Zeus doesn't mean you're a one-man army."

A few feet away, Leo lit a small cooking fire. He hummed as he pulled supplies out of his pack and his tool belt.

In the firelight, Piper's eyes seemed to dance. Jason had been studying them for days now, and he still couldn't decide what color they were.

"I know this must suck for you," he said. "Not just the quest, I mean. The way I appeared on the bus, the Mist messing with your mind, and making you think I was . . . you know."

She dropped her gaze. "Yeah, well. None of us asked for this. It's not your fault."

She tugged at the little braids on each side of her head. Again, Jason thought how glad he was that she'd lost the Aphrodite blessing. With the makeup and the dress and the perfect hair, she'd looked about twenty-five, glamorous, and completely out of his league. He'd never thought of beauty as a form of power, but that's the way Piper had seemed—*powerful.*

He liked regular Piper better—someone he could hang out with. But the weird thing was, he couldn't quite get that other image out of his head. It hadn't been an illusion. That side of Piper was there too. She just did her best to hide it.

"Back in the factory," Jason said, "you were you going to say something about your dad."

She traced her finger over the bricks, almost like she was writing out a scream she didn't want to vocalize. "Was I?"

"Piper," he said, "he's in some kind of trouble, isn't it?"

Over at the fire, Leo stirred some sizzling bell peppers and meat in a pan. "Yeah, baby! Almost there."

Piper looked on the verge of tears. "Jason...I can't talk about it."

"We're your friends. Let us help."

That seemed to make her feel worse. She took a shaky breath. "I wish I could, but—"

"And bingo!" Leo announced.

He came over with three plates stacked on his arms like a waiter. Jason had no idea where he'd gotten all the food, or how he'd put it together so fast, but it looked amazing: pepper and beef tacos with chips and salsa.

"Leo," Piper said in amazement. "How did you—?"

"Chef Leo's Taco Garage is fixing you up!" he said proudly. "And by the way, it's tofu, not beef, beauty queen, so don't freak. Just dig in!"

Jason wasn't sure about tofu, but the tacos tasted as good as they smelled. While they ate, Leo tried to lighten the mood and joke around. Jason was grateful Leo was with them. It made being with Piper a little less intense and uncomfortable. At the same time, he kind of wished he *was* alone with her; but he chided himself for feeling that way.

After Piper ate, Jason encouraged her to get some sleep. Without another word, she curled up and put her head in his lap. In two seconds she was snoring.

Jason looked up at Leo, who was obviously trying not to laugh.

They sat in silence for a few minutes, drinking lemonade Leo had made from canteen water and powdered mix.

"Good, huh?" Leo grinned.

"You should start a stand," Jason said. "Make some serious coin."

But as he stared at the embers of the fire, something began to bother him. "Leo... about this fire stuff you can do... is it true?"

Leo's smile faltered. "Yeah, well..." He opened his hand. A small ball of flame burst to life, dancing across his palm.

"That is so cool," Jason said. "Why didn't you say anything?"

Leo closed his hand and the fire went out. "Didn't want to look like a freak."

"I have lightning and wind powers," Jason reminded him. "Piper can turn beautiful and charm people into giving her BMWs. You're no more a freak than we are. And, hey, maybe you can fly, too. Like jump off a building and yell, 'Flame on!'"

Leo snorted. "If I did that, you would see a flaming kid falling to his death, and I would be yelling something a little stronger than 'Flame on!' Trust me, Hephaestus cabin doesn't see fire powers as cool. Nyssa told me they're super rare. When a demigod like me comes around, bad things happen. *Really* bad."

"Maybe it's the other way around," Jason suggested. "Maybe people with special gifts show up when bad things are happening because that's when they're needed most."

Leo cleared away the plates. "Maybe. But I'm telling you ... it's not always a gift."

Jason fell silent. "You're talking about your mom, aren't you? The night she died."

Leo didn't answer. He didn't have to. The fact that he was quiet, not joking around—that told Jason enough.

"Leo, her death wasn't your fault. Whatever happened that night—it wasn't because you could summon fire. This Dirt Woman, whoever she is, has been trying to ruin you for years, mess up your confidence, take away everything you care about. She's trying to make you feel like a failure. You're not. You're important."

"That's what she said." Leo looked up, his eyes full of pain. "She said I was meant to do something important—something that would make or break that big prophecy about the seven demigods. That's what scares me. I don't know if I'm up to it."

Jason wanted to tell him everything would be all right, but it would've sounded fake. Jason didn't know *what* would happen. They were demigods, which meant sometimes things didn't end okay. Sometimes you got eaten by the Cyclops.

If you asked most kids, "Hey, you want to summon fire or lightning or magical makeup?" they'd think it sounded pretty cool. But those powers went along with hard stuff, like sitting in a sewer in the middle of winter, running from monsters, losing your memory, watching your friends almost get cooked, and having dreams that warned you of your own death.

Leo poked at the remnants of his fire, turning over red-hot

coals with his bare hand. "You ever wonder about the other four demigods? I mean . . . if we're three of the ones from the Great Prophecy, who are the others? Where are they?"

Jason had thought about it, all right, but he tried to push it out of his mind. He had a horrible suspicion that *he* would be expected to lead those other demigods, and he was afraid he would fail.

You'll tear each other apart, Boreas had promised.

Jason had been trained never to show fear. He was sure of that from his dream with the wolves. He was supposed to act confident, even if he didn't feel it. But Leo and Piper were depending on him, and he was terrified of failing them. If he had to lead a group of six—six who might not get along—that would be even worse.

"I don't know," he said at last. "I guess the other four will show up when the time is right. Who knows? Maybe they're on some other quest right now."

Leo grunted. "I bet their sewer is nicer than ours."

The draft picked up, blowing toward the south end of the tunnel.

"Get some rest, Leo," Jason said. "I'll take first watch."

It was hard to measure time, but Jason figured his friends slept about four hours. Jason didn't mind. Now that he was resting, he didn't really feel the need for more sleep. He'd been conked out long enough on the dragon. Plus, he needed time to think about the quest, his sister Thalia, and Hera's warnings. He also didn't mind Piper's using him for a pillow. She had a cute way of breathing when she slept—inhaling through the nose, exhaling with a little puff through the mouth. He was almost disappointed when she woke up.

Finally they broke camp and started down the tunnel.

It twisted and turned and seemed to go on forever. Jason wasn't sure what to expect at the end—a dungeon, a mad scientist's lab, or maybe a sewer reservoir where all Porta-Potty sludge ends up, forming an evil toilet face large enough to swallow the world.

Instead, they found polished steel elevator doors, each one engraved with a cursive letter *M*. Next to the elevator was a directory, like for a department store.

"M for Macy's?" Piper guessed. "I think they have one in downtown Chicago."

"Or Monocle Motors still?" Leo said. "Guys, read the directory. It's messed up."

Parking, Kennels, Main Entrance	Sewer Level
Furnishings and Café M	1
Women's Fashion and Magical Appliances	2
Men's Wear and Weaponry	3
Cosmetics, Potions, Poisons & Sundries	4

"Kennels for what?" Piper said. "And what kind of department store has its entrance in a sewer?"

"Or sells poisons," Leo said. "Man, what does 'sundries' even mean? Is that like underwear?"

Jason took a deep breath. "When in doubt, start at the top."

• • •

The doors slid open on the fourth floor, and the scent of perfume wafted into the elevator. Jason stepped out first, sword ready.

"Guys," he said. "You've got to see this."

Piper joined him and caught her breath. "This is *not* Macy's."

The department store looked like the inside of a kaleidoscope. The entire ceiling was a stained glass mosaic with astrological signs around a giant sun. The daylight streaming through it washed everything in a thousand different colors. The upper floors made a ring of balconies around a huge central atrium, so they could see all the way down to the ground floor. Gold railings glittered so brightly, they were hard to look at.

Aside from the stained glass ceiling and the elevator, Jason couldn't see any other windows or doors, but two sets of glass escalators ran between the levels. The carpeting was a riot of oriental patterns and colors, and the racks of merchandise were just as bizarre. There was too much to take it at once, but Jason saw normal stuff like shirt racks and shoe trees mixed in with armored manikins, beds of nails, and fur coats that seemed to be moving.

Leo stepped to the railing and looked down. "Check it out."

In the middle of the atrium a fountain sprayed water twenty feet into the air, changing color from red to yellow to blue. The pool glittered with gold coins, and on either side of the fountain stood a gilded cage—like an oversize canary cage.

Inside one, a miniature hurricane swirled, and lightning flashed. Somebody had imprisoned the storm spirits, and the cage shuddered as they tried to get out. In the other, frozen like a statue, was a short, buff satyr, holding a tree-branch club.

"Coach Hedge!" Piper said. "We've got to get down there."

A voice said, "May I help you find something?"

All three of them jumped back.

A woman had just *appeared* in front of them. She wore an elegant black dress with diamond jewelry, and she looked like a retired fashion model—maybe fifty years old, though it was hard for Jason to judge. Her long dark hair swept over one shoulder, and her face was gorgeous in that surreal super-model way—thin and haughty and cold, not quite human. With their long red-painted nails, her fingers looked more like talons.

She smiled. "I'm so happy to see new customers. How may I help you?"

Leo glanced at Jason like, *All yours.*

"Um," Jason started, "is this your store?"

The woman nodded. "I found it abandoned, you know. I understand so many stores are, these days. I decided it would make the perfect place. I love collecting tasteful objects, helping people, and offering quality goods at a reasonable price. So this seemed a good . . . how do you say . . . first acquisition in this country."

She spoke with a pleasing accent, but Jason couldn't guess where from. Clearly she wasn't hostile, though. Jason started to relax. Her voice was rich and exotic. Jason wanted to hear more.

"So you're new to America?" he asked.

"I am . . . new," the woman agreed. "I am the Princess of Colchis. My friends call me Your Highness. Now, what are you looking for?"

Jason had heard of rich foreigners buying American department stores. Of course most of the time they didn't sell poisons, living fur coats, storm spirits, or satyrs, but still —with a nice voice like that, the Princess of Colchis couldn't be all bad.

Piper poked him in the ribs. "Jason . . ."

"Um, right. Actually, Your Highness . . ." He pointed to the gilded cage on the first floor. "That's our friend down there, Gleeson Hedge. The satyr. Could we . . . have him back, please?"

"Of course!" the princess agreed immediately. "I would love to show you my inventory. First, may I know your names?"

Jason hesitated. It seemed like a bad idea to give out their names. A memory tugged at the back of his mind—something Hera had warned him about, but it seemed fuzzy.

On the other hand, Her Highness was on the verge of cooperating. If they could get what they wanted without a fight, that would be better. Besides, this lady didn't seem like an enemy.

Piper started to say, "Jason, I wouldn't—"

"This is Piper," he said. "This is Leo. I'm Jason."

The princess fixed her eyes on him and, just for a moment,

her face literally glowed, blazing with so much anger, Jason could see her skull beneath her skin. Jason's mind was getting blurrier, but he knew something didn't seem right. Then the moment passed, and Her Highness looked like a normal elegant woman again, with a cordial smile and a soothing voice.

"Jason. What an interesting name," she said, her eyes as cold as the Chicago wind. "I think we'll have to make a special deal for you. Come, children. Let's go shopping."

XXVII

PIPER

PIPER WANTED TO RUN FOR THE ELEVATOR.

Her second choice: attack the weird princess now, because she was sure a fight was coming. The way the lady's face glowed when she'd heard Jason's name had been bad enough. Now Her Highness was smiling like nothing had happened, and Jason and Leo didn't seem to think anything was wrong.

The princess gestured toward the cosmetics counter. "Shall we start with the potions?"

"Cool," Jason said.

"Guys," Piper interrupted, "we're here to get the storm spirits and Coach Hedge. If this—*princess*—is really our friend—"

"Oh, I'm better than a friend, my dear," Her Highness said. "I'm a saleswoman." Her diamonds sparkled, and her eyes glittered like a snake's—cold and dark. "Don't worry. We'll work our way down to the first floor, eh?"

Leo nodded eagerly. "Sure, yeah! That sounds okay. Right, Piper?"

Piper did her best to stare daggers at him: *No, it is not okay!*

"Of course it's okay." Her Highness put her hands on Leo's and Jason's shoulders and steered them toward the cosmetics. "Come along, boys."

Piper didn't have much choice except to follow.

She hated department stores—mostly because she'd gotten caught stealing from several of them. Well, not exactly *caught*, and not exactly *stealing*. She'd talked salesmen into giving her computers, new boots, a gold ring, once even a lawn mower, though she had no idea why she wanted one. She never kept the stuff. She just did it to get her dad's attention. Usually she talked her neighborhood UPS guy into taking the stuff back. But of course the salesmen she duped always came to their senses and called the police, who eventually tracked her down.

Anyway, she wasn't thrilled to be back in a department store—especially one run by a crazy princess who glowed in the dark.

"And here," the princess said, "is the finest assortment of magical mixtures anywhere."

The counter was crammed with bubbling beakers and smoking vials on tripods. Lining the display shelves were crystal flasks—some shaped like swans or honey bear dispensers. The liquids inside were every color, from glowing white to polka-dotted. And the smells—ugh! Some were pleasant, like fresh-baked cookies or roses, but they were mixed with the scents of burning tires, skunk spray, and gym lockers.

The princess pointed to a bloodred vial—a simple test tube with a cork stopper. "This one will heal any disease."

"Even cancer?" Leo asked. "Leprosy? Hangnails?"

"Any disease, sweet boy. And this vial"—she pointed to a swan-shaped container with blue liquid inside—"will kill you very painfully."

"Awesome," Jason said. His voice sounded dazed and sleepy.

"Jason," Piper said. "We've got a job to do. Remember?" She tried to put power into her words, to snap him out of his trance with charmspeak, but her voice sounded shaky even to her. This princess woman scared her too much, made her confidence crumble, just the way she'd felt back in the Aphrodite cabin with Drew.

"Job to do," Jason muttered. "Sure. But shopping first, okay?"

The princess beamed at him. "Then we have potions for resisting fire—"

"Got that covered," Leo said.

"Indeed?" The princess studied Leo's face more closely. "You don't appear to be wearing my trademark sunscreen... but no matter. We also have potions that cause blindness, insanity, sleep, or—"

"Wait." Piper was still staring at the red vial. "Could that potion cure lost memory?"

The princess narrowed her eyes. "Possibly. Yes. Quite

possibly. Why, my dear? Have you forgotten something important?"

Piper tried to keep her expression neutral, but if that vial could cure Jason's memory...

Do I really want that? she wondered.

If Jason found out who he was, he might not even be her friend. Hera had taken away his memories for a reason. She'd told him it was the only way he'd survive at Camp Half-Blood. What if Jason found out that he was their enemy, or something? He might come out of his amnesia and decide he hated Piper. He might have a girlfriend wherever he came from.

It doesn't matter, she decided, which kind of surprised her.

Jason always looked so anguished when he tried to remember things. Piper hated seeing him that way. She wanted to help him because she cared about him, even if that meant losing him. And maybe it would make this trip through Her Craziness's department store worthwhile.

"How much?" Piper asked.

The princess got a faraway look in her eyes. "Well, now... The price is always tricky. I love helping people. Honestly, I do. And I always keep my bargains, but sometimes people try to cheat me." Her gaze drifted to Jason. "Once, for instance, I met a handsome young man who wanted a treasure from my father's kingdom. We made a bargain, and I promised to help him steal it."

"From your own dad?" Jason still looked half in a trance, but the idea seemed to bother him.

"Oh, don't worry," the princess said. "I demanded a high

price. The young man had to take me away with him. He was quite good-looking, dashing, strong..." She looked at Piper. "I'm sure, my dear, you understand how one might be attracted to such a hero, and want to help him."

Piper tried to control her emotions, but she probably blushed. She got the creepiest feeling the princess could read her thoughts.

She also found the princess's story disturbingly familiar. Pieces of old myths she'd read with her dad started coming together, but this woman couldn't be the one she was thinking of.

"At any rate," Her Highness continued, "my hero had to do many impossible tasks, and I'm not bragging when I say he couldn't have done them without me. I betrayed my own family to win the hero his prize. And still he cheated me of my payment."

"Cheated?" Jason frowned, as if trying to remember something important.

"That's messed up," Leo said.

Her Highness patted his cheek affectionately. "I'm sure you don't need to worry, Leo. You seem honest. You would always pay a fair price, wouldn't you?"

Leo nodded. "What were we buying again? I'll take two."

Piper broke in: "So, the vial, Your Highness—how much?"

The princess assessed Piper's clothes, her face, her posture, as if putting a price tag on one slightly used demigod.

"Would you give anything for it, my dear?" the princess asked. "I sense that you would."

The words washed over Piper as powerfully as a good

surfing wave. The force of the suggestion nearly lifted her off her feet. She wanted to pay any price. She wanted to say yes.

Then her stomach twisted. Piper realized she was being charmspoken. She'd sensed something like it before, when Drew spoke at the campfire, but this was a thousand times more potent. No wonder her friends were dazed. Was *this* was what people felt when Piper used charmspeak? A feeling of guilt settled over her.

She summoned all her willpower. "No, I won't pay *any* price. But a fair price, maybe. After that, we need to leave. Right, guys?"

Just for a moment, her words seemed to have some effect. The boys looked confused.

"Leave?" Jason said.

"You mean . . . after shopping?" Leo asked.

Piper wanted to scream, but the princess tilted her head, examining Piper with newfound respect.

"Impressive," the princess said. "Not many people could resist my suggestions. Are you a child of Aphrodite, my dear? Ah, yes—I should have seen it. No matter. Perhaps we should shop a while longer before you decide what to buy, eh?"

"But the vial—"

"Now, boys." She turned to Jason and Leo. Her voice was so much more powerful than Piper's, so full of confidence, Piper didn't stand a chance. "Would you like to see more?"

"Sure," Jason said.

"Okay," Leo said.

"Excellent," the princess said. "You'll need all the help you can get if you're to make it to the Bay Area."

Piper's hand moved to her dagger. She thought about her dream of the mountaintop—the scene Enceladus had shown her, a place she knew, where she was supposed to betray her friends in two days.

"The Bay Area?" Piper said. "Why the Bay Area?"

The princess smiled. "Well, that's where they'll die, isn't it?"

Then she led them toward the escalators, Jason and Leo still looking excited to shop.

XXVIII

PIPER

PIPER CORNERED THE PRINCESS as Jason and Leo went off to check out the living fur coats.

"You want them shopping for their deaths?" Piper demanded.

"Mmm." The princess blew dust off a display case of swords. "I'm a seer, my dear. I know your little secret. But we don't want to dwell on that, do we? The boys are having such fun."

Leo laughed as he tried on a hat that seemed to be made from enchanted raccoon fur. Its ringed tail twitched, and its little legs wiggled frantically as Leo walked. Jason was ogling the men's sportswear. Boys interested in shopping for clothes? A definite sign they were under an evil spell.

Piper glared at the princess. "Who are you?"

"I told you, my dear. I'm the Princess of Colchis."

"Where's Colchis?"

The princess's expression turned a little sad. "Where *was*

Colchis, you mean. My father ruled the far shores of the Black Sea, as far to the east as a Greek ship could sail in those days. But Colchis is no more—lost eons ago."

"Eons?" Piper asked. The princess looked no more than fifty, but a bad feeling started settling over Piper—something King Boreas had mentioned back in Quebec. "How old are you?"

The princess laughed. "A lady should avoid asking or answering that question. Let's just say the, ah, immigration process to enter your country took quite a while. My patron finally brought me through. She made all this possible." The princess swept her hand around the department store.

Piper's mouth tasted like metal. "Your patron . . ."

"Oh, yes. She doesn't bring just anyone through, mind you—only those who have special talents, such as me. And really, she insists on so little—a store entrance that must be underground so she can, ah, monitor my clientele; and a favor now and then. In exchange for a new life? Really, it was the best bargain I'd made in centuries."

Run, Piper thought. *We have to get out of here.*

But before she could even turn her thoughts into words, Jason called, "Hey, check it out!"

From a rack labeled DISTRESSED CLOTHING, he held up a purple T-shirt like the one he'd worn on the school field trip —except this shirt looked as if it had been clawed by tigers.

Jason frowned. "Why does this look so familiar?"

"Jason, it's like *yours*," Piper said. "Now we really have to leave." But she wasn't sure he could even hear her anymore through the princess's enchantment.

"Nonsense," the princess said. "The boys aren't done, are they? And yes, my dear. Those shirts are very popular—trade-ins from previous customers. It suits you."

Leo picked up an orange Camp Half-Blood tee with a hole through the middle, as if it had been hit by a javelin. Next to that was a dented bronze breastplate pitted with corrosion—acid, maybe?—and a Roman toga slashed to pieces and stained with something that looked disturbingly like dried blood.

"Your Highness," Piper said, trying to control her nerves. "Why don't you tell the boys how you betrayed your family? I'm sure they'd like to hear that story."

Her words didn't have any effect on the princess, but the boys turned, suddenly interested.

"More story?" Leo asked.

"I like more story!" Jason agreed.

The princess flashed Piper an irritated look. "Oh, one will do strange things for love, Piper. You should know that. I fell for that young hero, in fact, because your mother Aphrodite had me under a spell. If it wasn't for her—but I can't hold a grudge against a goddess, can I?"

The princess's tone made her meaning clear: *I can take it out on you.*

"But that hero took you with him when he fled Colchis," Piper remembered. "Didn't he, Your Highness? He married you just as he promised."

The look in the princess's eyes made Piper want to apologize, but she didn't back down.

"At first," Her Highness admitted, "it seemed he would

keep his word. But even after I helped him steal my father's treasure, he *still* needed my help. As we fled, my brother's fleet came after us. His warships overtook us. He would have destroyed us, but I convinced my brother to come aboard our ship first and talk under a flag of truce. He trusted me."

"And you killed your own brother," Piper said, the horrible story all coming back to her, along with a name—an infamous name that began with the letter *M*.

"What?" Jason stirred. For a moment he looked almost like himself. "Killed your own—"

"No," the princess snapped. "Those stories are lies. It was my new husband and his men who killed my brother, though they couldn't have done it without my deception. They threw his body into the sea, and the pursuing fleet had to stop and search for it so they could give my brother a proper burial. This gave us time to get away. All this, I did for my husband. And he forgot our bargain. He betrayed me in the end."

Jason still looked uncomfortable. "What did he do?"

The princess held the sliced-up toga against Jason's chest, as if measuring him for an assassination. "Don't you know the story, my boy? You of all people should. You were named for him."

"Jason," Piper said. "The *original* Jason. But then you're —you should be dead!"

The princess smiled. "As I said, a new life in a new country. Certainly I made mistakes. I turned my back on my own people. I was called a traitor, a thief, a liar, a murderess. But I acted out of love." She turned to the boys and gave them a pitiful look, batting her eyelashes. Piper could feel the sorcery washing over them, taking control more firmly than ever. "Wouldn't you do the same for someone you loved, my dears?"

"Oh, sure," Jason said.

"Okay," Leo said.

"Guys!" Piper ground her teeth in frustration. "Don't you see who she is? Don't you—"

"Let's continue, shall we?" the princess said breezily. "I believe you wanted to talk about a price for the storm spirits —and your satyr."

Leo got distracted on the second floor with the appliances.

"No way," he said. "Is that an armored forge?"

Before Piper could stop him, he hopped off the escalator and ran over to a big oval oven that looked like a barbecue on steroids.

When they caught up with him, the princess said, "You have good taste. This is the H-2000, designed by Hephaestus himself. Hot enough to melt Celestial bronze or Imperial gold."

Jason flinched as if he recognized that term. "Imperial gold?"

The princess nodded. "Yes, my dear. Like that weapon so cleverly concealed in your pocket. To be properly forged, Imperial gold had to be consecrated in the Temple of Jupiter on Capitoline Hill in Rome. Quite a powerful and rare metal, but like the Roman emperors, quite volatile. Be sure never to break that blade...." She smiled pleasantly. "Rome was *after* my time, of course, but I do hear stories. And now over here—this golden throne is one of my finest luxury items.

Hephaestus made it as a punishment for his mother, Hera. Sit in it and you'll be immediately trapped."

Leo apparently took this as an order. He began walking toward it in a trance.

"Leo, don't!" Piper warned.

He blinked. "How much for both?"

"Oh, the seat I could let you have for five great deeds. The forge, seven years of servitude. And for only a bit of your strength—" She led Leo into the appliance section, giving him prices on various items.

Piper didn't want to leave him alone with her, but she had to try reasoning with Jason. She pulled him aside and slapped him across the face.

"Ow," he muttered sleepily. "What was that for?"

"Snap out of it!" Piper hissed.

"What do you mean?"

"She's charmspeaking you. Can't you feel it?"

He knit his eyebrows. "She seems okay."

"She's not okay! She shouldn't even be alive! She was married to Jason—the *other* Jason—three thousand years ago. Remember what Boreas said—something about the souls no longer being confined to Hades? It's not just monsters who can't stay dead. She's come back from the Underworld!"

Jason shook his head uneasily. "She's not a ghost."

"No, she's worse! She's—"

"Children." The princess was back with Leo in tow. "If you please, we will now see what you came for. That is what you want, yes?"

Piper had to choke back a scream. She was tempted to

pull out her dagger and take on this witch herself, but she didn't like her chances—not in the middle of Her Highness's department store while her friends were under a spell. Piper couldn't even be sure they'd take her side in a fight. She had to figure out a better plan.

They took the escalator down to the base of the fountain. For the first time, Piper noticed two large bronze sundials —each about the size of a trampoline—inlaid on the marble tile floor to the north and south of the fountain. The gilded oversize canary cages stood to the east and west, and the farthest one held the storm spirits. They were so densely packed, spinning around like a super-concentrated tornado, that Piper couldn't tell how many there were—dozens, at least.

"Hey," Leo said, "Coach Hedge looks okay!"

They ran to the nearest canary cage. The old satyr seemed to have been petrified at the moment he was sucked into the sky above the Grand Canyon. He was frozen mid-shout, his club raised over his head like he was ordering the gym class to drop and give him fifty. His curly hair stuck up at odd angles. If Piper just concentrated on certain details—the bright orange polo shirt, the wispy goatee, the whistle around his neck—she could imagine Coach Hedge as his good old annoying self. But it was hard to ignore the stubby horns on his head, and the fact that he had furry goat legs and hooves instead of workout pants and Nikes.

"Yes," the princess said. "I always keep my wares in good condition. We can certainly barter for the storm spirits and the satyr. A package deal. If we come to terms, I'll even throw in the vial of healing potion, and you can go in peace." She gave Piper a shrewd look. "That's better than starting unpleas-antness, isn't it, dear?"

Don't trust her, warned a voice in her head. If Piper was right about this lady's identity, nobody would be leaving in peace. A fair deal wasn't possible. It was all a trick. But her friends were looking at her, nodding urgently and mouthing, *Say yes!* Piper needed more to time to think.

"We can negotiate," she said.

"Totally!" Leo agreed. "Name your price."

"Leo!" Piper snapped.

The princess chuckled. "Name my price? Perhaps not the best haggling strategy, my boy, but at least you know a thing's value. Freedom is very valuable indeed. You would ask me to release this satyr, who attacked my storm winds—"

"Who attacked us," Piper interjected.

Her Highness shrugged. "As I said, my patron asks me for small favors from time to time. Sending the storm spirits to abduct you—that was one. I assure you it was nothing per-sonal. And no harm done, as you came here, in the end, of your own free will! At any rate, you want the satyr freed, and you want my storm spirits—who are very valuable servants, by the way—so you can hand them over to that tyrant Aeolus. Doesn't seem quite fair, does it? The price will be high."

Piper could see that her friends were ready to offer any-thing, promise anything. Before they could speak, she played her last card.

"You're Medea," she said. "You helped the original Jason steal the Golden Fleece. You're one of the most evil villains in Greek mythology. Jason, Leo—don't trust her."

Piper put all the intensity she could gather into those words. She was utterly sincere, and it seemed to have some effect. Jason stepped away from the sorceress.

Leo scratched his head and looked around like he was coming out of a dream.

"What are we doing, again?"

"Boys!" The princess spread her hands in a welcoming gesture. Her diamond jewelry glittered, and her painted fingers curled like blood-tipped claws. "It's true, I'm Medea. But I'm so misunderstood. Oh, Piper, my dear, you don't know what it was like for women in the old days. We had no power, no leverage. Often we couldn't even choose our own husbands. But *I* was different. I chose my own destiny by becoming a sorceress. Is that so wrong? I made a pact with Jason: my help to win the fleece, in exchange for his love. A fair deal. He became a famous hero! Without me, he would've died unknown on the shores of Colchis."

Jason—Piper's Jason—scowled. "Then...you really did die three thousand years ago? You came back from the Underworld?"

"Death no longer holds me, young hero," Medea said. "Thanks to my patron, I am flesh and blood again."

"You...re-formed?" Leo blinked. "Like a monster?"

Medea spread her fingers, and steam hissed from her nails, like water splashed on hot iron. "You have no idea what's happening, do you, my dears? It is so much worse than a stirring of monsters from Tartarus. My patron knows that giants and monsters are not her greatest servants. *I* am mortal. I learn from my mistakes. And now that I have returned to the living, I will not be cheated again. Now, here is my price for what you ask."

"Guys," Piper said. "The original Jason left Medea because she was crazy and bloodthirsty."

"Lies!" Medea said.

"On the way back from Colchis, Jason's ship landed at another kingdom, and Jason agreed to dump Medea and marry the king's daughter."

"After I bore him two children!" Medea said. "Still he broke his promise! I ask you, was that right?"

Jason and Leo dutifully shook their heads, but Piper wasn't through.

"It may not have been right," she said, "but neither was Medea's revenge. She murdered her own children to get back at Jason. She poisoned his new wife and fled the kingdom."

Medea snarled. "An invention to ruin my reputation! The people of the Corinth—that unruly mob—killed my children and drove me out. Jason did nothing to protect me. He robbed me of everything. So yes, I sneaked back into the palace and poisoned his lovely new bride. It was only fair—a suitable price."

"You're insane," Piper said.

"I am the victim!" Medea wailed. "I died with my dreams shattered, but no longer. I know now not to trust heroes. When they come asking for treasures, they will pay a heavy price. Especially when the one asking has the name of Jason!"

The fountain turned bright red. Piper drew her dagger, but her hand was shaking almost too badly to hold it. "Jason, Leo—it's time to go. *Now.*"

"Before you've closed the deal?" Medea asked. "What of your quest, boys? And my price is so easy. Did you know this fountain is magic? If a dead man were to be thrown into it, even if he was chopped to pieces, he would pop back out fully formed—stronger and more powerful than ever."

"Seriously?" Leo asked.

"Leo, she's lying," Piper said. "She did that trick with somebody before—a king, I think. She convinced his daughters to cut him to pieces so he could come out of the water young and healthy again, but it just killed him!"

"Ridiculous," Medea said, and Piper could hear the power charged in every syllable. "Leo, Jason—my price is so simple. Why don't you two fight? If you get injured, or even killed, no problem. We'll just throw you into the fountain and you'll be better than ever. You *do* want to fight, don't you? You resent each other!"

"Guys, no!" Piper said. But they were already glaring at each other, as if it was just dawning on them how they really felt.

Piper had never felt more helpless. Now she understood what real sorcery looked like. She'd always thought magic meant wands and fireballs, but this was worse. Medea didn't just rely on poisons and potions. Her most potent weapon was her voice.

Leo scowled. "Jason's always the star. He always gets the attention and takes me for granted."

"You're annoying, Leo," Jason said. "You never take anything seriously. You can't even fix a dragon."

"Stop!" Piper pleaded, but both drew weapons—Jason his gold sword, and Leo a hammer from his tool belt.

"Let them go, Piper," Medea urged. "I'm doing you a favor. Let it happen now, and it will make your choice so much easier. Enceladus will be pleased. You could have your father back today!"

Medea's charmspeak didn't work on her, but the sorceress still had a persuasive voice. *Her father back today?* Despite her best intentions, Piper wanted that. She wanted her father back so much, it hurt.

"You work for Enceladus," she said.

Medea laughed. "Serve a giant? No. But we all serve the same greater cause—a patron you cannot begin to challenge. Walk away, child of Aphrodite. This does not have to be your death, too. Save yourself, and your father can go free."

Leo and Jason were still facing off, ready to fight, but they looked unsteady and confused—waiting for another order. Part of them had to be resisting, Piper hoped. This went completely against their nature.

"Listen to me, girl." Medea plucked a diamond off her bracelet and threw it into a spray of water from the fountain. As it passed through the multicolored light, Medea said, "O Iris, goddess of the rainbow, show me the office of Tristan McLean."

The mist shimmered, and Piper saw her father's study. Sitting behind his desk, talking on the phone, was her dad's assistant, Jane, in her dark business suit, her hair swirled in a tight bun.

"Hello, Jane," Medea said.

Jane hung up the phone calmly. "How can I help you, ma'am? Hello, Piper."

"You—" Piper was so angry she could hardly talk.

"Yes, child," Medea said. "Your father's assistant. Quite easy to manipulate. An organized mind for a mortal, but incredibly weak."

"Thank you, ma'am," Jane said.

"Don't mention it," Medea said. "I just wanted to congratulate you, Jane. Getting Mr. McLean to leave town so suddenly, take his jet to Oakland without alerting the press or the police—well done! No one seems to know where he's gone. And telling him his daughter's life was on the line— that was a nice touch to get his cooperation."

"Yes," Jane agreed in a bland tone, as if she were sleepwalking. "He was quite cooperative when he believed Piper was in danger."

Piper looked down at her dagger. The blade trembled in her hand. She couldn't use it for a weapon any better than Helen of Troy could, but it was still a looking glass, and what she saw in it was a scared girl with no chance of winning.

"I may have new orders for you, Jane," Medea said. "If the girl cooperates, it may be time for Mr. McLean to come home. Would you arrange a suitable cover story for his absence, just in case? And I imagine the poor man will need some time in a psychiatric hospital."

"Yes, ma'am. I will stand by."

The image faded, and Medea turned to Piper. "There, you see?"

"You lured my dad into a trap," Piper said. "You helped the giant—"

"Oh, please, dear. You'll work yourself into a fit! I've been preparing for this war for years, even before I was brought back to life. I'm a seer, as I said. I can tell the future as well as your little oracle. Years ago, still suffering in the Fields of Punishment, I had a vision of the seven in your so-called Great Prophecy. I saw your friend Leo here, and saw that he would be an important enemy someday. I stirred the consciousness of my patron, gave her this information, and she managed to wake just a little—just enough to visit him."

"Leo's mother," Piper said. "Leo, listen to this! She helped get your mother killed!"

"Uh-huh," Leo mumbled, in a daze. He frowned at his hammer. "So . . . I just attack Jason? That's okay?"

"Perfectly safe," Medea promised. "And Jason, strike him hard. Show me you are worthy of your namesake."

"No!" Piper ordered. She knew it was her last chance. "Jason, Leo—she's tricking you. Put down your weapons."

The sorceress rolled her eyes. "Please, girl. You're no match for me. I trained with my aunt, the immortal Circe. I can drive men mad or heal them with my voice. What hope do these puny young heroes have against me? Now, boys, kill each other!"

"Jason, Leo, listen to me." Piper put all of her emotion into her voice. For years she'd been trying to control herself and not show weakness, but now she poured everything into her words—her fear, her desperation, her anger. She knew she might be signing her dad's death warrant, but she cared too much about her friends to let them hurt each other. "Medea is charming you. It's part of her magic. You are best friends. Don't fight each other. Fight *her!*"

They hesitated, and Piper could feel the spell shatter.

Jason blinked. "Leo, was I just about to stab you?"

"Something about my mother...?" Leo frowned, then turned toward Medea. "You...you're working for Dirt Woman. You sent her to the machine shop." He lifted his arm. "Lady, I got a three-pound hammer with your name on it."

"Bah!" Medea sneered. "I'll simply collect payment another way."

She pressed one of the mosaic tiles on the floor, and the building rumbled. Jason swung his sword at Medea, but she dissolved into smoke and reappeared at the base of the escalator.

"You're slow, hero!" She laughed. "Take your frustration out on my pets!"

Before Jason could go after her, the giant bronze sundials at either end of the fountain swung open. Two snarling gold beasts—flesh-and-blood winged dragons—crawled out from the pits below. Each was the size of a camper van, maybe not large compared to Festus, but large enough.

"So that's what's in the kennels," Leo said meekly.

The dragons spread their wings and hissed. Piper could feel the heat coming off their glittering skin. One turned his angry orange eyes on her.

"Don't look them in the eye!" Jason warned. "They'll paralyze you."

"Indeed!" Medea was leisurely riding the escalator up, leaning against the handrail as she watched the fun. "These two dears have been with me a long time—sun dragons, you know, gifts from my grandfather Helios. They pulled my chariot when I left Corinth, and now they will be your destruction. Ta-ta!"

The dragons lunged. Leo and Jason charged to intercept. Piper was amazed how fearlessly the boys attacked—working like a team who had trained together for years.

Medea was almost to the second floor, where she'd be able to choose from a wide assortment of deadly appliances.

"Oh, no, you don't," Piper growled, and took off after her.

When Medea spotted Piper, she started climbing in earnest. She was quick for a three-thousand-year-old lady. Piper climbed at top speed, taking the steps three at a time, and still she couldn't catch her. Medea didn't stop at floor two. She hopped the next escalator and continued to ascend.

The potions, Piper thought. Of course that's what she would go for. She was famous for potions.

Down below, Piper heard the battle raging. Leo was blowing his safety whistle, and Jason was yelling to keep the dragons' attention. Piper didn't dare look—not while she was running with a dagger in her hand. She could just see herself tripping and stabbing herself in the nose. That would be super heroic.

She grabbed a shield from an armored manikin on floor three and continued to climb. She imagined Coach Hedge yelling in her mind, just like back in gym class at Wilderness School: *Move it, McLean! You call that escalator-climbing?*

She reached the top floor, breathing hard, but she was too late. Medea had reached the potions counter.

The sorceress grabbed a swan-shaped vial—the blue one that caused painful death—and Piper did the only thing that came to mind. She threw her shield.

Medea turned triumphantly just in time to get hit in the chest by a fifty-pound metal Frisbee. She stumbled backward, crashing over the counter, breaking vials and knocking down shelves. When the sorceress stood from the wreckage, her dress was stained a dozen different colors. Many of the stains were smoldering and glowing.

"Fool!" Medea wailed. "Do you have any idea what so many potions will do when mixed?"

"Kill you?" Piper said hopefully.

The carpet began to steam around Medea's feet. She coughed, and her face contorted in pain—or was she faking?

Below, Leo called, "Jason, help!"

Piper risked a quick look, and almost sobbed in despair. One of the dragons had Leo pinned to the floor. It was baring its fangs, ready to snap. Jason was all the way across the room battling the other dragon, much too far away to assist.

"You've doomed us all!" Medea screamed. Smoke was rolling across the carpet as the stain spread, throwing sparks and setting fires in the clothing racks. "You have only seconds before this concoction consumes everything and destroys the building. There's no time—"

CRASH! The stained glass ceiling splintered in a rain of multicolored shards, and Festus the bronze dragon dropped into the department store.

He hurtled into the fray, snatching up a sun dragon in each claw. Only now did Piper appreciate just how big and strong their metal friend was.

"That's my boy!" Leo yelled.

Festus flew halfway up the atrium, then hurled the sun dragons into the pits they'd come from. Leo raced to the fountain and pressed the marble tile, closing the sundials. They shuddered as the dragons banged against them, trying to get out, but for the moment they were contained.

Medea cursed in some ancient language. The whole fourth floor was on fire now. The air filled with noxious gas. Even with the roof open, Piper could feel the heat intensifying. She backed up to the edge of the railing, keeping her dagger pointed toward Medea.

"I will not be abandoned again!" The sorceress knelt and snatched up the red healing potion, which had somehow survived the crash. "You want your boyfriend's memory restored? Take me with you!"

Piper glanced behind her. Leo and Jason were on board Festus's back. The bronze dragon flapped his mighty wings, snatched the two cages with the satyr and the storm spirits in his claws, and began to ascend.

The building rumbled. Fire and the smoke curled up the walls, melting the railings, turning the air to acid.

"You'll never survive your quest without me!" Medea growled. "Your boy hero will stay ignorant forever, and your father will die. Take me with you!"

For one heartbeat, Piper was tempted. Then she saw Medea's grim smile. The sorceress was confident in her powers of persuasion, confident that she could always make a deal, always escape and win in the end.

"Not today, witch." Piper jumped over the side. She plummeted for only a second before Leo and Jason caught her, hauling her aboard the dragon.

She heard Medea screaming in rage as they soared through the broken roof and over downtown Chicago. Then the department store exploded behind them.

XXIX

LEO

LEO KEPT LOOKING BACK. HE HALF EXPECTED to see those nasty sun dragons toting a flying chariot with a screaming magical saleswoman throwing potions, but nothing followed them.

He steered the dragon toward the southwest. Eventually, the smoke from the burning department store faded in the distance, but Leo didn't relax until the suburbs of Chicago gave way to snowy fields, and the sun began to set.

"Good job, Festus." He patted the dragon's metal hide. "You did awesome."

The dragon shuddered. Gears popped and clicked in his neck.

Leo frowned. He didn't like those noises. If the control disk was failing again—No, hopefully it was something minor. Something he could fix.

"I'll give you a tune-up next time we land," Leo promised. "You've earned some motor oil and Tabasco sauce."

Festus whirled his teeth, but even that sounded weak. He flew at a steady pace, his great wings angling to catch the wind, but he was carrying a heavy load. Two cages in his claws plus three people on his back—the more Leo thought about it, the more worried he got. Even metal dragons had limits.

"Leo." Piper patted his shoulder. "You feeling okay?"

"Yeah... not bad for a brainwashed zombie." He hoped he didn't look as embarrassed as he felt. "Thanks for saving us back there, beauty queen. If you hadn't talked me out of that spell—"

"Don't worry about it," Piper said.

But Leo worried a lot. He felt terrible about how easily Medea had set him against his best friend. And those feelings hadn't come from nowhere—his resentment of the way Jason always got the spotlight and didn't really seem to need him. Leo did feel that way sometimes, even if he wasn't proud of it.

What bothered him more was the news about his mom. Medea had seen the future down in the Underworld. That was how her patron, the woman in the black earthen robes, had come to the machine shop seven years ago to scare him, ruin his life. That's how his mother had died—because of something Leo might do someday. So in a weird way, even if his fire powers weren't to blame, Mom's death was *still* his fault.

When they had left Medea in that exploding store, Leo had felt a little too good. He hoped she wouldn't make it out, and would go right back to the Fields of Punishment, where she belonged. Those feelings didn't make him proud, either.

And if souls were coming back from the Underworld... was it possible Leo's mom could be brought back?

He tried to put the idea aside. That was Frankenstein thinking. It wasn't natural. It wasn't right. Medea might've been brought back to life, but she hadn't seemed quite human, with the hissing nails and the glowing head and whatnot.

No, Leo's mom had passed on. Thinking any other way would just drive Leo nuts. Still, the thought kept poking at him, like an echo of Medea's voice.

"We're going to have to put down soon," he warned his friends. "Couple more hours, maybe, to make sure Medea's not following us. I don't think Festus can fly much longer than that."

"Yeah," Piper agreed. "Coach Hedge probably wants to get out of his canary cage, too. Question is—where are we going?"

"The Bay Area," Leo guessed. His memories of the department store were fuzzy, but he seemed to remember hearing that. "Didn't Medea say something about Oakland?"

Piper didn't respond for so long, Leo wondered if he'd said something wrong.

"Piper's dad," Jason put in. "Something's happened to your dad, right? He got lured into some kind of trap."

Piper let out a shaky breath. "Look, Medea said you would both *die* in the Bay Area. And besides...even if we went there, the Bay Area is huge! First we need to find Aeolus and drop off the storm spirits. Boreas said Aeolus was the only one who could tell us exactly where to go."

Leo grunted. "So how do we find Aeolus?"

Jason leaned forward. "You mean you don't see it?" He pointed ahead of them, but Leo didn't see anything except clouds and the lights of a few towns glowing in the dusk.

"What?" Leo asked.

"That...whatever it is," Jason said. "In the air."

Leo glanced back. Piper looked just as confused as he was.

"Right," Leo said. "Could you be more specific on the 'whatever-it-is' part?"

"Like a vapor trail," Jason said. "Except it's glowing. Really faint, but it's definitely there. We've been following it since Chicago, so I figured you saw it."

Leo shook his head. "Maybe Festus can sense it. You think Aeolus made it?"

"Well, it's a magic trail in the wind," Jason said. "Aeolus is the wind god. I think he knows we've got prisoners for him. He's telling us where to fly."

"Or it's another trap," Piper said.

Her tone worried Leo. She didn't just sound nervous. She sounded broken with despair, like they'd already sealed their fate, and like it was her fault.

"Pipes, you all right?" he asked.

"Don't call me that."

"Okay, fine. You don't like any of the names I make up for you. But if your dad's in trouble and we can help—"

"You can't," she said, her voice getting shakier. "Look, I'm tired. If you don't mind..."

She leaned back against Jason and closed her eyes.

All right, Leo thought—pretty clear signal she didn't want to talk.

They flew in silence for a while. Festus seemed to know where he was going. He kept his course, gently curving toward the southwest and hopefully Aeolus's fortress. Another wind god to visit, a whole new flavor of crazy— Oh, boy, Leo couldn't wait.

He had way too much on his mind to sleep, but now that he was out danger, his body had different ideas. His energy level was crashing. The monotonous beat of the dragon's wings made his eyes feel heavy. His head started to nod.

"Catch a few Z's," Jason said. "It's cool. Hand me the reins."

"Nah, I'm okay—"

"Leo," Jason said, "you're not a machine. Besides, I'm the only one who can see the vapor trail. I'll make sure we stay on course."

Leo's eyes started to close on their own. "All right. Maybe just..."

He didn't finish the sentence before slumping forward against the dragon's warm neck.

In his dream, he heard a voice full of static, like a bad AM radio: "Hello? Is this thing working?"

Leo's vision came into focus—sort of. Everything was hazy and gray, with bands of interference running across his sight. He'd never dreamed with a bad connection before.

He seemed to be in a workshop. Out of the corners of his eyes he saw bench saws, metal lathes, and tool cages. A forge glowed cheerfully against one wall.

It wasn't the camp forge—too big. Not Bunker 9—much warmer and more comfortable, obviously not abandoned.

Then Leo realized something was blocking the middle of his view—something large and fuzzy, and so close, Leo had to cross his eyes to see it properly. It was a large ugly face.

"Holy mother!" he yelped.

The face backed away and came into focus. Staring down at him was a bearded man in grimy blue coveralls. His face was lumpy and covered with welts, as if he'd been bitten by a million bees, or dragged across gravel. Possibly both.

"Humph," the man said. "Holy *father*, boy. I should think you'd know the difference."

Leo blinked. "Hephaestus?"

Being in the presence of his father for the first time, Leo probably should've been speechless or awestruck or something. But after what he'd been through the last couple of days, with Cyclopes and a sorceress and a face in the potty sludge, all Leo felt was a surge of complete annoyance.

"Now you show up?" he demanded. "After fifteen years? Great parenting, Fur Face. Where do you get off sticking your ugly nose into my dreams?"

The god raised an eyebrow. A little spark caught fire in his beard. Then he threw back his head and laughed so loudly, the tools rattled on the workbenches.

"You sound just like your mother," Hephaestus said. "I miss Esperanza."

"She's been dead seven years." Leo's voice trembled. "Not that you'd care."

"But I do care, boy. About both of you."

"Uh-huh. Which is why I never saw you before today."

The god made a rumbling sound in his throat, but he looked more uncomfortable than angry. He pulled a miniature motor from his pocket and began fiddling absently with the pistons—just the way Leo did when he was nervous.

"I'm not good with children," the god confessed. "Or people. Well, any organic life forms, really. I thought about speaking to you at your mom's funeral. Then again when you were in fifth grade... that science project you made, steam-powered chicken chucker. Very impressive."

"You saw that?"

Hephaestus pointed to the nearest worktable, where a shiny bronze mirror showed a hazy image of Leo asleep on the dragon's back.

"Is that me?" Leo asked. "Like—me right now, having this dream—looking at me having a dream?"

Hephaestus scratched his beard. "Now you've confused me. But yes—it's you. I'm always keeping an eye on you, Leo. But talking to you is, um... different."

"You're scared," Leo said.

"Grommets and gears!" the god yelled. "Of course not!"

"Yeah, you're scared." But Leo's anger seeped away. He'd spent years thinking about what he'd say to his dad if they ever met—how Leo would chew him out for being a deadbeat. Now, looking at that bronze mirror, Leo thought about his dad watching his progress over the years, even his stupid science experiments.

Maybe Hephaestus was still a jerk, but Leo kind of understood where he was coming from. Leo knew about running away from people, not fitting in. He knew about hiding out in a workshop rather than trying to deal with organic life forms.

"So," Leo grumbled, "you keep track of all your kids? You got like twelve back at camp. How'd you even— Never mind. I don't want to know."

Hephaestus might've blushed, but his face was so beat up and red, it was hard to tell. "Gods are different from mortals, boy. We can exist in many places at once—wherever people call on us, wherever our sphere of influence is strong. In fact, it's rare our entire essence is ever together in one place—our true form. It's dangerous, powerful enough to destroy any mortal who looks upon us. So, yes...lots of children. Add to that our different aspects, Greek and Roman—" The god's fingers froze on his engine project. "Er, that is to say, being a god is complicated. And yes, I try to keep an eye on all my children, but you especially."

Leo was pretty sure Hephaestus had almost slipped and said something important, but he wasn't sure what.

"Why contact me now?" Leo asked. "I thought the gods had gone silent."

"We have," Hephaestus grumped. "Zeus's orders—very strange, even for him. He's blocked all visions, dreams, and Iris-messages to and from Olympus. Hermes is sitting around bored out of his mind because he can't deliver the mail. Fortunately, I kept my old pirate broadcasting equipment."

Hephaestus patted a machine on the table. It looked like a combination satellite dish, V-6 engine, and espresso maker. Each time Hephaestus jostled the machine, Leo's dream flickered and changed color.

"Used this in the Cold War," the god said fondly. "Radio Free Hephaestus. Those were the days. I keep it around for pay-for-view, mostly, or making viral brain videos—"

"Viral brain videos?"

"But now it's come in handy again. If Zeus knew I was contacting you, he'd have my hide."

"Why is Zeus being such a jerk?"

"Hrumph. He excels at that, boy." Hephaestus called him *boy* as if Leo were an annoying machine part—an extra washer, maybe, that had no clear purpose, but that Hephaestus didn't want to throw away for fear he might need it someday.

Not exactly heartwarming. Then again, Leo wasn't sure he wanted to be called "son." Leo wasn't about to start calling this big awkward ugly guy "Dad."

Hephaestus got tired of his engine and tossed it over his shoulder. Before it could hit the floor, it sprouted helicopter wings and flew itself into a recycling bin.

"It was the second Titan War, I suppose," Hephaestus said. "That's what got Zeus upset. We gods were...well, embarrassed. Don't think there's any other way to say it."

"But you won," Leo said.

The god grunted. "We won because the demigods of"— again he hesitated, as if he'd almost made a slip—"of Camp Half-Blood took the lead. We won because our children fought our battles for us, smarter than we did. If we'd relied on Zeus's plan, we would've all gone down to Tartarus fighting the storm giant Typhon, and Kronos would've won. Bad enough mortals won our war for us, but then that young upstart, Percy Jackson—"

"The guy who's missing."

"Hmph. Yes. Him. He had the nerve to turn down our

offer of immortality and tell us to pay better attention to our children. Er, no offense."

"Oh, how could I take offense? Please, go on ignoring me."

"Mighty understanding of you..." Hephaestus frowned, then sighed wearily. "That was sarcasm, wasn't it? Machines don't have sarcasm, usually. But as I was saying, the gods felt ashamed, shown up by mortals. At first, of course, we were grateful. But after a few months, those feelings turned bitter. We're gods, after all. We need to be admired, looked up to, held in awe and admiration."

"Even if you're wrong?"

"Especially then! And to have Jackson refuse our gift, as if being mortal were somehow *better* than being a god... well, that stuck in Zeus's craw. He decided it was high time we got back to traditional values. Gods were to be respected. Our children were to be seen and not visited. Olympus was closed. At least that was *part* of his reasoning. And, of course, we started hearing of bad things stirring under the earth."

"The giants, you mean. Monsters re-forming instantly. The dead rising again. Little stuff like that?"

"Aye, boy." Hephaestus turned a knob on his pirate broadcasting machine. Leo's dream sharpened to full color, but the god's face was such a riot of red welts and yellow and black bruises, Leo wished it would go back to black and white.

"Zeus thinks he can reverse the tide," the god said, "lull the earth back to sleep as long as we stay quiet. None of us really believes that. And I don't mind saying, we're in no shape to fight another war. We barely survived the Titans. If we're repeating the old pattern, what comes next is even worse."

"The giants," Leo said. "Hera said demigods and gods had to join forces to defeat them. Is that true?"

"Mmm. I hate to agree with my mother about anything, but yes. Those giants are tough to kill, boy. They're a different breed."

"Breed? You make them sound like racehorses."

"Ha!" the god said. "More like war dogs. Back in the beginning, y'see, everything in creation came from the same parents—Gaea and Ouranos, Earth and Sky. They had their different batches of children—your Titans, your Elder Cyclopes, and so forth. Then Kronos, the head Titan—well, you've probably heard how he chopped up his father Ouranos with a scythe and took over the world. Then we gods came along, children of the Titans, and defeated *them*. But that wasn't the end of it. The earth bore a new batch of children, except they were sired by Tartarus, the spirit of the eternal abyss—the darkest, most evil place in the Underworld. Those children, the giants, were bred for one purpose—revenge on *us* for the fall of the Titans. They rose up to destroy Olympus, and they came awfully close."

Hephaestus's beard began to smolder. He absently swatted out the flames. "What my blasted mother Hera is doing now—she's a meddling fool playing a dangerous game, but she's right about one thing: you demigods have to unite. That's the only way to open Zeus's eyes, convince the Olympians they must accept your help. And that's the only way to defeat what's coming. You're a big part of that, Leo. "

The god's gaze seemed far away. Leo wondered if really could split himself into different parts—where else was he right now? Maybe his Greek side was fixing a car or going on a date, while his Roman side was watching a ball game and ordering pizza. Leo tried to imagine what it would feel like to have multiple personalities. He hoped it wasn't hereditary.

"Why me?" he asked, and as soon as he said it, more questions flooded out. "Why claim me now? Why not when I was thirteen, like you're supposed to? Or you could've claimed me at seven, before my mom died! Why didn't you find me earlier? Why didn't you warn me about *this*?"

Leo's hand burst into flames.

Hephaestus regarded him sadly. "Hardest part, boy. Letting my children walk their own paths. Interfering doesn't work. The Fates make sure of that. As for the claiming, you were a special case, boy. The timing had to be right. I can't explain it much more, but—"

Leo's dream went fuzzy. Just for a moment, it turned into a rerun of *Wheel of Fortune*. Then Hephaestus came back into focus.

"Blast," he said. "I can't talk much longer. Zeus is sensing an illegal dream. He is lord of the air, after all, including the airwaves. Just listen, boy: you have a role to play. Your friend Jason is right—fire is a gift, not a curse. I don't give that blessing to just anyone. They'll never defeat the giants without you, much less the mistress they serve. She's worse than any god or Titan."

"Who?" Leo demanded.

Hephaestus frowned, his image becoming fuzzier. "I told you. Yes, I'm pretty sure I told you. Just be warned: along the way, you're going to lose some friends and some valuable tools.

But that isn't your fault, Leo. Nothing lasts forever, not even the best machines. And everything can be reused."

"What do you mean? I don't like the sound of that."

"No, you shouldn't." Hephaestus's image was barely visible now, just a blob in the static. "Just watch out for—"

Leo's dream switched to *Wheel of Fortune* just as the wheel hit Bankrupt and the audience said, "Awwww!"

Then Leo snapped awake to Jason and Piper screaming.

XXX

LEO

THEY SPIRALED THROUGH THE DARK in a free fall, still on the dragon's back, but Festus's hide was cold. His ruby eyes were dim.

"Not again!" Leo yelled. "You can't fall again!"

He could barely hold on. The wind stung his eyes, but he managed to pull open the panel on the dragon's neck. He toggled the switches. He tugged the wires. The dragon's wings flapped once, but Leo caught a whiff of burning bronze. The drive system was overloaded. Festus didn't have the strength to keep flying, and Leo couldn't get to the main control panel on the dragon's head—not in midair. He saw the lights of a city below them—just flashes in the dark as they plummeted in circles. They had only seconds before they crashed.

"Jason!" he screamed. "Take Piper and fly out of here!"

"What?"

"We need to lighten the load! I might be able to reboot Festus, but he's carrying too much weight!"

"What about you?" Piper cried. "If you can't reboot him—"

"I'll be fine," Leo yelled. "Just follow me to the ground. Go!"

Jason grabbed Piper around the waist. They both unbuckled their harnesses, and in a flash they were gone—shooting into the air.

"Now," Leo said. "Just you and me, Festus—and two heavy cages. You can do it, boy!"

Leo talked to the dragon while he worked, falling at terminal velocity. He could see the city lights below him, getting closer and closer. He summoned fire in his hand so he could see what he was doing, but the wind kept extinguishing it.

He pulled a wire that he thought connected the dragon's nerve center to its head, hoping for a little wake-up jolt.

Festus groaned—metal creaking inside his neck. His eyes flickered weakly to life, and he spread his wings. Their fall turned into a steep glide.

"Good!" Leo said. "Come on, big boy. Come on!"

They were still flying in way too hot, and the ground was too close. Leo needed a place to land—fast.

There was a big river—no. Not good for a fire-breathing dragon. He'd never get Festus out from the bottom if he sank, especially in freezing temperatures. Then, on the riverbanks, Leo spotted a white mansion with a huge snowy lawn inside a tall brick perimeter fence—like some rich person's private compound, all of it blazing with light. A perfect landing field. He did his best to steer the dragon toward it, and Festus seemed to come back to life. They could make this!

Then everything went wrong. As they approached the

lawn, spotlights along the fence fixed on them, blinding Leo. He heard bursts like tracer fire, the sound of metal being cut to shreds—and *BOOM*.

Leo blacked out.

When Leo came to his senses, Jason and Piper were leaning over him. He was lying in the snow, covered in mud and grease. He spit a clump of frozen grass out of his mouth.

"Where—"

"Lie still." Piper had tears in her eyes. "You rolled pretty hard when—when Festus—"

"Where is he?" Leo sat up, but his head felt like it was floating. They'd landed inside the compound. Something had happened on the way in—gunfire?

"Seriously, Leo," Jason said. "You could be hurt. You shouldn't—"

Leo pushed himself to his feet. Then he saw the wreckage. Festus must have dropped the big canary cages as he came over the fence, because they'd rolled in different directions and landed on their sides, perfectly undamaged.

Festus hadn't been so lucky.

The dragon had disintegrated. His limbs were scattered across the lawn. His tail hung on the fence. The main section of his body had plowed a trench twenty feet wide and fifty feet long across the mansion's yard before breaking apart. What remained of his hide was a charred, smoking pile of scraps. Only his neck and head were somewhat intact, resting across a row of frozen rosebushes like a pillow.

"No," Leo sobbed. He ran to the dragon's head and stroked

its snout. The dragon's eyes flickered weakly. Oil leaked out of his ear.

"You can't go," Leo pleaded. "You're the best thing I ever fixed."

The dragon's head whirred its gears, as if it were purring. Jason and Piper stood next to him, but Leo kept his eyes fixed on the dragon.

He remembered what Hephaestus had said: *That isn't your fault, Leo. Nothing lasts forever, not even the best machines.*

His dad had been trying to warn him.

"It's not fair," he said.

The dragon clicked. Long *creak*. Two short *clicks*. *Creak*. *Creak*. Almost like a pattern . . . triggering an old memory in Leo's mind. Leo realized Festus was trying to say something. He was using Morse code—just like Leo's mom had taught him years ago. Leo listened more intently, translating the clicks into letters: a simple message repeating over and over.

"Yeah," Leo said. "I understand. I will. I promise."

The dragon's eyes went dark. Festus was gone.

Leo cried. He wasn't even embarrassed. His friends stood on either side, patting his shoulders, saying comforting things; but the buzzing in Leo's ears drowned out their words.

Finally Jason said, "I'm so sorry, man. What did you promise Festus?"

Leo sniffled. He opened the dragon's head panel, just to be sure, but the control disk was cracked and burned beyond repair.

"Something my dad told me," Leo said. "Everything can be reused."

"Your dad talked to you?" Jason asked. "When was this?"

Leo didn't answer. He worked at the dragon's neck hinges until the head was detached. It weighed about a hundred pounds, but Leo managed to hold it in his arms. He looked up at the starry sky and said, "Take him back to the bunker, Dad. Please, until I can reuse him. I've never asked you for anything."

The wind picked up, and the dragon's head floated out of Leo's arms like it weighed nothing. It flew into the sky and disappeared.

Piper looked at him in amazement. "He *answered* you?"

"I had a dream," Leo managed. "Tell you later."

He knew he owed his friends a better explanation, but Leo could barely speak. He felt like a broken machine himself—like someone had removed one little part of him, and now he'd never be complete. He might move, he might talk, he might keep going and do his job. But he'd always be off balance, never calibrated exactly right.

Still, he couldn't afford to break down completely. Otherwise, Festus had died for nothing. He had to finish this quest—for his friends, for his mom, for his dragon.

He looked around. The large white mansion glowed in the center of the grounds. Tall brick walls with lights and security cameras surrounded the perimeter, but now Leo could see—or rather *sense*—just how well those walls were defended.

"Where are we?" he asked. "I mean, what city?"

"Omaha, Nebraska," Piper said. "I saw a billboard as we flew in. But I don't know what this mansion is. We came in right behind you, but as you were landing, Leo, I swear it looked like—I don't know—"

"Lasers," Leo said. He picked up a piece of dragon wreckage and threw it toward the top of the fence. Immediately a turret popped up from the brick wall and a beam of pure heat incinerated the bronze plating to ashes.

Jason whistled. "Some defense system. How are we even alive?"

"Festus," Leo said miserably. "He took the fire. The lasers sliced him to bits as he came in so they didn't focus on you. I led him into a death trap."

"You couldn't have known," Piper said. "He saved our lives again."

"But what now?" Jason said. "The main gates are locked, and I'm guessing I can't fly us out of here without getting shot down."

Leo looked up the walkway at the big white mansion. "Since we can't go out, we'll have to go in."

JASON

JASON WOULD'VE DIED FIVE TIMES on the way to the front door if not for Leo.

First it was the motion-activated trapdoor on the sidewalk, then the lasers on the steps, then the nerve gas dispenser on the porch railing, the pressure-sensitive poison spikes in the welcome mat, and of course the exploding doorbell.

Leo deactivated all of them. It was like he could smell the traps, and he picked just the right tool out of his belt to disable them.

"You're amazing, man," Jason said.

Leo scowled as he examined the front door lock. "Yeah, amazing," he said. "Can't fix a dragon right, but I'm amazing."

"Hey, that wasn't your—"

"Front door's already unlocked," Leo announced.

Piper stared at the door in disbelief. "It is? All those traps, and the *door's* unlocked?"

Leo turned the knob. The door swung open easily. He stepped inside without hesitation.

Before Jason could follow, Piper caught his arm. "He's going to need some time to get over Festus. Don't take it personally."

"Yeah," Jason said. "Yeah, okay."

But still he felt terrible. Back in Medea's store, he'd said some pretty harsh stuff to Leo—stuff a friend shouldn't say, not to mention the fact he'd almost skewered Leo with a sword. If it hadn't been for Piper, they'd both be dead. And Piper hadn't gotten out of that encounter easily, either.

"Piper," he said, "I know I was in a daze back in Chicago, but that stuff about your dad—if he's in trouble, I want to help. I don't care if it's a trap or not."

Her eyes were always different colors, but now they looked shattered, as if she'd seen something she just couldn't cope with. "Jason, you don't know what you're saying. Please—don't make me feel worse. Come on. We should stick together."

She ducked inside.

"Together," Jason said to himself. "Yeah, we're doing great with that."

Jason's first impression of the house: Dark.

From the echo of his footsteps he could tell the entry hall was enormous, even bigger than Boreas's penthouse; but the only illumination came from the yard lights outside. A faint glow peeked through the breaks in the thick velvet curtains. The windows rose about ten feet tall. Spaced between them along the walls were life-size metal statues. As Jason's eyes adjusted, he saw sofas arranged in a ∪ in the middle of the room, with a central coffee table and one large chair at the far end. A massive chandelier glinted overhead. Along the back wall stood a row of closed doors.

"Where's the light switch?" His voice echoed alarmingly through the room.

"Don't see one," Leo said.

"Fire?" Piper suggested.

Leo held out his hand, but nothing happened. "It's not working."

"Your fire is out? Why?" Piper asked.

"Well, if I knew that—"

"Okay, okay," she said. "What do we do—explore?"

Leo shook his head. "After all those traps outside? Bad idea."

Jason's skin tingled. He hated being a demigod. Looking around, he didn't see a comfortable room to hang out in. He imagined vicious storm spirits lurking in the curtains, dragons under the carpet, a chandelier made of lethal ice shards, ready to impale them.

"Leo's right," he said. "We're not separating again—not like in Detroit."

"Oh, thank you for reminding me of the Cyclopes." Piper's voice quavered. "I needed that."

"It's a few hours until dawn," Jason guessed. "Too cold to wait outside. Let's bring the cages in and make camp in this room. Wait for daylight; then we can decide what to do."

Nobody offered a better idea, so they rolled in the cages

with Coach Hedge and the storm spirits, then settled in. Thankfully, Leo didn't find any poison throw pillows or electric whoopee cushions on the sofas.

Leo didn't seem in the mood to make more tacos. Besides, they had no fire, so they settled for cold rations.

As Jason ate, he studied the metal statues along the walls. They looked like Greek gods or heroes. Maybe that was a good sign. Or maybe they were used for target practice. On the coffee table sat a tea service and a stack of glossy brochures, but Jason couldn't make out the words. The big chair at the other end of the table looked like a throne. None of them tried to sit in it.

The canary cages didn't make the place any less creepy. The *venti* kept churning in their prison, hissing and spinning, and Jason got the uncomfortable feeling they were watching him. He could sense their hatred for the children of Zeus—the lord of the sky who'd ordered Aeolus to imprison their kind. The *venti* would like nothing better than to tear Jason apart.

As for Coach Hedge, he was still frozen mid-shout, his cudgel raised. Leo was working on the cage, trying to open it with various tools, but the lock seemed to be giving him a hard time. Jason decided not to sit next to him in case Hedge suddenly unfroze and went into ninja goat mode.

Despite how wired he felt, once his stomach was full, Jason started to nod off. The couches were a little too comfortable —a lot better than a dragon's back—and he'd taken the last two watches while his friends slept. He was exhausted.

Piper had already curled up on the other sofa. Jason wondered if she was really asleep or dodging a conversation about her dad. Whatever Medea had meant in Chicago, about Piper getting her dad back if she cooperated—it didn't sound good. If Piper had risked her own dad to save them, that made Jason feel even guiltier.

And they were running out of time. If Jason had his days straight, this was early morning of December 20. Which meant tomorrow was the winter solstice.

"Get some sleep," Leo said, still working on the locked cage. "It's your turn."

Jason took a deep breath. "Leo, I'm sorry about that stuff I said in Chicago. That wasn't me. You're not annoying and you *do* take stuff seriously—especially your work. I wish I could do half the things you can do."

Leo lowered his screwdriver. He looked at the ceiling and shook his head like, *What am I gonna do with this guy?*

"I try very hard to be annoying," Leo said. "Don't insult my ability to *annoy*. And how am I supposed to resent you if you go apologizing? I'm a lowly mechanic. You're like the prince of the sky, son of the Lord of the Universe. I'm *supposed* to resent you."

"Lord of the Universe?"

"Sure, you're all—*bam!* Lightning man. And 'Watch me fly. I am the eagle that soars—'"

"Shut up, Valdez."

Leo managed a little smile. "Yeah, see. I *do* annoy you."

"I apologize for apologizing."

"Thank you." He went back to work, but the tension had eased between them. Leo still looked sad and exhausted—just not quite so angry.

"Go to sleep, Jason," he ordered. "It's gonna take a few hours to get this goat man free. Then I still got to figure out how to make the winds a smaller holding cell, 'cause I am *not* lugging that canary cage to California."

"You did fix Festus, you know," Jason said. "You gave him a purpose again. I think this quest was the high point of his life."

Jason was afraid he'd blown it and made Leo mad again, but Leo just sighed.

"I hope," he said. "Now, sleep, man. I want some time without you organic life forms."

Jason wasn't quite sure what that meant, but he didn't argue. He closed his eyes and had a long, blissfully dreamless sleep.

He only woke when the yelling started.

"Ahhhgggggggh!"

Jason leaped to his feet. He wasn't sure what was more jarring—the full sunlight that now bathed the room, or the screaming satyr.

"Coach is awake," Leo said, which was kind of unnecessary. Gleeson Hedge was capering around on his furry hindquarters, swinging his club and yelling, "Die!" as he smashed the tea set, whacked the sofas, and charged at the throne.

"Coach!" Jason yelled.

Hedge turned, breathing hard. His eyes were so wild, Jason was afraid he might attack. The satyr was still wearing his orange polo shirt and his coach's whistle, but his horns were clearly visible above his curly hair, and his beefy hindquarters were definitely all goat. Could you call a goat *beefy*? Jason put the thought aside.

"You're the new kid," Hedge said, lowering his club. "Jason." He looked at Leo, then Piper, who'd apparently also just woken up. Her hair looked like it had become a nest for a friendly hamster.

"Valdez, McLean," the coach said. "What's going on? We were at the Grand Canyon. The *anemoi thuellai* were attacking and—" He zeroed in on the storm spirit cage, and his eyes went back to DEFCON 1. "Die!"

"Whoa, Coach!" Leo stepped in his path, which was pretty brave, even though Hedge was six inches shorter. "It's okay. They're locked up. We just sprang you from the other cage."

"Cage? Cage? What's going on? Just because I'm a satyr doesn't mean I can't have you doing plank push-ups, Valdez!"

Jason cleared his throat. "Coach—Gleeson—um, whatever you want us to call you. You saved us at the Grand Canyon. You were totally brave."

"Of course I was!"

"The extraction team came and took us to Camp Half-Blood. We thought we'd lost you. Then we got word the storm spirits had taken you back to their—um, operator, Medea."

"That witch! Wait—that's impossible. She's mortal. She's dead."

"Yeah, well," Leo said, "somehow she got not dead anymore."

Hedge nodded, his eyes narrowing. "So! You were sent on a dangerous quest to rescue me. Excellent!"

"Um." Piper got to her feet, holding out her hands so Coach Hedge wouldn't attack her. "Actually, Glee—can I still call you Coach Hedge? Gleeson seems *wrong*. We're on a quest for something else. We kind of found you by accident."

"Oh." The coach's spirits seemed to deflate, but only for a second. Then his eyes lit up again. "But there are no accidents! Not on quests. This was *meant* to happen! So, this is the witch's lair, eh? Why is everything gold?"

"Gold?" Jason looked around. From the way Leo and Piper caught their breath, he guessed they hadn't noticed yet either.

The room was full of gold—the statues, the tea set Hedge had smashed, the chair that was definitely a throne. Even the curtains—which seemed to have opened by themselves at daybreak—appeared to be woven of gold fiber.

"Nice," Leo said. "No wonder they got so much security."

"This isn't—" Piper stammered. "This isn't Medea's place, Coach. It's some rich person's mansion in Omaha. We got away from Medea and crash-landed here."

"It's destiny, cupcakes!" Hedge insisted. "I'm meant to protect you. What's the quest?"

Before Jason could decide if he wanted to explain or just shove Coach Hedge back into his cage, a door opened at the far end of the room.

A pudgy man in a white bathrobe stepped out with a golden toothbrush in his mouth. He had a white beard and one of those long, old-fashioned sleeping caps pressed down over his white hair. He froze when he saw them, and the toothbrush fell out of his mouth.

He glanced into the room behind him and called, "Son? Lit, come out here, please. There are strange people in the throne room."

Coach Hedge did the obvious thing. He raised his club and shouted, "Die!"

XXXII

JASON

It took all three of them to hold back the satyr.

"Whoa, Coach!" Jason said. "Bring it down a few notches."

A younger man charged into the room. Jason guessed he must be Lit, the old guy's son. He was dressed in pajama pants with a sleeveless T-shirt that said CORNHUSKERS, and he held a sword that looked like it could husk a lot of things besides corn. His ripped arms were covered in scars, and his face, framed by curly dark hair, would've been handsome if it wasn't also sliced up.

Lit immediately zeroed in on Jason like he was the biggest threat, and stalked toward him, swinging his sword overhead.

"Hold on!" Piper stepped forward, trying for her best calming voice. "This is just a misunderstanding! Everything's fine."

Lit stopped in his tracks, but he still looked wary.

It didn't help that Hedge was screaming, "I'll get them! Don't worry!"

"Coach," Jason pleaded, "they may be friendly. Besides, we're trespassing in their house."

"Thank you!" said the old man in the bathrobe. "Now, who are you, and why are you here?"

"Let's all put our weapons down," Piper said. "Coach, you first."

Hedge clenched his jaw. "Just one thwack?"

"No," Piper said.

"What about a compromise? I'll kill them first, and if it turns out they were friendly, I'll apologize."

"No!" Piper insisted.

"Meh." Coach Hedge lowered his club.

Piper gave Lit a friendly *sorry-about-that* smile. Even with her hair messed up and wearing two-day-old clothes, she looked extremely cute, and Jason felt a little jealous she was giving Lit that smile.

Lit huffed and sheathed his sword. "You speak well, girl— fortunately for your friends, or I would've run them through."

"Appreciate it," Leo said. "I try not to get run through before lunchtime."

The old man in the bathrobe sighed, kicking the teapot that Coach Hedge had smashed. "Well, since you're here. Please, sit down."

Lit frowned. "Your Majesty—"

"No, no, it's fine, Lit," the old man said. "New land, new customs. They may sit in my presence. After all, they've seen me in my nightclothes. No sense observing formalities." He did his best to smile, though it looked a little forced. "Welcome to my humble home. I am King Midas."

• • •

"Midas? Impossible," said Coach Hedge. "He died."

They were sitting on the sofas now, while the king reclined on his throne. Tricky to do that in a bathrobe, and Jason kept worrying the old guy would forget and uncross his legs. Hopefully he was wearing golden boxers under there.

Lit stood behind the throne, both hands on his sword, glancing at Piper and flexing his muscular arms just to be annoying. Jason wondered if *he* looked that ripped holding a sword. Sadly, he doubted it.

Piper sat forward. "What our satyr friend means, Your Majesty, is that you're the second mortal we've met who should be—sorry—dead. King Midas lived thousands of years ago."

"Interesting." The king gazed out the windows at the brilliant blue skies and the winter sunlight. In the distance, downtown Omaha looked like a cluster of children's blocks —way too clean and small for a regular city.

"You know," the king said, "I think I *was* a bit dead for a while. It's strange. Seems like a dream, doesn't it, Lit?"

"A very long dream, Your Majesty."

"And yet, now we're here. I'm enjoying myself very much. I like being alive better."

"But how?" Piper asked. "You didn't happen to have a . . . patron?"

Midas hesitated, but there was a sly twinkle in his eyes. "Does it matter, my dear?"

"We could kill them again," Hedge suggested.

"Coach, not helping," Jason said. "Why don't you go outside and stand guard?"

Leo coughed. "Is that safe? They've got some serious security."

"Oh, yes," the king said. "Sorry about that. But it's lovely stuff, isn't it? Amazing what gold can still buy. Such excellent toys you have in this country!"

He fished a remote control out of his bathrobe pocket and pressed a few buttons—a pass code, Jason guessed.

"There," Midas said. "Safe to go out now."

Coach Hedge grunted. "Fine. But if you need me . . ." He winked at Jason meaningfully. Then he pointed at himself, pointed two fingers at their hosts, and sliced a finger across his throat. Very subtle sign language.

"Yeah, thanks," Jason said.

After the satyr left, Piper tried another diplomatic smile. "So . . . you don't know how you got here?"

"Oh, well, yes. Sort of," the king said. He frowned at Lit. "Why did we pick Omaha, again? I know it wasn't the weather."

"The oracle," Lit said.

"Yes! I was told there was an oracle in Omaha." The king shrugged. "Apparently I was mistaken. But this is a rather nice house, isn't it? Lit—it's short for Lityerses, by the way —horrible name, but his mother insisted—Lit has plenty of wide-open space to practice his swordplay. He has quite a reputation for that. They called him the Reaper of Men back in the old days."

"Oh." Piper tried to sound enthusiastic. "How nice."

Lit's smile was more of a cruel sneer. Jason was now one hundred percent sure he didn't like this guy, and he was starting to regret sending Hedge outside.

"So," Jason said. "All this gold—"

The king's eyes lit up. "Are you here for gold, my boy? Please, take a brochure!"

Jason looked at the brochures on the coffee table. The title said *GOLD: Invest for Eternity.* "Um, you sell gold?"

"No, no," the king said. "I *make* it. In uncertain times like these, gold is the wisest investment, don't you think? Governments fall. The dead rise. Giants attack Olympus. But gold retains its value!"

Leo frowned. "I've seen that commercial."

"Oh, don't be fooled by cheap imitators!" the king said. "I assure you, I can beat any price for a serious investor. I can make a wide assortment of gold items at a moment's notice."

"But..." Piper shook her head in confusion. "Your Majesty, you gave up the golden touch, didn't you?"

The king looked astonished. "Gave it up?"

"Yes," Piper said. "You got it from some god—"

"Dionysus," the king agreed. "I'd rescued one of his satyrs, and in return, the god granted me one wish. I chose the golden touch."

"But you accidentally turned your own daughter to gold," Piper remembered. "And you realized how greedy you'd been. So you repented."

"Repented!" King Midas looked at Lit incredulously. "You see, son? You're away for a few thousand years, and the story gets twisted all around. My dear girl, did those stories ever *say* I'd lost my magic touch?"

"Well, I guess not. They just said you learned how to reverse it with running water, and you brought your daughter back to life."

"That's all true. Sometimes I still have to reverse my touch. There's no running water in the house because I don't want accidents"—he gestured to his statues—"but we chose to live next to a river just in case. Occasionally, I'll forget and pat Lit on the back—"

Lit retreated a few steps. "I hate that."

"I *told* you I was sorry, son. At any rate, gold is wonderful. Why would I give it up?"

"Well..." Piper looked truly lost now. "Isn't that the point of the story? That you learned your lesson?"

Midas laughed. "My dear, may I see your backpack for a moment? Toss it here."

Piper hesitated, but she wasn't eager to offend the king. She dumped everything out of the pack and tossed it to Midas. As soon as he caught it, the pack turned to gold, like frost spreading across the fabric. It still looked flexible and soft, but definitely gold. The king tossed it back.

"As you see, I can still turn anything to gold," Midas said. "That pack is magic now, as well. Go ahead—put your little storm spirit enemies in there."

"Seriously?" Leo was suddenly interested. He took the bag from Piper and held it up to the cage. As soon as he unzipped the backpack, the winds stirred and howled in protest. The cage bars shuddered. The door of the prison flew open and the winds got vacuumed straight into the pack. Leo zipped it shut and grinned. "Gotta admit. That's cool."

"You see?" Midas said. "My golden touch a *curse*? Please. I didn't learn any lesson, and life isn't a story, girl. Honestly, my daughter Zoe was much more pleasant as a gold statue."

"She talked a lot," Lit offered.

"Exactly! And so I turned her back to gold." Midas pointed. There in the corner was a golden statue of a girl with a shocked expression, as if she were thinking, *Dad!*

"That's horrible!" Piper said.

"Nonsense. She doesn't mind. Besides, if I'd learned my lesson, would I have gotten these?"

Midas pulled off his oversize sleeping cap, and Jason didn't know whether to laugh or get sick. Midas had long fuzzy gray ears sticking up from his white hair—like Bugs Bunny's, but they weren't rabbit ears. They were donkey ears.

"Oh, wow," Leo said. "I didn't need to see that."

"Terrible, isn't it?" Midas sighed. "A few years after the golden touch incident, I judged a music contest between Apollo and Pan, and I declared Pan the winner. Apollo, sore loser, said I must have the ears of an ass, and *voilà*. This was my reward for being truthful. I tried to keep them a secret. Only my barber knew, but he couldn't help blabbing." Midas pointed out another golden statue—a bald man in a toga, holding a pair of shears. "That's him. He won't be telling anyone's secrets again."

The king smiled. Suddenly he didn't strike Jason as a harmless old man in a bathrobe. His eyes had a merry glow to them—the look of a madman who knew he was mad, accepted his madness, and enjoyed it. "Yes, gold has many uses. I think that *must* be why I was brought back, eh Lit? To bankroll our patron."

Lit nodded. "That and my good sword arm."

Jason glanced at his friends. Suddenly the air in the room seemed much colder.

"So you do have a patron," Jason said. "You work for the giants."

King Midas waved his hand dismissively. "Well, I don't care for giants myself, of course. But even supernatural armies need to get paid. I do owe my patron a great debt. I tried to explain that to the last group that came through, but they were very unfriendly. Wouldn't cooperate at all."

Jason slipped his hand into his pocket and grabbed his gold coin. "The last group?"

"Hunters," Lit snarled. "Blasted girls from Artemis."

Jason felt a spark of electricity—a *literal* spark—travel down his spine. He caught a whiff of electrical fire like he'd just melted some of the springs in the sofa.

His *sister* had been here.

"When?" he demanded. "What happened?"

Lit shrugged. "Few days ago? I didn't get to kill them, unfortunately. They were looking for some evil wolves, or something. Said they were following a trail, heading west. Missing demigod—I don't recall."

Percy Jackson, Jason thought. Annabeth had mentioned the Hunters were looking for him. And in Jason's dream of the burned-out house in the redwoods, he'd heard enemy wolves baying. Hera had called them her keepers. It had to be connected somehow.

Midas scratched his donkey ears. "Very unpleasant young ladies, those Hunters," he recalled. "They absolutely refused to be turned into gold. Much of the security system outside I installed to keep that sort of thing from happening again, you know. I don't have time for those who aren't serious investors."

Jason stood warily and glanced at his friends. They got the message.

"Well," Piper said, managing a smile. "It's been a great visit. Welcome back to life. Thanks for the gold bag."

"Oh, but you can't leave!" Midas said. "I know you're not serious investors, but that's all right! I have to rebuild my collection."

Lit was smiling cruelly. The king rose, and Leo and Piper moved away from him.

"Don't worry," the king assured them. "You don't *have* to be turned to gold. I give all my guests a choice—join my collection, or die at the hands of Lityerses. Really, it's good either way."

Piper tried to use her charmspeak. "Your Majesty, you can't—"

Quicker than any old man should've been able to move, Midas lashed out and grabbed her wrist.

"No!" Jason yelled.

But a frost of gold spread over Piper, and in a heartbeat she was a glittering statue. Leo tried to summon fire, but he'd forgotten his power wasn't working. Midas touched his hand, and Leo transformed into solid metal.

Jason was so horrified he couldn't move. His friends—just *gone.* And he hadn't been able to stop it.

Midas smiled apologetically. "Gold trumps fire, I'm afraid." He waved around him at all the gold curtains and furniture. "In this room, my power dampens all others: fire ... even charmspeak. Which leaves me only one more trophy to collect."

"Hedge!" Jason yelled. "Need help in here!"

For once, the satyr didn't charge in. Jason wondered if the

lasers had gotten him, or if he was sitting at the bottom of a trap pit.

Midas chuckled. "No goat to the rescue? Sad. But don't worry, my boy. It's really not painful. Lit can tell you."

Jason fixed on an idea. "I choose combat. You said I could choose to fight Lit instead."

Midas looked mildly disappointed, but he shrugged. "I said you could *die* fighting Lit. But of course, if you wish."

The king backed away, and Lit raised his sword.

"I'm going to enjoy this," Lit said. "I am the Reaper of Men!"

"Come on, Cornhusker." Jason summoned his own weapon. This time it came up as a javelin, and Jason was glad for the extra length.

"Oh, gold weapon!" Midas said. "Very nice."

Lit charged.

The guy was fast. He slashed and sliced, and Jason could barely dodge the strikes, but his mind went into a different mode—analyzing patterns, learning Lit's style, which was all offense, no defense.

Jason countered, sidestepped, and blocked. Lit seemed surprised to find him still alive.

"What is that style?" Lit growled. "You don't fight like a Greek."

"Legion training," Jason said, though he wasn't sure how he knew that. "It's Roman."

"Roman?" Lit struck again, and Jason deflected his blade. "What is *Roman*?"

"News flash," Jason said. "While you were dead, Rome defeated Greece. Created the greatest empire of all time."

"Impossible," Lit said. "Never even heard of them."

Jason spun on one heel, smacked Lit in the chest with the butt of his javelin, and sent him toppling into Midas's throne.

"Oh, dear," Midas said. "Lit?"

"I'm fine," Lit growled.

"You'd better help him up," Jason said.

Lit cried, "Dad, no!"

Too late. Midas put his hand on his son's shoulder, and suddenly a very angry-looking gold statue was sitting on Midas's throne.

"Curses!" Midas wailed. "That was a naughty trick, demigod. I'll get you for that." He patted Lit's golden shoulder. "Don't worry, son. I'll get you down to the river right after I collect this prize."

Midas raced forward. Jason dodged, but the old man was fast, too. Jason kicked the coffee table into the old man's legs and knocked him over, but Midas wouldn't stay down for long.

Then Jason glanced at Piper's golden statue. Anger washed over him. He was the son of Zeus. He could *not* fail his friends.

He felt a tugging sensation in his gut, and the air pressure dropped so rapidly that his ears popped. Midas must've felt it too, because he stumbled to his feet and grabbed his donkey ears.

"Ow! What are you doing?" he demanded. "My power is supreme here!"

Thunder rumbled. Outside, the sky turned black.

"You know another good use for gold?" Jason said.

Midas raised his eyebrows, suddenly excited. "Yes?"

"It's an excellent conductor of electricity."

Jason raised his javelin, and the ceiling exploded. A lightning bolt ripped through the roof like it was an eggshell, connected with the tip of Jason's spear, and sent out arcs of energy that blasted the sofas to shreds. Chunks of ceiling plaster crashed down. The chandelier groaned and snapped off its chain, and Midas screamed as it pinned him to the floor. The glass immediately turned into gold.

When the rumbling stopped, freezing rain poured into the building. Midas cursed in Ancient Greek, thoroughly pinned under his chandelier. The rain soaked everything, turning the gold chandelier back to glass. Piper and Leo were slowly changing too, along with the other statues in the room.

Then the front door burst open, and Coach Hedge charged in, club ready. His mouth was covered with dirt, snow, and grass.

"What'd I miss?" he asked.

"Where were you?" Jason demanded. His head was spinning from summoning the lightning bolt, and it was all he could do to keep from passing out. "I was screaming for help."

Hedge belched. "Getting a snack. Sorry. Who needs killing?"

"No one, now!" Jason said. "Just grab Leo. I'll get Piper."

"Don't leave me like this!" Midas wailed.

All around him the statues of his victims were turning to flesh—his daughter, his barber, and a whole lot of angry-looking guys with swords.

Jason grabbed Piper's golden bag and his own supplies.

Then he threw a rug over the golden statue of Lit on the throne. Hopefully that would keep the Reaper of Men from turning back to flesh—at least until after Midas's victims did.

"Let's get out of here," Jason told Hedge. "I think these guys will want some quality time with Midas."

XXXIII

PIPER

PIPER WOKE UP COLD AND SHIVERING.

She'd had the worst dream about an old guy with donkey ears chasing her around and shouting, *You're it!*

"Oh, god." Her teeth chattered. "He turned me to gold!"

"You're okay now." Jason leaned over and tucked a warm blanket around her, but she still felt as cold as a Boread.

She blinked, trying to figure out where they were. Next to her, a campfire blazed, turning the air sharp with smoke. Firelight flickered against rock walls. They were in a shallow cave, but it didn't offer much protection. Outside, the wind howled. Snow blew sideways. It might've been day or night. The storm made it too dark to tell.

"L-L-Leo?" Piper managed.

"Present and un-gold-ified." Leo was also wrapped in blankets. He didn't look great, but better than Piper felt. "I got the precious metal treatment too," he said. "But I came out of it faster. Dunno why. We had to dunk you in the river to get you back completely. Tried to dry you off, but...it's really, really cold."

"You've got hypothermia," Jason said. "We risked as much nectar as we could. Coach Hedge did a little nature magic—"

"Sports medicine." The coach's ugly face loomed over her. "Kind of a hobby of mine. Your breath might smell like wild mushrooms and Gatorade for a few days, but it'll pass. You probably won't die. Probably."

"Thanks," Piper said weakly. "How did you beat Midas?"

Jason told her the story, putting most of it down to luck.

The coach snorted. "Kid's being modest. You should've seen him. Hi-yah! Slice! Boom with the lightning!"

"Coach, you didn't even see it," Jason said. "You were outside eating the lawn."

But the satyr was just warming up. "Then I came in with my club, and we dominated that room. Afterward, I told him, 'Kid, I'm proud of you! If you could just work on your upper body strength—'"

"Coach," said Jason.

"Yeah?"

"Shut up, please."

"Sure." The coach sat down at the fire and started chewing his cudgel.

Jason put his hand on Piper's forehead and checked her temperature. "Leo, can you stoke the fire?"

"On it." Leo summoned a baseball-sized clump of flames and lobbed it into the campfire.

"Do I look that bad?" Piper shivered.

"Nah," Jason said.

"You're a terrible liar," she said. "Where are we?"

"Pikes Peak," Jason said. "Colorado."

"But that's, what—five hundred miles from Omaha?"

"Something like that," Jason agreed. "I harnessed the storm spirits to bring us this far. They didn't like it—went a little faster than I wanted, almost crashed us into the mountainside before I could get them back in the bag. I'm not going to be trying that again."

"Why are we here?"

Leo sniffed. "That's what *I* asked him."

Jason gazed into the storm as if watching for something. "That glittery wind trail we saw yesterday? It was still in the sky, though it had faded a lot. I followed it until I couldn't see it anymore. Then—honestly I'm not sure. I just felt like this was the right place to stop."

"'Course it is." Coach Hedge spit out some cudgel splinters. "Aeolus's floating palace should be anchored above us, right at the peak. This is one of his favorite spots to dock."

"Maybe that was it." Jason knit his eyebrows. "I don't know. Something else, too . . ."

"The Hunters were heading west," Piper remembered. "Do you think they're around here?"

Jason rubbed his forearm as if the tattoos were bothering him. "I don't see how anyone could survive on the mountain right now. The storm's pretty bad. It's already the evening before the solstice, but we didn't have much choice except to wait out the storm here. We had to give you some time to rest before we tried moving."

He didn't need to convince her. The wind howling outside the cave scared her, and she couldn't stop shivering.

"We have to get you warm." Jason sat next to her and held out his arms a little awkwardly. "Uh, you mind if I . . ."

"I suppose." She tried to sound nonchalant.

He put his arms around her and held her. They scooted closer to the fire. Coach Hedge chewed on his club and spit splinters into the fire.

Leo broke out some cooking supplies and started frying burger patties on an iron skillet. "So, guys, long as you're cuddled up for story time . . . something I've been meaning to tell you. On the way to Omaha, I had this dream. Kinda hard to understand with the static and the *Wheel of Fortune* breaking in—"

"*Wheel of Fortune*?" Piper assumed Leo was kidding, but when he looked up from his burgers, his expression was deadly serious.

"The thing is," he said, "my dad Hephaestus talked to me."

Leo told them about his dream. In the firelight, with the wind howling, the story was even creepier. Piper could imagine the static-filled voice of the god warning about giants who were the sons of Tartarus, and about Leo losing some friends along the way.

She tried to concentrate on something good: Jason's arms around her, the warmth slowly spreading into her body, but she was terrified. "I don't understand. If demigods and gods have to work together to kill the giants, why would the gods stay silent? If they need us—"

"Ha," said Coach Hedge. "The gods *hate* needing humans. They like to be needed *by* humans, but not the other way around. Things will have to get a whole lot worse before Zeus admits he made a mistake closing Olympus."

"Coach," Piper said, "that was almost an intelligent comment."

Hedge huffed. "What? I'm intelligent! I'm not surprised you cupcakes haven't heard of the Giant War. The gods don't like to talk about it. Bad PR to admit you needed mortals to help beat an enemy. That's just embarrassing."

"There's more, though," Jason said. "When I dreamed about Hera in her cage, she said Zeus was acting unusually paranoid. And Hera—she said she went to those ruins because a voice had been speaking in her head. What if someone's influencing the gods, like Medea influenced us?"

Piper shuddered. She'd had a similar thought—that some force they couldn't see was manipulating things behind the scenes, helping the giants. Maybe the same force was keeping Enceladus informed about their movements, and had even knocked their dragon out of the sky over Detroit. Perhaps Leo's sleeping Dirt Woman, or another servant of hers . . .

Leo set hamburger buns on the skillet to toast. "Yeah, Hephaestus said something similar, like Zeus was acting weirder than usual. But what bothered me was the stuff my dad *didn't* say. Like a couple of times he was talking about the demigods, and how he had so many kids and all. I don't know. He acted like getting the greatest demigods together was going to be almost impossible—like Hera was trying, but it was a really stupid thing to do, and there was some secret Hephaestus wasn't supposed to tell me."

Jason shifted. Piper could feel the tension in his arms.

"Chiron was the same way back at camp," he said. "He mentioned a sacred oath not to discuss—something. Coach, you know anything about that?"

"Nah. I'm just a satyr. They don't tell us the juicy stuff. Especially an old—" He stopped himself.

"An old guy like you?" Piper asked. "But you're not that old, are you?"

"Hundred and six," the coach muttered.

Leo coughed. "Say what?"

"Don't catch your panties on fire, Valdez. That's just fifty-three in human years. Still, yeah, I made some enemies on the Council of Cloven Elders. I've been a protector a *long* time. But they started saying I was getting unpredictable. Too violent. Can you imagine?"

"Wow." Piper tried not to look at her friends. "That's hard to believe."

Coach scowled. "Yeah, then finally we get a good war going with the Titans, and do they put me on the front lines? No! They send me as far away as possible—the Canadian frontier, can you believe it? Then after the war, they put me out to pasture. The Wilderness School. Bah! Like I'm too old to be helpful just because I like playing offense. All those flower-pickers on the Council—talking about nature."

"I thought satyrs liked nature," Piper ventured.

"Shoot, I love nature," Hedge said. "Nature means big

things killing and eating little things! And when you're a —you know—vertically challenged satyr like me, you get in good shape, you carry a big stick, and you don't take nothing from no one! That's nature." Hedge snorted indignantly. "Flower-pickers. Anyway, I hope you got something vegetarian cooking, Valdez. I don't do flesh."

"Yeah, Coach. Don't eat your cudgel. I got some tofu patties here. Piper's a vegetarian too. I'll throw them on in a second."

The smell of frying burgers filled the air. Piper usually hated the smell of cooking meat, but her stomach rumbled like it wanted to mutiny.

I'm losing it, she thought. *Think broccoli. Carrots. Lentils.*

Her stomach wasn't the only thing rebelling. Lying by the fire, with Jason holding her, Piper's conscience felt like a hot bullet slowing working its way toward her heart. All the guilt she'd been holding in for the last week, since the giant Enceladus had first sent her a dream, was about to kill her.

Her friends wanted to help her. Jason even said he'd walk into a trap to save her dad. And Piper had shut them out.

For all she knew, she'd already doomed her father when she attacked Medea.

She choked back a sob. Maybe she'd done the right thing in Chicago by saving her friends, but she'd only delayed her problem. She could never betray her friends, but the tiniest part of her was desperate enough to think, *What if I did?*

She tried to imagine what her dad would say. *Hey, Dad, if you were ever chained up by a cannibal giant and I had to betray a couple of friends to save you, what should I do?*

Funny, that had never come up when they did Any Three Questions. Her dad would never take the question seriously, of course. He'd probably tell her one of Grandpa Tom's old stories—something with glowing hedgehogs and talking birds—and then laugh about it as if the advice was silly.

Piper wished she remembered her grandpa better. Sometimes she dreamed about that little two-room house in Oklahoma. She wondered what it would've been like to grow up there.

Her dad would think that was nuts. He'd had spent his whole life running away from that place, distancing himself from the rez, playing any role except Native American. He'd always told Piper how lucky she was to grow up rich and well cared-for, in a nice house in California.

She'd learned to be vaguely uncomfortable about her ancestry—like Dad's old pictures from the eighties, when he had feathered hair and crazy clothes. *Can you believe I ever looked like that?* he'd say. Being Cherokee was the same way for him—something funny and mildly embarrassing.

But what else were they? Dad didn't seem to know. Maybe that's why he was always so unhappy, changing roles. Maybe that's why Piper started stealing things, looking for something her dad couldn't give her.

Leo put tofu patties on the skillet. The wind kept raging. Piper thought of an old story her dad had told her . . . one that maybe *did* answer some of her questions.

One day in second grade she'd come home in tears and demanded why her father had named her Piper. The kids were making fun of her because Piper Cherokee was a kind of airplane.

Her dad laughed, as if that had never occurred to him. "No, Pipes. Fine airplane. That's not how I named you. Grandpa Tom picked out your name. First time he heard you cry, he said you had a powerful voice—better than any reed flute piper. He said you'd learn to sing the hardest Cherokee songs, even the snake song."

"The snake song?"

Dad told her the legend—how one day a Cherokee woman had seen a snake playing too near her children and killed it with a rock, not realizing it was the king of rattlesnakes. The snakes prepared for war on the humans, but the woman's husband tried to make peace. He promised he'd do anything to repay the rattlesnakes. The snakes held him to his word. They told him to send his wife to the well so the snakes could bite her and take her life in exchange. The man was heartbroken, but he did what they asked. Afterward, the snakes were impressed that the man had given up so much and kept his promise. They taught him the snake song for all the Cherokee to use. From that point on, if any Cherokee met a snake and sang that song, the snake would recognize the Cherokee as a friend, and would not bite.

"That's awful!" Piper had said. "He let his wife die?"

Her dad spread his hands. "It was a hard sacrifice. But one life brought generations of peace between snakes and Cherokee. Grandpa Tom believed that Cherokee music could solve almost any problem. He thought you'd know lots of songs, and be the greatest musician of the family. That's why we named you Piper."

A hard sacrifice. Had her grandfather foreseen something about her, even when she was a baby? Had he sensed she was a child of Aphrodite? Her dad would probably tell her that was crazy. Grandpa Tom was no oracle.

But still...she'd made a promise to help on this quest. Her friends were counting on her. They'd saved her when Midas had turned her to gold. They'd brought her back to life. She couldn't repay them with lies.

Gradually, she started to feel warmer. She stopped shivering and settled against Jason's chest. Leo handed out the food. Piper didn't want to move, talk, or do anything to disrupt the moment. But she had to.

"We need to talk." She sat up so she could face Jason. "I don't want to hide anything from you guys anymore."

They looked at her with their mouths full of burger. Too late to change her mind now.

"Three nights before the Grand Canyon trip," she said, "I had a dream vision—a giant, telling me my father had been taken hostage. He told me I had to cooperate, or my dad would be killed."

The flames crackled.

Finally Jason said, "Enceladus? You mentioned that name before."

Coach Hedge whistled. "Big giant. Breathes fire. Not somebody I'd want barbecuing my daddy goat."

Jason gave him a *shut up* look. "Piper, go on. What happened next?"

"I—I tried to reach my dad, but all I got was his personal assistant, and she told me not to worry."

"Jane?" Leo remembered. "Didn't Medea say something about controlling her?"

Piper nodded. "To get my dad back, I had to sabotage this quest. I didn't realize it would be the three of us. Then after we started the quest, Enceladus sent me another warning: He told me he wanted you two dead. He wants me to lead you to a mountain. I don't know exactly which one, but it's in the Bay Area—I could see the Golden Gate Bridge from the summit. I have to be there by noon on the solstice, tomorrow. An exchange."

She couldn't meet her friends' eyes. She waited for them to yell at her, or turn their backs, or kick her out into the snowstorm.

Instead, Jason scooted next to her and put his arm around her again. "God, Piper. I'm so sorry."

Leo nodded. "No kidding. You've been carrying this around for a week? Piper, we could *help* you."

She glared at them. "Why don't you yell at me or something? I was ordered to kill you!"

"Aw, come on," Jason said. "You've saved us both on this quest. I'd put my life in your hands any day."

"Same," Leo said. "Can I have a hug too?"

"You don't get it!" Piper said. "I've probably just killed my dad, telling you this."

"I doubt it." Coach Hedge belched. He was eating his

tofu burger folded inside the paper plate, chewing it all like a taco. "Giant hasn't gotten what he wants yet, so he still needs your dad for leverage. He'll wait until the deadline passes, see if you show up. He wants you to divert the quest to this mountain, right?"

Piper nodded uncertainly.

"So that means Hera is being kept somewhere else," Hedge reasoned. "And she has to be saved by the same day. So you have to choose—rescue your dad, or rescue Hera. If you go after Hera, *then* Enceladus takes care of your dad. Besides, Enceladus would never let you go even if you cooperated. You're obviously one of the seven in the Great Prophecy."

One of the seven. She'd talked about this before with Jason and Leo, and she supposed it must be true, but she still had trouble believing it. She didn't feel that important. She was just a stupid child of Aphrodite. How could she be worth deceiving and killing?

"So we have no choice," she said miserably. "We have to save Hera, or the giant king gets unleashed. That's our quest. The world depends on it. And Enceladus seems to have ways of watching me. He isn't stupid. He'll know if we change course and go the wrong way. He'll kill my dad."

"He's not going to kill your dad," Leo said. "We'll save him."

"We don't have time!" Piper cried. "Besides, it's a trap."

"We're your friends, beauty queen," Leo said. "We're not going to let your dad die. We just gotta figure out a plan."

Coach Hedge grumbled. "Would help if we knew where this mountain was. Maybe Aeolus can tell you that. The Bay

Area has a bad reputation for demigods. Old home of the Titans, Mount Othrys, sits over Mount Tam, where Atlas holds up the sky. I hope that's not the mountain you saw."

Piper tried to remember the vista in her dreams. "I don't think so. This was inland."

Jason frowned at the fire, like he was trying to remember something.

"Bad reputation...that doesn't seem right. The Bay Area..."

"You think you've been there?" Piper asked.

"I..." He looked like he was almost on the edge of a breakthrough. Then the anguish came back into his eyes. "I don't know. Hedge, what happened to Mount Othrys?"

Hedge took another bite of paper and burger. "Well, Kronos built a new palace there last summer. Big nasty place, was going to be the headquarters for his new kingdom and all. Weren't any battles there, though. Kronos marched on Manhattan, tried to take Olympus. If I remember right, he left some other Titans in charge of his palace, but after Kronos got defeated in Manhattan, the whole palace just crumbled on its own."

"No," Jason said.

Everyone looked at him.

"What do you mean, 'No'?" Leo asked.

"That's not what happened. I—" He tensed, looking toward the cave entrance. "Did you hear that?"

For a second, nothing. Then Piper heard it: howls piercing the night.

XXXIV

PIPER

"WOLVES," PIPER SAID. "THEY SOUND CLOSE."

Jason rose and summoned his sword. Leo and Coach Hedge got to their feet too. Piper tried, but black spots danced before her eyes.

"Stay there," Jason told her. "We'll protect you."

She gritted her teeth. She hated feeling helpless. She didn't *want* anyone to protect her. First the stupid ankle. Now stupid hypothermia. She wanted to be on her feet, with her dagger in her hand.

Then, just outside the firelight at the entrance of the cave, she saw a pair of red eyes glowing in dark.

Okay, she thought. Maybe a little protection is fine.

More wolves edged into the firelight—black beasts bigger than Great Danes, with ice and snow caked on their fur. Their fangs gleamed, and their glowing red eyes looked disturbingly intelligent. The wolf in front was almost as tall as a horse, his mouth stained as if he'd just made a fresh kill.

Piper pulled her dagger out of its sheath.

Then Jason stepped forward and said something in Latin.

Piper didn't think a dead language would have much effect on wild animals, but the alpha wolf curled his lip. The fur stood up along his spine. One of his lieutenants tried to advance, but the alpha wolf snapped at his ear. Then all of the wolves backed into the dark.

"Dude, I gotta study Latin." Leo's hammer shook in his hand. "What'd you say, Jason?"

Hedge cursed. "Whatever it was, it wasn't enough. Look."

The wolves were coming back, but the alpha wolf wasn't with them. They didn't attack. They waited—at least a dozen now, in a rough semicircle just outside the firelight, blocking the cave exit.

The coach hefted his club. "Here's the plan. I'll kill them all, and you guys escape."

"Coach, they'll rip you apart," Piper said.

"Nah, I'm good."

Then Piper saw the silhouette of a man coming through the storm, wading through the wolf pack.

"Stick together," Jason said. "They respect a pack. And Hedge, no crazy stuff. We're not leaving you or anyone else behind."

Piper got a lump in her throat. She was the weak link in their "pack" right now. No doubt the wolves could smell her fear. She might as well be wearing a sign that said FREE LUNCH.

The wolves parted, and the man stepped into the firelight. His hair was greasy and ragged, the color of fireplace soot, topped with a crown of what looked like finger bones. His robes were tattered fur—wolf, rabbit, raccoon, deer, and several others Piper couldn't identify. The furs didn't look cured, and from the smell, they weren't very fresh. His frame was lithe and muscular, like a distance runner's. But the most horrible thing was his face. His thin pale skin was pulled tight over his skull. His teeth were sharpened like fangs. His eyes glowed bright red like his wolves'—and they fixed on Jason with absolute hatred.

"*Ecce,*" he said, "*filli Romani.*"

"Speak English, wolf man!" Hedge bellowed.

The wolf man snarled. "Tell your faun to mind his tongue, son of Rome. Or he'll be my first snack."

Piper remembered that *faun* was the Roman name for *satyr.* Not exactly helpful information. Now, if she could remember who this wolf guy was in Greek mythology, and how to defeat him, *that* she could use.

The wolf man studied their little group. His nostrils twitched. "So it's true," he mused. "A child of Aphrodite. A son of Hephaestus. A faun. And a child of Rome, of Lord Jupiter, no less. All together, without killing each other. How interesting."

"You were told about us?" Jason asked. "By whom?"

The man snarled—perhaps a laugh, perhaps a challenge. "Oh, we've been patrolling for you all across the west, demigod, hoping we'd be the first to find you. The giant king will reward me well when he rises. I am Lycaon, king of the wolves. And my pack is hungry."

The wolves snarled in the darkness.

Out of the corner of her eye, Piper saw Leo put up his hammer and slip something else from his tool belt—a glass bottle full of clear liquid.

Piper racked her brain trying to place the wolf guy's name. She knew she'd heard it before, but she couldn't remember details.

Lycaon glared at Jason's sword. He moved to each side as if looking for an opening, but Jason's blade moved with him.

"Leave," Jason ordered. "There's no food for you here."

"Unless you want tofu burgers," Leo offered.

Lycaon bared his fangs. Apparently he wasn't a tofu fan.

"If I had my way," Lycaon said with regret, "I'd kill you first, son of Jupiter. Your father made me what I am. I was the powerful mortal king of Arcadia, with fifty fine sons, and Zeus slew them all with his lightning bolts."

"Ha," Coach Hedge said. "For good reason!"

Jason glanced over his shoulder. "Coach, you know this clown?"

"*I* do," Piper answered. The details of the myth came back to her—a short, horrible story she and her father had laughed at over breakfast. She wasn't laughing now.

"Lycaon invited Zeus to dinner," she said. "But the king wasn't sure it was really Zeus. So to test his powers, Lycaon tried to feed him human flesh. Zeus got outraged—"

"And killed my sons!" Lycaon howled. The wolves behind him howled too.

"So Zeus turned him into a wolf," Piper said. "They call ...they call werewolves *lycanthropes*, named after him, the first werewolf."

"The king of wolves," Coach Hedge finished. "An immortal, smelly, vicious mutt."

Lycaon growled. "I will tear you apart, faun!"

"Oh, you want some goat, buddy? 'Cause I'll give you goat."

"Stop it," Jason said. "Lycaon, you said you *wanted* to kill me first, but . . . ?"

"Sadly, Child of Rome, you are spoken for. Since this one" —he waggled his claws at Piper—"has failed to kill you, you are to be delivered alive to the Wolf House. One of my compatriots has asked for the honor of killing you herself."

"Who?" Jason said.

The wolf king snickered. "Oh, a great admirer of yours. Apparently, you made quite an impression on her. She will take care of you soon enough, and really I cannot complain. Spilling your blood at the Wolf House should mark my new territory quite well. Lupa will think twice about challenging my pack."

Piper's heart tried to jump out of her chest. She didn't understand everything Lycaon had said, but a woman who wanted to kill Jason? Medea, she thought. Somehow, she must've survived the explosion.

Piper struggled to her feet. Spots danced before her eyes again. The cave seemed to spin.

"You're going to leave now," Piper said, "before we destroy you."

She tried to put power into the words, but she was too weak. Shivering in her blankets, pale and sweaty and barely able to hold a knife, she couldn't have looked very threatening.

Lycaon's red eyes crinkled with humor. "A brave try, girl.

I admire that. Perhaps I'll make your end quick. Only the son of Jupiter is needed alive. The rest of you, I'm afraid, are dinner."

At that moment, Piper knew she was going to die. But at least she'd die on her feet, fighting next to Jason.

Jason took a step forward. "You're not killing anyone, wolf man. Not without going through me."

Lycaon howled and extended his claws. Jason slashed at him, but his golden sword passed straight through as if the wolf king wasn't there.

Lycaon laughed. "Gold, bronze, steel—none of these are any good against my wolves, son of Jupiter."

"Silver!" Piper cried. "Aren't werewolves hurt by silver?"

"We don't have any silver!" Jason said.

Wolves leaped into the firelight. Hedge charged forward with an elated "Woot!"

But Leo struck first. He threw his glass bottle and it shattered on the ground, splattering liquid all over the wolves —the unmistakable smell of gasoline. He shot a burst of fire at the puddle, and a wall of flames erupted.

Wolves yelped and retreated. Several caught fire and had to run back into the snow. Even Lycaon looked uneasily at the barrier of flames now separating his wolves from the demigods.

"Aw, c'mon," Coach Hedge complained. "I can't hit them if they're way over there."

Every time a wolf came closer, Leo shot a new wave of fire from his hands, but each effort seemed to make him a little more tired, and the gasoline was already dying down. "I can't summon any more gas!" Leo warned. Then his face turned red. "Wow, that came out wrong. I mean the *burning* kind. Gonna take the tool belt a while to recharge. What you got, man?"

"Nothing," Jason said. "Not even a weapon that works."

"Lightning?" Piper asked.

Jason concentrated, but nothing happened. "I think the snowstorm is interfering, or something."

"Unleash the *venti*!" Piper said.

"Then we'll have nothing to give Aeolus," Jason said. "We'll have come all this way for nothing."

Lycaon laughed. "I can smell your fear. A few more minutes of life, heroes. Pray to whatever gods you wish. Zeus did not grant me mercy, and you will have none from me."

The flames began to sputter out. Jason cursed and dropped his sword. He crouched like he was ready to go hand-to-hand. Leo pulled his hammer out of his pack. Piper raised her dagger—not much, but it was all she had. Coach Hedge hefted his club, and he was the only one who looked excited about dying.

Then a ripping sound cut through the wind—like a piece of tearing cardboard. A long stick sprouted from the neck of the nearest wolf—the shaft of a silver arrow. The wolf writhed and fell, melting into a puddle of shadow.

More arrows. More wolves fell. The pack broke in confusion. An arrow flashed toward Lycaon, but the wolf king caught it in midair. Then he yelled in pain. When he dropped the arrow, it left a charred, smoking gash across his palm. Another arrow caught him in the shoulder, and the wolf king staggered.

"Curse them!" Lycaon yelled. He growled at his pack, and the wolves turned and ran. Lycaon fixed Jason with those glowing red eyes. "This isn't over, boy."

The wolf king disappeared into the night.

Seconds later, Piper heard more wolves baying, but the sound was different—less threatening, more like hunting dogs on the scent. A smaller white wolf burst into the cave, followed by two more.

Hedge said, "Kill it?"

"No!" Piper said. "Wait."

The wolves tilted their heads and studied the campers with huge golden eyes.

A heartbeat later, their masters appeared: a troop of hunters in white-and-gray winter camouflage, at least half a dozen. All of them carried bows, with quivers of glowing silver arrows on their backs.

Their faces were covered with parka hoods, but clearly they were all girls. One, a little taller than the rest, crouched in the firelight and snatched up the arrow that had wounded Lycaon's hand.

"So close." She turned to her companions. "Phoebe, stay with me. Watch the entrance. The rest of you, follow Lycaon. We can't lose him now. I'll catch up with you."

The other hunters mumbled agreement and disappeared, heading after Lycaon's pack.

The girl in white turned toward them, her face still hidden

in her parka hood. "We've been following that demon's trail for over a week. Is everyone all right? No one got bit?"

Jason stood frozen, staring at the girl. Piper realized something about her voice sounded familiar. It was hard to pin down, but the way she spoke, the way she formed her words, reminded her of Jason.

"You're her," Piper guessed. "You're Thalia."

The girl tensed. Piper was afraid she might draw her bow, but instead she pulled down her parka hood. Her hair was spiky black, with a silver tiara across her brow. Her face had a super-healthy glow to it, as if she were a little more than human, and her eyes were brilliant blue. She was the girl from Jason's photograph.

"Do I know you?" Thalia asked.

Piper took a breath. "This might be a shock, but—"

"Thalia." Jason stepped forward, his voice trembling. "I'm Jason, your brother."

X X X V

LEO

Leo figured he had the worst luck in the group, and that was saying a lot. Why didn't *he* get to have the long-lost sister or the movie star dad who needed rescuing? All he got was a tool belt and a dragon that broke down halfway through the quest. Maybe it was the stupid curse of the Hephaestus cabin, but Leo didn't think so. His life had been unlucky way before he got to camp.

A thousand years from now, when this quest was being told around a campfire, he figured people would talk about brave Jason, beautiful Piper, and their sidekick Flaming Valdez, who accompanied them with a bag of magic screwdrivers and occasionally fixed tofu burgers.

If that wasn't bad enough, Leo fell in love with every girl he saw—as long as she was totally out of his league.

When he first saw Thalia, Leo immediately thought she was *way* too pretty to be Jason's sister. Then he thought he'd better not say that or he'd get in trouble. He liked her dark hair, her blue eyes, and her confident attitude. She looked like the kind of girl who could stomp anybody on the ball court or the battlefield, and wouldn't give Leo the time of day—just Leo's type!

For a minute, Jason and Thalia faced each other, stunned. Then Thalia rushed forward and hugged him.

"My gods! She told me you were dead!" She gripped Jason's face and seemed to be examining everything about it. "Thank Artemis, it *is* you. That little scar on your lip—you tried to eat a stapler when you were two!"

Leo laughed. "Seriously?"

Hedge nodded like he approved of Jason's taste. "Staplers —excellent source of iron."

"W-wait," Jason stammered. "Who told you I was dead? What happened?"

At the cave entrance, one of the white wolves barked. Thalia looked back at the wolf and nodded, but she kept her hands on Jason's face, like she was afraid he might vanish. "My wolf is telling me I don't have much time, and she's right. But we *have* to talk. Let's sit."

Piper did better than that. She collapsed. She would've cracked her head on the cave floor if Hedge hadn't caught her.

Thalia rushed over. "What's wrong with her? Ah—never mind. I see. Hypothermia. Ankle." She frowned at the satyr. "Don't you know nature healing?"

Hedge scoffed. "Why do you think she looks *this* good? Can't you smell the Gatorade?"

Thalia looked at Leo for the first time, and of course it was an accusatory glare, like *Why did you let the goat be a doctor?* As if that was Leo's fault.

"You and the satyr," Thalia ordered, "take this girl to my friend at the entrance. Phoebe's an excellent healer."

"It's cold out there!" Hedge said. "I'll freeze my horns off."

But Leo knew when they weren't wanted. "Come on, Hedge. These two need time to talk."

"Humph. Fine," the satyr muttered. "Didn't even get to brain anybody."

Hedge carried Piper toward the entrance. Leo was about to follow when Jason called, "Actually, man, could you, um, stick around?"

Leo saw something in Jason's eyes he didn't expect: Jason was asking for support. He wanted somebody else there. He was scared.

Leo grinned. "Sticking around is my specialty."

Thalia didn't look too happy about it, but the three of them sat at the fire. For a few minutes, nobody spoke. Jason studied his sister like she was a scary device—one that might explode if handled incorrectly. Thalia seemed more at ease, as if she was used to stumbling across stranger things than long-lost relatives. But still she regarded Jason in a kind of amazed trance, maybe remembering a little two-year-old who tried to eat a stapler. Leo took a few pieces of copper wire out of his pockets and twisted them together.

Finally he couldn't stand the silence. "So ... the Hunters of Artemis. This whole 'not dating' thing—is that like *always*, or more of a seasonal thing, or what?"

Thalia stared at him as if he'd just evolved from pond scum. Yeah, he was *definitely* liking this girl.

Jason kicked him in the shin. "Don't mind Leo. He's just trying to break the ice. But, Thalia... what happened to our family? Who told you I was dead?"

Thalia tugged at a silver bracelet on her wrist. In the firelight, in her winter camouflage, she almost looked like Khione the snow princess—just as cold and beautiful.

"Do you remember anything?" she asked.

Jason shook his head. "I woke up three days ago on a bus with Leo and Piper."

"Which wasn't our fault," Leo added hastily. "Hera stole his memories."

Thalia tensed. "Hera? How do you know that?"

Jason explained about their quest—the prophecy at camp, Hera getting imprisoned, the giant taking Piper's dad, and the winter solstice deadline. Leo chimed in to add the important stuff: how he'd fixed the bronze dragon, could throw fireballs, and made excellent tacos.

Thalia was a good listener. Nothing seemed to surprise her—the monsters, the prophecies, the dead rising. But when Jason mentioned King Midas, she cursed in Ancient Greek.

"I knew we should've burned down his mansion," she said. "That man's a menace. But we were so intent on following Lycaon— Well, I'm glad you got away. So Hera's been... what, hiding you all these years?"

"I don't know." Jason brought out the photo from his pocket. "She left me just enough memory to recognize your face."

Thalia looked at the picture, and her expression softened. "I'd forgotten about that. I left it in Cabin One, didn't I?"

Jason nodded. "I think Hera wanted for us to meet. When we landed here, at this cave... I had a feeling it was important. Like I knew you were close by. Is that crazy?"

"Nah," Leo assured him. "We were absolutely destined to meet your hot sister."

Thalia ignored him. Probably she just didn't want to let on how much Leo impressed her.

"Jason," she said, "when you're dealing with the gods, *nothing* is too crazy. But you can't trust Hera, especially since we're children of Zeus. She *hates* all children of Zeus."

"But she said something about Zeus giving her my life as a peace offering. Does that make any sense?"

The color drained from Thalia's face. "Oh, gods. Mother wouldn't have... You don't remember— No, of course you don't."

"What?" Jason asked.

Thalia's features seemed to grow older in the firelight, like her immortality wasn't working so well. "Jason... I'm not sure how to say this. Our mom wasn't exactly stable. She caught Zeus's eye because she was a television actress, and she *was* beautiful, but she didn't handle the fame well. She drank, pulled stupid stunts. She was always in the tabloids. She could never get enough attention. Even before you were born, she and I argued all the time. She... she knew Dad was Zeus, and I think that was too much for her to take. It was like the ultimate achievement for her to attract the lord of the sky, and she couldn't accept it when he left. The thing about the gods . . . well, they don't hang around."

Leo remembered his own mom, the way she'd assured him over and over that his dad would be back someday. But she'd never acted mad about it. She didn't seem to want Hephaestus for herself—only so Leo could know his father. She'd dealt with working a dead-end job, living in a tiny apartment, never having enough money—and she'd seemed fine with it. As long as she had Leo, she always said, life would be okay.

He watched Jason's face—looking more and more devastated as Thalia described their mom—and for once, Leo didn't feel jealous of his friend. Leo might have lost his mom. He might have had some hard times. But at least he remembered her. He found himself tapping out a Morse code message on his knee: *Love you.* He felt bad for Jason, not having memories like that—not having anything to fall back on.

"So . . ." Jason didn't seem able to finish the question.

"Jason, you got friends," Leo told him. "Now you got a sister. You're not alone."

Thalia offered her hand, and Jason took it.

"When I was about seven," she said, "Zeus started visiting Mom again. I think he felt bad about wrecking her life, and he seemed—different somehow. A little older and sterner, more fatherly toward me. For a while, Mom improved. She loved having Zeus around, bringing her presents, causing the sky to rumble. She always wanted more attention. That's the year you were born. Mom . . . well, I never got along with her, but you gave me a reason to hang around. You were so cute.

And I didn't trust Mom to look after you. Of course, Zeus eventually stopped coming by again. He probably couldn't stand Mom's demands anymore, always pestering him to let her visit Olympus, or to make her immortal or eternally beautiful. When he left for good, Mom got more and more unstable. That was about the time the monsters started attacking me. Mom blamed Hera. She claimed the goddess was coming after you too—that Hera had barely tolerated my birth, but *two* demigod children from the same family was too big an insult. Mom even said she hadn't wanted to name you Jason, but Zeus insisted, as a way to appease Hera because the goddess liked that name. I didn't know what to believe."

Leo fiddled with his copper wires. He felt like an intruder. He shouldn't be listening to this, but it also made him feel like he was getting to know Jason for the first time—like maybe being here now made up for those four months at Wilderness School, when Leo had just imagined they'd had a friendship.

"How did you guys get separated?" he asked.

Thalia squeezed her brother's hand. "If I'd known you were alive...gods, things would've been so different. But when you were two, Mom packed us in the car for a family vacation. We drove up north, toward the wine country, to this park she wanted to show us. I remember thinking it was strange because Mom never took us anywhere, and she was acting super nervous. I was holding your hand, walking you toward this big building in the middle of the park, and..." She took a shaky breath. "Mom told me to go back to the car and get the picnic basket. I didn't want to leave you alone with her, but it was only for a few minutes. When I came back...Mom was kneeling on the stone steps, hugging herself and crying. She said—she said you were gone. She said Hera claimed you and you were as good as dead. I didn't know what she'd done. I was afraid she'd completely lost her mind. I ran all over the place looking for you, but you'd just vanished. She had to drag me away, kicking and screaming. For the next few days I was hysterical. I don't remember everything, but I called the police on Mom and they questioned her for a long time. Afterward, we fought. She told me I'd betrayed her, that I should support her, like *she* was the only one who mattered. Finally I couldn't stand it. Your disappearance was the last straw. I ran away from home, and I never went back, not even when Mom died a few years ago. I thought you were gone forever. I never told anyone about you—not even Annabeth or Luke, my two best friends. It was just too painful."

"Chiron knew." Jason's voice sounded far away. "When I got to camp, he took one look at me and said, 'You should be dead.'"

"That doesn't make sense," Thalia insisted. "I never told him."

"Hey," Leo said. "Important thing is you've got each other now, right? You two are lucky."

Thalia nodded. "Leo's right. Look at you. You're *my* age. You've grown up."

"But where have I been?" Jason said. "How could I be missing all that time? And the Roman stuff..."

Thalia frowned. "The Roman stuff?"

"Your brother speaks Latin," Leo said. "He calls gods by their Roman names, and he's got tattoos." Leo pointed out the marks on Jason's arm. Then he gave Thalia the rundown about the other weird stuff that had happened: Boreas turning into Aquilon, Lycaon calling Jason a "child of Rome," and the wolves backing off when Jason spoke Latin to them.

Thalia plucked her bowstring. "Latin. Zeus sometimes spoke Latin, the second time he stayed with Mom. Like I said, he seemed different, more formal."

"You think he was in his Roman aspect?" Jason asked. "And that's why I think of myself as a child of Jupiter?"

"Possibly," Thalia said. "I've never heard of something like that happening, but it might explain why you think in Roman terms, why you can speak Latin rather than Ancient Greek. That would make you unique. Still, it doesn't explain how you've survived without Camp Half-Blood. A child of Zeus, or Jupiter, or whatever you want to call him—you would've been hounded by monsters. If you were on your own, you should've died years ago. I know *I* wouldn't have been able to survive without friends. You would've needed training, a safe haven—"

"He wasn't alone," Leo blurted out. "We've heard about others like him."

Thalia looked at him strangely. "What do you mean?"

Leo told her about the slashed-up purple shirt in Medea's department store, and the story the Cyclopes told about the child of Mercury who spoke Latin.

"Isn't there anywhere else for demigods?" Leo asked. "I mean besides Camp Half-Blood? Maybe some crazy Latin teacher has been abducting children of the gods or something, making them think like Romans."

As soon as he said it, Leo realized how stupid the idea sounded. Thalia's dazzling blue eyes studied him intently, making him feel like a suspect in a lineup.

"I've been all over the country," Thalia mused. "I've never seen evidence of a crazy Latin teacher, or demigods in purple shirts. Still..." Her voice trailed off, like she'd just had a troubling thought.

"What?" Jason asked.

Thalia shook her head. "I'll have to talk to the goddess. Maybe Artemis will guide us."

"She's still talking to you?" Jason asked. "Most of the gods have gone silent."

"Artemis follows her own rules," Thalia said. "She has to be careful not to let Zeus know, but she thinks Zeus is being ridiculous closing Olympus. She's the one who set us on the trail of Lycaon. She said we'd find a lead to a missing friend of ours."

"Percy Jackson," Leo guessed. "The guy Annabeth is looking for."

Thalia nodded, her face full of concern.

Leo wondered if anyone had ever looked that worried all the times *he'd* disappeared. He kind of doubted it.

"So what would Lycaon have to do with it?" Leo asked. "And how does it connect to us?"

"We need to find out soon," Thalia admitted. "If your deadline is tomorrow, we're wasting time. Aeolus could tell you—"

The white wolf appeared again at the doorway and yipped insistently.

"I have to get moving." Thalia stood. "Otherwise I'll lose the other Hunters' trail. First, though, I'll take you to Aeolus's palace."

"If you can't, it's okay," Jason said, though he sounded kind of distressed.

"Oh, please." Thalia smiled and helped him up. "I haven't had a brother in years. I think I can stand a few minutes with you before you get annoying. Now, let's go!"

XXXVI

LEO

WHEN LEO SAW HOW WELL PIPER AND HEDGE were being treated, he was thoroughly offended.

He'd imagined them freezing their hindquarters off in the snow, but the Hunter Phoebe had set up this silver tent pavilion thing right outside the cave. How she'd done it so fast, Leo had no idea, but inside was a kerosene heater keeping them toasty warm and a bunch of comfy throw pillows. Piper looked back to normal, decked out in a new parka, gloves, and camo pants like a Hunter. She and Hedge and Phoebe were kicking back, drinking hot chocolate.

"Oh, no way," Leo said. "We've been sitting in a *cave* and you get the luxury tent? Somebody give me hypothermia. I want hot chocolate and a parka!"

Phoebe sniffed. "Boys," she said, like it was the worst insult she could think of.

"It's all right, Phoebe," Thalia said. "They'll need extra coats. And I think we can spare some chocolate."

Phoebe grumbled, but soon Leo and Jason were also dressed in silvery winter clothes that were incredibly light-weight and warm. The hot chocolate was first-rate.

"Cheers!" said Coach Hedge. He crunched down his plastic thermos cup.

"That cannot be good for your intestines," Leo said.

Thalia patted Piper on the back. "You up for moving?"

Piper nodded. "Thanks to Phoebe, yeah. You guys are really good at this wilderness survival thing. I feel like I could run ten miles."

Thalia winked at Jason. "She's tough for a child of Aphrodite. I like this one."

"Hey, I could run ten miles too," Leo volunteered. "Tough Hephaestus kid here. Let's hit it."

Naturally, Thalia ignored him.

It took Phoebe exactly six seconds to break camp, which Leo could not believe. The tent self-collapsed into a square the size of a pack of chewing gum. Leo wanted to ask her for the blueprints, but they didn't have time.

Thalia ran uphill through the snow, hugging a tiny little path on the side of the mountain, and soon Leo was regretting trying to look macho, because the Hunters left him in the dust.

Coach Hedge leaped around like a happy mountain goat, coaxing them on like he used to do on track days at school. "Come on, Valdez! Pick up the pace! Let's chant. *I've got a girl in Kalamazoo—*"

"Let's not," Thalia snapped.

So they ran in silence.

Leo fell in next to Jason at the back of the group. "How you doing, man?"

Jason's expression was enough of an answer: *Not good.*

"Thalia takes it so calmly," Jason said. "Like it's no big deal that I appeared. I didn't know what I was expecting, but ... she's not like me. She seems so much more *together.*"

"Hey, she's not fighting amnesia," Leo said. "Plus, she's had more time to get used to this whole demigod thing. You fight monsters and talk to gods for a while, you probably get used to surprises."

"Maybe," Jason said. "I just wish I understood what happened when I was two, why my mom got rid of me. Thalia ran away because of *me.*"

"Hey, whatever's happened, it wasn't your fault. And your sister is pretty cool. She's a *lot* like you."

Jason took that in silence. Leo wondered if he'd said the right things. He wanted to make Jason feel better, but this was way outside his comfort zone.

Leo wished he could reach inside his tool belt and pick just the right wrench to fix Jason's memory—maybe a little hammer—bonk the sticking spot and make everything run right. That would be a lot easier than trying to talk it through. *Not good with organic life forms.* Thanks for those inherited traits, Dad.

He was so lost in thought, he didn't realize the Hunters had stopped. He slammed into Thalia and nearly sent them both down the side of the mountain the hard way. Fortunately, the Hunter was light on her feet. She steadied them both, then pointed up.

"That," Leo choked, "is a really large rock."

They stood near the summit of Pikes Peak. Below them the world was blanketed in clouds. The air was so thin, Leo could hardly breathe. Night had set in, but a full moon shone and the stars were incredible. Stretching out to the north and south, peaks of other mountains rose from the clouds like islands—or teeth.

But the real show was above them. Hovering in the sky, about a quarter mile away, was a massive free-floating island of glowing purple stone. It was hard to judge its size, but Leo figured it was at least as wide as a football stadium and just as tall. The sides were rugged cliffs, riddled with caves, and every once in a while a gust of wind burst out with a sound like a pipe organ blast. At the top of the rock, brass walls ringed some kind of a fortress.

The only thing connecting Pikes Peak to the floating island was a narrow bridge of ice that glistened in the moonlight.

Then Leo realized the bridge wasn't exactly ice, because it wasn't solid. As the winds changed direction, the bridge snaked around—blurring and thinning, in some places even breaking into a dotted line like the vapor trail of a plane.

"We're not seriously crossing that," Leo said.

Thalia shrugged. "I'm not a big fan of heights, I'll admit. But if you want to get to Aeolus's fortress, this is the only way."

"Is the fortress always hanging there?" Piper asked. "How can people not notice it sitting on top of Pikes Peak?"

"The Mist," Thalia said. "Still, mortals do notice it indirectly. Some days, Pikes Peak looks purple. People say it's a trick of the light, but actually it's the color of Aeolus's palace, reflecting off the mountain face."

"It's enormous," Jason said.

Thalia laughed. "You should see Olympus, little brother."

"You're serious? You've been there?"

Thalia grimaced as if it wasn't a good memory. "We should go across in two different groups. The bridge is fragile."

"That's reassuring," Leo said. "Jason, can't you just fly us up there?"

Thalia laughed. Then she seemed to realize Leo's question wasn't a joke. "Wait . . . Jason, you can *fly*?"

Jason gazed up at the floating fortress. "Well, sort of. More like I can control the winds. But the winds up here are so strong, I'm not sure I'd want to try. Thalia, you mean . . . you can't fly?"

For a second, Thalia looked genuinely afraid. Then she got her expression under control. Leo realized she was a lot more scared of heights than she was letting on.

"Truthfully," she said, "I've never tried. Might be better if we stuck to the bridge."

Coach Hedge tapped the ice vapor trail with his hoof, then jumped onto the bridge. Amazingly, it held his weight. "Easy! I'll go first. Piper, come on, girl. I'll give you a hand."

"No, that's okay," Piper started to say, but the coach grabbed her hand and dragged her up the bridge.

When they were about halfway, the bridge still seemed to be holding them just fine.

Thalia turned to her Hunter friend. "Phoebe, I'll be back soon. Go find the others. Tell them I'm on my way."

"You sure?" Phoebe narrowed her eyes at Leo and Jason, like they might kidnap Thalia or something.

"It's fine," Thalia promised.

Phoebe nodded reluctantly, then raced down the mountain path, the white wolves at her heels.

"Jason, Leo, just be careful where you step," Thalia said. "It hardly ever breaks."

"It hasn't met me yet," Leo muttered, but he and Jason led the way up the bridge.

Halfway up, things went wrong, and of course it was Leo's fault. Piper and Hedge had already made it safely to the top and were waving at them, encouraging them to keep climbing, but Leo got distracted. He was thinking about bridges —how he would design something way more stable than this shifting ice vapor business if this were his palace. He was pondering braces and support columns. Then a sudden revelation stopped him in his tracks.

"Why do they have a bridge?" he asked.

Thalia frowned. "Leo, this isn't a good place to stop. What do you mean?"

"They're wind spirits," Leo said. "Can't they fly?"

"Yes, but sometimes they need a way to connect to the world below."

"So the bridge isn't always here?" Leo asked.

Thalia shook her head. "The wind spirits don't like to anchor to the earth, but sometimes it's necessary. Like now. They know you're coming."

Leo's mind was racing. He was so excited he could almost feel his body's temperature rising. He couldn't quite put his thoughts into words, but he knew he was on to something important.

"Leo?" Jason said. "What are you thinking?"

"Oh, gods," Thalia said. "Keep moving. Look at your feet."

Leo shuffled backward. With horror, he realized his body temperature really *was* rising, just as it had years ago at that picnic table under the pecan tree, when his anger had gotten away from him. Now, excitement was causing the reaction. His pants steamed in the cold air. His shoes were literally smoking, and the bridge didn't like it. The ice was thinning.

"Leo, stop it," Jason warned. "You're going to melt it."

"I'll try," Leo said. But his body was overheating on its own, running as fast as his thoughts. "Listen, Jason, what did Hera call you in that dream? She called you a *bridge*."

"Leo, seriously, cool down," Thalia said. "I don't what you're talking about, but the bridge is—"

"Just listen," Leo insisted. "If Jason is a bridge, what's he connecting? Maybe two different places that normally don't get along—like the air palace and the ground. You had to be somewhere before this, right? And Hera said you were an exchange."

"An exchange." Thalia's eyes widened. "Oh, gods."

Jason frowned. "What are you two talking about?"

Thalia murmured something like a prayer. "I understand now why Artemis sent me here. Jason—she told me to hunt for Lycaon and I would find a clue about Percy. *You* are the clue. Artemis wanted us to meet so I could hear your story."

"I don't understand," he protested. "I don't have a story. I don't remember anything."

"But Leo's right," Thalia said. "It's all connected. If we just knew where—"

Leo snapped his fingers. "Jason, what did you call that place in your dream? That ruined house. The Wolf House?"

Thalia nearly choked. "The Wolf House? Jason, why didn't you tell me that! *That's* where they're keeping Hera?"

"You know where it is?" Jason asked.

Then the bridge dissolved. Leo would've fallen to his death, but Jason grabbed his coat and pulled him to safety. The two of them scrambled up the bridge, and when they turned, Thalia was on the other side of a thirty-foot chasm. The bridge was continuing to melt.

"Go!" Thalia shouted, backing down the bridge as it crumbled. "Find out where the giant is keeping Piper's dad. Save him! I'll take the Hunters to the Wolf House and hold it until you can get there. We can do both!"

"But where *is* the Wolf House?" Jason shouted.

"You know where it is, little brother!" She was so far away now that they could barely hear her voice over the wind. Leo was pretty sure she said: "I'll see you there. I promise."

Then she turned and raced down the dissolving bridge.

Leo and Jason had no time to stand around. They climbed for their lives, the ice vapor thinning under their feet. Several times, Jason grabbed Leo and used the winds to keep them aloft, but it was more like bungee jumping than flying.

When they reached the floating island, Piper and Coach Hedge pulled them aboard just as the last of the vapor bridge vanished. They stood gasping for breath at the base of a stone stairway chiseled into the side of the cliff, leading up to the fortress.

Leo looked back down. The top of Pikes Peak floated below them in a sea of clouds, but there was no sign of Thalia. And Leo had just burned their only exit.

"What happened?" Piper demanded. "Leo, why are your clothes smoking?"

"I got a little heated," he gasped. "Sorry, Jason. Honest. I didn't—"

"It's all right," Jason said, but his expression was grim. "We've got less than twenty-four hours to rescue a goddess and Piper's dad. Let's go see the king of the winds."

XXXVII

JASON

JASON HAD FOUND HIS SISTER AND lost her in less than an hour. As they climbed the cliffs of the floating island, he kept looking back, but Thalia was gone.

Despite what she'd said about meeting him again, Jason wondered. She'd found a new family with the Hunters, and a new mother in Artemis. She seemed so confident and comfortable with her life, Jason wasn't sure if he'd ever be part of it. And she seemed so set on finding her friend Percy. Had she ever searched for Jason that way?

Not fair, he told himself. *She thought you were dead.*

He could barely tolerate what she'd said about their mom. It was almost like Thalia had handed him a baby—a really loud, ugly baby—and said, *Here, this is yours. Carry it.* He didn't want to carry it. He didn't want to look at it or claim it. He didn't want to know that he had an unstable mother who'd gotten rid of him to appease a goddess. No wonder Thalia had run away.

Then he remembered the Zeus cabin at Camp Half-Blood —that tiny little alcove Thalia had used as a bunk, out of sight from the glowering statue of the sky god. Their dad wasn't much of a bargain, either. Jason understood why Thalia had renounced that part of her life too, but he was still resentful. He couldn't be so lucky. He was left holding the bag —literally.

The golden backpack of winds was strapped over his shoulders. The closer they got to Aeolus's palace, the heavier the bag got. The winds struggled, rumbling and bumping around.

The only one who seemed in a good mood was Coach Hedge. He kept bounding up the slippery staircase and trotting back down. "Come on, cupcakes! Only a few thousand more steps!"

As they climbed, Leo and Piper left Jason in his silence. Maybe they could sense his bad mood. Piper kept glancing back, worried, as if he were the one who'd almost died of hypothermia rather than she. Or maybe she was thinking about Thalia's idea. They'd told her what Thalia had said on the bridge—how they could save both her dad and Hera—but Jason didn't really understand how they were going to do that, and he wasn't sure if the possibility had made Piper more hopeful or just more anxious.

Leo kept swatting his own legs, checking for signs that his pants were on fire. He wasn't steaming anymore, but the incident on the ice bridge had really freaked Jason out. Leo hadn't seemed to realize that he had smoke coming out his ears and flames dancing through his hair. If Leo started spontaneously combusting every time he got excited, they were going to have a tough time taking him anywhere. Jason imagined trying to get food at a restaurant. *I'll have a cheeseburger and—Ahhh! My friend's on fire! Get me a bucket!*

Mostly, though, Jason worried about what Leo had said. Jason didn't want to be a bridge, or an exchange, or anything else. He just wanted to know where he'd come from. And Thalia had looked so unnerved when Leo mentioned the burned-out house in his dreams—the place the wolf Lupa had told him was his starting point. How did Thalia know that place, and why did she assume Jason could find it?

The answer seemed close. But the nearer Jason got to it, the less it cooperated, like the winds on his back.

Finally they arrived at the top of the island. Bronze walls marched all the way around the fortress grounds, though Jason couldn't imagine who would possibly attack this place. Twenty-foot-high gates opened for them, and a road of polished purple stone led up to the main citadel—a white-columned rotunda, Greek style, like one of the monuments in Washington, D.C.—except for the cluster of satellite dishes and radio towers on the roof.

"That's bizarre," Piper said.

"Guess you can't get cable on a floating island," Leo said. "Dang, check this guy's front yard."

The rotunda sat in the center of a quarter-mile circle. The grounds were amazing in a scary way. They were divided into four sections like big pizza slices, each one representing a season.

The section on their right was an icy waste, with bare trees and a frozen lake. Snowmen rolled across the landscape as the wind blew, so Jason wasn't sure if they were decorations or alive.

To their left was an autumn park with gold and red trees. Mounds of leaves blew into patterns—gods, people, animals that ran after each other before scattering back into leaves.

In the distance, Jason could see two more areas behind the rotunda. One looked like a green pasture with sheep made out of clouds. The last section was a desert where tumbleweeds scratched strange patterns in the sand like Greek letters, smiley faces, and a huge advertisement that read: *WATCH AEOLUS NIGHTLY!*

"One section for each of the four wind gods," Jason guessed. "Four cardinal directions."

"I'm loving that pasture." Coach Hedge licked his lips. "You guys mind—"

"Go ahead," Jason said. He was actually relieved to send the satyr off. It would be hard enough getting on Aeolus's good side without Coach Hedge waving his club and screaming, "Die!"

While the satyr ran off to attack springtime, Jason, Leo, and Piper walked down the road to the steps of the palace. They passed through the front doors into a white marble foyer decorated with purple banners that read OLYMPIAN WEATHER CHANNEL, and some that just read ow!

"Hello!" A woman floated up to them. *Literally* floated. She was pretty in that elfish way Jason associated with nature spirits at Camp Half-Blood—petite, slightly pointy ears, and an ageless face that could've been sixteen or thirty. Her brown eyes twinkled cheerfully. Even though there was no wind, her dark hair blew in slow motion, shampoo-commercial style. Her white gown billowed around her like parachute material. Jason couldn't tell if she had feet, but if so, they didn't touch the floor. She had a white tablet computer in her hand. "Are you from Lord Zeus?" she asked. "We've been expecting you."

Jason tried to respond, but it was a little hard to think straight, because he'd realized the woman was see-through. Her shape faded in and out like she was made of fog.

"Are you a ghost?" he asked.

Right away he knew he'd insulted her. The smile turned into a pout. "I'm an *aura*, sir. A wind nymph, as you might expect, working for the lord of the winds. My name is Mellie. We don't have *ghosts*."

Piper came to the rescue. "No, of course you don't! My friend simply mistook you for Helen of Troy, the most beautiful mortal of all time. It's an easy mistake."

Wow, she was good. The compliment seemed a little over the top, but Mellie the aura blushed. "Oh . . . well, then. So you *are* from Zeus?"

"Er," Jason said, "I'm the son of Zeus, yeah."

"Excellent! Please, right this way." She led them through some security doors into another lobby, consulting her tablet as she floated. She didn't look where she was going, but apparently it didn't matter as she drifted straight through a marble column with no problem. "We're out of prime time now, so that's good," she mused. "I can fit you in right before his 11:12 spot."

"Um, okay," Jason said.

The lobby was a pretty distracting place. Winds blasted

around them, so Jason felt like he was pushing through an invisible crowd. Doors blew open and slammed by themselves.

The things Jason *could* see were just as bizarre. Paper airplanes of all different sizes and shapes sped around, and other wind nymphs, *aurai*, would occasionally pluck them out of the air, unfold and read them, then toss them back into the air, where the planes would refold themselves and keep flying.

An ugly creature fluttered past. She looked like a mix between an old lady and a chicken on steroids. She had a wrinkled face with black hair tied in a hairnet, arms like a human plus wings like a chicken, and a fat, feathered body with talons for feet. It was amazing she could fly at all. She kept drifting around and bumping into things like a parade balloon.

"Not an *aura?*" Jason asked Mellie as the creature wobbled by.

Mellie laughed. "That's a harpy, of course. Our, ah, ugly stepsisters, I suppose you would say. Don't you have harpies on Olympus? They're spirits of violent gusts, unlike us *aurai*. We're all gentle breezes."

She batted her eyes at Jason.

"'Course you are," he said.

"So," Piper prompted, "you were taking us to see Aeolus?"

Mellie led them through a set of doors like an airlock. Above the interior door, a green light blinked.

"We have a few minutes before he starts," Mellie said cheerfully. "He probably won't kill you if we go in now. Come along!"

XXXVIII

JASON

JASON'S JAW DROPPED. THE CENTRAL SECTION of Aeolus's fortress was as big as a cathedral, with a soaring domed roof covered in silver. Television equipment floated randomly through the air—cameras, spotlights, set pieces, potted plants. And there was no floor. Leo almost fell into the chasm before Jason pulled him back.

"Holy—!" Leo gulped. "Hey, Mellie. A little warning next time!"

An enormous circular pit plunged into the heart of the mountain. It was probably half a mile deep, honeycombed with caves. Some of the tunnels probably led straight outside. Jason remembered seeing winds blast out of them when they'd been on Pikes Peak. Other caves were sealed with some glistening material like glass or wax. The whole cavern bustled with harpies, *aurai*, and paper airplanes, but for someone who couldn't fly, it would be a very long, very fatal fall.

"Oh, my," Mellie gasped. "I'm so sorry." She unclipped a walkie-talkie from somewhere inside her robes and spoke into it: "Hello, sets? Is that Nuggets? Hi, Nuggets. Could we get a floor in the main studio, please? Yes, a solid one. Thanks."

A few seconds later, an army of harpies rose from the pit—three dozen or so demon chicken ladies, all carrying squares of various building material. They went to work hammering and gluing—and using large quantities of duct tape, which didn't reassure Jason. In no time there was a makeshift floor snaking out over the chasm. It was made of plywood, marble blocks, carpet squares, wedges of grass sod—just about anything.

"That can't be safe," Jason said.

"Oh, it is!" Mellie assured him. "The harpies are very good."

Easy for her to say. She just drifted across without touching the floor, but Jason decided he had the best chance at surviving, since he could fly, so he stepped out first. Amazingly, the floor held.

Piper gripped his hand and followed him. "If I fall, you're catching me."

"Uh, sure." Jason hoped he wasn't blushing.

Leo stepped out next. "You're catching me, too, Superman. But I ain't holding your hand."

Mellie led them toward the middle of the chamber, where a loose sphere of flat-panel video screens floated around a kind of control center. A man hovered inside, checking monitors and reading paper airplane messages.

The man paid them no attention as Mellie brought them forward. She pushed a forty-two-inch Sony out of their way and led them into the control area.

Leo whistled. "I *got* to get a room like this."

The floating screens showed all sorts of television programs. Some Jason recognized—news broadcasts, mostly—but some programs looked a little strange: gladiators fighting, demigods battling monsters. Maybe they were movies, but they looked more like reality shows.

At the far end of the sphere was a silky blue backdrop like a cinema screen, with cameras and studio lights floating around it.

The man in the center was talking into an earpiece phone. He had a remote control in each hand and was pointing them at various screens, seemingly at random.

He wore a business suit that looked like the sky—blue mostly, but dappled with clouds that changed and darkened and moved across the fabric. He looked like he was in his sixties, with a shock of white hair, but he had a ton of stage makeup on, and that smooth plastic-surgery look to his face, so he appeared not really young, not really old, just *wrong*—like a Ken doll someone had halfway melted in a microwave. His eyes darted back and forth from screen to screen, like he was trying to absorb everything at once. He muttered things into his phone, and his mouth kept twitching. He was either amused, or crazy, or both.

Mellie floated toward him. "Ah, sir, Mr. Aeolus, these demigods—"

"Hold it!" He held up a hand to silence her, then pointed at one of the screens. "Watch!"

It was one of those storm-chaser programs, where insane thrill-seekers drive after tornados. As Jason watched, a Jeep plowed straight into a funnel cloud and got tossed into the sky.

Aeolus shrieked with delight. "The Disaster Channel. People do that *on purpose!*" He turned toward Jason with a mad grin. "Isn't that amazing? Let's watch it again."

"Um, sir," Mellie said, "this is Jason, son of—"

"Yes, yes, I remember," Aeolus said. "You're back. How did it go?"

Jason hesitated. "Sorry? I think you've mistaken me—"

"No, no, Jason Grace, aren't you? It was—what—last year? You were on your way to fight a sea monster, I believe."

"I—I don't remember."

Aelous laughed. "Must not have been a very good sea monster! No, I remember every hero who's ever come to me for aid. Odysseus—gods, he docked at my island for a month! At least you only stayed a few days. Now, watch this video. These ducks get sucked straight into—"

"Sir," Mellie interrupted. "Two minutes to air."

"Air!" Aeolus exclaimed. "I love air. How do I look? Makeup!"

Immediately a small tornado of brushes, blotters, and cotton balls descended on Aeolus. They blurred across his face in a cloud of flesh-tone smoke until his coloration was even more gruesome than before. Wind swirled through his hair and left it sticking up like a frosted Christmas tree.

"Mr. Aeolus." Jason slipped off the golden backpack. "We brought you these rogue storm spirits."

"Did you!" Aeolus looked at the bag like it was a gift from a fan—something he really didn't want. "Well, how nice."

Leo nudged him, and Jason offered the bag. "Boreas sent us to capture them for you. We hope you'll accept them and stop—you know—ordering demigods to be killed."

Aeolus laughed, and looked incredulously at Mellie. "Demigods be killed—did I order that?"

Mellie checked her computer tablet. "Yes, sir, fifteenth of September. 'Storm spirits released by the death of Typhon, demigods to be held responsible,' etc. . . . yes, a general order for them all to be killed."

"Oh, pish," Aeolus said. "I was just grumpy. Rescind that order, Mellie, and um, who's on guard duty—Teriyaki?—Teri, take these storm spirits down to cell block Fourteen E, will you?"

A harpy swooped out of nowhere, snatched the golden bag, and spiraled into the abyss.

Aeolus grinned at Jason. "Now, sorry about that kill-on-sight business. But gods, I really was mad, wasn't I?" His face suddenly darkened, and his suit did the same, the lapels flashing with lightning. "You know . . . I remember now. Almost seemed like a voice was telling me to give that order. A little cold tingle on the back of my neck."

Jason tensed. A cold tingle on the back of his neck . . . Why did that sound so familiar? "A . . . um, voice in your head, sir?"

"Yes. How odd. Mellie, *should* we kill them?"

"No, sir," she said patiently. "They just brought us the storm spirits, which makes everything all right."

"Of course." Aeolus laughed. "Sorry. Mellie, let's send the demigods something nice. A box of chocolates, perhaps."

"A box of chocolates to *every* demigod in the world, sir?"

"No, too expensive. Never mind. Wait, it's time! I'm on!"

Aeolus flew off toward the blue screen as newscast music started to play.

Jason looked at Piper and Leo, who seemed just as confused as he was.

"Mellie," he said, "is he . . . always like that?"

She smiled sheepishly. "Well, you know what they say. If you don't like his mood, wait five minutes. That expression 'whichever way the wind blows'—that was based on him."

"And that thing about the sea monster," Jason said. "*Was* I here before?"

Mellie blushed. "I'm sorry, I don't remember. I'm Mr. Aeolus's new assistant. I've been with him longer than most, but still—not that long."

"How long do his assistants usually last?" Piper asked.

"Oh . . ." Mellie thought for a moment. "I've been doing this for . . . twelve hours?"

A voice blared from floating speakers: "And now, weather every twelve minutes! Here's your forecaster for Olympian Weather—the OW! channel—Aeolus!"

Lights blazed on Aeolus, who was now standing in front of the blue screen. His smile was unnaturally white, and he looked like he'd had so much caffeine his face was about to explode.

"Hello, Olympus! Aeolus, master of the winds here, with weather every twelve! We'll have a low-pressure system moving over Florida today, so expect milder temperatures since Demeter wishes to spare the citrus farmers!" He gestured at the blue screen, but when Jason checked the monitors, he saw that a digital image was being projected behind Aeolus, so it looked like he was standing in front of a U.S. map with animated smiley suns and frowny storm clouds. "Along the eastern seaboard—oh, hold on." He tapped his earpiece. "Sorry, folks! Poseidon is angry with Miami today, so it looks like that Florida freeze is back on! Sorry, Demeter. Over in the Midwest, I'm not sure what St. Louis did to offend Zeus, but you can expect winter storms! Boreas himself is being called down to punish the area with ice. Bad news, Missouri! No, wait. Hephaestus feels sorry for central Missouri, so you all will have much more moderate temperatures and sunny skies."

Aeolus kept going like that—forecasting each area of the country and changing his prediction two or three times as he got messages over his earpiece—the gods apparently putting in orders for various winds and weather.

"This can't be right," Jason whispered. "Weather isn't this random."

Mellie smirked. "And how often are the mortal weathermen right? They talk about fronts and air pressure and moisture, but the weather surprises them all the time. At least Aeolus tells us *why* it's so unpredictable. Very hard job, trying to appease all the gods at once. It's enough to drive anyone..."

She trailed off, but Jason knew what she meant. *Mad.* Aeolus was completely mad.

"And that's the weather," Aeolus concluded. "See you in twelve minutes, because I'm sure it'll change!"

The lights shut off, the video monitors went back to random coverage, and just for a moment, Aeolus's face sagged with weariness. Then he seemed to remember he had guests, and he put a smile back on.

"So, you brought me some rogue storm spirits," Aeolus said. "I suppose . . . thanks! And did you want something else? I assume so. Demigods always do."

Mellie said, "Um, sir, this is Zeus's son."

"Yes, yes. I know that. I said I remembered him from before."

"But, sir, they're here from *Olympus*."

Aeolus looked stunned. Then he laughed so abruptly, Jason almost jumped into the chasm. "You mean you're here on behalf of your father this time? Finally! I *knew* they would send someone to renegotiate my contract!"

"Um, what?" Jason asked.

"Oh, thank goodness!" Aeolus sighed with relief. "It's been what, three thousand years since Zeus made me master of the winds. Not that I'm ungrateful, of course! But really, my contract is so vague. Obviously I'm immortal, but 'master of the winds.' What does that mean? Am I a nature spirit? A demigod? A god? I *want* to be god of the winds, because the benefits are *so* much better. Can we start with that?"

Jason looked at his friends, mystified.

"Dude," Leo said, "you think we're here to promote you?"

"You are, then?" Aeolus grinned. His business suit turned completely blue—not a cloud in the fabric. "Marvelous! I mean, I think I've shown quite a bit of initiative with the weather channel, eh? And of course I'm in the press all the time. So many books have been written about me: *Into Thin Air, Up in the Air, Gone with the Wind*—"

"Er, I don't think those are about you," Jason said, before he noticed Mellie shaking her head.

"Nonsense," Aeolus said. "Mellie, they're biographies of me, aren't they?"

"Absolutely, sir," she squeaked.

"There, you see? I don't read. Who has time? But obviously the mortals love me. So, we'll change my official title to *god of the winds*. Then, about salary and staff—"

"Sir," Jason said, "we're not from Olympus."

Aeolus blinked. "But—"

"I'm the son of Zeus, yes," Jason said, "but we're not here to negotiate your contract. We're on a quest and we need your help."

Aeolus's expression hardened. "Like last time? Like *every* hero who comes here? Demigods! It's always about *you*, isn't it?"

"Sir, please, I don't remember last time, but if you helped me once before—"

"I'm always helping! Well, sometimes I'm destroying, but mostly I'm helping, and sometimes I'm asked to do both at the same time! Why, Aeneas, the first of your kind—"

"My kind?" Jason asked. "You mean, demigods?"

"Oh, please!" Aeolus said. "I mean your *line* of demigods. You know, Aeneas, son of Venus—the only surviving hero of Troy. When the Greeks burned down his city, he escaped to

Italy, where he founded the kingdom that would eventually become Rome, blah, blah, blah. *That's* what I meant."

"I don't get it," Jason admitted.

Aeolus rolled his eyes. "The point being, I was thrown in the middle of that conflict, too! Juno calls up: 'Oh, Aeolus, destroy Aeneas's ships for me. I don't like him.' Then Neptune says, 'No, you don't! That's my territory. Calm the winds.' Then Juno is like, 'No, wreck his ships, or I'll tell Jupiter you're uncooperative!' Do you think it's easy juggling requests like that?"

"No," Jason said. "I guess not."

"And don't get me started on Amelia Earhart! I'm *still* getting angry calls from Olympus about knocking *her* out of the sky!"

"We just want information," Piper said in her most calming voice. "We hear you know everything."

Aeolus straightened his lapels and looked slightly mollified. "Well . . . *that's* true, of course. For instance, I know that *this* business here"—he waggled his fingers at the three of them—"this harebrained scheme of Juno's to bring you all together is likely to end in bloodshed. As for you, Piper McLean, I know your father is in serious trouble." He held out his hand, and a scrap of paper fluttered into his grasp. It was a photo of Piper with a guy who must've been her dad. His face *did* look familiar. Jason was pretty sure he'd seen him in some movies.

Piper took the photo. Her hands were shaking. "This—this is from his wallet."

"Yes," Aeolus said. "All things lost in the wind eventually

come to me. The photo blew away when the Earthborn captured him."

"The what?" Piper asked.

Aeolus waved aside the question and narrowed his eyes at Leo. "Now, *you*, son of Hephaestus . . . yes, I see your future." Another paper fell into the wind god's hands—an old tattered drawing done in crayons.

Leo took it as if it might be coated in poison. He staggered backward.

"Leo?" Jason said. "What is it?"

"Something I—I drew when I was a kid." He folded it quickly and put it in his coat. "It's . . . yeah, it's nothing."

Aeolus laughed. "Really? Just the key to your success! Now, where were we? Ah, yes, you wanted information. Are you sure about that? Sometimes information can be dangerous."

He smiled at Jason like he was issuing a challenge. Behind him, Mellie shook her head in warning.

"Yeah," Jason said. "We need to find the lair of Enceladus."

Aeolus's smile melted. "The giant? Why would you want to go there? He's horrible! He doesn't even watch my program!"

Piper held up the photo. "Aeolus, he's got my father. We need to rescue him and find out where Hera is being held captive."

"Now, *that's* impossible," Aeolus said. "Even *I* can't see that, and believe me, I've tried. There's a veil of magic over Hera's location—very strong, impossible to locate."

"She's at a place called the Wolf House," Jason said.

"Hold on!" Aelous put a hand to his forehead and closed

his eyes. "I'm getting something! Yes, she's at a place called the Wolf House! Sadly, I don't know where that is."

"Enceladus does," Piper persisted. "If you help us find him, we could get the location of the goddess—"

"Yeah," Leo said, catching on. "And if we save her, she'd be really grateful to you—"

"And Zeus might promote you," Jason finished.

Aeolus's eyebrows crept up. "A promotion—and all you want from me is the giant's location?"

"Well, if you could get us there, too," Jason amended, "that would be great."

Mellie clapped her hands in excitement. "Oh, he could do that! He often sends helpful winds—"

"Mellie, quiet!" Aeolus snapped. "I have half a mind to fire you for letting these people in under false pretenses."

Her face paled. "Yes, sir. Sorry, sir."

"It wasn't her fault," Jason said. "But about that help..."

Aelous tilted his head as if thinking. Then Jason realized the wind lord was listening to voices in his earpiece.

"Well... Zeus approves," Aeolus muttered. "He says... he says it would be better if you could avoid saving her until after the weekend, because he has a big party planned—Ow! That's Aphrodite yelling at him, reminding him that the solstice starts at dawn. She says I should help you. And Hephaestus ...yes. Hmm. Very rare they agree on anything. Hold on..."

Jason smiled at his friends. Finally, they were having some good luck. Their godly parents were standing up for them.

Back toward the entrance, Jason heard a loud belch. Coach

Hedge waddled in from the lobby, grass all over his face. Mellie saw him coming across the makeshift floor and caught her breath. "Who is *that*?"

Jason stifled a cough. "That? That's just Coach Hedge. Uh, Gleeson Hedge. He's our..." Jason wasn't sure what to call him: *teacher, friend, problem?*

"Our guide."

"He's *so* goatly," Mellie murmured.

Behind her, Piper poofed out her cheeks, pretending to vomit.

"What's up, guys?" Hedge trotted over. "Wow, nice place. Oh! Sod squares."

"Coach, you just ate," Jason said. "And we're using the sod as a floor. This is, ah, Mellie—"

"An *aura*." Hedge smiled winningly. "Beautiful as a summer breeze."

Mellie blushed.

"And Aeolus here was just about to help us," Jason said.

"Yes," the wind lord muttered. "It seems so. You'll find Enceladus on Mount Diablo."

"Devil Mountain?" Leo asked. "That doesn't sound good."

"I remember that place!" Piper said. "I went there once with my dad. It's just east of San Francisco Bay."

"The Bay Area again?" The coach shook his head. "Not good. Not good at all."

"Now..." Aeolus began to smile. "As to getting you there—"

Suddenly his face went slack. He bent over and tapped his earpiece as if it were malfunctioning. When he straightened again, his eyes were wild. Despite the makeup, he looked like an old man—an old, very frightened man. "She hasn't spoke to me for centuries. I can't—yes, yes I understand."

He swallowed, regarding Jason as if he had suddenly turned into a giant cockroach. "I'm sorry, son of Jupiter. New orders. You all have to die."

Mellie squeaked. "But—but, sir! Zeus said to help them. Aphrodite, Hephaestus—"

"Mellie!" Aeolus snapped. "Your job is already on the line. Besides, there are some orders that transcend even the wishes of the gods, especially when it comes to the forces of nature."

"*Whose* orders?" Jason said. "Zeus will fire you if you don't help us!"

"I doubt it." Aeolus flicked his wrist, and far below them, a cell door opened in the pit. Jason could hear storm spirits screaming out of it, spiraling up toward them, howling for blood.

"Even Zeus understands the order of things," Aeolus said. "And if *she* is waking—by all the gods—she cannot be denied. Good-bye, heroes. I'm terribly sorry, but I'll have to make this quick. I'm back on the air in four minutes."

Jason summoned his sword. Coach Hedge pulled out his club. Mellie the aura yelled, "No!"

She dived at their feet just as the storm spirits hit with hurricane force, blasting the floor to pieces, shredding the carpet samples and marble and linoleum into what should've been lethal projectiles, had Mellie's robes not spread out like a shield and absorbed the brunt of the impact. The five of them fell into the pit, and Aeolus screamed above them, "Mellie, you are *so* fired!"

"Quick," Mellie yelled. "Son of Zeus, do you have any power over the air?"

"A little!"

"Then help me, or you're all dead!" Mellie grabbed his hand, and an electric charge went through Jason's arm. He understood what she needed. They had to control their fall and head for one of the open tunnels. The storm spirits were following them down, closing rapidly, bringing with them a cloud of deadly shrapnel.

Jason grabbed Piper's hand. "Group hug!"

Hedge, Leo, and Piper tried to huddle together, hanging on to Jason and Mellie as they fell.

"This is NOT GOOD!" Leo yelled.

"Bring it on, gas bags!" Hedge yelled up at the storm spirits. "I'll pulverize you!"

"He's magnificent," Mellie sighed.

"Concentrate?" Jason prompted.

"Right!" she said.

They channeled the wind so their fall became more of a tumble into the nearest open chute. Still, they slammed into the tunnel at painful speed and went rolling over each other down a steep vent that was not designed for people. There was no way they could stop.

Mellie's robes billowed around her. Jason and the others clung to her desperately, and they began to slow down, but the storm spirits were screaming into the tunnel behind them.

"Can't—hold—long," Mellie warned. "Stay together! When the winds hit—"

"You're doing great, Mellie," Hedge said. "My own mama was an *aura*, you know. She couldn't have done better herself."

"Iris-message me?" Mellie pleaded.

Hedge winked.

"Could you guys plan your date later?" Piper screamed. "Look!"

Behind them, the tunnel was turning dark. Jason could feel his ears pop as the pressure built.

"Can't hold them," Mellie warned. "But I'll try to shield you, do you one more favor."

"Thanks, Mellie," Jason said. "I hope you get a new job."

She smiled, and then dissolved, wrapping them in a warm gentle breeze. Then the real winds hit, shooting them into the sky so fast, Jason blacked out.

XXXIX

PIPER

PIPER DREAMED SHE WAS ON THE Wilderness School dorm roof.

The desert night was cold, but she'd brought blankets, and with Jason next to her, she didn't need any more warmth.

The air smelled of sage and burning mesquite. On the horizon, the Spring Mountains loomed like jagged black teeth, the dim glow of Las Vegas behind them.

The stars were so bright, Piper had been afraid they wouldn't be able to see the meteor shower. She didn't want Jason to think she'd dragged him up here on false pretenses. (Even though her pretenses had been *totally* false.) But the meteors did not disappoint. One streaked across the sky almost every minute—a line of white, yellow, or blue fire. Piper was sure her Grandpa Tom would have some Cherokee myth to explain them, but at the moment she was busy creating her own story.

Jason took her hand—*finally*—and pointed as two meteors skipped across the atmosphere and formed a cross.

"Wow," he said. "I can't believe Leo didn't want to see this."

"Actually, I didn't invite him," Piper said casually.

Jason smiled. "Oh, yeah?"

"Mm-hmm. You ever feel like three would be a crowd?"

"Yeah," Jason admitted. "Like right now. You know how much trouble we'd get in if we got caught up here?"

"Oh, I'd make up something," Piper said. "I can be very persuasive. So you want to dance, or what?"

He laughed. His eyes were amazing, and his smile was even better in the starlight. "With no music. At night. On a rooftop. Sounds dangerous."

"I'm a dangerous girl."

"That, I can believe."

He stood and offered her his hand. They slow danced a few steps, but it quickly turned into a kiss. Piper almost couldn't kiss him again, because she was too busy smiling.

Then her dream changed—or maybe she was dead in the Underworld—because she found herself back in Medea's department store.

"Please let this be a dream," she murmured, "and not my eternal punishment."

"No, dear," said a woman's honey-sweet voice. "No punishment."

Piper turned, afraid she'd see Medea, but a different

woman stood next to her, browsing through the fifty-percent-off rack.

The woman was gorgeous—shoulder-length hair, a graceful neck, perfect features, and an amazing figure tucked into jeans and a snowy white top.

Piper had seen her share of actresses—most of her dad's dates were knockout beautiful—but this lady was different. She was elegant without trying, fashionable without effort, stunning without makeup. After seeing Aeolus with his silly face-lifts and cosmetics, Piper thought this woman looked even more astonishing. There was nothing artificial about her.

Yet as Piper watched, the woman's appearance changed. Piper couldn't decide the color of her eyes, or the exact color of her hair. The woman became more and more beautiful, as if her image were aligning itself to Piper's thoughts—getting as close as possible to Piper's ideal of beauty.

"Aphrodite," Piper said. "Mom?"

The goddess smiled. "You're only dreaming, my sweet. If anyone wonders, I wasn't here. Okay?"

"I—" Piper wanted to ask a thousand questions, but they all crowded together in her head.

Aphrodite held up a turquoise dress. Piper thought it looked awesome, but the goddess made a face. "This isn't my color, is it? Pity, it's cute. Medea really does have some lovely things here."

"This—this building exploded," Piper stammered. "I saw it."

"Yes," Aphrodite agreed. "I suppose that's why everything's on sale. Just a memory, now. And I'm sorry to pull you out of your other dream. Much more pleasant, I know."

Piper's face burned. She didn't know whether she was more angry or embarrassed, but mostly she felt hollow with disappointment. "It wasn't real. It never even happened. So why do I remember it so vividly?"

Aphrodite smiled. "Because you are my daughter, Piper. You see possibilities much more vividly than others. You see what *could* be. And it still might be—don't give up. Unfortunately—" The goddess gestured around the department store. "You have other trials to face, first. Medea will be back, along with many other enemies. The Doors of Death have opened."

"What do you mean?"

Aphrodite winked at her. "You're a smart one, Piper. You know."

A cold feeling settled over her. "The sleeping woman, the one Medea and Midas called their patron. She's managed to open a new entrance from the Underworld. She's letting the dead escape back into the world."

"Mmm. And not just *any* dead. The worst, the most powerful, the ones most likely to hate the gods."

"The monsters are coming back from Tartarus the same way," Piper guessed. "That's why they don't stay disintegrated."

"Yes. Their *patron*, as you call her, has a special relationship with Tartarus, the spirit of the pit." Aphrodite held up a gold sequined top. "No . . . this would make me look ridiculous."

Piper laughed uneasily. "You? You can't look anything but perfect."

"You're sweet," Aphrodite said. "But beauty is about finding the right fit, the most natural fit. To be perfect, you have to feel perfect about yourself—avoid trying to be something you're not. For a goddess, that's especially hard. We can change so easily."

"My dad thought you were perfect." Piper's voice quavered. "He never got over you."

Aphrodite's gaze became distant. "Yes...Tristan. Oh, he was amazing. So gentle and kind, funny and handsome. Yet he had so much sadness inside."

"Could we please not talk about him in the past tense?"

"I'm sorry, dear. I didn't want to leave your father, of course. It's always so hard, but it was for the best. If he had realized who I actually was—"

"Wait—he didn't *know* you were a goddess?"

"Of course not." Aphrodite sounded offended. "I wouldn't do that to him. For most mortals, that's simply too hard to accept. It can ruin their lives! Ask your friend Jason—*lovely* boy, by the way. His poor mother was destroyed when she found out she'd fallen in love with Zeus. No, it was much better Tristan believed that I was a mortal woman who left him without explanation. Better a bittersweet memory than an immortal, unattainable goddess. Which brings me to an important matter..."

She opened her hand and showed Piper a glowing glass vial of pink liquid. "This is one of Medea's kinder mixtures. It erases only recent memories. When you save your father, *if* you can save him, you should give him this."

Piper couldn't believe what she was hearing. "You want me to dope my dad? You want me to make him forget what he's been through?"

Aphrodite held up the vial. The liquid cast a pink glow over her face. "Your father acts confident, Piper, but he walks a fine line between two worlds. He's worked his whole life to deny the old stories about gods and spirits, yet he fears those stories might be real. He fears that he's shut off an important part of himself, and someday it will destroy him. Now he's been captured by a giant. He's living a nightmare. Even if he survives...if he has to spend the rest of his life with those memories, knowing that gods and spirits walk the earth, it will shatter him. That's what our enemy hopes for. She will break him, and thus break your spirit."

Piper wanted to shout that Aphrodite was wrong. Her dad was the strongest person she knew. Piper would never take his memories the way Hera had taken Jason's.

But somehow she couldn't stay angry with Aphrodite. She remembered what her dad had said months ago, at the beach at Big Sur: *If I really believed in Ghost Country, or animal spirits, or Greek gods...I don't think I could sleep at night. I'd always be looking for somebody to blame.*

Now Piper wanted someone to blame, too.

"Who is she?" Piper demanded. "The one controlling the giants?"

Aphrodite pursed her lips. She moved to the next rack, which held battered armor and ripped togas, but Aphrodite looked through them as if they were designer outfits.

"You have a strong will," she mused. "I'm never given much credit among the gods. My children are laughed at. They're dismissed as conceited and shallow."

"Some of them are."

Aphrodite laughed. "Granted. Perhaps I'm conceited and shallow, too, sometimes. A girl has to indulge. Oh, this is nice." She picked up a burned and stained bronze breastplate and held it up for Piper to see. "No?"

"No," Piper said. "Are you going to answer my question?"

"Patience, my sweet," the goddess said. "My point is that love is the most powerful motivator in the world. It spurs mortals to greatness. Their noblest, bravest acts are done for love."

Piper pulled out her dagger and studied its reflective blade. "Like Helen starting the Trojan War?"

"Ah, Katoptris." Aphrodite smiled. "I'm glad you found it. I get so much flack for that war, but honestly, Paris and Helen were a cute couple. And the heroes of that war are immortal now—at least in the memories of men. Love is powerful, Piper. It can bring even the gods to their knees. I told this to my son Aeneas when he escaped from Troy. He thought he had failed. He thought he was a loser! But he traveled to Italy—"

"And became the forebear of Rome."

"Exactly. You see, Piper, my children can be quite powerful. *You* can be quite powerful, because my lineage is unique. I am closer to the beginning of creation than any other Olympian."

Piper struggled to remember about Aphrodite's birth. "Didn't you . . . rise from the sea? Standing on a seashell?"

The goddess laughed. "That painter Botticelli had quite an imagination. I never stood on a seashell, thank you very much. But yes, I rose from the sea. The first beings to rise from Chaos were the Earth and Sky—Gaea and Ouranos. When their son the Titan Kronos killed Ouranos—"

"By chopping him to pieces with a scythe," Piper remembered.

Aphrodite wrinkled her nose. "Yes. The pieces of Ouranos fell into the sea. His immortal essence created sea foam. And from that foam—"

"You were born. I remember now. So you're—"

"The last child of Ouranos, who was greater than the gods or the Titans. So, in a strange way, I'm the eldest Olympian god. As I said, love is a powerful force. And you, my daughter, are much more than a pretty face. Which is why you already know who is waking the giants, and who has the power to open doors into the deepest parts of the earth."

Aphrodite waited, as if she could sense Piper slowly putting together the pieces of a puzzle, which made a dreadful picture.

"Gaea," Piper said. "The earth itself. That's our enemy."

She hoped Aphrodite would say no, but the goddess kept her eyes on the rack of tattered armor. "She has slumbered for eons, but she is slowly waking. Even asleep, she is powerful, but once she wakes . . . we will be doomed. You must defeat the giants before that happens, and lull Gaea back into her slumber. Otherwise the rebellion has only begun. The dead will continue to rise. Monsters will regenerate with even greater speed. The giants will lay waste to the birthplace of the gods. And if they do that, all civilization will burn."

"But *Gaea*? Mother Earth?"

"Do not underestimate her," Aphrodite warned. "She is a cruel deity. She orchestrated Ouranos's death. *She* gave Kronos the sickle and urged him to kill his own father. While the Titans ruled the world, she slumbered in peace. But when the gods overthrew them, Gaea woke again in all her anger and gave birth to a new race—the giants—to destroy Olympus once and for all."

"And it's happening again," Piper said. "The rise of the giants."

Aphrodite nodded. "Now you know. What will you do?"

"Me?" Piper clenched her fists. "What am I supposed to do? Put on a pretty dress and sweet-talk Gaea into going back to sleep?"

"I wish that would work," Aphrodite said. "But no, you will have to find your own strengths, and fight for what you love. Like my favored ones, Helen and Paris. Like my son Aeneas."

"Helen and Paris died," Piper said.

"And Aeneas became a hero," the goddess countered. "The first great hero of Rome. The result will depend on you, Piper, but I will tell you this: The seven greatest demigods must be gathered to defeat the giants, and that effort will not succeed without you. When the two sides meet . . . you will be the mediator. You will determine whether there is friendship or bloodshed."

"What two sides?"

Piper's vision began to dim.

"You must wake soon, my child," said the goddess. "I do not always agree with Hera, but she's taken a bold risk, and

I agree it must be done. Zeus has kept the two sides apart for too long. Only together will you have the power to save Olympus. Now, wake, and I hope you like the clothes I picked out."

"What clothes?" Piper demanded, but the dream faded to black.

PIPER

PIPER WOKE AT A TABLE AT A SIDEWALK CAFÉ.

For a second, she thought she was still dreaming. It was a sunny morning. The air was brisk but not unpleasant for sitting outside. At the other tables, a mix of bicyclists, business people, and college kids sat chatting and drinking coffee.

She could smell eucalyptus trees. Lots of foot traffic passed in front of quaint little shops. The street was lined with bottlebrush trees and blooming azaleas as if winter was a foreign concept.

In other words: she was in California.

Her friends sat in chairs around her—all of them with their hands calmly folded across their chests, dozing pleasantly. And they all had new clothes on. Piper looked down at her own outfit and gasped. "Mother!"

She yelled louder than she meant. Jason flinched, bumping the table with his knees, and then all of them were awake.

"What?" Hedge demanded. "Fight who? Where?"

"Falling!" Leo grabbed the table. "No—not falling. Where are we?"

Jason blinked, trying to get his bearings. He focused on Piper and made a little choking sound. "What are you wearing?"

Piper probably blushed. She was wearing the turquoise dress she'd seen in her dream, with black leggings and black leather boots. She had on her favorite silver charm bracelet, even though she'd left that back home in L.A., and her old snowboarding jacket from her dad, which amazingly went with the outfit pretty well. She pulled out Katoptris, and judging from the reflection in the blade, she'd gotten her hair done, too.

"It's nothing," she said. "It's my—" She remembered Aphrodite's warning not to mention that they'd talked. "It's nothing."

Leo grinned. "Aphrodite strikes again, huh? You're gonna be the best-dressed warrior in town, beauty queen."

"Hey, Leo." Jason nudged his arm. "You look at yourself recently?"

"What...oh."

All of them had been give a makeover. Leo was wearing pinstriped pants, black leather shoes, a white collarless shirt with suspenders, and his tool belt, Ray-Ban sunglasses, and a porkpie hat.

"God, Leo." Piper tried not to laugh. "I think my dad wore that to his last premiere, minus the tool belt."

"Hey, shut up!"

"I think he looks good," said Coach Hedge. "'Course, I look better."

The satyr was a pastel nightmare. Aphrodite had given him a baggy canary yellow zoot suit with two-tone shoes that fit over his hooves. He had a matching yellow broad-brimmed hat, a rose-colored shirt, a baby blue tie, and a blue carnation in his lapel, which Hedge sniffed and then ate.

"Well," Jason said, "at least your mom overlooked me."

Piper knew that wasn't exactly true. Looking at him, her heart did a little tap dance. Jason was dressed simply in jeans and a clean purple T-shirt, like he'd worn at the Grand Canyon. He had new track shoes on, and his hair was newly trimmed. His eyes were the same color as the sky. Aphrodite's message was clear: *This one needs no improvement.*

And Piper agreed.

"Anyway," she said uncomfortably, "how did we get here?"

"Oh, that would be Mellie," Hedge said, chewing happily on his carnation. "Those winds shot us halfway across the country, I'd guess. We would've been smashed flat on impact, but Mellie's last gift—a nice soft breeze—cushioned our fall."

"And she got fired for us," Leo said. "Man, we suck."

"Ah, she'll be fine," Hedge said. "Besides, she couldn't help herself. I've got that effect on nymphs. I'll send her a message when we're through with this quest and help her figure something out. That is one *aura* I could settle down with and raise a herd of baby goats."

"I'm going to be sick," Piper said. "Anyone else want coffee?"

"Coffee!" Hedge's grin was stained blue from the flower. "I love coffee!"

"Um," Jason said, "but—money? Our packs?"

Piper looked down. Their packs were at their feet, and everything seemed to still be there. She reached into her coat pocket and felt two things she hadn't expected. One was a wad of cash. The other was a glass vial—the amnesia potion. She left the vial in her pocket and brought out the money.

Leo whistled. "Allowance? Piper, your mom rocks!"

"Waitress!" Hedge called. "Six double espressos, and whatever these guys want. Put it on the girl's tab."

It didn't take them long to figure out where they were. The menus said "Café Verve, Walnut Creek, CA." And according to the waitress, it was 9 A.M. on December 21, the winter solstice, which gave them three hours until Enceladus's deadline.

They didn't have to wonder where Mount Diablo was, either. They could see it on the horizon, right at the end of the street. After the Rockies, Mount Diablo didn't look very large, nor was it covered in snow. It seemed downright peaceful, its golden creases marbled with gray-green trees. But size was deceptive with mountains, Piper knew. It was probably much bigger up close. And appearances were deceptive too. Here they were—back in California—supposedly her home —with sunny skies, mild weather, laid-back people, and a plate of chocolate chip scones with coffee. And only a few miles away, somewhere on that peaceful mountain, a superpowerful, super-evil giant was about to have her father for lunch.

Leo pulled something out of his pocket—the old crayon drawing Aeolus had given him. Aphrodite must've thought it was important if she'd magically transferred it to his new outfit.

"What is that?" Piper asked.

Leo folded it up gingerly again and put it away. "Nothing. You don't want to see my kindergarten artwork."

"It's more than that," Jason guessed. "Aeolus said it was the key to our success."

Leo shook his head. "Not today. He was talking about . . . later."

"How can you be sure?" Piper asked.

"Trust me," Leo said. "Now—what's our game plan?"

Coach Hedge belched. He'd already had three espressos and a plate of doughnuts, along with two napkins and another flower from the vase on the table. He would've eaten the silverware, except Piper had slapped his hand.

"Climb the mountain," Hedge said. "Kill everything except Piper's dad. Leave."

"Thank you, General Eisenhower," Jason grumbled.

"Hey, I'm just saying!"

"Guys," Piper said. "There's more you need to know."

It was tricky, because she couldn't mention her mom; but she told them she'd figured some things out in her dreams. She told them about their real enemy: Gaea.

"Gaea?" Leo shook his head. "Isn't that Mother Nature? She's supposed to have, like, flowers in her hair and birds singing around her and deer and rabbits doing her laundry."

"Leo, that's Snow White," Piper said.

"Okay, but—"

"Listen, cupcake." Coach Hedge dabbed the espresso out of his goatee. "Piper's telling us some serious stuff, here. Gaea's no softie. I'm not even sure *I* could take her."

Leo whistled. "Really?"

Hedge nodded. "This earth lady—she and her old man the sky were nasty customers."

"Ouranos," Piper said. She couldn't help looking up at the blue sky, wondering if it had eyes.

"Right," Hedge said. "So Ouranos, he's not the best dad. He throws their first kids, the Cyclopes, into Tartarus. That makes Gaea mad, but she bides her time. Then they have another set of kids—the twelve Titans—and Gaea is afraid they'll get thrown into prison too. So she goes up to her son Kronos—"

"The big bad dude," Leo said. "The one they defeated last summer."

"Right. And Gaea's the one who gives him the scythe, and tells him, 'Hey, why don't I call your dad down here? And while he's talking to me, distracted, you can cut him to pieces. Then you can take over the world. Wouldn't that be great?'"

Nobody said anything. Piper's chocolate chip scone didn't look so appetizing anymore. Even though she'd heard the story before, she still couldn't quite get her mind around it. She tried to imagine a kid so messed up, he would kill his own dad just for power. Then she imagined a mom so messed up, she would convince her son to do it.

"Definitely not Snow White," she decided.

"Nah, Kronos was a bad guy," Hedge said. "But Gaea is

literally the *mother* of all bad guys. She's so old and powerful, so *huge*, that it's hard for her to be fully conscious. Most of the time, she sleeps, and that's the way we like her—snoring."

"But she talked to me," Leo said. "How can she be asleep?"

Gleeson brushed crumbs off his canary yellow lapel. He was on his sixth espresso now, and his pupils were as big as quarters. "Even in her sleep, part of her consciousness is active —dreaming, keeping watch, doing little things like causing volcanoes to explode and monsters to rise. Even now, she's not fully awake. Believe me, you don't want to see her fully awake."

"But she's getting more powerful," Piper said. "She's causing the giants to rise. And if their king comes back—this guy Porphyrion—"

"He'll raise an army to destroy the gods," Jason put in. "Starting with Hera. It'll be another war. And Gaea will wake up fully."

Gleeson nodded. "Which is why it's a good idea for us to stay off the ground as much as possible."

Leo looked warily at Mount Diablo. "So...climbing a mountain. That would be bad."

Piper's heart sank. First, she'd been asked to betray her friends. Now they were trying to help her rescue her dad even though they knew they were walking into a trap. The idea of fighting a giant had been scary enough. But the idea that Gaea was behind it—a force more powerful than a god or Titan...

"Guys, I can't ask you to do this," Piper said. "This is too dangerous."

"You kidding?" Gleeson belched and showed them his blue carnation smile. "Who's ready to beat stuff up?"

XLI

LEO

LEO HOPED THE TAXI COULD TAKE THEM all the way to the top.

No such luck. The cab made lurching, grinding sounds as it climbed the mountain road, and halfway up they found the ranger's station closed, a chain blocking the way.

"Far as I can go," the cabbie said. "You sure about this? Gonna be a long walk back, and my car's acting funny. I can't wait for you."

"We're sure." Leo was the first one out. He had a bad feeling about what was wrong with the cab, and when he looked down he saw he was right. The wheels were sinking into the road like it was made of quicksand. Not fast—just enough to make the driver think he had a transmission problem or a bad axle—but Leo knew different.

The road was hard-packed dirt. No reason at all it should have been soft, but already Leo's shoes were starting to sink. Gaea was messing with them.

While his friends got out, Leo paid the cabbie. He was generous—heck, why not? It was Aphrodite's money. Plus, he had a feeling he might never be coming off this mountain.

"Keep the change," he said. "And get out of here. Quick."

The driver didn't argue. Soon all they could see was his dust trail.

The view from the mountain was pretty amazing. The whole inland valley around Mount Diablo was a patchwork of towns—grids of tree-lined streets and nice middle-class suburbs, shops, and schools. All these normal people living normal lives—the kind Leo had never known.

"That's Concord," Jason said, pointing to the north. "Walnut Creek below us. To the south, Danville, past those hills. And that way…"

He pointed west, where a ridge of golden hills held back a layer of fog, like the rim of a bowl. "That's the Berkeley Hills. The East Bay. Past that, San Francisco."

"Jason?" Piper touched his arm. "You remember something? You've been here?"

"Yes…no." He gave her an anguished look. "It just seems important."

"That's Titan land." Coach Hedge nodded toward the west. "Bad place, Jason. Trust me, this is as close to 'Frisco as we want to get."

But Jason looked toward the foggy basin with such longing that Leo felt uneasy. Why did Jason seem so connected with that place—a place Hedge said was evil, full of bad magic and old enemies? What if Jason came from here? Everybody kept hinting Jason was an enemy, that his arrival at Camp Half-Blood was a dangerous mistake.

No, Leo thought. Ridiculous. Jason was their friend.

Leo tried to move his foot, but his heels were now completely embedded in the dirt.

"Hey, guys," he said. "Let's keep moving."

The others noticed the problem.

"Gaea is stronger here," Hedge grumbled. He popped his hooves free from his shoes, then handed the shoes to Leo. "Keep those for me, Valdez. They're nice."

Leo snorted. "Yes, sir, Coach. Would you like them polished?"

"That's varsity thinking, Valdez." Hedge nodded approvingly. "But first, we'd better hike up this mountain while we still can."

"How do we know where the giant is?" Piper asked.

Jason pointed toward the peak. Drifting across the summit was a plume of smoke. From a distance, Leo had thought it was a cloud, but it wasn't. Something was burning.

"Smoke equals fire," Jason said. "We'd better hurry."

The Wilderness School had taken Leo on several forced marches. He thought he was in good shape. But climbing a mountain when the earth was trying to swallow his feet was like jogging on a flypaper treadmill.

In no time, Leo had rolled up the sleeves on his collarless shirt, even though the wind was cold and sharp. He wished Aphrodite had given him walking shorts and some more comfortable shoes, but he was grateful for the Ray-Bans that kept the sun out of his eyes. He slipped his hands into his tool belt and started summoning supplies—gears, a tiny wrench, some strips of bronze. As he walked, he built—not really thinking about it, just fiddling with pieces.

By the time they neared the crest of the mountain, Leo was the most fashionably dressed sweaty, dirty hero ever. His hands were covered in machine grease.

The little object he'd made was like a windup toy—the kind that rattles and walks across a coffee table. He wasn't sure what it could do, but he slipped it into his tool belt.

He missed his army coat with all its pockets. Even more than that, he missed Festus. He could use a fire-breathing bronze dragon right now. But Leo knew Festus would not be coming back—at least, not in his old form.

He patted the picture in his pocket—the crayon drawing he'd made at the picnic table under the pecan tree when he was five years old. He remembered Tía Callida singing as he worked, and how upset he'd been when the winds had snatched the picture away. *It isn't time yet, little hero,* Tía Callida had told him. *Someday, yes. You'll have your quest. You will find your destiny, and your hard journey will finally make sense.*

Now Aeolus had returned the picture. Leo knew that meant his destiny was getting close; but the journey was as frustrating as this stupid mountain. Every time Leo thought they'd reached the summit, it turned out to be just another ridge with an even higher one behind it.

First things first, Leo told himself. Survive today. Figure out crayon drawing of destiny later.

Finally Jason crouched behind a wall of rock. He gestured for the others to do the same. Leo crawled up next to him. Piper had to pull Coach Hedge down.

"I don't want to get my outfit dirty!" Hedge complained.

"Shhh!" Piper said.

Reluctantly, the satyr knelt.

Just over the ridge where they were hiding, in the shadow of the mountain's final crest, was a forested depression about the size of a football field, where the giant Enceladus had set up camp.

Trees had been cut down to make a towering purple bonfire. The outer rim of the clearing was littered with extra logs and construction equipment—an earthmover; a big crane thing with rotating blades at the end like an electric shaver—must be a tree harvester, Leo thought—and a long metal column with an ax blade, like a sideways guillotine—a hydraulic ax.

Why a giant needed construction equipment, Leo wasn't sure. He didn't see how the creature in front of him could even fit in the driver's seat. The giant Enceladus was so large, so horrible, Leo didn't want to look at him.

But he forced himself to focus on the monster.

To start with, he was thirty feet tall—easily as tall as the treetops. Leo was sure the giant could've seen them behind their ridge, but he seemed intent on the weird purple bonfire, circling it and chanting under his breath. From the waist up, the giant appeared humanoid, his muscular chest clad in bronze armor, decorated with flame designs. His arms were completely ripped. Each of his biceps was bigger than Leo. His skin was bronze but sooty with ash. His face was crudely shaped, like a half-finished clay figure, but his eyes glowed white, and his hair was matted in shaggy dreadlocks down to his shoulders, braided with bones.

From the waist down, he was even more terrifying. His legs were scaly green, with claws instead of feet—like the forelegs of a dragon. In his hand, Enceladus held a spear the size of a flagpole. Every so often he dipped its tip in the fire, turning the metal molten red.

"Okay," Coach Hedge whispered. "Here's the plan—"

Leo elbowed him. "You're not charging him alone!"

"Aw, c'mon."

Piper choked back a sob. "Look."

Just visible on the other side of the bonfire was a man tied to a post. His head slumped like he was unconscious, so Leo couldn't make out his face, but Piper didn't seem to have any doubts.

"Dad," she said.

Leo swallowed. He wished this were a Tristan McLean movie. Then Piper's dad would be faking unconsciousness. He'd untie his bonds and knock out the giant with some cleverly hidden anti-giant gas. Heroic music would start to play, and Tristan McLean would make his amazing escape, running away in slow motion while the mountainside exploded behind him.

But this wasn't a movie. Tristan McLean was half dead and about to be eaten. The only people who could stop it —three fashionably dressed teenaged demigods and a megalomaniac goat.

"There's four of us," Hedge whispered urgently. "And only one of him."

"Did you miss the fact that he's thirty feet tall?" Leo asked.

"Okay," Hedge said. "So you, me, and Jason distract him. Piper sneaks around and frees her dad."

They all looked at Jason.

"What?" Jason asked. "I'm not the leader."

"Yes," Piper said. "You are."

They'd never really talked about it, but no one disagreed, not even Hedge. Coming this far had been a team effort, but when it came to a life-and-death decision, Leo knew Jason was the one to ask. Even if he had no memory, Jason had a kind of balance to him. You could just tell he'd been in battles before, and he knew how to keep his cool. Leo wasn't exactly the trusting type, but he trusted Jason with his life.

"I hate to say it," Jason sighed, "but Coach Hedge is right. A distraction is Piper's best chance."

Not a good chance, Leo thought. Not even a survivable chance. Just their *best* chance.

They couldn't sit there all day and talk about it, though. It had to be close to noon—the giant's deadline—and the ground was still trying to pull them down. Leo's knees had already sunk two inches into the dirt.

Leo looked at the construction equipment and got a crazy

idea. He brought out the little toy he'd made on the climb, and he realized what it could do—*if* he was lucky, which he almost never was.

"Let's boogie," he said. "Before I come to my senses."

XLII

LEO

THE PLAN WENT WRONG ALMOST IMMEDIATELY. Piper scrambled along the ridge, trying to keep her head down, while Leo, Jason, and Coach Hedge walked straight into the clearing.

Jason summoned his golden lance. He brandished it over his head and yelled, "Giant!" Which sounded pretty good, and a lot more confident than Leo could've managed. He was thinking more along the lines of, "We are pathetic ants! Don't kill us!"

Enceladus stopped chanting at the flames. He turned toward them and grinned, revealing fangs like a saber-toothed tiger's.

"Well," the giant rumbled. "What a nice surprise."

Leo didn't like the sound of that. His hand closed on his windup gadget. He stepped sideways, edging his way toward the bulldozer.

Coach Hedge shouted, "Let the movie star go, you big ugly cupcake! Or I'm gonna plant my hoof right up your—"

"Coach," Jason said. "Shut up."

Enceladus roared with laughter. "I've forgotten how funny satyrs are. When we rule the world, I think I'll keep your kind around. You can entertain me while I eat all the other mortals."

"Is that a compliment?" Hedge frowned at Leo. "I don't think that was a compliment."

Enceladus opened his mouth wide, and his teeth began to glow.

"Scatter!" Leo yelled.

Jason and Hedge dove to the left as the giant blew fire —a furnace blast so hot even Festus would've been jealous. Leo dodged behind the bulldozer, wound up his homemade device, and dropped it into the driver's seat. Then he ran to the right, heading for the tree harvester.

Out of the corner of his eye, he saw Jason rise and charge the giant. Coach Hedge ripped off his canary yellow jacket, which was now on fire, and bleated angrily. "I *liked* that outfit!" Then he raised his club and charged, too.

Before they could get very far, Enceladus slammed his spear against the ground. The entire mountain shook.

The shockwave sent Leo sprawling. He blinked, momentarily stunned. Through a haze of grassfire and bitter smoke, he saw Jason staggering to his feet on the other side of the clearing. Coach Hedge was knocked out cold. He'd fallen forward and hit his head on a log. His furry hindquarters were sticking straight up, with his canary yellow pants around his knees—a view Leo really didn't need.

The giant bellowed, "I see you, Piper McLean!" He turned and blew fire at a line of bushes to Leo's right. Piper ran into the clearing like a flushed quail, the underbrush burning behind her.

Enceladus laughed. "I'm happy you've arrived. And you brought me my prizes!"

Leo's gut twisted. This was the moment Piper had warned them about. They'd played right into Enceladus's hands.

The giant must've read Leo's expression, because he laughed even louder. "That's right, son of Hephaestus. I didn't expect you all to stay alive this long, but it doesn't matter. By bringing you here, Piper McLean has sealed the deal. If she betrays you, I'm as good as my word. She can take her father and go. What do I care about a movie star?"

Leo could see Piper's dad more clearly now. He wore a ragged dress shirt and torn slacks. His bare feet were caked with mud. He wasn't completely unconscious, because he lifted his head and groaned—yep, Tristan McLean all right. Leo had seen that face in enough movies. But he had a nasty cut down the side of his face, and he looked thin and sickly —not heroic at all.

"Dad!" Piper yelled.

Mr. McLean blinked, trying to focus. "Pipes...? Where..."

Piper drew her dagger and faced Enceladus. "Let him go!"

"Of course, dear," the giant rumbled. "Swear your loyalty to me, and we have no problem. Only these others must die."

Piper looked back and forth between Leo and her dad.

"He'll kill you," Leo warned. "Don't trust him!"

"Oh, come now," Enceladus bellowed. "You know I was born to fight Athena herself? Mother Gaea made each of us giants with a specific purpose, designed to fight and destroy a particular god. I was Athena's nemesis, the *anti*-Athena, you might say. Compared to some of my brethren—I am small! But I am clever. And I keep my bargain with you, Piper McLean. It's part of my plan!"

Jason was on his feet now, lance ready; but before he could act, Enceladus roared—a call so loud it echoed down the valley and was probably heard all the way to San Francisco.

At the edge the woods, half a dozen ogre-like creatures rose up. Leo realized with nauseating certainty that they hadn't simply been hiding there. They'd risen straight out of the earth.

The ogres shuffled forward. They were small compared to Enceladus, about seven feet tall. Each one of them had six arms—one pair in the regular spot, then an extra pair sprouting out the top of their shoulders, and another set shooting from the sides of their rib cages. They wore only ragged leather loincloths, and even across the clearing, Leo could smell them. Six guys who never bathed, with six armpits each. Leo decided if he survived this day, he'd have to take a three-hour shower just to forget the stench.

Leo stepped toward Piper. "What—what are those?"

Her blade reflected the purple light of the bonfire. "Gegenees."

"In English?" Leo asked.

"The Earthborn," she said. "Six-armed giants who fought Jason—the *first* Jason."

"Very good, my dear!" Enceladus sounded delighted. "They used to live on a miserable place in Greece called Bear Mountain. Mount Diablo is much nicer! They are lesser children of Mother Earth, but they serve their purpose. They're good with construction equipment—"

"Vroom, vroom!" one of the Earthborn bellowed, and the others took up the chant, each moving his six hands as though driving a car, as if it were some kind of weird religious ritual. "Vroom, vroom!"

"Yes, thank you, boys," Encedalus said. "They also have a score to settle with heroes. Especially anyone named Jason."

"Yay-son!" the Earthborn screamed. They all picked up clumps of earth, which solidified in their hands, turning to nasty pointed stones. "Where Yay-son? Kill Yay-son!"

Enceladus smiled. "You see, Piper, you have a choice. Save your father, or ah, *try* to save your friends and face certain death."

Piper stepped forward. Her eyes blazed with such rage, even the Earthborn backed away. She radiated power and beauty, but it had nothing to do with her clothes or her makeup.

"You will not take the people I love," she said. "None of them."

Her words rippled across the clearing with such force, the Earthborn muttered, "Okay. Okay, sorry," and began to retreat.

"Stand your ground, fools!" Enceladus bellowed. He

snarled at Piper. "This is why we wanted you alive, my dear. You could have been so useful to us. But as you wish. Earthborn! I will show you Jason."

Leo's heart sank. But the giant didn't point to Jason. He pointed to the other side of the bonfire, where Tristan McLean hung helpless and half conscious.

"There is Jason," Enceladus said with pleasure. "Tear him apart!"

Leo's biggest surprise: One look from Jason, and all three of them knew the game plan. When had that happened, that they could read each other so well?

Jason charged Enceladus, while Piper rushed to her father, and Leo dashed for the tree harvester, which stood between Mr. McLean and the Earthborn.

The Earthborn were fast, but Leo ran like a storm spirit. He leaped toward the harvester from five feet away and slammed into the driver's seat. His hands flew across the controls, and the machine responded with unnatural speed—coming to life as if it knew how important this was.

"Ha!" Leo screamed, and swung the crane arm through the bonfire, toppling burning logs onto the Earthborn and spraying sparks everywhere. Two giants went down under a fiery avalanche and melted back into the earth—hopefully to stay for a while.

The other four ogres stumbled across burning logs and hot coals while Leo brought the harvester around. He smashed a button, and on the end of the crane arm the wicked rotating blades began to whir.

Out of the corner of his eye, he could see Piper at the stake, cutting her father free. On the other side of the clearing, Jason fought the giant, somehow managing to dodge his massive spear and blasts of fire breath. Coach Hedge was still heroically passed out with his goat tail sticking up in the air.

The whole side of the mountain would soon be ablaze. The fire wouldn't bother Leo, but if his friends got trapped up here— No. He had to act quickly.

One of the Earthborn—apparently not the most intelligent one—charged the tree harvester, and Leo swung the crane arm in his direction. As soon as the blades touched the ogre, he dissolved like wet clay and splattered all over the clearing. Most of him flew into Leo's face.

He spit clay out of his mouth and turned the harvester toward the three remaining Earthborn, who backed up quickly.

"Bad vroom-vroom!" one yelled.

"Yeah, that's right!" Leo yelled at them. "You want some bad vroom-vroom? Come on!"

Unfortunately, they did. Three ogres with six arms, each throwing large, hard rocks at super speed—and Leo knew it was over. Somehow, he launched himself in a backward somersault off the harvester half a second before a boulder demolished the driver's seat. Rocks slammed into metal. By the time Leo stumbled to his feet, the harvester looked like a crushed soda can, sinking in the mud.

"Dozer!" Leo yelled.

The ogres were picking up more clumps of earth, but this time they were glaring in Piper's direction.

Thirty feet away, the bulldozer roared to life. Leo's make-shift gadget had done its job, burrowing into the earthmover's controls and giving it a temporary life of its own. It roared toward the enemy.

Just as Piper cut her father free and caught him in her arms, the giants launched their second volley of stones. The dozer swiveled in the mud, skidding to intercept, and most of the rocks slammed into its shovel. The force was so great it pushed the dozer back. Two rocks ricocheted and struck their throwers. Two more Earthborn melted into clay. Unfortunately, one rock hit the dozer's engine, sending up a cloud of oily smoke, and the dozer groaned to a stop. Another great toy broken.

Piper dragged her father below the ridge. The last Earthborn charged after her.

Leo was out of tricks, but he couldn't let that monster get to Piper. He ran forward, straight through the flames, and grabbed something—*anything*—from his tool belt.

"Hey, stupid!" he yelled, and threw a screwdriver at the Earthborn.

It didn't kill the ogre, but it sure got his attention. The screwdriver sank hilt-deep into the Earthborn's forehead like he was made of Play-Doh.

The Earthborn yelped in pain and skittered to a halt. He pulled out the screwdriver, turned and glared at Leo. Sadly, this last ogre looked like the biggest and nastiest of the bunch. Gaea had really gone all out creating him—with extra muscle upgrades, deluxe ugly face, the whole package.

Oh, great, Leo thought. I've made a friend.

"You die!" the Earthborn roared. "Friend of Yay-son dies!"

The ogre scooped up handfuls of dirt, which immediately hardened into rock cannonballs.

Leo's mind went blank. He reached into his tool belt, but he couldn't think of anything that would help. He was supposed to be clever—but he couldn't craft or build or tinker his way out of this one.

Fine, he thought. I'll go out blaze-of-glory style.

He burst into flames, yelled, "Hephaestus!" and charged at the ogre barehanded.

He never got there.

A blur of turquoise and black flashed behind the ogre. A gleaming bronze blade sliced up one side of the Earthborn and down the other.

Six large arms dropped to the ground, boulders rolling out of their useless hands. The Earthborn looked down, very surprised. He mumbled, "Arms go bye-bye."

Then he melted into the ground.

Piper stood there, breathing hard, her dagger covered with clay. Her dad sat at the ridge, dazed and wounded, but still alive.

Piper's expression was ferocious—almost crazy, like a cornered animal. Leo was glad she was on his side.

"Nobody hurts my friends," she said, and with a sudden warm feeling, Leo realized she was talking about him. Then she yelled, "Come on!"

Leo saw that the battle wasn't over. Jason was still fighting the giant Enceladus—and it wasn't going well.

XLIII

JASON

WHEN JASON'S LANCE BROKE, he knew he was dead.

The battle had started well enough. Jason's instincts kicked in, and his gut told him he'd dueled opponents almost this big before. Size and strength equaled slowness, so Jason just had to be quicker—pace himself, wear out his opponent, and avoid getting smashed or flame-broiled.

He rolled away from the giant's first spear thrust and jabbed Enceladus in the ankle. Jason's javelin managed to pierce the thick dragon hide, and golden *ichor*—the blood of immortals—trickled down the giant's clawed foot.

Enceladus bellowed in pain and blasted him with fire. Jason scrambled away, rolling behind the giant, and struck again behind his knee.

It went on like that for seconds, minutes—it was hard to judge. Jason heard combat across the clearing—construction equipment grinding, fire roaring, monsters shouting, and rocks smashing into metal. He heard Leo and Piper yelling defiantly, which meant they were still alive. Jason tried not to think about it. He couldn't afford to get distracted.

Enceladus's spear missed him by a millimeter. Jason kept dodging, but the ground stuck to his feet. Gaea was getting stronger, and the giant was getting faster. Enceladus might be slow, but he wasn't dumb. He began anticipating Jason's moves, and Jason's attacks were only annoying him, making him more enraged.

"I'm not some minor monster," Enceladus bellowed. "I am a giant, born to destroy gods! Your little gold toothpick can't kill me, boy."

Jason didn't waste energy replying. He was already tired. The ground clung to his feet, making him feel like he weighed an extra hundred pounds. The air was full of smoke that burned his lungs. Fires roared around him, stoked by the winds, and the temperature was approaching the heat of an oven.

Jason raised his javelin to block the giant's next strike—a big mistake. *Don't fight force with force,* a voice chided him— the wolf Lupa, who'd told him that long ago. He managed to deflect the spear, but it grazed his shoulder, and his arm went numb.

He backed up, almost tripping over a burning log.

He had to delay—to keep the giant's attention fixed on him while his friends dealt with the Earthborn and rescued Piper's dad. He couldn't fail.

He retreated, trying to lure the giant to the edge of the clearing. Enceladus could sense his weariness. The giant smiled, baring his fangs.

"The mighty Jason Grace," he taunted. "Yes, we know about you, son of Jupiter. The one who led the assault on Mount Othrys. The one who single-handedly slew the Titan Krios and toppled the black throne."

Jason's mind reeled. He didn't know these names, yet they made his skin tingle, as if his body remembered the pain his mind didn't.

"What are you talking about?" he asked. He realized his mistake when Enceladus breathed fire.

Distracted, Jason moved too slowly. The blast missed him, but heat blistered his back. He slammed into the ground, his clothes smoldering. He was blinded from ash and smoke, choking as he tried to breathe.

He scrambled back as the giant's spear cleaved the ground between his feet.

Jason managed to stand.

If he could only summon one good blast of lightning—but he was already drained, and in this condition, the effort might kill him. He didn't even know if electricity would harm the giant.

Death in battle is honorable, said Lupa's voice.

That's real comforting, Jason thought.

One last try: Jason took a deep breath and charged.

Enceladus let him approach, grinning with anticipation. At the last second, Jason faked a strike and rolled between the giant's legs. He came up quickly, thrusting with all his might, ready to stab the giant in the small of his back, but Enceladus anticipated the trick. He stepped aside with too much speed and agility for a giant, as if the earth were helping him move.

He swept his spear sideways, met Jason's javelin—and with a snap like a shotgun blast, the golden weapon shattered.

The explosion was hotter than the giant's breath, blinding Jason with golden light. The force knocked him off his feet and squeezed the breath out of him.

When he regained his focus, he was sitting at the rim of a crater. Enceladus stood at the other side, staggering and confused. The javelin's destruction had released so much energy, it had blasted a perfect cone-shaped pit thirty feet deep, fusing the dirt and rock into a slick glassy substance. Jason wasn't sure how he'd survived, but his clothes were steaming. He was out of energy. He had no weapon. And Enceladus was still very much alive.

Jason tried to get up, but his legs were like lead. Enceladus blinked at the destruction, then laughed. "Impressive! Unfortunately, that was your last trick, demigod."

Enceladus leaped the crater in a single bound, planting his feet on either side of Jason. The giant raised his spear, its tip hovering six feet over Jason's chest.

"And now," Enceladus said, "my first sacrifice to Gaea!"

XLIV

JASON

TIME SEEMED TO SLOW DOWN, WHICH WAS really frustrating, since Jason still couldn't move. He felt himself sinking into the earth like the ground was a waterbed—comfortable, urging him to relax and give up. He wondered if the stories of the Underworld were true. Would he end up in the Fields of Punishment or Elysium? If he couldn't remember any of his deeds, would they still count? He wondered if the judges would take that into consideration, or if his dad, Zeus, would write him a note: "Please excuse Jason from eternal damnation. He has had amnesia."

Jason couldn't feel his arms. He could see the tip of the spear coming toward his chest in slow motion. He knew he should move, but he couldn't seem to do it. Funny, he thought. All that effort to stay alive, and then, *boom*. You just lie there helplessly while a fire-breathing giant impales you.

Leo's voice yelled, "Heads up!"

A large black metal wedge slammed into Enceladus with a massive *thunk!* The giant toppled over and slid into the pit.

"Jason, get up!" Piper called. Her voice energized him, shook him out of his stupor. He sat up, his head groggy, while Piper grabbed him under his arms and hauled him to his feet.

"Don't die on me," she ordered. "You are *not* dying on me."

"Yes, ma'am." He felt light-headed, but she was about the most beautiful thing he'd ever seen. Her hair was smoldering. Her face was smudged with soot. She had a cut on her arm, her dress was torn, and she was missing a boot. Beautiful.

About a hundred feet behind her, Leo was standing over a piece of construction equipment—a long cannonlike thing with a single massive piston, the edge broken clean off.

Then Jason looked down in the crater and saw where the other end of the hydraulic ax had gone. Enceladus was struggling to rise, an ax blade the size of a washing machine stuck in his breastplate.

Amazingly, the giant managed to pull the ax blade free. He yelled in pain and the mountain trembled. Golden ichor soaked the front of his armor, but Enceladus stood.

Shakily, he bent down and retrieved his spear.

"Good try." The giant winced. "But I cannot be beaten."

As they watched, the giant's armor mended itself, and the ichor stopped flowing. Even the cuts on his dragon-scale legs, which Jason had worked so hard to make, were now just pale scars.

Leo ran up to them, saw the giant, and cursed. "What *is* it with this guy? Die, already!"

"My fate is preordained," Enceladus said. "Giants cannot be killed by gods or heroes."

"Only by both," Jason said. The giant's smile faltered, and Jason saw in his eyes something like fear. "It's true, isn't it? Gods and demigods have to work together to kill you."

"You will not live long enough to try!" The giant started stumbling up the crater's slope, slipping on the glassy sides.

"Anyone have a god handy?" Leo asked.

Jason's heart filled with dread. He looked at the giant below them, struggling to get out of the pit, and he knew what had to happen.

"Leo," he said, "if you've got a rope in that tool belt, get it ready."

He leaped at the giant with no weapon but his bare hands.

"Enceladus!" Piper yelled. "Look behind you!"

It was an obvious trick, but her voice was so compelling, even Jason bought it. The giant said, "What?" and turned like there was an enormous spider on his back.

Jason tackled his legs at just the right moment. The giant lost his balance. Enceladus slammed into the crater and slid to the bottom. While he tried to rise, Jason put his arms around the giant's neck. When Enceladus struggled to his feet, Jason was riding his shoulders.

"Get off!" Enceladus screamed. He tried to grab Jason's legs, but Jason scrabbled around, squirming and climbing over the giant's hair.

Father, Jason thought. *If I've ever done anything good, anything you approved of, help me now. I offer my own life—just save my friends.*

Suddenly he could smell the metallic scent of a storm. Darkness swallowed the sun. The giant froze, sensing it too.

Jason yelled to his friends, "Hit the deck!"

And every hair on his head stood straight up.

Crack!

Lightning surged through Jason's body, straight through Enceladus, and into the ground. The giant's back stiffened, and Jason was thrown clear. When he regained his bearings, he was slipping down the side of the crater, and the crater was cracking open. The lightning bolt had split the mountain itself. The earth rumbled and tore apart, and Enceladus's legs slid into the chasm. He clawed helplessly at the glassy sides of the pit, and just for a moment managed to hold on to the edge, his hands trembling.

He fixed Jason with a look of hatred. "You've won nothing, boy. My brothers are rising, and they are ten times as strong as I. We will destroy the gods at their roots! You will die, and Olympus will die with—"

The giant lost his grip and fell into the crevice.

The earth shook. Jason fell toward the rift.

"Grab hold!" Leo yelled.

Jason's feet were at the edge of the chasm when he grabbed the rope, and Leo and Piper pulled him up.

They stood together, exhausted and terrified, as the chasm closed like an angry mouth. The ground stopped pulling at their feet.

For now, Gaea was gone.

The mountainside was on fire. Smoke billowed hundreds

of feet into the air. Jason spotted a helicopter—maybe fire-fighters or reporters—coming toward them.

All around them was carnage. The Earthborn had melted into piles of clay, leaving behind only their rock missiles and some nasty bits of loincloth, but Jason figured they would re-form soon enough. Construction equipment lay in ruins. The ground was scarred and blackened.

Coach Hedge started to move. He sat up with a groan and rubbed his head. His canary yellow pants were now the color of Dijon mustard mixed with mud.

He blinked and looked around him at the battle scene. "Did I do this?"

Before Jason could reply, Hedge picked up his club and got shakily to his feet. "Yeah, you wanted some hoof? I gave you some hoof, cupcakes! Who's the goat, huh?"

He did a little dance, kicking rocks and making what were probably rude satyr gestures at the piles of clay.

Leo cracked a smile, and Jason couldn't help it—he started to laugh. It probably sounded a little hysterical, but it was such a relief to be alive, he didn't care.

Then a man stood up across the clearing. Tristan McLean staggered forward. His eyes were hollow, shell-shocked, like someone who'd just walked through a nuclear wasteland.

"Piper?" he called. His voice cracked. "Pipes, what—what is—"

He couldn't complete the thought. Piper ran over to him and hugged him tightly, but he almost didn't seem to know her.

Jason had felt a similar way—that morning at the Grand

Canyon, when he woke with no memory. But Mr. McLean had the opposite problem. He had too *many* memories, too much trauma his mind just couldn't handle. He was coming apart.

"We need to get him out of here," Jason said.

"Yeah, but how?" Leo said. "He's in no shape to walk."

Jason glanced up at the helicopter, which was now circling directly overhead. "Can you make us a bullhorn or something?" he asked Leo. "Piper has some talking to do."

XLV

PIPER

BORROWING THE HELICOPTER WAS EASY. Getting her dad on board was not.

Piper needed only a few words through Leo's improvised bullhorn to convince the pilot to land on the mountain. The Park Service copter was big enough for medical evacuations or search and rescue, and when Piper told the very nice ranger pilot lady that it would be a great idea to fly them to the Oakland Airport, she readily agreed.

"No," her dad muttered, as they picked him up off the ground. "Piper, what—there were monsters—there were monsters—"

She needed both Leo's and Jason's help to hold him, while Coach Hedge gathered their supplies. Fortunately Hedge had put his pants and shoes back on, so Piper didn't have to explain the goat legs.

It broke Piper's heart to see her dad like this—pushed beyond the breaking point, crying like a little boy. She didn't know what the giant had done to him exactly, how the monsters had shattered his spirit, but she didn't think she could stand to find out.

"It'll be okay, Dad," she said, making her voice as soothing as possible. She didn't want to charmspeak her own father, but it seemed the only way. "These people are my friends. We're going to help you. You're safe now."

He blinked, and looked up at helicopter rotors. "Blades. They had a machine with so many blades. They had six arms..."

When they got him to the bay doors, the pilot came over to help. "What's wrong with him?" she asked.

"Smoke inhalation," Jason suggested. "Or heat exhaustion."

"We should get him to a hospital," the pilot said.

"It's okay," Piper said. "The airport is good."

"Yeah, the airport is good," the pilot agreed immediately. Then she frowned, as if uncertain why she'd changed her mind. "Isn't he Tristan McLean, the movie star?"

"No," Piper said. "He only looks like him. Forget it."

"Yeah," the pilot said. "Only looks like him. I—" She blinked, confused. "I forgot what I was saying. Let's get going."

Jason raised his eyebrows at Piper, obviously impressed, but Piper felt miserable. She didn't want to twist people's minds, convince them of things they didn't believe. It felt so bossy, so *wrong*—like something Drew would do back at camp, or Medea in her evil department store. And how would it help her father? She couldn't convince him he would be okay, or that nothing had happened. His trauma was just too deep.

Finally they got him on board, and the helicopter took off. The pilot kept getting questions over her radio, asking her where she was going, but she ignored them. They veered away from the burning mountain and headed toward the Berkeley Hills.

"Piper." Her dad grasped her hand and held on like he was afraid he'd fall. "It's you? They told me—they told me you would die. They said . . . horrible things would happen."

"It's me, Dad." It took all her willpower not to cry. She had to be strong for him. "Everything's going to be okay."

"They were monsters," he said. "Real monsters. Earth spirits, right out of Grandpa Tom's stories—and the Earth Mother was angry with me. And the giant, Tsul'kälû, breathing fire—" He focused on Piper again, his eyes like broken glass, reflecting a crazy kind of light. "They said you were a demigod. Your mother was . . ."

"Aphrodite," Piper said. "Goddess of love."

"I—I—" He took a shaky breath, then seemed to forget how to exhale.

Piper's friends were careful not to watch. Leo fiddled with a lug nut from his tool belt. Jason gazed at the valley below —the roads backing up as mortals stopped their cars and gawked at the burning mountain. Gleeson chewed on the stub of his carnation, and for once the satyr didn't look in the mood to yell or boast.

Tristan McLean wasn't supposed to be seen like this. He was a star. He was confident, stylish, suave—always in control. That was the public image he projected. Piper had seen the image falter before. But this was different. Now it was broken, gone.

"I didn't know about Mom," Piper told him. "Not until you were taken. When we found out where you were, we came right away. My friends helped me. No one will hurt you again."

Her dad couldn't stop shivering. "You're heroes—you and your friends. I can't believe it. You're a *real* hero, not like me. Not playing a part. I'm so proud of you, Pipes." But the words were muttered listlessly, in a semi-trance.

He gazed down on the valley, and his grip on Piper's hand went slack. "Your mother never told me."

"She thought it was for the best." It sounded lame, even to Piper, and no amount of charmspeak could change that. But she didn't tell her dad what Aphrodite had really worried about: *If he has to spend the rest of his life with those memories, knowing that gods and spirits walk the earth, it will shatter him.*

Piper felt inside the pocket of her jacket. The vial was still there, warm to her touch.

But how could she erase his memories? Her dad finally knew who she was. He was proud of her, and for once she was his hero, not the other way around. He would never send her away now. They shared a secret.

How could she go back to the way things were?

She held his hand, speaking to him about small things— her time at the Wilderness School, her cabin at Camp Half-Blood. She told him how Coach Hedge ate carnations and got knocked on his butt on Mount Diablo, how Leo had tamed a dragon, and how Jason had made wolves back down by talking in Latin. Her friends smiled reluctantly as she recounted their adventures. Her dad seemed to relax as she talked, but he didn't smile. Piper wasn't even sure he heard her.

As they passed over the hills into the East Bay, Jason tensed. He leaned so far out the doorway Piper was afraid he'd fall.

He pointed. "What is that?"

Piper looked down, but she didn't see anything interesting —just hills, woods, houses, little roads snaking through the canyons. A highway cut through a tunnel in the hills, connecting the East Bay with the inland towns.

"Where?" Piper asked.

"That road," he said. "The one that goes through the hills."

Piper picked up the com helmet the pilot had given her and relayed the question over the radio. The answer wasn't very exciting.

"She says it's Highway 24," Piper reported. "That's the Caldecott Tunnel. Why?"

Jason stared intently at the tunnel entrance, but he said nothing. It disappeared from view as they flew over downtown Oakland, but Jason still stared into the distance, his expression almost as unsettled as Piper's dad's.

"Monsters," her dad said, a tear tracing his cheek. "I live in a world of monsters."

XLVI

PIPER

AIR TRAFFIC CONTROL DIDN'T WANT TO let an unscheduled helicopter land at the Oakland Airport—until Piper got on the radio. Then it turned out to be no problem.

They unloaded on the tarmac, and everyone looked at Piper.

"What now?" Jason asked her.

She felt uncomfortable. She didn't want to be in charge, but for her dad's sake, she had to appear confident. She had no plan. She'd just remembered that he'd flown into Oakland, which meant his private plane would still be here. But today was the solstice. They had to save Hera. They had no idea where to go or if they were even too late. And how could she leave her dad in this condition?

"First thing," she said. "I—I have to get my dad home. I'm sorry, guys."

Their faces fell.

"Oh," Leo said. "I mean, absolutely. He needs you right now. We can take it from here."

"Pipes, no." Her dad had been sitting in the helicopter doorway, a blanket around his shoulders. But he stumbled to his feet. "You have a mission. A quest. I can't—"

"I'll take care of him," said Coach Hedge.

Piper stared at him. The satyr was the last person she'd expected to offer. "You?" she asked.

"I'm a protector," Gleeson said. "That's my job, not fighting."

He sounded a little crestfallen, and Piper realized maybe she shouldn't have recounted how he got knocked unconscious in the last battle. In his own way, maybe the satyr was as sensitive as her dad.

Then Hedge straightened, and set his jaw. "Of course, I'm good at fighting, too." He glared at them all, daring them to argue.

"Yes," Jason said.

"Terrifying," Leo agreed.

The coach grunted. "But I'm a protector, and I can do this. Your dad's right, Piper. You need to carry on with the quest."

"But..." Piper's eyes stung, as if she were back in the forest fire. "Dad..."

He held out his arms, and she hugged him. He felt frail. He was trembling so much, it scared her.

"Let's give them a minute," Jason said, and they took the pilot a few yards down the tarmac.

"I can't believe it," her dad said. "I failed you."

"No, Dad!"

"The things they did, Piper, the visions they showed me..."

"Dad, listen." She took out the vial from her pocket. "Aphrodite gave me this, for you. It takes away your recent memories. It'll make it like none of this ever happened."

He gazed at her, as if translating her words from a foreign language. "But you're a hero. I would forget that?"

"Yes," Piper whispered. She forced an assuring tone into her voice. "Yes, you would. It'll be like—like before."

He closed his eyes and took a shaky breath. "I love you, Piper. I always have. I—I sent you away because I didn't want you exposed to my life. Not the way I grew up—the poverty, the hopelessness. Not the Hollywood insanity either. I thought—I thought I was protecting you." He managed a brittle laugh. "As if your life without me was better, or safer."

Piper took his hand. She'd heard him talk about protecting her before, but she'd never believed it. She'd always thought he was just rationalizing. Her dad seemed so confident and easygoing, like his life was a joyride. How could he claim she needed protecting from that?

Finally Piper understood he'd been acting for her benefit, trying not to show how scared and insecure he was. He really *had* been trying to protect her. And now his ability to cope had been destroyed.

She offered him the vial. "Take it. Maybe someday we'll be ready to talk about this again. When you're ready."

"When I'm ready," he murmured. "You make it sound like—like I'm the one growing up. I'm supposed to be the parent." He took the vial. His eyes glimmered with a small desperate hope. "I love you, Pipes."

"Love you, too, Dad."

He drank the pink liquid. His eyes rolled up into his head, and he slumped forward. Piper caught him, and her friends ran up to help.

"Got him," Hedge said. The satyr stumbled, but he was strong enough to hold Tristan McLean upright. "I already asked our ranger friend to call up his plane. It's on the way now. Home address?"

Piper was about to tell him. Then a thought occurred to her. She checked her dad's pocket, and his BlackBerry was still there. It seemed bizarre that he'd still have something so normal after all he'd been through, but she guessed Enceladus hadn't seen any reason to take it.

"Everything's on here," Piper said. "Address, his chauffeur's number. Just watch out for Jane."

Hedge's eyes lit up, like he sensed a possible fight. "Who's Jane?"

By the time Piper explained, her dad's sleek white Gulfstream had taxied next to the helicopter.

Hedge and the flight attendant got Piper's dad on board. Then Hedge came down one last time to say his good-byes. He gave Piper a hug and glared at Jason and Leo. "You cupcakes take care of this girl, you hear? Or I'm gonna make you do push-ups."

"You got it, Coach," Leo said, a smile tugging at his mouth.

"No push-ups," Jason promised.

Piper gave the old satyr one more hug. "Thank you, Gleeson. Take care of him, please."

"I got this, McLean," he assured her. "They got root beer and veggie enchiladas on this flight, and one hundred percent linen napkins—yum! I could get used to this."

Trotting up the stairs, he lost one shoe, and his hoof was visible for just a second. The flight attendant's eyes widened, but she looked away and pretended nothing was wrong. Piper figured she'd probably seen stranger things, working for Tristan McLean.

When the plane was heading down the runaway, Piper started to cry. She'd been holding it in too long and she just couldn't anymore. Before she knew it, Jason was hugging her, and Leo stood uncomfortably nearby, pulling Kleenex out of his tool belt.

"Your dad's in good hands," Jason said. "You did amazing."

She sobbed into his shirt. She allowed herself to be held for six deep breaths. Seven. Then she couldn't indulge herself anymore. They needed her. The helicopter pilot was already looking uncomfortable, like she was starting to wonder why she'd flown them here.

"Thank you, guys," Piper said. "I—"

She wanted to tell them how much they meant to her. They'd sacrificed everything, maybe even their quest, to help her. She couldn't repay them, couldn't even put her gratitude into words. But her friends' expressions told her they understood.

Then, right next to Jason, the air began to shimmer. At first Piper thought it was heat off the tarmac, or maybe gas fumes from the helicopter, but she'd seen something like this before in Medea's fountain. It was an Iris message. An image appeared in the air—a dark-haired girl in silver winter camouflage, holding a bow.

Jason stumbled back in surprise. "Thalia!"

"Thank the gods," said the Hunter. The scene behind her was hard to make out, but Piper heard yelling, metal clashing on metal, and explosions.

"We've found her," Thalia said. "Where are you?"

"Oakland," he said. "Where are you?"

"The Wolf House! Oakland is good; you're not too far. We're holding off the giant's minions, but we can't hold them forever. Get here before sunset, or it's all over."

"Then it's not too late?" Piper cried. Hope surged through her, but Thalia's expression quickly dampened it.

"Not yet," Thalia said. "But Jason—it's worse than I realized. Porphyrion is rising. Hurry."

"But where is the Wolf House?" he pleaded.

"Our last trip," Thalia said, her image starting to flicker. "The park. Jack London. Remember?"

This made no sense to Piper, but Jason looked like he'd been shot. He tottered, his face pale, and the Iris message disappeared.

"Bro, you all right?" Leo asked. "You know where she is?"

"Yes," Jason said. "Sonoma Valley. Not far. Not by air."

Piper turned to the ranger pilot, who'd been watching all this with an increasingly puzzled expression.

"Ma'am," Piper said with her best smile. "You don't mind helping us one more time, do you?"

"I don't mind," the pilot agreed.

"We can't take a mortal into battle," Jason said. "It's too dangerous." He turned to Leo. "Do you think you could fly this thing?"

"Um . . ." Leo's expression didn't exactly reassure Piper. But then he put his hand on the side of the helicopter, concentrating hard, as if listening to the machine.

"Bell 412HP utility helicopter," Leo said. "Composite four-blade main rotor, cruising speed twenty-two knots, service ceiling twenty-thousand feet. The tank is near full. Sure, I can fly it."

Piper smiled at the ranger again. "You don't have a problem with an under-aged unlicensed kid borrowing your copter, do you? We'll return it."

"I—" The pilot nearly choked on the words, but she got them out: "I don't have a problem with that."

Leo grinned. "Hop in, kids. Uncle Leo's gonna take you for a ride."

XLVII

LEO

FLY A HELICOPTER? SURE, WHY NOT. Leo had done plenty of crazier things that week.

The sun was going down as they flew north over the Richmond Bridge, and Leo couldn't believe the day had gone so quickly. Once again, nothing like ADHD and a good fight to the death to make time fly.

Piloting the chopper, he went back and forth between confidence and panic. If he didn't think about it, he found himself automatically flipping the right switches, checking the altimeter, easing back on the stick, and flying straight. If he allowed himself to consider what he was doing, he started freaking out. He imagined his Aunt Rosa yelling at him in Spanish, telling him he was a delinquent lunatic who was going to crash and burn. Part of him suspected she was right.

"Going okay?" Piper asked from the copilot's seat. She sounded more nervous than he was, so Leo put on a brave face.

"Aces," he said. "So what's the Wolf House?"

Jason knelt between their seats. "An abandoned mansion in the Sonoma Valley. A demigod built it—Jack London."

Leo couldn't place the name. "He an actor?"

"Writer," Piper said. "Adventure stuff, right? *Call of the Wild? White Fang?*"

"Yeah," Jason said. "He was a son of Mercury—I mean, Hermes. He was an adventurer, traveled the world. He was even a hobo for a while. Then he made a fortune writing. He bought a big ranch in the country and decided to build this huge mansion—the Wolf House."

"Named that 'cause he wrote about wolves?" Leo guessed.

"Partially," Jason said. "But the site, and the reason he wrote about wolves—he was dropping hints about his personal experience. There're a lot of holes in his life story—how he was born, who his dad was, why he wandered around so much—stuff you can only explain if you know he was a demigod."

The bay slipped behind them, and the helicopter continued north. Ahead of them, yellow hills rolled out as far as Leo could see.

"So Jack London went to Camp Half-Blood," Leo guessed.

"No," Jason said. "No, he didn't."

"Bro, you're freaking me out with the mysterious talk. Are you remembering your past or not?"

"Pieces," Jason said. "Only pieces. None of it good. The Wolf House is on sacred ground. It's where London started his journey as a child—where he found out he was a demigod. That's why he returned there. He thought he could live there, claim that land, but it wasn't meant for him. The Wolf House was cursed. It burned in a fire a week before he and his wife were supposed to move in. A few years later, London died, and his ashes were buried on the site."

"So," Piper said, "how do you know all this?"

A shadow crossed Jason's face. Probably just a cloud, but Leo could swear the shape looked like an eagle.

"I started my journey there too," Jason said. "It's a powerful place for demigods, a dangerous place. If Gaea can claim it, use its power to entomb Hera on the solstice and raise Porphyrion—that might be enough to awaken the earth goddess fully."

Leo kept his hand on the joystick, guiding the chopper at full speed—racing toward the north. He could see some weather ahead—a spot of darkness like a cloudbank or a storm, right where they were going.

Piper's dad had called him a hero earlier. And Leo couldn't believe some of the things he'd done—smacking around Cyclopes, disarming exploding doorbells, battling six-armed ogres with construction equipment. They seemed like they had happened to another person. He was just Leo Valdez, an orphaned kid from Houston. He'd spent his life running away, and part of him still wanted to run. What was he thinking, flying toward a cursed mansion to fight more evil monsters?

His mom's voice echoed in his head: *Nothing is unfixable.*

Except the fact that you're gone forever, Leo thought.

Seeing Piper and her dad back together had really driven that home. Even if Leo survived this quest and saved Hera,

Leo wouldn't have any happy reunions. He wouldn't be going back to a loving family. He wouldn't see his mom.

The helicopter shuddered. Metal creaked, and Leo could almost imagine the tapping was Morse code: *Not the end. Not the end.*

He leveled out the chopper, and the creaking stopped. He was just hearing things. He couldn't dwell on his mom, or the idea that kept bugging him—that Gaea was bringing souls back from the Underworld—so why couldn't he make some good come out of it? Thinking like that would drive him crazy. He had a job to do.

He let his instincts take over—just like flying the helicopter. If he thought about the quest too much, or what might happen afterward, he'd panic. The trick was not to think—just get through it.

"Thirty minutes out," he told his friends, though he wasn't sure how he knew. "If you want to get some rest, now's a good time."

Jason strapped himself into the back of the helicopter and passed out almost immediately. Piper and Leo stayed wide-awake.

After a few minutes of awkward silence, Leo said, "Your dad'll be fine, you know. Nobody's gonna mess with him with that crazy goat around."

Piper glanced over, and Leo was struck by how much she'd changed. Not just physically. Her presence was stronger. She seemed more... *here.* At Wilderness School she'd spent the semester trying not to be seen, hiding out in the back row of the classroom, the back of the bus, the corner of the lunchroom as far as possible from the loud kids. Now she would be impossible to miss. It didn't matter what she was wearing —you'd *have* to look at her.

"My dad," she said thoughtfully. "Yeah, I know. I was thinking about Jason. I'm worried about him."

Leo nodded. The closer they got to that bank of dark clouds, the more Leo worried, too. "He's starting to remember. That's got to make him a little edgy."

"But what if... what if he's a different person?"

Leo had had the same thought. If the Mist could affect their memories, could Jason's whole personality be an illusion, too? If their friend wasn't their friend, and they were heading into a cursed mansion—a dangerous place for demigods —what would happen if Jason's full memory came back in the middle of a battle?

"Nah," Leo decided. "After all we've been through? I can't see it. We're a team. Jason can handle it."

Piper smoothed her blue dress, which was tattered and burned from their fight on Mount Diablo. "I hope you're right. I need him..." She cleared her throat. "I mean I need to trust him...."

"I know," Leo said. After seeing her dad break down, Leo understood Piper couldn't afford to lose Jason as well. She'd just watched Tristan McLean, her cool suave movie star dad, reduced to near insanity. Leo could barely stand to watch that, but for *Piper*— Wow, Leo couldn't even imagine. He figured that would make her insecure about herself, too. If weakness was inherited, she'd be wondering, could *she* break down the same way her dad did?

"Hey, don't worry," Leo said. "Piper, you're the strongest, most powerful beauty queen I've ever met. You can trust yourself. For what it's worth, you can trust me too."

The helicopter dipped in a wind shear, and Leo almost jumped out of his skin. He cursed and righted the chopper.

Piper laughed nervously. "Trust you, huh?"

"Ah, shut up, already." But he grinned at her, and for a second, it felt like he was just relaxing comfortably with a friend.

Then they hit the storm clouds.

XLVIII

LEO

At first, Leo thought rocks were pelting the windshield. Then he realized it was sleet. Frost built up around the edges of the glass, and slushy waves of ice blotted out his view.

"An ice storm?" Piper shouted over the engine and the wind. "Is it supposed to be this cold in Sonoma?"

Leo wasn't sure, but something about this storm seemed conscious, malevolent—like it was intentionally slamming them.

Jason woke up quickly. He crawled forward, grabbing their seats for balance. "We've got to be getting close."

Leo was too busy wrestling with the stick to reply. Suddenly it wasn't so easy to drive the chopper. Its movements turned sluggish and jerky. The whole machine shuddered in the icy wind. The helicopter probably hadn't been prepped for cold-weather flying. The controls refused to respond, and they started to lose altitude.

Below them, the ground was a dark quilt of trees and fog. The ridge of a hill loomed in front of them and Leo yanked the stick, just clearing the treetops.

"There!" Jason shouted.

A small valley opened up before them, with the murky shape of a building in the middle. Leo aimed the helicopter straight for it. All around them were flashes of light that reminded Leo of the tracer fire at Midas's compound. Trees cracked and exploded at the edges of the clearing. Shapes moved through the mist. Combat seemed to be everywhere.

He set down the helicopter in an icy field about fifty yards from the house and killed the engine. He was about to relax when he heard a whistling sound and saw a dark shape hurtling toward them out of the mist.

"Out!" Leo screamed.

They leaped from the helicopter and barely cleared the rotors before a massive *BOOM* shook the ground, knocking Leo off his feet and splattering ice all over him.

He got up shakily and saw that the world's largest snowball —a chunk of snow, ice, and dirt the size of a garage—had completely flattened the Bell 412.

"You all right?" Jason ran up to him, Piper at his side. They both looked fine except for being speckled with snow and mud.

"Yeah." Leo shivered. "Guess we owe that ranger lady a new helicopter."

Piper pointed south. "Fighting's over there." Then she frowned. "No . . . it's all around us."

She was right. The sounds of combat rang across the valley. The snow and mist made it hard to tell for sure, but there seemed to be a circle of fighting all around the Wolf House.

Behind them loomed Jack London's dream home—a massive ruin of red and gray stones and rough-hewn timber beams. Leo could imagine how it had looked before it burned down—a combination log cabin and castle, like a billionaire lumberjack might build. But in the mist and sleet, the place had a lonely, haunted feel. Leo could totally believe the ruins were cursed.

"Jason!" a girl's voice called.

Thalia appeared from the fog, her parka caked with snow. Her bow was in her hand, and her quiver was almost empty. She ran toward them, but made it only a few steps before a six-armed ogre—one of the Earthborn—burst out of the storm behind her, a raised club in each hand.

"Look out!" Leo yelled. They rushed to help, but Thalia had it under control. She launched herself into a flip, notching an arrow as she pivoted like a gymnast and landed in a kneeling position. The ogre got a silver arrow right between the eyes and melted into a pile of clay.

Thalia stood and retrieved her arrow, but the point had snapped off. "That was my last one." She kicked the pile of clay resentfully. "Stupid ogre."

"Nice shot, though," Leo said.

Thalia ignored him as usual (which no doubt meant she thought he was as cool as ever). She hugged Jason and nodded to Piper. "Just in time. My Hunters are holding a perimeter around the mansion, but we'll be overrun any minute."

"By Earthborn?" Jason asked.

"*And* wolves—Lycaon's minions." Thalia blew a fleck of ice off her nose. "Also storm spirits—"

"But we gave them to Aeolus!" Piper protested.

"Who tried to kill us," Leo reminded her. "Maybe he's helping Gaea again."

"I don't know," Thalia said. "But the monsters keep re-forming almost as fast as we can kill them. We took the Wolf House with no problem: surprised the guards and sent them straight to Tartarus. But then this freak snowstorm blew in. Wave after wave of monsters started attacking. Now we're surrounded. I don't know who or what is leading the assault, but I think they planned this. It was a trap to kill anyone who tried to rescue Hera."

"Where is she?" Jason asked.

"Inside," Thalia said. "We tried to free her, but we can't figure out how to break the cage. It's only a few minutes until the sun goes down. Hera thinks that's the moment when Porphyrion will be reborn. Plus, most monsters are stronger at night. If we don't free Hera soon—"

She didn't need to finish the thought.

Leo, Jason, and Piper followed her into the ruined mansion.

Jason stepped over the threshold and immediately collapsed.

"Hey!" Leo caught him. "None of that, man. What's wrong?"

"This place..." Jason shook his head. "Sorry...It came rushing back to me."

"So you *have* been here," Piper said.

"We both have," Thalia said. Her expression was grim, like she was reliving someone's death. "This is where my mom took us when Jason was a child. She left him here, told me he was dead. He just disappeared."

"She gave me to the wolves," Jason murmured. "At Hera's insistence. She gave me to Lupa."

"That part I didn't know." Thalia frowned. "Who is Lupa?"

An explosion shook the building. Just outside, a blue mushroom cloud billowed up, raining snowflakes and ice like a nuclear blast made of cold instead of heat.

"Maybe this isn't the time for questions," Leo suggested. "Show us the goddess."

Once inside, Jason seemed to get his bearings. The house was built in a giant U, and Jason led them between the two wings to an outside courtyard with an empty reflecting pool. At the bottom of the pool, just as Jason had described from his dream, two spires of rock and root tendrils had cracked through the foundation.

One of the spires was much bigger—a solid dark mass about twenty feet high, and to Leo it looked like a stone body bag. Underneath the mass of fused tendrils he could make out the shape of a head, wide shoulders, a massive chest and arms, like the creature was stuck waist deep in the earth. No, not stuck—*rising.*

On the opposite end of the pool, the other spire was smaller and more loosely woven. Each tendril was as thick as a telephone pole, with so little space between them that Leo doubted he could've gotten his arm through. Still, he could see inside. And in the center of the cage stood Tía Callida.

She looked exactly like Leo remembered: dark hair covered with a shawl, the black dress of a widow, a wrinkled face with glinting, scary eyes.

She didn't glow or radiate any sort of power. She looked like a regular mortal woman, his good old psychotic babysitter.

Leo dropped into the pool and approached the cage. "*Hola, Tía.* Little bit of trouble?"

She crossed her arms and sighed in exasperation. "Don't inspect me like I'm one of your machines, Leo Valdez. Get me out of here!"

Thalia stepped next to him and looked at the cage with distaste—or maybe she was looking at the goddess. "We tried everything we could think of, Leo, but maybe my heart wasn't in it. If it was up to me, I'd just leave her in there."

"Ohh, Thalia Grace," the goddess said. "When I get out of here, you'll be sorry you were ever born."

"Save it!" Thalia snapped. "You've been nothing but a curse to every child of Zeus for ages. You sent a bunch of intestinally challenged cows after my friend Annabeth—"

"She was disrespectful!"

"You dropped a statue on my legs."

"It was an accident!"

"*And* you took my brother!" Thalia's voice cracked with emotion. "Here—on this spot. You ruined our lives. We should leave you to Gaea!"

"Hey," Jason intervened. "Thalia—Sis—I know. But this isn't the time. You should help your Hunters."

Thalia clenched her jaw. "Fine. For you, Jason. But if you ask me, she isn't worth it."

Thalia turned, leaped out of the pool, and stormed from the building.

Leo turned to Hera with grudging respect. "Intestinally challenged cows?"

"Focus on the cage, Leo," she grumbled. "And Jason—you are wiser than your sister. I chose my champion well."

"I'm not your champion, lady," Jason said. "I'm only helping you because you stole my memories and you're better than the alternative. Speaking of which, what's going on with that?"

He nodded to the other spire that looked like the king-size granite body bag. Was Leo imagining it, or had it grown taller since they'd gotten here?

"That, Jason," Hera said, "is the king of the giants being reborn."

"Gross," Piper said.

"Indeed," Hera said. "Porphyrion, the strongest of his kind. Gaea needed a great deal of power to raise him again —*my* power. For weeks I've grown weaker as my essence was used to grow him a new form."

"So you're like a heat lamp," Leo guessed. "Or fertilizer."

The goddess glared at him, but Leo didn't care. This old lady had been making his life miserable since he was a baby. He totally had rights to rag on her.

"Joke all you wish," Hera said in a clipped tone. "But at sundown, it will be too late. The giant will awake. He will offer me a choice: marry him, or be consumed by the earth. And I cannot marry him. We will all be destroyed. And as we die, Gaea will awaken."

Leo frowned at the giant's spire. "Can't we blow it up or something?"

"Without me, you do not have the power," Hera said. "You might as well try to destroy a mountain."

"Done that once today," Jason said.

"Just hurry up and let me out!" Hera demanded.

Jason scratched his head. "Leo, can you do it?"

"I don't know." Leo tried not to panic. "Besides, if she's a goddess, why hasn't she busted herself out?"

Hera paced furiously around her cage, cursing in Ancient Greek. "Use your brain, Leo Valdez. I *picked* you because you're intelligent. Once trapped, a god's power is useless. Your own father trapped me once in a golden chair. It was humiliating! I had to beg—*beg* him for my freedom and apologize for throwing him off Olympus."

"Sounds fair," Leo said.

Hera gave him the godly stink-eye. "I've watched you since you were a child, son of Hephaestus, because I knew you could aid me at this moment. If anyone can find a way to destroy this *abomination*, it is you."

"But it's not a machine. It's like Gaea thrust her hand out of the ground and..." Leo felt dizzy. The line of their prophecy came back to him: *The forge and dove shall break the cage.* "Hold on. I do have an idea. Piper, I'm going to need your help. And we're going to need time."

The air turned brittle with cold. The temperature dropped so fast, Leo's lips cracked and his breath changed to mist. Frost coated the walls of the Wolf House. *Venti* rushed in

—but instead of winged men, these were shaped like horses, with dark storm-cloud bodies and manes that crackled with lightning. Some had silver arrows sticking out of their flanks. Behind them came red-eyed wolves and the six-armed Earthborn.

Piper drew her dagger. Jason grabbed an ice-covered plank off the pool floor. Leo reached into his tool belt, but he was so shaken up, all he produced was a tin of breath mints. He shoved them back in, hoping nobody had noticed, and drew a hammer instead.

One of the wolves padded forward. It was dragging a human-size statue by the leg. At the edge of the pool, the wolf opened its maw and dropped the statue for them to see —an ice sculpture of a girl, an archer with short spiky hair and a surprised look on her face.

"Thalia!" Jason rushed forward, but Piper and Leo pulled him back. The ground around Thalia's statue was already webbed with ice. Leo feared if Jason touched her, he might freeze too.

"Who did this?" Jason yelled. His body crackled with electricity. "I'll kill you myself!"

From somewhere behind the monsters, Leo heard a girl's laughter, clear and cold. She stepped out of the mist in her snowy white dress, a silver crown atop her long black hair. She regarded them with those deep brown eyes Leo had thought were so beautiful in Quebec.

"*Bon soir, mes amis,*" said Khione, the goddess of snow. She gave Leo a frosty smile. "Alas, son of Hephaestus, you say you need time? I'm afraid time is one tool you do not have."

XLIX

JASON

AFTER THE FIGHT ON MOUNT DIABLO, Jason didn't think he could ever feel more afraid or devastated.

Now his sister was frozen at his feet. He was surrounded by monsters. He'd broken his golden sword and replaced it with a piece of wood. He had approximately five minutes until the king of the giants busted out and destroyed them. Jason had already pulled his biggest ace, calling down Zeus's lightning when he'd fought Enceladus, and he doubted he'd have the strength or the cooperation from above to do it again. Which meant his only assets were one whiny imprisoned goddess, one sort-of girlfriend with a dagger, and Leo, who apparently thought he could defeat the armies of darkness with breath mints.

On top of all this, Jason's worst memories were flooding back. He knew for certain he'd done many dangerous things in his life, but he'd never been closer to death than he was right now.

The enemy was beautiful. Khione smiled, her dark eyes glittering, as a dagger of ice grew in her hand.

"What've you done?" Jason demanded.

"Oh, so many things," the snow goddess purred. "Your sister's not dead, if that's what you mean. She and her Hunters will make fine toys for our wolves. I thought we'd defrost them one at a time and hunt them down for amusement. Let *them* be the prey for once."

The wolves snarled appreciatively.

"Yes, my dears." Khione kept her eyes on Jason. "Your sister almost killed their king, you know. Lycaon's off in a cave somewhere, no doubt licking his wounds, but his minions have joined us to take revenge for their master. And soon Porphyrion will arise, and we shall rule the world."

"Traitor!" Hera shouted. "You meddlesome, D-list goddess! You aren't worthy to pour my wine, much less rule the world."

Khione sighed. "Tiresome as ever, Queen Hera. I've been wanting to shut you up for millennia."

Khione waved her hand, and ice encased the prison, sealing in the spaces between the earthen tendrils.

"That's better," the snow goddess said. "Now, demigods, about your death—"

"You're the one who tricked Hera into coming here," Jason said. "You gave Zeus the idea of closing Olympus."

The wolves snarled, and the storm spirits whinnied, ready to attack, but Khione held up her hand. "Patience, my loves. If he wants to talk, what matter? The sun is setting, and time is on our side. Of course, Jason Grace. Like snow, my voice is quiet and gentle, and very cold. It's easy for me to whisper to the other gods, especially when I am only confirming their own deepest fears. I also whispered in Aeolus's ear that he should issue an order to kill demigods. It is a small service for Gaea, but I'm sure I will be well rewarded when her sons the giants come to power."

"You could've killed us in Quebec," Jason said. "Why let us live?"

Khione wrinkled her nose. "Messy business, killing you in my father's house, especially when he insists on meeting all visitors. I did *try*, you remember. It would've been lovely if he'd agreed to turn you to ice. But once he'd given you guarantee of safe passage, I couldn't openly disobey him. My father is an old fool. He lives in fear of Zeus and Aeolus, but he's still powerful. Soon enough, when my new masters have awakened, I will depose Boreas and take the throne of the North Wind, but not just yet. Besides, my father did have a point. Your quest was suicidal. I fully expected you to fail."

"And to help us with that," Leo said, "you knocked our dragon out of the sky over Detroit. Those frozen wires in his head—that was *your* fault. You're gonna pay for that."

"You're also the one who kept Enceladus informed about us," Piper added. "We've been plagued by snowstorms the whole trip."

"Yes, I feel so close to all of you now!" Khione said. "Once you made it past Omaha, I decided to asked Lycaon to track you down so Jason could die here, at the Wolf House." Khione smiled at him. "You see, Jason, your blood spilled on this sacred ground will taint it for generations. Your demigod brethren will be outraged, especially when they find the bodies of these two from Camp Half-Blood. They'll believe the Greeks have conspired with giants. It will be . . . delicious."

Piper and Leo didn't seem to understand what she was saying. But Jason knew. His memories were returning enough for him to realize how dangerously effective Khione's plan could be.

"You'll set demigods against demigods," he said.

"It's so easy!" said Khione. "As I told you, I only encourage what you would do anyway."

"But why?" Piper spread her hands. "Khione, you'll tear the world apart. The giants will destroy everything. You don't want that. Call off your monsters."

Khione hesitated, then laughed. "Your persuasive powers are improving, girl. But I am a goddess. You can't charm-speak me. We wind gods are creatures of chaos! I'll overthrow Aeolus and let the storms run free. If we destroy the mortal world, all the better! They never honored me, even in Greek times. Humans and their talk of global warming. Pah! I'll cool them down quickly enough. When we retake the ancient places, I will cover the Acropolis in snow."

"The ancient places." Leo's eyes widened. "That's what Enceladus meant about destroy the roots of the gods. He meant Greece."

"You could join me, son of Hephaestus," Khione said. "I know you find me beautiful. It would be enough for my plan if these other two were to die. Reject that ridiculous destiny the Fates have given you. Live and be my champion, instead. Your skills would be quite useful."

Leo looked stunned. He glanced behind him, like Khione might be talking to somebody else. For a second Jason was worried. He figured Leo didn't have beautiful goddesses make him offers like this every day.

Then Leo laughed so hard, he doubled over. "Yeah, join you. Right. Until you get bored of me and turn me into a Leosicle? Lady, nobody messes with my dragon and gets away with it. I can't believe I thought you were hot."

Khione's face turned red. "Hot? You dare insult me? I am cold, Leo Valdez. Very, very cold."

She shot a blast of wintry sleet at the demigods, but Leo held up his hand. A wall of fire roared to life in front of them, and the snow dissolved in a steamy cloud.

Leo grinned. "See, lady, that's what happens to snow in Texas. It—freaking—melts."

Khione hissed. "Enough of this. Hera is failing. Porphyrion is rising. Kill the demigods. Let them be our king's first meal!"

Jason hefted his icy wooden plank—a stupid weapon to die fighting with—and the monsters charged.

L

JASON

A WOLF LAUNCHED ITSELF AT JASON. He stepped back and swung his scrap wood into the beast's snout with a satisfying crack. Maybe only silver could kill it, but a good old-fashioned board could still give it a Tylenol headache.

He turned toward the sound of hooves and saw a storm spirit horse bearing down on him. Jason concentrated and summoned the wind. Just before the spirit could trample him, Jason launched himself into the air, grabbed the horse's smoky neck, and pirouetted onto its back.

The storm spirit reared. It tried to shake Jason, then tried to dissolve into mist to lose him; but somehow Jason stayed on. He willed the horse to remain in solid form, and the horse seemed unable to refuse. Jason could feel it fighting against him. He could sense its raging thoughts—complete chaos straining to break free. It took all Jason's willpower to impose his own wishes and bring the horse under control. He thought about Aeolus, overseeing thousands and thousands of spirits like this, some much worse. No wonder the Master of the Winds had gone a little mad after centuries of that pressure. But Jason had only one spirit to master, and he *had* to win.

"You're mine now," Jason said.

The horse bucked, but Jason held fast. Its mane flickered as it circled around the empty pool, its hooves causing miniature thunderstorms—tempests—whenever they touched.

"Tempest?" Jason said. "Is that your name?"

The horse spirit shook its mane, evidently pleased to be recognized.

"Fine," Jason said. "Now, let's fight."

He charged into battle, swinging his icy piece of wood, knocking aside wolves and plunging straight through other *venti*. Tempest was a strong spirit, and every time he plowed through one of his brethren, he discharged so much electricity, the other spirit vaporized into a harmless cloud of mist.

Through the chaos, Jason caught glimpses of his friends. Piper was surrounded by Earthborn, but she seemed to be holding her own. She was so impressive-looking as she fought, almost glowing with beauty, that the Earthborn stared at her in awe, forgetting that they were supposed to kill her. They'd lower their clubs and watch dumbfounded as she smiled and charged them. They'd smile back—until she sliced them apart with her dagger, and they melted into mounds of mud.

Leo had taken on Khione herself. While fighting a goddess should've been suicide, Leo was the right man for the job. She kept summoning ice daggers to throw at him, blasts of winter air, tornadoes of snow. Leo burned through all of it. His whole body flickered with red tongues of flame like he'd been doused with gasoline. He advanced on the goddess, using two silver-tipped ball-peen hammers to smash any monsters that got in his way.

Jason realized that Leo was the only reason they were still alive. His fiery aura was heating up the whole courtyard, countering Khione's winter magic. Without him, they would've been frozen like the Hunters long ago. Wherever Leo went, ice melted off the stones. Even Thalia started to defrost a little when Leo stepped near her.

Khione slowly backed away. Her expression went from enraged to shocked to slightly panicked as Leo got closer.

Jason was running out of enemies. Wolves lay in dazed heaps. Some slunk away into the ruins, yelping from their wounds. Piper stabbed the last Earthborn, who toppled to the ground in a pile of sludge. Jason rode Tempest through the last *ventus*, breaking it into vapor. Then he wheeled around and saw Leo bearing down on the goddess of snow.

"You're too late," Khione snarled. "He's awake! And don't think you've won anything here, demigods. Hera's plan will never work. You'll be at each other's throats before you can ever stop us."

Leo set his hammers ablaze and threw them at the goddess, but she turned into snow—a white powdery image of herself. Leo's hammers slammed into the snow woman, breaking it into a steaming mound of mush.

Piper was breathing hard, but she smiled up at Jason. "Nice horse."

Tempest reared on his hind legs, arcing electricity across his hooves. A complete show-off.

Then Jason heard a cracking sound behind him. The melting ice on Hera's cage sloughed off in a curtain of slush, and the goddess called, "Oh, don't mind me! Just the queen of the heavens, dying over here!"

Jason dismounted and told Tempest to stay put. The three demigods jumped into the pool and ran to the spire.

Leo frowned. "Uh, Tía Callida, are you getting shorter?"

"No, you dolt! The earth is claiming me. Hurry!"

As much as Jason disliked Hera, what he saw inside the cage alarmed him. Not only was Hera sinking, the ground was rising around her like water in a tank. Liquid rock had already covered her shins. "The giant wakes!" Hera warned. "You only have seconds!"

"On it," Leo said. "Piper, I need your help. Talk to the cage."

"What?" she said.

"Talk to it. Use everything you've got. Convince Gaea to sleep. Lull her into a daze. Just slow her down, try to get the tendrils to loosen while I—"

"Right!" Piper cleared her throat and said, "Hey, Gaea. Nice night, huh? Boy, I'm tired. How about you? Ready for some sleep?"

The more she talked, the more confident she sounded. Jason felt his own eyes getting heavy, and he had to force himself not to focus on her words. It seemed to have some effect on the cage. The mud was rising more slowly. The tendrils seemed to soften just a little—becoming more like tree root than rock. Leo pulled a circular saw out of his tool belt. How it fit in there, Jason had no idea. Then Leo looked at the cord and grunted in frustration. "I don't have anywhere to plug it in!"

The spirit horse Tempest jumped into the pit and whinnied.

"Really?" Jason asked.

Tempest dipped his head and trotted over to Leo. Leo looked dubious, but he held up the plug, and a breeze whisked it into the horse's flank. Lighting sparked, connecting with the prongs of the plug, and the circular saw whirred to life.

"Sweet!" Leo grinned. "Your horse comes with AC outlets!"

Their good mood didn't last long. On the other side of the pool, the giant's spire crumbled with a sound like a tree snapping in half. Its outer sheath of tendrils exploded from the top down, raining stone and wood shards as the giant shook himself free and climbed out of the earth.

Jason hadn't thought anything could be scarier than Enceladus.

He was wrong.

Porphyrion was even taller, and even more ripped. He didn't radiate heat, or show any signs of breathing fire, but there was something more terrible about him—a kind of strength, even magnetism, as if the giant were so huge and dense he had his own gravitational field.

Like Enceladus, the giant king was humanoid from the waist up, clad in bronze armor, and from the waist down he had scaly dragon's legs; but his skin was the color of lima beans. His hair was green as summer leaves, braided in long locks and decorated with weapons—daggers, axes, and full-size swords, some of them bent and bloody—maybe trophies taken from demigods eons before. When the giant opened his eyes, they were blank white, like polished marble. He took a deep breath.

"Alive!" he bellowed. "Praise to Gaea!"

Jason made a heroic little whimpering sound he hoped his friends couldn't hear. He was very sure no demigod could solo this guy. Porphyrion could lift mountains. He could crush Jason with one finger.

"Leo," Jason said.

"Huh?" Leo's mouth was wide open. Even Piper seemed dazed.

"You guys keep working," Jason said. "Get Hera free!"

"What are you going to do?" Piper asked. "You can't seriously—"

"Entertain a giant?" Jason said. "I've got no choice."

"Excellent!" the giant roared as Jason approached. "An appetizer! Who are you—Hermes? Ares?"

Jason thought about going with that idea, but something told him not to.

"I'm Jason Grace," he said. "Son of Jupiter."

Those white eyes bored into him. Behind him, Leo's circular saw whirred, and Piper talked to the cage in soothing tones, trying to keep the fear out of her voice.

Porphyrion threw back his head and laughed. "Outstanding!" He looked up at the cloudy night sky. "So, Zeus, you sacrifice a son to me? The gesture is appreciated, but it will not save you."

The sky didn't even rumble. No help from above. Jason was on his own.

He dropped his makeshift club. His hands were covered in splinters, but that didn't matter now. He had to buy Leo and Piper some time, and he couldn't do that without a proper weapon.

It was time to act a whole lot more confident than he felt.

"If you knew who I was," Jason yelled up at the giant, "you'd be worried about me, not my father. I hope you enjoyed your two and a half minutes of rebirth, giant, because I'm going to send you right back to Tartarus."

The giant's eyes narrowed. He planted one foot outside the pool and crouched to get a better look at his opponent. "So . . . we'll start by boasting, will we? Just like old times! Very well, demigod. I am Porphryion, king of the giants, son of Gaea. In olden times, I rose from Tatarus, the abyss of my father, to challenge the gods. To start the war, I stole Zeus's queen." He grinned at the goddess's cage. "Hello, Hera."

"My husband destroyed you once, monster!" Hera said. "He'll do it again!"

"But he didn't, my dear! Zeus wasn't powerful enough to kill me. He had to rely on a puny demigod to help, and even then, we almost won. This time, we will complete what we started. Gaea is waking. She has provisioned us with many fine servants. Our armies will shake the earth—and we will destroy you at the roots."

"You wouldn't dare," Hera said, but she was weakening. Jason could hear it in her voice. Piper kept whispering to the cage, and Leo kept sawing, but the earth was still rising inside Hera's prison, covering her up to her waist.

"Oh, yes," the giant said. "The Titans sought to attack

your new home in New York. Bold, but ineffective. Gaea is wiser and more patient. And we, her greatest children, are much, much stronger than Kronos. We know how to kill you Olympians once and for all. You must be dug up completely like rotten trees—your eldest roots torn out and burned."

The giant frowned at Piper and Leo, as if he'd just noticed them working at the cage. Jason stepped forward and yelled to get back Porphyrion's attention.

"You said a demigod killed you," he shouted. "How, if we're so puny?"

"Ha! You think I would explain it to you? I was created to be Zeus's replacement, born to destroy the lord of the sky. I shall take his throne. I shall take his wife—or, if she will not have me, I will let the earth consume her life force. What you see before you, child, is only my weakened form. I will grow stronger by the hour, until I am invincible. But I am already quite capable of smashing you to a grease spot!"

He rose to his full height and held out his hand. A twenty-foot spear shot from the earth. He grasped it, then stomped the ground with his dragon's feet. The ruins shook. All around the courtyard, monsters started to regather—storm spirits, wolves, and Earthborn, all answering the giant king's call.

"Great," Leo muttered. "We needed more enemies."

"Hurry," Hera said.

"I know!" Leo snapped.

"Go to sleep, cage," Piper said. "Nice, sleepy cage. Yes, I'm talking to a bunch of earthen tendrils. This isn't weird at all."

Porphyrion raked his spear across the top of the ruins, destroying a chimney and spraying wood and stone across the courtyard. "So, child of Zeus! I have finished my boasting. Now it's your turn. What were you saying about destroying me?"

Jason looked at the ring of monsters, waiting impatiently for their master's order to tear them to shreds. Leo's circular saw kept whirring, and Piper kept talking, but it seemed hopeless. Hera's cage was almost completely filled with earth.

"I'm the son of Jupiter!" he shouted, and just for effect, he summoned the winds, rising a few feet off the ground. "I'm a child of Rome, consul to demigods, praetor of the First Legion." Jason didn't know quite what he was saying, but he rattled off the words like he'd said them many times before. He held out his arms, showing the tattoo of the eagle and SPQR, and to his surprise the giant seemed to recognize it.

For a moment, Porphyrion actually looked uneasy.

"I slew the Trojan sea monster," Jason continued. "I toppled the black throne of Kronos, and destroyed the Titan Krios with my own hands. And now I'm going to destroy you, Porphyrion, and feed you to your own wolves."

"Wow, dude," Leo muttered. "You been eating red meat?"

Jason launched himself at the giant, determined to tear him apart.

The idea of fighting a forty-foot-tall immortal bare handed was so ridiculous, even the giant seemed surprised. Half flying, half leaping, Jason landed on the giant's scaly reptilian knee and climbed up the giant's arm before Porphyrion even realized what had happened.

"You dare?" the giant bellowed.

Jason reached his shoulders and ripped a sword out of the giant's weapon-filled braids. He yelled, "For Rome!" and drove the sword into the nearest convenient target—the giant's massive ear.

Lightning streaked out of the sky and blasted the sword, throwing Jason free. He rolled when he hit the ground. When he looked up, the giant was staggering. His hair was on fire, and the side of his face was blackened from lightning. The sword had splintered in his ear. Golden ichor ran down his jaw. The other weapons were sparking and smoldering in his braids.

Porphyrion almost fell. The circle of monsters let out a collective growl and moved forward—wolves and ogres fixing their eyes on Jason.

"No!" Porphyrion yelled. He regained his balance and glared at the demigod. "I will kill him myself."

The giant raised his spear and it began to glow. "You want to play with lightning, boy? You forget. I am the bane of Zeus. I was created to destroy your father, which means I know exactly what will kill *you*."

Something in Porphyrion's voice told Jason he wasn't bluffing.

Jason and his friends had had a good run. The three of them had done amazing things. Yeah, even *heroic* things. But as the giant raised his spear, Jason knew there was no way he could deflect this strike.

This was the end.

"Got it!" Leo yelled.

"Sleep!" Piper said, so forcefully, the nearest wolves fell to the ground and began snoring.

The stone and wood cage crumbled. Leo had sawed through the base of the thickest tendril and apparently cut off the cage's connection to Gaea. The tendrils turned to dust. The mud around Hera disintegrated. The goddess grew in size, glowing with power.

"Yes!" the goddess said. She threw off her black robes to reveal a white gown, her arms bedecked with golden jewelry. Her face was both terrible and beautiful, and a golden crown glowed in her long black hair. "Now I shall have my revenge!"

The giant Porphyrion backed away. He said nothing, but he gave Jason one last look of hatred. His message was clear: *Another time.* Then he slammed his spear against the earth, and the giant disappeared into the ground like he'd dropped down a chute.

Around the courtyard, monsters began to panic and retreat, but there was no escape for them.

Hera glowed brighter. She shouted, "Cover your eyes, my heroes!"

But Jason was too much in shock. He understood too late.

He watched as Hera turned into a supernova, exploding in a ring of force that vaporized every monster instantly. Jason fell, light searing into his mind, and his last thought was that his body was burning.

PIPER

"Jason!"

Piper kept calling his name as she held him, though she'd almost lost hope. He'd been unconscious for two minutes now. His body was steaming, his eyes rolled back in his head. She couldn't tell if he was even breathing.

"It's no use, child." Hera stood over them in her simple black robes and shawl.

Piper hadn't seen the goddess go nuclear. Thankfully she'd closed her eyes, but she could see the aftereffects. Every vestige of winter was gone from the valley. No signs of battle, either. The monsters had been vaporized. The ruins had been restored to what they were before—still ruins, but with no evidence that they'd been overrun by a horde of wolves, storm spirits, and six-armed ogres.

Even the Hunters had been revived. Most waited at a respectful distance in the meadow, but Thalia knelt by Piper's side, her hand on Jason's forehead.

Thalia glared up at the goddess. "This is your fault. Do something!"

"Do not address me that way, girl. I am the queen—"

"Fix him!"

Hera's eyes flickered with power. "I *did* warn him. I would never intentionally hurt the boy. He was to be my champion. I told them to close their eyes before I revealed my true form."

"Um..." Leo frowned. "True form is bad, right? So why did you do it?"

"I unleashed my power to help you, fool!" Hera cried. "I became pure energy so I could disintegrate the monsters, restore this place, and even save these miserable Hunters from the ice."

"But mortals can't look upon you in that form!" Thalia shouted. "You've killed him!"

Leo shook his head in dismay. "That's what our prophecy meant. *Death unleash, through Hera's rage.* Come on, lady. You're a goddess. Do some voodoo magic on him! Bring him back."

Piper half heard their conversation, but mostly she was focused on Jason's face. "He's breathing!" she announced.

"Impossible," Hera said. "I wish it were true, child, but no mortal has ever—"

"Jason," Piper called, putting every bit of her willpower into his name. She could *not* lose him. "Listen to me. You can do this. Come back. You're going to be fine."

Nothing happened. Had she imagined his breath stirring?

"Healing is not a power of Aphrodite," Hera said regretfully. "Even I cannot fix this, girl. His mortal spirit—"

"Jason," Piper said again, and she imagined her voice resonating through the earth, all the way down to the Underworld. "Wake up."

He gasped, and his eyes flew open. For a moment they were full of light—glowing pure gold. Then the light faded and his eyes were normal again. "What—what happened?"

"Impossible!" Hera said.

Piper wrapped him in a hug until he groaned, "Crushing me."

"Sorry," she said, so relieved, she laughed while wiping a tear from her eye.

Thalia gripped her brother's hand. "How do you feel?"

"Hot," he muttered. "Mouth is dry. And I saw something . . . really terrible."

"That was Hera," Thalia grumbled. "Her Majesty, the Loose Cannon."

"That's it, Thalia Grace," said the goddess. "I will turn you into an aardvark, so help me—"

"Stop it, you two," Piper said. Amazingly, they both shut up.

Piper helped Jason to his feet and gave him the last nectar from their supplies.

"Now . . ." Piper faced Thalia and Hera. "Hera—Your Majesty—we couldn't have rescued you without the Hunters. And Thalia, you never would've seen Jason again—*I* wouldn't have met him—if it weren't for Hera. You two make nice, because we've got bigger problems."

They both glared at her, and for three long seconds, Piper wasn't sure which one of them was going to kill her first.

Finally Thalia grunted. "You've got spirit, Piper." She pulled a silver card from her parka and tucked it into the pocket of Piper's snowboarding jacket. "You ever want to be a Hunter, call me. We could use you."

Hera crossed her arms. "Fortunately for *this* Hunter, you have a point, daughter of Aphrodite." She assessed Piper, as if seeing her clearly for the time. "You wondered, Piper, why I chose you for this quest, why I didn't reveal your secret in the beginning, even when I knew Enceladus was using you. I must admit, until this moment I was not sure. Something told me you would be vital to the quest. Now I see I was right. You're even stronger than I realized. And you are correct about the dangers to come. We must work together."

Piper's face felt warm. She wasn't sure how to respond to Hera's compliment, but Leo stepped in.

"Yeah," he said, "I don't suppose that Porphyrion guy just melted and died, huh?"

"No," Hera agreed. "By saving me, and saving this place, you prevented Gaea from waking. You have bought us some time. But Porphyrion has risen. He simply knew better than to stay here, especially since he has not yet regained his full power. Giants can only be killed by a combination of god and demigod, working together. Once you freed me—"

"He ran away," Jason said. "But to where?"

Hera didn't answer, but a sense of dread washed over Piper. She remembered what Porphyrion had said about killing the Olympians by pulling up their roots. *Greece.* She looked at Thalia's grim expression, and guessed the Hunter had come to the same conclusion.

"I need to find Annabeth," Thalia said. "She has to know what's happened here."

"Thalia..." Jason gripped her hand. "We never got to talk about this place, or—"

"I know." Her expression softened. "I lost you here once. I don't want to leave you again. But we'll meet soon. I'll rendezvous with you back at Camp Half-Blood." She glanced at Hera. "You'll see them there safely? It's the least you can do."

"It's not your place to tell me—"

"Queen Hera," Piper interceded.

The goddess sighed. "Fine. Yes. Just off with you, Hunter!"

Thalia gave Jason a hug and said her good-byes. When the Hunters were gone, the courtyard seemed strangely quiet. The dry reflecting pool showed no sign of the earthen tendrils that had brought back the giant king or imprisoned Hera. The night sky was clear and starry. The wind rustled in the redwoods. Piper thought about that night in Oklahoma when she and her dad had slept in Grandpa Tom's front yard. She thought about the night on the Wilderness School dorm roof, when Jason had kissed her—in her Mist-altered memories, anyway.

"Jason, what happened to you here?" she asked. "I mean— I know your mom abandoned you here. But you said it was sacred ground for demigods. Why? What happened after you were on your own?"

Jason shook his head uneasily. "It's still murky. The wolves..."

"You were given a destiny," Hera said. "You were given into my service."

Jason scowled. "Because you forced my mom to do that. You couldn't stand knowing Zeus had two children with my mom. Knowing that he'd fallen for her *twice*. I was the price you demanded for leaving the rest of my family alone. "

"It was the right choice for you as well, Jason," Hera insisted. "The second time your mother managed to snare Zeus's affections, it was because she imagined him in a different aspect—the aspect of Jupiter. Never before had this happened—two children, Greek and Roman, born into the same family. You *had* to be separated from Thalia. This is where all demigods of your kind start their journey."

"Of his kind?" Piper asked.

"She means Roman," Jason said. "Demigods are left here. We meet the she-wolf goddess, Lupa, the same immortal wolf that raised Romulus and Remus."

Hera nodded. "And if you are strong enough, you live."

"But..." Leo looked mystified. "What happened after that? I mean, Jason never made it to camp."

"Not to Camp Half-Blood, no," Hera agreed.

Piper felt as if the sky were spiraling above her, making her dizzy. "You went somewhere else. That's where you've been all these years. Somewhere else for demigods—but where?"

Jason turned to the goddess. "The memories are coming back, but not the location. You're not going to tell me, are you?"

"No," Hera said. "That is part of your destiny, Jason. You must find your own way back. But when you do . . . you will unite two great powers. You will give us hope against the giants, and more importantly—against Gaea herself."

"You want us to help you," Jason said, "but you're holding back information."

"Giving you answers would make those answers invalid," Hera said. "That is the way of the Fates. You must forge your own path for it to mean anything. Already, you three have surprised me. I would not have thought it possible..."

The goddess shook her head. "Suffice to say, you have performed well, demigods. But this is only the beginning. Now you must return to Camp Half-Blood, where you will begin planning for the next phase."

"Which you won't tell us about," Jason grumped. "And I suppose you destroyed my nice storm spirit horse, so we'll have to walk home?"

Hera waved aside the question. "Storm spirits are creatures of chaos. I did not destroy that one, though I have no idea where he went, or whether you'll see him again. But there is an easier way home for you. As you have done me a great service, so I can help you—at least this once. Farewell, demigods, for now."

The world turned upside down, and Piper almost blacked out.

When she could see straight again, she was back at camp, in the dining pavilion, in the middle of dinner. They were standing on the Aphrodite cabin's table, and Piper had one foot in Drew's pizza. Sixty campers rose at once, gawking at them in astonishment.

Whatever Hera had done to shoot them across the country, it wasn't good for Piper's stomach. She could barely control her nausea. Leo wasn't so lucky. He jumped off the table, ran to the nearest bronze brazier, and threw up in it—which was probably not a great burnt offering for the gods.

"Jason?" Chiron trotted forward. No doubt the old centaur had seen thousands of years' worth of weird stuff, but even he looked totally flabbergasted. "What— How—?"

The Aphrodite campers stared up at Piper with their mouths open. Piper figured she must look awful.

"Hi," she said, as casually as she could. "We're back."

LII

PIPER

PIPER DIDN'T REMEMBER MUCH ABOUT the rest of the night. They told their story and answered a million questions from the other campers, but finally Chiron saw how tired they were and ordered them to bed.

It felt so good to sleep on a real mattress, and Piper was so exhausted, she crashed immediately, which spared her any worry about what it would be like returning to the Aphrodite cabin.

The next morning she woke in her bunk, feeling reinvigorated. The sun came through the windows along with a pleasant breeze. It might've been spring instead of winter. Birds sang. Monsters howled in the woods. Breakfast smells wafted from the dining pavilion—bacon, pancakes, and all sorts of wonderful things.

Drew and her gang were frowning down at her, their arms crossed.

"Morning." Piper sat up and smiled. "Beautiful day."

"You're going to make us late for breakfast," Drew said, "which means *you* get to clean the cabin for inspection."

A week ago, Piper would've either punched Drew in the face, or hidden back under her covers. Now she thought about the Cyclopes in Detroit, Medea in Chicago, Midas turning her to gold in Omaha. Looking at Drew, who used to bother her, Piper laughed.

Drew's smug expression crumbled. She backed up, then remembered she was supposed to be angry. "What are you—"

"Challenging you," Piper said. "How about noon in the arena? You can choose the weapons."

She got out of bed, stretched leisurely, and beamed at her cabinmates. She spotted Mitchell and Lacy, who'd helped her pack for the quest. They were smiling tentatively, their eyes flitting from Piper to Drew like this might be a very interesting tennis game.

"I missed you guys!" Piper announced. "We're going to have a great time when I'm senior counselor."

Drew turned bug juice red. Even her closest lieutenants looked a little nervous. This wasn't in their script.

"You—" Drew spluttered. "You ugly little witch! I've been here the longest. You can't just—"

"Challenge you?" Piper said. "Sure, I can. Camp rules: I've been claimed by Aphrodite. I've completed a quest, which is one more than *you've* completed. If I feel I can do a better job, I can challenge you. Unless you just want to step down. Did I get all that right, Mitchell?"

"Just right, Piper." Mitchell was grinning. Lacy was bouncing up and down like she was trying to achieve liftoff.

A few of the other kids started to grin, as if they were enjoying the different colors Drew's face was turning.

"Step down?" Drew shrieked. "You're crazy!"

Piper shrugged. Then fast as a viper she pulled Katoptris from under her pillow, unsheathed the dagger, and thrust the point under Drew's chin. Everybody else backed up fast. One guy crashed into a makeup table and sent up a plume of pink powder.

"A duel, then," Piper said cheerfully. "If you don't want to wait until noon, now is fine. You've turned this cabin into a dictatorship, Drew. Silena Beauregard knew better than that. Aphrodite is about love and beauty. *Being* loving. *Spreading* beauty. Good friends. Good times. Good deeds. Not just looking good. Silena made mistakes, but in the end she stood by her friends. That's why she was a hero. I'm going to set things right, and I've got a feeling Mom will be on my side. Want to find out?"

Drew went cross-eyed looking down the blade of Piper's dagger.

A second passed. Then two. Piper didn't care. She was absolutely happy and confident. It must've shown in her smile.

"I . . . step down," Drew grumbled. "But if you think I'm ever going to forget this, McLean—"

"Oh, I hope you won't," Piper said. "Now, run along to the dining pavilion, and explain to Chiron why we're late. There's been a change of leadership."

Drew backed to the door. Even her closest lieutenants didn't follow her. She was about to leave when Piper said, "Oh, and Drew, honey?"

The former counselor looked back reluctantly.

"In case you think I'm not a true daughter of Aphrodite," Piper said, "don't even *look* at Jason Grace. He may not know it yet, but he's *mine*. If you even try to make a move, I will load you into a catapult and shoot you across Long Island Sound."

Drew turned around so fast, she ran into the doorframe. Then she was gone.

The cabin was silent. The other campers stared at Piper. This was the part she was unsure of. She didn't want to rule by fear. She wasn't like Drew, but she didn't know if they'd accept her.

Then, spontaneously, the Aphrodite campers cheered so loudly, they must've been heard all across camp. They herded Piper out of the cabin, raised her on their shoulders, and carried her all the way to the dining pavilion—still in her pajamas, her hair still a mess, but she didn't care. She'd never felt better.

By afternoon, Piper had changed into comfortable camp clothes and led the Aphrodite cabin through their morning activities. She was ready for free time.

Some of the buzz of her victory had faded because she had an appointment at the Big House.

Chiron met her on the front porch in human form, compacted into his wheelchair. "Come inside, my dear. The video conference is ready."

The only computer at camp was in Chiron's office, and the whole room was shielded in bronze plating.

"Demigods and technology don't mix," Chiron explained. "Phone calls, texting, even browsing the Internet—all these things can attract monsters. Why, just this fall at a school in Cincinnati, we had to rescue a young hero who Googled the gorgons and got a little more than he bargained for, but never mind that. Here at camp, you're protected. Still . . . we try to be cautious. You'll only be able to talk for a few minutes."

"Got it," Piper said. "Thank you, Chiron."

He smiled and wheeled himself out of the office. Piper hesitated before clicking the call button. Chiron's office had a cluttered, cozy feel. One wall was covered with T-shirts from different conventions—PARTY PONIES '09 VEGAS, PARTY PONIES '10 HONOLULU, et cetera. Piper didn't know who the Party Ponies were, but judging from the stains, scorch marks, and weapon holes in the T-shirts, they must've had some pretty wild meetings. On the shelf over Chiron's desk sat an old-fashioned boom box with cassette tapes labeled "Dean Martin" and "Frank Sinatra" and "Greatest Hits of the 40s." Chiron was so old, Piper wondered if that meant 1940s, 1840s, or maybe just A.D. 40.

But most of the office's wall space was plastered with photos of demigods, like a hall of fame. One of the newer shots showed a teenage guy with dark hair and green eyes. Since he stood arm in arm with Annabeth, Piper assumed the guy must be Percy Jackson. In some of the older photos, she recognized famous people: businessmen, athletes, even some actors that her dad knew.

"Unbelievable," she muttered.

Piper wondered if her photo would go on that wall some-day. For the first time, she felt like she was part of something bigger than herself. Demigods had been around for centuries. Whatever she did, she did for all of them.

She took a deep breath and made the call. The video screen popped up.

Gleeson Hedge grinned at her from her dad's office. "Seen the news?"

"Kind of hard to miss," Piper said. "I hope you know what you're doing."

Chiron had shown her a newspaper at lunch. Her dad's mysterious return from nowhere had made the front page. His personal assistant Jane had been fired for covering up his disappearance and failing to notify the police. A new staff had been hired and personally vetted by Tristan McLean's "life coach," Gleeson Hedge. According to the paper, Mr. McLean claimed to have no memory of the last week, and the media was totally eating up the story. Some thought it was a clever marketing ploy for a movie—maybe McLean was going to play an amnesiac? Some thought he'd been kidnapped by terrorists, or rabid fans, or had heroically escaped from ransom seekers using his incredible King of Sparta fighting skills. Whatever the truth, Tristan McLean was more famous than ever.

"It's going great," Hedge promised. "But don't worry. We're going to keep him out of the public eye for the next month or so until things cool down. Your dad's got more important things to do—like resting, and talking to his daughter."

"Don't get too comfortable out there in Hollywood, Gleeson," Piper said.

Hedge snorted. "You kidding? These people make Aeolus look sane. I'll be back as soon as I can, but your dad's gotta get back on his feet first. He's a good guy. Oh, and by the way, I took care of that other little matter. The Park Service in the Bay Area just got an anonymous gift of a new helicopter. And that ranger pilot who helped us? She's got a very lucrative offer to fly for Mr. McLean."

"Thanks, Gleeson," Piper said. "For everything."

"Yeah, well. I don't try to be awesome. It just comes natural. Speaking of Aeolus's place, meet your dad's new assistant."

Hedge was nudged out of the way, and a pretty young lady grinned into the camera.

"Mellie?" Piper stared, but it was definitely her: the *aura* who'd helped them escape from Aeolus's fortress. "You're working for my dad now?"

"Isn't it great?"

"Does he know you're a—you know—wind spirit?"

"Oh, no. But I love this job. It's—um—a breeze."

Piper couldn't help but laugh. "I'm glad. That's awesome. But where—"

"Just a sec." Mellie kissed Gleeson on the cheek. "Come on, you old goat. Stop hogging the screen."

"What?" Hedge demanded. But Mellie steered him away and called, "Mr. McLean? She's on!"

A second later, Piper's dad appeared.

He broke into a huge grin. "Pipes!"

He looked great—back to normal, with his sparkling brown eyes, his half-day beard, his confident smile, and his newly trimmed hair like he was ready to shoot a scene. Piper was relieved, but she also felt a little sad. Back to normal wasn't necessarily what she'd wanted.

In her mind, she started the clock. On a normal call like this, on a workday, she hardly ever got her dad's attention for longer than thirty seconds.

"Hey," she said weakly. "You feeling okay?"

"Honey, I'm so sorry to worry you with this disappearance business. I don't know..." His smile wavered, and she could tell he was trying to remember—grasping for a memory that should have been there, but wasn't. "I'm not sure what happened, honestly. But I'm fine. Coach Hedge has been a godsend."

"A godsend," she repeated. Funny choice of words.

"He told me about your new school," Dad said. "I'm sorry the Wilderness School didn't work out, but you were right. Jane was wrong. I was a fool to listen to her."

Ten seconds left, maybe. But at least her dad sounded sincere, like he really did feel remorseful.

"You don't remember anything?" she said, a bit wistfully.

"Of course I do," he said.

A chill went down her neck. "You do?"

"I remember that I love you," he said. "And I'm proud of you. Are you happy at your new school?"

Piper blinked. She wasn't going to cry now. After all she'd been through, that would be ridiculous. "Yeah, Dad. It's more like a camp, not a school, but...Yeah, I think I'll be happy here."

"Call me as often as you can," he said. "And come home for Christmas. And Pipes..."

"Yes?"

He touched the screen as if trying to reach through with his hand. "You're a wonderful young lady. I don't tell you that often enough. You remind me so much of your mother. She'd be proud. And Grandpa Tom"—he chuckled—"he always said you'd be the most powerful voice in our family. You're going to outshine me some day, you know. They're going to remember me as Piper McLean's father, and that's the best legacy I can imagine."

Piper tried to answer, but she was afraid she'd break down. She just touched his fingers on the screen and nodded.

Mellie said something in the background, and her dad sighed. "Studio calling. I'm sorry, honey." And he did sound genuinely annoyed to go.

"It's okay, Dad," she managed. "Love you."

He winked. Then the video call went black.

Forty-five seconds? Maybe a full minute.

Piper smiled. A small improvement, but it was progress.

At the commons area, she found Jason relaxing on a bench, a basketball between his feet. He was sweaty from working out, but he looked great in his orange tank top and shorts. His various scars and bruises from the quest were healing, thanks to some medical attention from the Apollo cabin. His arms and legs were well muscled and tan—distracting as always. His close-cropped blond hair caught the afternoon light so it looked like it was turning to gold, Midas style.

"Hey," he said. "How did it go?"

It took her a second to focus on his question. "Hmm? Oh, yeah. Fine."

She sat next to him and they watched the campers going

back and forth. A couple of Demeter girls were playing tricks on two of the Apollo guys—making grass grow around their ankles as they shot baskets. Over at the camp store, the Hermes kids were putting up a sign that read: FLYING SHOES, SLIGHTLY USED, 50% OFF TODAY! Ares kids were lining their cabin with fresh barbed wire. The Hypnos cabin was snoring away. A normal day at camp.

Meanwhile, the Aphrodite kids were watching Piper and Jason, and trying to pretend they weren't. Piper was pretty sure she saw money change hands, like they were placing bets on a kiss.

"Get any sleep?" she asked him.

He looked at her as if she'd been reading his thoughts. "Not much. Dreams."

"About your past?"

He nodded.

She didn't push him. If he wanted to talk, that was fine, but she knew him better than to press the subject. She didn't even worry that her knowledge of him was mostly based on three months of false memories. *You can sense possibilities,* her mother had said. And Piper was determined to make those possibilities a reality.

Jason spun his basketball. "It's not good news," he warned. "My memories aren't good for—for any of us."

Piper was pretty sure he'd been about to say *for us*—as in the two of them, and she wondered if he'd remembered a girl from his past. But she didn't let it bother her. Not on a sunny winter day like this, with Jason next to her.

"We'll figure it out," she promised.

He looked at her hesitantly, like he wanted very much to believe her. "Annabeth and Rachel are coming in for the meeting tonight. I should probably wait until then to explain..."

"Okay." She plucked a blade of grass by her foot. She knew there were dangerous things in store for both of them. She would have to compete with Jason's past, and they might not even survive their war against the giants. But right now, they were both alive, and she was determined to enjoy this moment.

Jason studied her warily. His forearm tattoo was faint blue in the sunlight. "You're in a good mood. How can you be so sure things will work out?"

"Because you're going to lead us," she said simply. "I'd follow you anywhere."

Jason blinked. Then slowly, he smiled. "Dangerous thing to say."

"I'm a dangerous girl."

"That, I believe."

He got up and brushed off his shorts. He offered her a hand. "Leo says he's got something to show us out in the woods. You coming?"

"Wouldn't miss it." She took his hand and stood up.

For a moment, they kept holding hands. Jason tilted his head. "We should get going."

"Yep," she said. "Just a sec."

She let go of his hand, and took a card from her pocket —the silver calling card that Thalia had given her for the Hunters of Artemis. She dropped it into a nearby eternal fire and watched it burn. There would be no breaking hearts in

Aphrodite cabin from now on. That was one rite of passage they didn't need.

Across the green, her cabinmates looking disappointed that they hadn't witnessed a kiss. They started cashing in their bets.

But that was all right. Piper was patient, and she could see lots of good possibilities.

"Let's go," she told Jason. "We've got adventures to plan."

LIII

LEO

Leo hadn't felt this jumpy since he offered tofu burgers to the werewolves. When he got to the limestone cliff in the forest, he turned to the group and smiled nervously. "Here we go."

He willed his hand to catch fire, and set it against the door. His cabinmates gasped.

"Leo!" Nyssa cried. "You're a fire user!"

"Yeah, thanks," he said. "I know."

Jake Mason, who was out of his body cast but still on crutches, said, "Holy Hephaestus. That means—it's so rare that—"

The massive stone door swung open, and everyone's mouth dropped. Leo's flaming hand seemed insignificant now. Even Piper and Jason looked stunned, and they'd seen enough amazing things lately.

Only Chiron didn't look surprised. The centaur knit his

bushy eyebrows and stroked his beard, as if the group was about to walk through a minefield.

That made Leo even more nervous, but he couldn't change his mind now. His instincts told him he was meant to share this place—at least with the Hephaestus cabin—and he couldn't hide it from Chiron or his two best friends.

"Welcome to Bunker Nine," he said, as confidently as he could. "C'mon in."

The group was silent as they toured the facility. Everything was just as Leo had left it—giant machines, worktables, old maps and schematics. Only one thing had changed. Festus's head was sitting on the central table, still battered and scorched from his final crash in Omaha.

Leo went over to it, a bitter taste in his mouth, and stroked the dragon's forehead. "I'm sorry, Festus. But I won't forget you."

Jason put a hand on Leo's shoulder. "Hephaestus brought it here for you?"

Leo nodded.

"But you can't repair him," Jason guessed.

"No way," Leo said. "But the head is going to be reused. Festus will be going with us."

Piper came over and frowned. "What do you mean?"

Before Leo could answer, Nyssa cried out, "Guys, look at this!"

She was standing at one of the worktables, flipping through a sketchbook—diagrams for hundreds of different machines and weapons.

"I've never seen anything like these," Nyssa said. "There are more amazing ideas here than in Daedalus's workshop. It would take a century just to prototype them all."

"Who built this place?" Jake Mason said. "And why?"

Chiron stayed silent, but Leo focused on the wall map he'd seen during his first visit. It showed Camp Half-Blood with a line of triremes in the Sound, catapults mounted in the hills around the valley, and spots marked for traps, trenches, and ambush sites.

"It's a wartime command center," he said. "The camp was attacked once, wasn't it?"

"In the Titan War?" Piper asked.

Nyssa shook her head. "No. Besides, that map looks *really* old. The date . . . does that say 1864?"

They all turned to Chiron.

The centaur's tail swished fretfully. "This camp has been attacked many times," he admitted. "That map is from the last Civil War."

Apparently, Leo wasn't the only one confused. The other Hephaestus campers looked at each other and frowned.

"Civil War . . ." Piper said. "You mean the American Civil War, like a hundred and fifty years ago?"

"Yes and no," Chiron said. "The two conflicts—mortal and demigod—mirrored each other, as they usually do in Western history. Look at any civil war or revolution from the fall of Rome onward, and it marks a time when demigods also fought one another. But *that* Civil War was particularly horrible. For American mortals, it is still their bloodiest conflict of all time—worse than their casualties in the two World

Wars. For demigods, it was equally devastating. Even back then, this valley was Camp Half-Blood. There was a horrible battle in these woods lasting for days, with terrible losses on both sides."

"Both sides," Leo said. "You mean the camp split apart?"

"No," Jason spoke up. "He means two different groups. Camp Half-Blood was one side in the war."

Leo wasn't sure he wanted an answer, but he asked, "Who was the other?"

Chiron glanced up at the tattered BUNKER 9 banner, as if remembering the day it was raised.

"The answer is dangerous," he warned. "It is something I swore upon the River Styx never to speak of. After the American Civil War, the gods were so horrified by the toll it took on their children, that they swore it would never happen again. The two groups were separated. The gods bent all their will, wove the Mist as tightly as they could, to make sure the enemies never remembered each other, never met on their quests, so that bloodshed could be avoided. This map is from the final dark days of 1864, the last time the two groups fought. We've had several close calls since then. The nineteen sixties were particularly dicey. But we've managed to avoid another civil war—at least so far. Just as Leo guessed, this bunker was a command center for the Hephaestus cabin. In the last century, it has been reopened a few times, usually as a hiding place in times of great unrest. But coming here is dangerous. It stirs old memories, awakens the old feuds. Even when the Titans threatened last year, I did not think it worth the risk to use this place."

Suddenly Leo's sense of triumph turned to guilt. "Hey, look, this place found *me*. It was meant to happen. It's a good thing."

"I hope you're right," Chiron said.

"I am!" Leo pulled the old drawing out of his pocket and spread it on the table for everyone to see.

"There," he said proudly. "Aeolus returned that to me. I drew it when I was five. That's my destiny."

Nyssa frowned. "Leo, it's a crayon drawing of a boat."

"Look." He pointed at the largest schematic on the bulletin board—the blueprint showing a Greek trireme. Slowly, his cabinmates' eyes widened as they compared the two designs. The number of masts and oars, even the decorations on the shields and sails were exactly the same as on Leo's drawing.

"That's impossible," Nyssa said. "That blueprint has to be a century old at least."

"'*Prophecy—Unclear—Flight*,'" Jake Mason read from the notes on the blueprint. "It's a diagram for a flying ship. Look, that's the landing gear. And weaponry—Holy Hephaestus: rotating ballista, mounted crossbows, Celestial bronze plating. That thing would be one spankin' hot war machine. Was it ever made?"

"Not yet," Leo said. "Look at the masthead."

There was no doubt—the figure at the front of the ship was the head of a dragon. A very particular dragon.

"Festus," Piper said. Everyone turned and looked at the dragon's head sitting on the table.

"He's meant to be our masthead," Leo said. "Our good

luck charm, our eyes at sea. I'm supposed to build this ship. I'm gonna call it the *Argo II*. And guys, I'll need your help."

"The *Argo II*." Piper smiled. "After Jason's ship."

Jason looked a little uncomfortable, but he nodded. "Leo's right. That ship is just what we need for our journey."

"What journey?" Nyssa said. "You just got back!"

Piper ran her fingers over the old crayon drawing. "We've got to confront Porphyrion, the giant king. He said he would destroy the gods at their roots."

"Indeed," Chiron said. "Much of Rachel's Great Prophecy is still a mystery to me, but one thing is clear. You three— Jason, Piper, and Leo—are among the seven demigods who must take on that quest. You must confront the giants in their homeland, where they are strongest. You must stop them before they can wake Gaea fully, before they destroy Mount Olympus."

"Um…" Nyssa shifted. "You don't mean Manhattan, do you?"

"No," Leo said. "The original Mount Olympus. We have to sail to Greece."

LIV

LEO

It took a few minutes for that to settle in. Then the other Hephaestus campers started asking questions all at once. Who were the other four demigods? How long would it take to build the boat? Why didn't everyone get to go to Greece?

"Heroes!" Chiron struck his hoof on the floor. "All the details are not clear yet, but Leo is correct. He will need your help to build the *Argo II*. It is perhaps the greatest project Cabin Nine has even undertaken, even greater than the bronze dragon."

"It'll take a year at least," Nyssa guessed. "Do we have that much time?"

"You have six months at most," Chiron said. "You should sail by summer solstice, when the gods' power is strongest. Besides, we evidently cannot trust the wind gods, and the summer winds are the least powerful and easiest to navigate. You dare not sail any later, or you may be too late to stop the giants. You must avoid ground travel, using only air and sea, so this vehicle is perfect. Jason being the son of the sky god..."

His voice trailed off, but Leo figured Chiron was thinking about his missing student, Percy Jackson, the son of Poseidon. He would've been good on this voyage, too.

Jake Mason turned to Leo. "Well, one thing's for sure. *You* are now senior counselor. This is the biggest honor the cabin has ever had. Anyone object?"

Nobody did. All his cabinmates smiled at him, and Leo could almost feel their cabin's curse breaking, their sense of hopelessness melting away.

"It's official, then," Jake said. "You're the man."

For once, Leo was speechless. Ever since his mom died, he'd spent his life on the run. Now he'd found a home and a family. He'd found a job to do. And as scary as it was, Leo wasn't tempted to run—not even a little.

"Well," he said at last, "if you guys elect me leader, you must be even crazier than I am. So let's build a spankin' hot war machine!"

LV

JASON

JASON WAITED ALONE IN CABIN ONE.

Annabeth and Rachel were due any minute for the head counselors' meeting, and Jason needed time to think.

His dreams the night before had been worse than he'd wanted to share—even with Piper. His memory was still foggy, but bits and pieces were coming back. The night Lupa had tested him at the Wolf House, to decide if he would be a pup or food. Then the long trip south to...he couldn't remember, but he had flashes of his old life. The day he'd gotten his tattoo. The day he'd been raised on a shield and proclaimed a praetor. His friends' faces: Dakota, Gwendolyn, Hazel, Bobby. And Reyna. Definitely there'd been a girl named Reyna. He wasn't sure what she'd meant to him, but the memory made him question what he felt about Piper— and wonder if he was doing something wrong. The problem was, he liked Piper a lot.

Jason moved his stuff to the corner alcove where his sister

had once slept. He put Thalia's photograph back on the wall so he didn't feel alone. He stared up at the frowning statue of Zeus, mighty and proud, but the statue didn't scare him anymore. It just made him feel sad.

"I know you can hear me," Jason said to the statue.

The statue said nothing. Its painted eyes seemed to stare at him.

"I wish I could talk with you in person," Jason continued, "but I understand you can't do that. The Roman gods don't like to interact with mortals so much, and—well, you're the king. You've got to set an example."

More silence. Jason had hoped for something—a bigger than usual rumble of thunder, a bright light, a smile. No, never mind. A smile would've been creepy.

"I remember some things," he said. The more he talked, the less self-conscious he felt. "I remember that it's hard being a son of Jupiter. Everyone is always looking at me to be a leader, but I always feel alone. I guess you feel the same way up on Olympus. The other gods challenge your decisions. Sometimes you've got to make hard choices, and the others criticize you. And you can't come to my aid like other gods might. You've got to keep me at a distance so it doesn't look like you're playing favorites. I guess I just wanted to say..."

Jason took a deep breath. "I understand all that. It's okay. I'm going to try to do my best. I'll try to make you proud. But I could really use some guidance, Dad. If there's anything you can do—help me so I can help my friends. I'm afraid I'll get them killed. I don't know how to protect them."

The back of his neck tingled. He realized someone was

standing behind him. He turned and found a woman in a black hooded robe, with a goatskin cloak over her shoulders and a sheathed Roman sword—a *gladius*—in her hands.

"Hera," he said.

She pushed back her hood. "To you, I have always been Juno. And your father has already sent you guidance, Jason. He sent you Piper and Leo. They're not just your responsibility. They are also your friends. Listen to them, and you will do well."

"Did Jupiter send you here to tell me that?"

"No one sends me anywhere, hero," she said. "I am not a messenger."

"But you got me into this. Why did you send me to this camp?"

"I think you know," Juno said. "An exchange of leaders was necessary. It was the only way to bridge to gap."

"I didn't agree to it."

"No. But Zeus gave your life to me, and I am helping you fulfill your destiny."

Jason tried to control his anger. He looked down at his orange camp shirt and the tattoos on his arm, and he knew these things should not go together. He had become a contradiction—a mixture as dangerous as anything Medea could cook up.

"You're not giving me all my memories," he said. "Even though you promised."

"Most will return in time," Juno said. "But you must find your own way back. You need these next months with your new friends, your new home. You're gaining their trust. By the time you sail in your ship, you will be a leader at this camp. And you will be ready to be a peacemaker between two great powers."

"What if you're not telling the truth?" he asked. "What if you're doing this to cause another civil war?"

Juno's expression was impossible to read—amusement? Disdain? Affection? Possibly all three. As much as she appeared human, Jason knew she was not. He could still see that blinding light—the true form of the goddess that had seared itself into his brain. She was Juno and Hera. She existed in many places at once. Her reasons for doing something were never simple.

"I am the goddess of family," she said. "My family has been divided for too long."

"They divided us so we don't kill each other," Jason said. "That seems like a pretty good reason."

"The prophecy demands that we change. The giants will rise. Each can only be killed by a god and demigod working together. Those demigods must be the seven greatest of the age. As it stands, they are divided between two places. If we remain divided, we cannot win. Gaea is counting on this. You must unite the heroes of Olympus and sail together to meet the giants on the ancient battlegrounds of Greece. Only then will the gods be convinced to join you. It will be the most dangerous quest, the most important voyage, ever attempted by the children of the gods."

Jason looked up again at the glowering statue of his father.

"It's not fair," Jason said. "I could ruin everything."

"You could," Juno agreed. "But gods need heroes. We always have."

"Even you? I thought you hated heroes."

The goddess gave him a dry smile. "I have that reputation. But if you want the truth, Jason, I often envy other gods their mortal children. You demigods can span both worlds. I think this helps your godly parents—even Jupiter, curse him—to understand the mortal world better than I."

Juno sighed so unhappily that despite his anger, Jason almost felt sorry for her.

"I am the goddess of marriage," she said. "It is not in my nature to be faithless. I have only two godly children—Ares and Hephaestus—both of whom are disappointments. I have no mortal heroes to do my bidding, which is why I am so often bitter toward demigods—Heracles, Aeneas, all of them. But it is also why I favored the first Jason, a pure mortal, who had no godly parent to guide him. And why I am glad Zeus gave you to me. You will be my champion, Jason. You will be the greatest of heroes, and bring unity to the demigods, and thus to Olympus."

Her words settled over him, as heavy as sandbags. Two days ago, he'd been terrified by the idea of leading demigods into a Great Prophecy, sailing off to battle the giants and save the world.

He was still terrified, but something had changed. He no longer felt alone. He had friends now, and a home to fight for. He even had a patron goddess looking out for him, which had to count for something, even if she seemed a little untrustworthy.

Jason had to stand up and accept his destiny, just as he had done when he faced Porphyrion with his bare hands. Sure, it seemed impossible. He might die. But his friends were counting on him.

"And if I fail?" he asked.

"Great victory requires great risk," she admitted. "Fail, and there will be bloodshed like we have never seen. Demigods will destroy one another. The giants will overrun Olympus. Gaea will wake, and the earth will shake off everything we have built over five millennia. It will be the end of us all."

"Great. Just great."

Someone pounded on the cabin doors.

Juno pulled her hood back over her face. Then she handed Jason the sheathed *gladius*. "Take this for the weapon you lost. We will speak again. Like it or not, Jason, I am your sponsor, and your link to Olympus. We need each other."

The goddess vanished as the doors creaked open, and Piper walked in.

"Annabeth and Rachel are here," she said. "Chiron has summoned the council."

JASON

THE COUNCIL WAS NOTHING LIKE Jason imagined. For one thing, it was in the Big House rec room, around a Ping-Pong table, and one of the satyrs was serving nachos and sodas. Somebody had brought Seymour the leopard head in from the living room and hung him on the wall. Every once in a while, a counselor would toss him a Snausage.

Jason looked around the room and tried to remember everyone's name. Thankfully, Leo and Piper were sitting next to him—it was their first meeting as senior counselors. Clarisse, leader of the Ares cabin, had her boots on the table, but nobody seemed to care. Clovis from Hypnos cabin was snoring in the corner while Butch from Iris cabin was seeing how many pencils he could fit in Clovis's nostrils. Travis Stoll from Hermes was holding a lighter under a Ping-Pong ball to see if it would burn, and Will Solace from Apollo was absently wrapping and unwrapping an Ace bandage around his wrist. The counselor from Hecate cabin,

Lou Ellen something-or-other, was playing "got-your-nose" with Miranda Gardiner from Demeter, except that Lou Ellen really *had* magically disconnected Miranda's nose, and Miranda was trying to get it back.

Jason had hoped Thalia would show. She'd promised, after all—but she was nowhere to be seen. Chiron had told him not to worry about it. Thalia often got sidetracked fighting monsters or running quests for Artemis, and she would probably arrive soon. But still, Jason worried.

Rachel Dare, the oracle, sat next to Chiron at the head of the table. She was wearing her Clarion Academy school uniform dress, which seemed a bit odd, but she smiled at Jason.

Annabeth didn't look so relaxed. She wore armor over her camp clothes, with her knife at her side and her blond hair pulled back in a ponytail. As soon as Jason walked in, she fixed him with an expectant look, as if she were trying to extract information out of him by sheer willpower.

"Let's come to order," Chiron said. "Lou Ellen, please give Miranda her nose back. Travis, if you'd kindly extinguish the flaming Ping-Pong ball, and Butch, I think twenty pencils is really too many for any human nostril. Thank you. Now, as you can see, Jason, Piper, and Leo have returned successfully ... more or less. Some of you have heard parts of their story, but I will let them fill you in."

Everyone looked at Jason. He cleared his throat and began the story. Piper and Leo chimed in from time to time, filling in the details he forgot.

It only took a few minutes, but it seemed like longer with everyone watching him. The silence was heavy, and for so many ADHD demigods to sit still listening for that long, Jason knew the story must have sounded pretty wild. He ended with Hera's visit right before the meeting.

"So Hera was *here*," Annabeth said. "Talking to you."

Jason nodded. "Look, I'm not saying I trust her—"

"That's smart," Annabeth said.

"—but she isn't making this up about another group of demigods. That's where I came from."

"Romans." Clarisse tossed Seymour a Snausage. "You expect us to believe there's another camp with demigods, but they follow the Roman forms of the gods. And we've never even heard of them."

Piper sat forward. "The gods have kept the two groups apart, because every time they see each other, they try to kill each other."

"I can respect that," Clarisse said. "Still, why haven't we ever run across each other on quests?"

"Oh, yes," Chiron said sadly. "You have, many times. It's always a tragedy, and always the gods do their best to wipe clean the memories of those involved. The rivalry goes all the way back to the Trojan War, Clarisse. The Greeks invaded Troy and burned it to the ground. The Trojan hero Aeneas escaped, and eventually made his way to Italy, where he founded the race that would someday become Rome. The Romans grew more and more powerful, worshipping the same gods but under different names, and with slightly different personalities."

"More warlike," Jason said. "More united. More about expansion, conquest, and discipline."

"Yuck," Travis put in.

Several of the others looked equally uncomfortable, though Clarisse shrugged like it sounded okay to her.

Annabeth twirled her knife on the table. "And the Romans hated the Greeks. They took revenge when they conquered the Greek isles, and made them part of the Roman Empire."

"Not exactly *hated* them," Jason said. "The Romans admired Greek culture, and were a little jealous. In return, the Greeks thought the Romans were barbarians, but they respected their military power. So during Roman times, demigods started to divide—either Greek or Roman."

"And it's been that way ever since," Annabeth guessed. "But this is crazy. Chiron, where were the Romans during the Titan War? Didn't they want to help?"

Chiron tugged at his beard. "They *did* help, Annabeth. While you and Percy were leading the battle to save Manhattan, who do think conquered Mount Othrys, the Titans' base in California?"

"Hold on," Travis said. "You said Mount Othrys just crumbled when we beat Kronos."

"No," Jason said. He remembered flashes of the battle—a giant in starry armor and a helm mounted with ram's horns. He remembered his army of demigods scaling Mount Tam, fighting through hordes of snake monsters. "It didn't just fall. We destroyed their palace. I defeated the Titan Krios myself."

Annabeth's eyes were as stormy as a *ventus*. Jason could almost see her thoughts moving, putting the pieces together. "The Bay Area. We demigods were always told to stay away from it because Mount Othrys was there. But that wasn't the only reason, was it? The Roman camp—it's got to be somewhere near San Francisco. I bet it was put there to keep watch on the Titans' territory. Where is it?"

Chiron shifted in his wheelchair. "I cannot say. Honestly, even *I* have never been trusted with that information. My counterpart, Lupa, is not exactly the sharing type. Jason's memory, too, has been burned away."

"The camp's heavily veiled with magic," Jason said. "And heavily guarded. We could search for years and never find it."

Rachel Dare laced her fingers. Of all the people in the room, only she didn't seem nervous about the conversation. "But you'll try, won't you? You'll build Leo's boat, the *Argo II*. And before you make for Greece, you'll sail for the Roman camp. You'll need their help to confront the giants."

"Bad plan," Clarisse warned. "If those Romans see a warship coming, they'll assume we're attacking."

"You're probably right," Jason agreed. "But we have to try. I was sent here to learn about Camp Half-Blood, to try to convince you the two camps don't have to be enemies. A peace offering."

"Hmm," Rachel said. "Because Hera is convinced we need both camps to win the war with the giants. Seven heroes of Olympus—some Greek, some Roman."

Annabeth nodded. "Your Great Prophecy—what's the last line?"

"And foes bear arms to the Doors of Death."

"Gaea has opened the Doors of Death," Annabeth said. "She's letting out the worst villains of the Underworld to fight us. Medea, Midas—there'll be more, I'm sure. Maybe the line means that the Roman and Greek demigods will unite, and find the doors, and close them."

"Or it could mean they fight each other at the doors of death," Clarisse pointed out. "It doesn't say we'll cooperate."

There was silence as the campers let that happy thought sink in.

"I'm going," Annabeth said. "Jason, when you get this ship built, let me go with you."

"I was hoping you'd offer," Jason said. "You of all people —we'll need you."

"Wait." Leo frowned. "I mean that's cool with me and all. But why Annabeth of all people?"

Annabeth and Jason studied one another, and Jason knew she had put it together. She saw the dangerous truth.

"Hera said my coming here was an exchange of leaders," Jason said. "A way for the two camps to learn of each other's existence."

"Yeah?" Leo said. "So?"

"An exchange goes two ways," Jason said. "When I got here, my memory was wiped. I didn't know who I was or where I belonged. Fortunately, you guys took me in and I found a new home. I know you're not my enemy. The Roman camp—they're not so friendly. You prove your worth quickly, or you don't survive. They may not be so nice to him, and if they learn where he comes from, he's going to be in serious trouble."

"Him?" Leo said. "Who are you talking about?"

"My boyfriend," Annabeth said grimly. "He disappeared

around the same time Jason appeared. If Jason came to Camp Half-Blood—"

"Exactly," Jason agreed. "Percy Jackson is at the other camp, and he probably doesn't even remember who he is."

Gods in *The Lost Hero*

Aeolus   The Greek god of the winds. Roman form: Aeolus

Aphrodite   The Greek goddess of love and beauty. She was marred to Hephaestus, but she loved Ares, the god of war. Roman form: Venus

Apollo   The Greek god of the sun, prophecy, music, and healing; the son of Zeus, and the twin of Artemis. Roman form: Apollo

Ares   The Greek god of war; the son of Zeus and Hera, and half brother to Athena. Roman form: Mars

Artemis   The Greek goddess of the hunt and the moon; the daughter of Zeus and the twin of Apollo. Roman form: Diana

Boreas   The Greek god of the north wind, one of the four directional *anemoi* (wind gods); the god of winter; father of Khione. Roman form: Aquilon

Demeter   The Greek goddess of agriculture, a daughter of the Titans Rhea and Kronos. Roman form: Ceres

Dionysus The Greek god of wine; the son of Zeus. Roman form: Bacchus

Gaea The Greek personification of Earth. Roman form: Terra

Hades According to Greek mythology, ruler of the Underworld and god of the dead. Roman form: Pluto

Hecate The Greek goddess of magic; the only child of the Titans Perses and Asteria. Roman form: Trivia

Hephaestus The Greek god of fire and crafts and of blacksmiths; the son of Zeus and Hera, and married to Aphrodite. Roman form: Vulcan

Hera The Greek goddess of marriage; Zeus's wife and sister. Roman form: Juno

Hermes The Greek god of travelers, communication, and thieves; son of Zeus. Roman form: Mercury

Hypnos The Greek god of sleep; the (fatherless) son of Nyx (Night) and brother of Thanatos (Death). Roman form: Somnus

Iris The Greek goddess of the rainbow, and a messenger of the gods; the daughter of Thaumas and Electra. Roman form: Iris

Janus The Roman god of gates, doors, and doorways, as well as beginnings and endings.

Khione The Greek goddess of snow; daughter of Boreas

Notus The Greek god of the south wind, one of the four directional *anemoi* (wind gods). Roman form: Favonius

Ouranos The Greek personification of the sky. Roman form: Uranus

Pan The Greek god of the wild; the son of Hermes. Roman form: Faunus

Pompona The Roman goddess of plenty

Poseidon The Greek god of the sea; son of the Titans Kronos and Rhea, and brother of Zeus and Hades. Roman form: Neptune

Zeus The Greek god of the sky and king of the gods. Roman form: Jupiter

Coming Fall 2011

The Heroes of Olympus, Book Two

THE SON OF NEPTUNE

Praise for The Percy Jackson Series by Rick Riordan:

The Lightning Thief

"Perfectly paced, with electrifying moments
chasing each other like heartbeats."

—*The New York Times Book Review*

The Sea of Monsters

★ "In a feat worthy of his heroic subjects, Riordan crafts
a sequel stronger than his compelling debut."

—*Publishers Weekly* (starred review)

The Titan's Curse

"All in all, a winner of Olympic proportions."

—*School Library Journal*

The Battle of the Labyrinth

★ "Look no further for the next Harry Potter; meet
Percy Jackson, as legions of fans already have."

—*Kirkus Reviews* (starred review)

The Last Olympian

"The hordes of young readers who have devoured Rick Riordan's
books ... will no doubt gulp down this concluding volume as
greedily as they would a plateful of ambrosia, or maybe pizza."

—*The Wall Street Journal*

Praise for The Kane Chronicles Book 1: The Red Pyramid *by Rick Riordan:*

★ "The first volume in the Kane Chronicles, this fantasy adventure delivers what fans loved about the Percy Jackson and the Olympians series: young protagonists with previously unsuspected magical powers, a riveting story marked by headlong adventure, a complex background rooted in ancient mythology, and wry, witty twenty-first-century narration."
—*ALA Booklist* (starred review)

"Riordan fans young and old will eat this new book up."
—*The New York Times Book Review*

"Fans of the Riordan magic—equal parts danger, myth, and irreverence—will embrace this new series with open arms."
—*Horn Book*

"This tale explodes into action from chapter one.... Readers pining for Percy Jackson will find new heroes in Carter and Sadie Kane."
—*Kirkus Reviews*

"Once again, Riordan masterfully meshes modern life with mythology and history, reinvigorating dusty artifacts such as the Rosetta stone and revitalizing ancient Egyptian story lines."
—*The Los Angeles Times*

★ "A truly original take on Egyptian mythology...A must-have book."
—*School Library Journal* (starred review)

"For anyone who was afraid he couldn't top his Percy Jackson series or his initial title in the *39 Clues,* fear no more. Riordan mined Greek myths for the lineage of his campers at Half-Blood. Now he drills into the depths of Egyptian history and lore for the page-turning Kane Chronicles. Riordan has a field day...imparting Egyptian history as he weaves his spellbinding tale. Plenty of humor keeps things light.... Readers will be clamoring for the next installment."
—*Shelf Awareness*

About the Author

Rick Riordan is the author of the *New York Times* #1 best-selling The Kane Chronicles, Book One: *The Red Pyramid*, as well as all the books in the *New York Times* #1 best-selling Percy Jackson and the Olympians series: T*he Lightning Thief*; *The Sea of Monsters*; *The Titan's Curse*; *The Battle of the Labyrinth*; and *The Last Olympian*. His previous novels for adults include the hugely popular Tres Navarre series, winner of the top three awards in the mystery genre. He lives in San Antonio, Texas, with his wife and two sons. To learn more about Rick, visit his Web site at www.rickriordan.com.